PEOPLE
TO
FOLLOW

PEOPLE
TO
FOLLOW

A Novel

Olivia Worley

WEDNESDAY BOOKS
NEW YORK

First published in the United States by Wednesday Books, an imprint of St. Martin's Publishing Group

PEOPLE TO FOLLOW. Copyright © 2023 by Olivia Worley. All rights reserved. Printed in the United States of America. For information, address St. Martin's Publishing Group, 120 Broadway, New York, NY 10271.

Designed by Jen Edwards

www.wednesdaybooks.com

The Library of Congress Cataloging-in-Publication Data is available upon request.

ISBN 978-1-250-88134-2 (trade paperback)
ISBN 978-1-250-88138-0 (hardcover)
ISBN 978-1-250-88135-9 (ebook)

Our books may be purchased in bulk for promotional, educational, or business use. Please contact your local bookseller or the Macmillan Corporate and Premium Sales Department at 1-800-221-7945, extension 5442, or by email at MacmillanSpecialMarkets@macmillan.com.

First Edition: 2023

10 9 8 7 6 5 4 3 2 1

For Mom and Dad

PEOPLE
TO
FOLLOW

KIRA

It's a view you could kill for. Or maybe it's to die for. As the boat sails forward, those are the two phrases that run through my head. I don't really know why, except that they feel true—because this is the kind of place you can only describe in clichés.

Lawrence Island rises out of the waves like a mirage, an oasis of land after miles of sea so clear and blue it shouldn't be real. The dock leads up to a beach, blinding white, dotted with palm trees and glittering rocks. Farther on, there's a terrace, a pool, and then, looking over it all, the house. It's Spanish-style, three stories of stucco and a clay roof, with curved windows and iron balconies, more palms flanking the sides like royal guards.

As we near the dock, I take a moment to breathe in the salty air, the humidity already teasing my hair into its natural wave. I fix my ponytail, raking unruly pieces back into order, and then close my eyes, letting the sun bake my cheeks, my bare shoulders.

This place would be perfect for the kind of content my followers want to see: workout videos on the beach. Vlogs where I make guilt-free virgin daiquiris. Pictures of me in a sponsored leggings set, stretching against a backdrop of sea and sky. But I gave my phone to a PA at the airport, so for the next three weeks, my followers will have to settle for posts I scheduled back home in Dallas.

For the next three weeks, I get to disappear.

"You okay?" Max Overby asks from across the small boat.

My face goes hot. So much for disappearing.

"Yeah," I tell him. "Sorry."

Right away, I regret it. I'm always apologizing for things I don't need to, instinct from years of hearing Ms. Tammy's hoarse shouts in the studio. *Toes pointed. No sickling. Eyes up, Lyons. Do you think the floor is going to fall out from under you?*

Max adjusts his glasses, blue eyes bright behind them. It makes me weirdly nervous, so I look at his camera instead. I don't know who Max had to charm for permission to bring the camera with him, since we were supposed to leave our devices behind, but he hasn't put it away since we got on the boat.

"This an interview?" I ask, raising an eyebrow.

"No. Genuine concern." He puts the camera away, a crooked smile curving on his lips. "You looked a little seasick."

A warm, wobbly feeling rushes through me, which I did *not* sign up for, so I look down at his sneakers, the crew socks sticking out from them. They're green with little cartoon sea turtles. Wait, did Max Overby coordinate his socks with the marine life? And why do I find that so attractive?

Eyes up, Lyons.

"Just not a fan of boats," I say, picking the first real excuse I can think of. "I've seen *Jaws* and *Titanic*. As far as I'm concerned, sea travel should be avoided at all costs."

Max laughs, warm. "Okay, but what if I see your *Jaws* and

Titanic and raise you the entire Final Destination series? Rules out air travel, car travel, *and* roller coasters."

A smile tugs at my lips, but I force it down—because 1) having a crush on the first lanky boy who asks me how I'm doing is totally embarrassing, and 2) I'm almost positive that this is how Max drags the secrets out of his documentary subjects before they even know what hit them.

I hadn't met him until today, but I've known about Max since his documentary blew up on YouTube last year, the one exposing Jared Sky, who runs one of the most-followed commentary channels, as a serial catfish. From there, Max's small following grew into a horde of fans—some of whom, I'd argue, are more drawn to his sharp jawline and six-foot frame than they are to his journalistic prowess, but that's just my opinion. As, you know, another girl who is also apparently charmed by those things, as much as that makes me want to scream into the nearest suitcase.

Logan Costello, on the other hand, is not impressed.

"Are you gonna be filming this whole time?" she asks Max, narrowing her hazel eyes. The breeze blows dark strands out of her loose ponytail, making them dance around her pale face. "Like, I'm pretty sure the crew has it covered. Unless the camera is just a film-bro fashion statement, in which case, might I suggest therapy?"

Max turns pink, and I bite my cheek to stifle a laugh. Logan comes off as a little harsh, I guess, but from what I've seen of her content, sharp and dry is her brand of humor. Before she joined the Bounce House, Logan's videos genuinely cracked me up, from tips on how to repel men on the dance floor to random stories told straight to the camera. But after getting picked up by the biggest TikTok collective around, she mostly did their usual stuff: spon-con, dances, and vlogs. Then, two months ago, she left without explanation. There's all kinds of rumors about why she quit, but if you ask me, it was a good move. I know there's only so much you can know about a person from their socials, but the longer Logan stayed with the Bounce House, the less she seemed like herself.

"Tilly said it was fine." Max shrugs, running a hand through his messy brown hair. "No internet connectivity."

Logan frowns. "Wait, are you actually making a documentary about this?"

"Yeah, maybe."

"A documentary about a TV show about disconnecting from social media." Corinne Lecompte leans back against the boat's railing, thoughtfully scrunching her nose, where freckles splash across her brown skin. "Meta."

I smile, wishing I could text Alex to let him know that I'm about to spend three weeks with his Twitch idol. My fifteen-year-old brother is almost always plugged into a video on his phone, and most of the time, it's one of Corinne's streams. I'm not much of a gamer, but she seems pretty badass. There are hardly any women on the most-followed streamer lists, especially Black women, so not only is Corinne breaking boundaries, but it looks like she's crushing them. This past spring, when a toxic alpha-male streamer started trolling her, Corinne challenged him to a match in a battle-royale game—and totally destroyed him, obviously. Her following surpassed his within hours, and it's only been growing since then. But she hasn't been going live lately, which I only know because Alex has been complaining about it for weeks. Mentally, I promise him that I'll ask Corinne what's been going on, once I stop feeling intimidated by how effortlessly cool she looks in her green coverall romper and platform sneakers.

A scoff draws my attention to Aaron Tyler Banks, sitting as far from everyone as he can manage—which isn't very, since the boat is barely big enough to fit the five of us, the driver, and our bags. Scowling at Max, Aaron squirts sunscreen into his hands and smears it onto his pasty, freckle-covered skin. "Whatever you think you're filming, you officially do *not* have permission to use my face."

Max shoots him a look. "You signed the release forms, didn't you?"

"Yeah, for the actual show. Not your little project."

Aaron's snarky expression is an echo of the one that used to be on my TV all the time, back when he was the lovable, mischievous star of *The Magnificent Millers*. Except now, all of that youthful glow is gone. Aaron can't be older than twenty-two, but he's got dark circles under his eyes, and his light-ginger hairline is already retreating. He looks even worse than he did in the tabloid photo of his DUI arrest, his shocked sixteen-year-old face seared into my memory, slack-jawed and sweaty, mixed together with Dad's voice.

Listen, Kicks, he told me, pointing at Aaron's photo on the news. It was only a few months after *Dance It Out* premiered. I was twelve and still not used to the strange reality of my dance studio being streamed into every living room in the country. *The show, all this social media stuff . . . promise me it won't turn you into a kid like him.* Dad paused. *Or if it does, promise me you'll at least have a better-looking mug shot.* We laughed it off together, but to this day, I've taken his advice to heart.

The boat slows to a stop, bobbing against the dock. As the motor quiets to a dull rumble, my heart picks up speed. Part of me is aware that this whole thing might be an unbelievably stupid idea. I, of all people, should know that reality TV isn't the best way to take a break, even if that's technically the point of all this: leaving our phones behind and living *IRL,* as the show's slightly on-the-nose title would suggest. Except I've been ignoring the part where three weeks off the grid also comes with cameras in my face 24/7.

I may not have thought this all the way through.

"You made it!" A tiny figure waves from the dock: Tilly, the PA we've been in touch with throughout the casting process. "Come on up, the gang's all here."

Tilly could be anywhere between eighteen and twenty-five—I really couldn't say which. There's something ageless about her energy, camp counselor meets suburban mom. With another enthusiastic grin, she starts hauling suitcases as big as she is off of the other boat, already docked, as the five other cast members start to disembark.

A girl steps out first, silky red hair billowing from under a floppy sun hat.

No. Is that . . .

"Kira?" McKayleigh Hill locks eyes with me, glossy mouth hanging open in shock. For half a second, I think she's about to throw a fit, demand I leave, but then she flashes a bright white grin. Her Alabama accent oozes out of her, stevia-sweet. "Get the heck up here and give me a hug, girl! It's been forever!"

I genuinely would rather leap into the Caribbean, but even though fitness is my thing, I don't think I have it in me to swim fifteen miles back to the mainland. There's no escape. Taking a deep breath, I lift my bags and climb out of the boat.

McKayleigh imprisons me in a tight hug, her Marc Jacobs Daisy perfume overpowering.

"I can't believe you're here, too! We're gonna have *so* much fun." She releases me, her bright green eyes conspiratorial. "I mean, look at this island! The other *Dance It Out* girls are gonna die when this airs, right?"

"Yeah, I guess." I can't form a more coherent response, because I'm too stunned to speak. It's been years since I've seen McKayleigh in person, but her smile hasn't changed a bit. It's the same one she always used when she was fourteen to disguise backhanded compliments or distract the judges from forgotten choreography, and now here it is, beaming down at me. McKayleigh Hill, the girl who bullied me on national TV for years, is standing in front of me acting like we're the best of friends.

And I'm not the only one who seems startled to see her. Stepping onto the dock, Logan looks like she's seen a ghost.

McKayleigh stares back, that fake-friendly smile still painted on. "Logan. It's been a minute."

My nerves twist into irritation. I should've known the producers would pull some crap like this. If the history between me and McKayleigh wasn't enough, she's also one of the cofounders of the Bounce House—as in, the content collective that Logan just quit. Or got kicked out of, if you believe some of the rumors.

And clearly, the producers didn't stop there. The blood drains from Logan's face as two more people climb onto the dock: Zane Rivers and Graham West, completing the Bounce House trio. Both of them freeze when they see her.

Zane recovers first. "Logan. Didn't realize you'd be here."

"Yeah, I'm sensing a theme," she snaps.

He smiles, running a hand over his stubbled jaw. "As friendly as ever, huh?"

Technically, all three of them—Zane, McKayleigh, and Graham—are the founders of the Bounce House, but everyone knows it's Zane's brainchild. Everything about him screams "leader": at twenty-two, Zane's the oldest—McKayleigh's twenty, Graham's nineteen, and Logan's eighteen—and he physically towers over them, too. But between Zane's man-bun, his vegan-lifestyle content, and the tattoos covering his toned arms, I feel like the ideal thing for Zane to lead would be either a SoulCycle class or a cult.

Graham gives a nervous laugh, pulling off his beanie and running a hand through his jet-black hair. While Zane looks totally at home on an island, Graham, with his all-black clothes and porcelain complexion, looks like he should be anywhere else. I'm genuinely impressed by his commitment to the e-boy aesthetic, even in eighty-degree weather.

"Mom, Dad," Graham teases. "Stop fighting. The other kids are watching."

Zane's laugh is half-hearted, and Graham shrinks, picking at the strap of his guitar case. Like the rest of the Bounce House, Graham has millions of followers, although I'm not really sure why. Not that Graham isn't good—he's got a really nice voice—but something about all three of them just seems so . . . fake, I guess. Like they're living, breathing brands, which technically they are. We all are. My manager is always going on about my brand, what we need to do to sell it. It's part of why I came here, what I wanted to get away from.

Now, though, I'm not sure what I was thinking.

Normally, I don't mind silence, but the tension between the Bounce House and Logan heats to a simmer. Something about this whole thing is making me itch, a creeping feeling all over my body. When someone new emerges from the boat, I'm grateful for the interruption.

"Oh my god." Elody Hart pushes designer sunglasses up into her blond hair, revealing ice-blue eyes. "This is so cute. It's, like, a real island."

"As opposed to a fake one?" Aaron mumbles, adjusting the back of his boat shoe.

Elody steps onto the dock and stares at him blankly, a hand on her hourglass hip. She's one of those girls who's famous for being unbelievably hot, her grid a patchwork of bikini pics, lip-sync thirst traps, and dead-eyed selfies. Outwardly, Elody's probably the least relatable eighteen-year-old in the world, but a lot of people seem to connect with her story: raised in a trailer park in Florida, Elody lived with a single mom and bills piling up on the counter until a few viral pictures launched her into stardom.

It's always cool to see other creators who didn't grow up rich—unlike McKayleigh, whose family moved from a multimillion-dollar mansion in Alabama to another in Highland Park the second she got cast on *Dance It Out*—but watching Elody now, I can't help but feel intimidated. I always figured she edited the crap out of her pictures, but she's just as flawless in person, even as she frowns at Aaron like she's trying to place him.

Suddenly, she gasps. "Wait, Aaron Tyler Banks. I thought you died, like, four years ago."

He blinks. "What?"

"Ohhh, my bad, babe." A catlike grin creeps onto her filler-plumped lips. "That was just your career."

A loud laugh booms from the boat.

"Broooo, you just got *roasted*!" Cole Bryan tosses his bags onto the dock and leaps down after them, pulling a backward baseball cap over his mop of blond hair. Seeing Aaron's red face, he laughs harder, giving him a frat-boy slap on the back. "Nah, dude, I'm just playing. Rub your sunscreen on it and you'll be good." He elbows Elody. "Am I right?"

She scrunches up her face. "Um, ew?"

For some reason, that makes him laugh even harder.

I fight a groan. If you asked me who I was *least* hoping to see here, it would have been Cole Bryan. Somehow, he's pulled in millions of subscribers with his prank videos, all of which share the same sense of "humor": explosions, air horns, or misogyny. A few months ago, Cole got exposed for some old tweets that were pretty much everything you'd expect from someone like him, in all the worst ways. His apology video is still burned into my brain—fake tears, ring light reflecting in his muddy eyes, and the eerie sense that someone on the other side of the camera was holding him hostage. It was clearly a load of BS, but I guess it was enough for *IRL* to overlook it and bring him on the show. It sucks, but it shouldn't surprise me. Cole's a straight cis white guy, and they take to getting canceled like monsters that grow an extra head when you chop one off.

"All right!" Tilly chirps. "You all got everything off the boats?" When no one says otherwise, she gives another excited clap. "Great! Go ahead and head on up to the house. I'll make sure everything's set down here, and then I'll show you your rooms in a few."

Cole whoops. "Let's roll, squad!"

I take a breath, reaching for my suitcase. Nowhere to go but forward.

Someone curses behind me: Logan, struggling to balance two stuffed duffels on her bony shoulders. I start toward her, but Zane beats me to it, reaching out a meaty hand.

"Need some help?"

Logan glares, her eyes flaring greener in the sun. "I'm good, thanks."

"Come on." He laughs, friendly. "You're built like a toothpick. I really don't mind—"

"I said I'm good." With another blistering look at Zane, Logan hauls up her bags and storms down the dock.

Cole nudges Max. "Yo, camera dude, you better start recording. We're getting some first-class Bounce House drama right now. Hold up." He clears his throat, and then puts on his fratty version of an announcer voice: "This just in—Logan Costello, ex-member of the Bounce House, totally rejects her ex-lover Zane Rivers right in front of the whole island! Zane, bro, what do you have to say to the people?"

Zane makes a face. "We aren't 'ex-lovers,' man. Grow up."

"Hey, not judging if the rumors are true. Logan's a little too tall, but I'd hit it."

I would really like to push Cole into the water, I think.

"Come on," Max says, lowering his camera. "Not cool."

Cole laughs. "Relax, bro, I'm just playing. Like, I did the work and shit. I respect women now."

Max rolls his eyes, walking faster to leave Cole behind.

"Dude, it was just a joke," he calls after him. "Right, fitness girl?"

He winks at me, like this is a little inside joke of ours, and my stomach roils. If this is day one and I'm already on a nickname basis with Cole Bryan, then maybe I really *do* need to jump into the Caribbean. And also rethink every life choice I've ever made. But instead, I breathe out through my nose and remember what's gotten me through these past five years in the public eye: keeping my cool. Not playing into the drama. And definitely not giving people like Cole Bryan the attention they want but don't deserve.

I pick up speed, keeping my focus locked on the house.

"For real?" Cole mumbles. "None of you guys can take a joke."

"Weird," Corinne says as she walks by. "Didn't realize you were making any."

He pulls a face. "I thought girl gamers were supposed to be cool."

"Yeah, well . . ." She turns and walks backward, giving him finger guns. "I'm all about breaking down stereotypes."

Corinne shoots me a look as she passes, like, *God help us.* I give one back that says, *Please restrain me if I try to muzzle Cole Bryan, or actually maybe don't.* She laughs, and watching her walk away, I'm grateful that someone who seems normal is here. At least I might make a friend.

Feeling another pair of eyes on me, I turn to find my only other potential friend so far: Max, that same crooked grin on his face.

"Feeling better?"

"What?" My chest flutters. Okay, so "potential friend" is maybe not the right term, if we're being specific, but that's beside the point.

He gestures at the dock. "Now that we're on dry land."

I cross my arms. "To be determined."

"Fair." He laughs. "Keep me updated."

"Still looking for that interview?"

"Too obvious?"

"No, not at all." I point at his camera. "You've only had that thing out for . . . the whole time we've been here?"

He puts a hand to his heart like I just stabbed him. "Brutal. But I respect the journalistic advice. I'll try to be less obvious, fitness girl."

Somehow, Cole's nickname sounds less atrocious coming from Max.

I try not to smile as I quote Cole right back to him. "You're welcome, camera dude."

As I turn away and keep walking, I can't help it. The smile stretches across my face, warm and giddy. It's very possible that this show will be a disaster. But maybe it's exactly what I need.

Fifteen miles from the mainland, and so much farther from home, from everything waiting for me there: college applications and career decisions. Endless messages and comments and emails from all the people who need me to be something I'm not so sure I can be anymore.

But here, on this island, I have the chance to just *be*. I could stand on the shore and scream into the sea and no one would hear me.

We're completely, perfectly alone.

ELODY

Oh my god, *finally*. Following Tilly into the air-conditioned house, I could literally cry. Seriously, if she took one more second unlocking it—I swear, it's like this girl has never seen a door in her life—I was going to die from the heat. And once I did, I would absolutely come back as a ghost and haunt her tiny ass, because the humidity is totally ruining my blowout, and that's a worse crime than killing me with heat exhaustion.

"Welcome," Tilly says, "to real life."

I roll my eyes. We're really committing to the brand, huh? But when I look at the mirror in the entryway—my hair is doing better than I thought, thank god—I catch everyone else's faces as they take in the house. They're, like, losing their minds.

Turning away from my reflection, I take a second to appreciate it, too. It *is* a pretty nice house, even if the décor is a little much, with all the potted palms and wicker furniture, everything white, white, white so the bright blue water pops through the massive windows. Like, we get it, babe. We're on an island.

A few steps ahead of me, Max Overby has his camera out, sweeping it around like the little moviemaker he is. He pans through the open-concept first floor, going from the big sectional, cushy chairs, and TV in the living-room area to the beachy wood and stainless steel of the kitchen. There's a dining area, too, with a long table and ten chairs, like we're all about to have an adorable family dinner—which makes me want to laugh and also gag a little, because *imagine* me eating dinner with someone as random as Aaron Tyler Banks. On purpose. My followers would murder me.

As we step into the living room, Logan pulls at one of the piercings going up her ear. She's one of those edgy girls who needs to put, like, four holes in each earlobe as a screw-you to society, or whatever. But maybe I would, too, if all of TikTok was starting rumors about why I left the Bounce House. I mean, the *Bounce House*. I know millions of people follow them, but can you imagine being part of something with such a stupid name? I don't know why she left, but maybe Logan had the right idea. Right now, though, she just looks worried.

"Not a lot of places to hide in here," she says, staring up at the second floor.

Logan's got a point. It's literally the perfect setup for reality TV. The white wooden staircase leads up to this indoor balcony kind of thing that wraps around the whole floor, like someone might come out and start doing that one scene from that one Shakespeare play where everyone dies. You could walk right out of any of the doors up there, lean over the balcony railing, and see everything going down on the first floor. The only place that's kind of hidden is the third floor, where another staircase winds up and then disappears.

"What's with all the cameras?" Corinne asks, looking up at one of the many pointing down at us.

I shake out my hair with my fingers, hoping it still looks

good—because I don't pay my stylist this much to *not* be the hottest girl in the room, even from the ceiling.

"Oh, yeah. The cameras," Tilly says. "I know it's a little weird, but this is standard reality-TV stuff, *Big Brother* style. They're pretty much everywhere. Except the bathrooms, of course." She laughs. "Don't worry."

"Facts," Cole says. "I'm gonna have to do a real paint job later. Heads up."

McKayleigh wrinkles her nose. "Ew. Are you four?"

"Airport burritos, dude."

Gross. I've been kind of excited about this whole thing, but the thought of being trapped on an island with Cole makes me want to hop back on the boat. Like, I know about his old tweets and everything, but I'm pretty sure the most offensive thing about Cole Bryan is his entire personality.

"The house is amazing, though, right?" Tilly goes on. "We really lucked out to get it, too. The owners are pretty reclusive."

"The Lawrences?" Corinne asks, looking at a potted palm like she's trying to figure out if it's real. News flash: definitely not.

"Actually, I'm not sure who they are," Tilly says. "I mean, I don't know if Lawrence is their name. All I know is they've owned the island for decades, but besides family and close friends, they haven't let anyone in. Our showrunner has a connection, so that's how we got it."

"Well, doesn't that just dill your pickle?" McKayleigh smiles, twirling a lock of iron-curled red hair. "We must be special."

Like, I've got to hand it to her. McKayleigh's name may be an actual crime, but it just fits her perfectly, doesn't it?

"Yeah, this is sick," Graham says, pulling on his dangly cross earring.

Ugh. I don't get why everyone wears those now. You'd think it's some kind of second coming, but I'm pretty sure the only divine inspiration is coming from K-pop or Harry Styles. Makes sense for Graham, though. His whole *thing* is just copying people with actual personalities. He acts like some kind of musician, but the only songs he posts are covers, feat. the most constipated singing face I've ever seen.

Next to Graham, Zane checks his reflection in one of the big windows looking out to the beach, rubbing at his stubbly jaw. "I can't wait to meditate out there, man."

My eyes are literally going to fall out if I keep rolling them like this. But I guess I should feel bad for the Bounce House. They were hot shit for, like, two seconds, and now people are already getting bored of them and the whole TikTok-house thing. Maybe I'd be super annoying, too, if I had such an embarrassing career.

A phone chimes, and on instinct, I reach for my purse, even though I leave mine on silent, because hello? I'm not a sociopath. Everyone else grabs for their pockets, too, but we all know there's only one phone in the room. The rest are back on the mainland.

Tilly gets her phone out of her fanny pack and squints at the screen.

"Oh! Speaking of our showrunner, I've got to take this. You guys can go ahead and get settled upstairs. Your rooms are marked, so just look for your names, and meet me back down here in ten for the tour!"

Tilly scurries away, leaving us alone.

"Onward and upward, kids." Aaron claps his hands like he's everyone's dad, or something.

Speaking of people with embarrassing careers.

Everyone starts to haul their stuff up to the second floor, but looking at the number of steps and knowing how many outfits I shoved into my bags, I get a better idea.

"Hey, babe."

Max practically jumps, pushing his glasses up his nose like he can't believe I know he exists. I smile, nudging my bags with my sandal.

"Help me with these? I promise I'm a strong independent woman, or whatever, but I'm really not feeling this manual-labor moment right now, and I bet those skinny arms are stronger than they look."

"Oh." He blinks, like he's literally short-circuiting. It's so cute. "Um . . ."

"Thanks."

I give his little twig arm a squeeze, and then bounce up the stairs, giving him a full view of how good I look in these shorts. What can I say? I have a thing for artistic nerds. It's so cute how they take themselves so seriously, how they act all confident and charming until two seconds of flirting can turn them into a puddle. And, like, I *guess* Max Overby isn't the worst thing to look at.

Upstairs, Kira and Corinne are moving into the first room to the right, and when I get closer, I can see a sign on the door with the three of our names on it. Of *course* I'm rooming with two people who give me total teacher's-pet energy, but I can't complain. One door down, Logan and McKayleigh are walking into their room like they already want to kill each other. So, yeah. I'll take my chances with little miss cardio and the gamer girl.

"Oh my god, cute," I announce, posing in the doorway. "Not gonna lie, I was hoping for my own room, but I love this for us. Three little beds. It's like camp, or something."

I'm joking, because ew, who goes to camp? But neither of them laugh, just stare up at the ceiling.

"Yeah, if camp was some kind of high-level security base," Corinne says, pulling nervously at one of her curls.

Kira rubs at her arms like she's cold. "It's kind of weird, right? Cameras in our rooms?"

"I mean, sure." I flop onto the nicest-looking bed and sink into the soft white covers. "But it's a thing. Haven't you seen those dating shows where they, like, film people hooking up with that weird night-vision filter? Wait, ew, do you think that's what these are for?" I sit up, gaping. "Actually, that sounds kind of hot. I might do it."

Corinne stares at me with actual terror in her eyes. "Or maybe . . . don't?"

"Oh my god, I'm kidding. Don't be such a prude."

Someone knocks on the door.

"Elody?" Max cracks it open without looking in.

Speaking of people I might hook up with on camera . . .

"Your stuff is out here," he says.

I grin. "You don't have to hide, babe. We're not naked."

He opens the door a little more so I can see his face.

"Yet," I finish.

Max turns red, looking everywhere in the room but at me.

God, it's just so easy.

"Thanks for bringing up my stuff, babe. You're, like, a literal star."

"Max!" Cole stomps down the hallway before he can say anything else. "You, me, and Graham are on the third floor, bro. It's about to be *lit*!"

As Cole stomps away again, Max sighs. "Well, I'd hate to miss one second of *that,* so . . ."

He disappears into the hallway, creaking our door shut behind him. Kira watches with her brown Bambi eyes like she's stuck in headlights, or something.

"Stare much?" I ask her. Guess I'm not the only one with eyes on Max, but whatever. Kira seems sweet and all, but come on. It's not even a competition.

"Sorry, I was just . . ." Kira pauses as she opens one of the drawers in her bedside table. Seeing what's inside, she frowns. "There's stuff in here."

"What kind of stuff?" Corinne asks.

Kira reaches into the drawer and pulls out a little card, reading from it. "'Dear influencers.'"

Corinne sighs as she unpacks a pair of thrift-store-looking overalls and, like, three different comic-book T-shirts, like she really needs everyone to know she's *not like other girls*. "I hate that word."

"Isn't that what we are, though?" I ask.

"I mean, sure, but the concept of calling yourself a person with *influence . . .*" Corinne makes a face. "It never sits right."

"Oh, are you one of those people who wants to be a 'creator'?" I put air quotes around it. "No offense, but isn't that even more cringe?"

She doesn't have to answer, because duh. It is. I don't "create" anything except posts that make people either horny or jealous or both. Doesn't keep me from taking the paychecks, babe.

"What does it say?" Corinne asks Kira, ignoring me.

Kira reads it out loud. "*Welcome to Lawrence Island. In these drawers, you'll each find a few gifts, courtesy of your Sponsor, which, as per your contract, you've agreed to use on camera. Enjoy the gifts, and enjoy your stay.*"

"Of course they want us to sell stuff," Corinne says.

"See? Influence, babe. It's in the job title." Lying on my stomach, I reach for my drawer and go through what's inside: some bikini tops, a pair of sunglasses, and a fitness watch, unboxed. I take it out and hold it up.

"Okay, these are so 2015, but also . . ." I slide it onto my wrist. "I can't say no to anything pink."

Corinne is already tapping at her watch, squinting at it like she might try to take it apart and put it back together. "There's a messaging app on here. Weird way to 'unplug,' but I'll take it."

"Doesn't seem like they're connected to Wi-Fi or anything," Kira says.

Corinne sighs. "Yeah, just tried to send an update to my family. The messages won't go through."

I groan. "Seriously? Like, look at this place. They should at least have the budget for Wi-Fi."

"The price we must pay for *real life*," Corinne says drily.

I lean back on my pillows with extra dramatic flair. I know not having phones is, like, the whole point here, but it's going to be harder than I thought. I should at *least* be allowed to complain about it.

"Well, if anyone needs pointe shoes . . . apparently, I have some?" With a confused look, Kira reaches into her drawer and pulls out a pair of pink ballet slippers. "But I don't know how they expect me to use these on camera."

"Oh my god, you should totally do a little dance for the show," I tell her.

She puts the shoes back. "I don't really do that anymore."

"What, show off?"

"Dance," she says, closing the drawer.

Someone knocks on the door, and thank god, because I really don't need a monologue about Kira's competition dance trauma, or whatever. I sit up, wondering if Max is back for more, but then McKayleigh opens the door, giving us the fakest smile I've ever seen. I don't even pretend I'm not disappointed.

"Hi, girls!" She looks around the room, pulling at the watch on her wrist like it's a nervous tic. "So sorry to barge in on y'all, but I think Tilly's ready for the tour."

McKayleigh looks over her shoulder, and that's when I notice

Logan glaring in the hallway a good five feet away. When she catches me looking, Logan glances down, fixing her ponytail, as if she doesn't purposefully wear it all messy. I almost laugh. Logan and McKayleigh, former fake *besties,* are forced to room together for ten minutes and they're already about to bite each other's heads off.

Suddenly, I feel a burst of new energy, jumping to my feet like I just pounded a bunch of espresso shots. Some people have cardio. I have other people's drama. And I'm starting to think this is going to be fun.

I strut out the door and into the hallway.

"Come on, babes," I call back after my roommates, launching into my best Tilly impression and giving McKayleigh a grin. "It's time for real life!"

MAX

Islands give me the creeps. Private ones especially. Something about it strikes me as completely delusional—the idea that people fantasize about being miles from the nearest hospital as a way of, you know, *relaxing*.

Still, I can't say it isn't incredible to look at. As Tilly leads us through the doors and onto the back patio, I pull out my camera and capture it: beach all around, water as far as I can see. Without the house to orient us, it would be hard to know which way is which. Nothing but sand, trees, and rocky dips down to the sea, which stretches all the way to the horizon.

Maybe it's the New Yorker in me, but I don't trust it. All this space makes me claustrophobic, like the endless water and sky makes the island even smaller than it is. Cramped. This is the kind of place where you say and do wild things just to fill it up, the kind that separates truth from lies like a sieve.

Lucky for me, I've got a camera to catch whatever falls through the cracks.

"That view, right?" Tilly muses, cupping her hand over her eyes as she looks out at the water. "Really takes your breath away."

Zane nods thoughtfully, like he's looking at a painting. "The ocean is so powerful, man."

I'm pretty sure we're looking at a sea, but I won't be a jerk about semantics. No matter what you call it, Zane has a point. I think of what Kira said earlier about *Jaws* and *Titanic*. We were joking, but there's something uniquely terrifying about huge bodies of water.

"We're pretty far out from the mainland, right?" I ask, trying not to sound too freaked out by the idea.

"Fifteen miles," Kira answers. I turn to look at her, but she avoids my gaze, moving like she's going to tuck a strand of light-brown hair behind her ear even though it's already in a short pony-tail. "Right?"

"Fifteen miles," Tilly repeats, nodding to the right. "Come on. We'll loop around this way."

As we follow Tilly, I glance at Kira again. I'm not really a workout-video kind of guy—Elody made that pretty clear earlier with her comment about my arms—so I haven't paid much atten-tion to Kira Lyons since she was on that dance show that my sister used to watch. From the episodes I caught, I remember Kira being good—incredible, honestly, and not just for a twelve-year-old—but she never seemed to get the attention. That was always reserved for McKayleigh and her stage mom to end all stage moms. Now, Kira still has that cute, big-eyed thing about her, but hardened some-how, straight posture and tight shoulders. She also can't be taller than, like, five foot two, but there's something intimidating about her. Maybe it's the fact that she could probably kick my ass if she wanted to.

"Here we are." Tilly stops at the front terrace. "Back where we started."

She gestures widely at the beach in the distance, where one of the boats that brought us here still bobs in the water. The other must've left when we were moving in. Waves crash against the shore, which might be an issue for audio, but I'll worry about that once I know where I'm even going with this. That's the best part of what I do: following an impulse, chipping away until the story comes through like a statue from a block of marble. And with ten influencers trapped on an island without their phones, a story is bound to be here. A good one. I already couldn't believe my luck when I first got on the boat and Logan was there—so when the three other most controversial members of the Bounce House showed up on the dock, it was like I hit the jackpot.

I've heard rumors about crazy shit going down at their parties, from the probably true (a minor lawsuit when fireworks singed a model's famously insured hair) to the definitely embellished (wannabe TikTokers getting so lost in the winding mansion halls that they're never seen or heard from again). And now, with all the drama around Logan leaving, it's like this documentary is being handed to me all garnished on a silver platter.

Still, I can't shake the weird feeling I've had since we docked, like something's off. Panning up to the house, I realize what it is: the cameras. More of them, security-style ones mounted on the roof, angled down toward us. And look, I know—as a YouTuber, I probably shouldn't be so creeped out, but that's the thing. The only camera I ever get in front of is my own.

"You guys are welcome to use the pool whenever you want," Tilly says, bringing my attention back to the terrace. "The pool house, too, although there's not much in there."

I pan to the small cottage on the left of the pool, the saltwater blue reflecting in its shut doors.

"But really, make yourselves at home. We want things to feel as organic and fun as possible. Just a bunch of cool creators hanging out on a private island!" Tilly smiles and glances down at her phone. A worried line creases her forehead.

"Okay, no offense," Elody says. "But can we wrap this up? It's, like, a million degrees."

"Of course." Tilly shoves her phone back in her pocket. "Let's head back inside and meet in the living room. There's a few quick things I want to discuss."

As the group starts moving back to the house, I do another quick sweep, landing on Zane. He glares at me over his tattooed shoulder, and I lower my camera. I'm not a Zane Rivers fan—I mean, the guy's most-watched TikTok is a thirst trap featuring a zucchini that I genuinely believe is now entitled to financial compensation—but I should cool it with the filming if I'm ever going to get any of the Bounce House to talk to me on the record.

As I zip my camera into my bag, someone materializes at my side like a ghost.

"Jesus, Aaron."

"I wasn't kidding earlier," he says, jabbing his freckly chin at my camera bag. "I'm not giving you consent to use my face in whatever garbage this is."

"Weird." I push my glasses up my nose. "A few months ago, you were pretty persistent about being on my channel." Watching his scowl get deeper, I shrug. "Look, we're gonna be here for a few weeks. If you're still sitting on that story, I'm all ears."

Aaron stares at me for a few seconds, and then looks away, squinting in the sunlight. "Thanks, but no thanks. That story needs more than a kid using Mommy and Daddy's connections to get ahead."

My jaw tightens. Sure, my parents are both in the industry, but neither of them has documentary connections. My mom produces rom-coms and my dad does a late-night talk show. It's not like either of them called up eight hundred thousand friends and forced them to subscribe to my channel. It's not like they did the work for me, the hours of research and filming and editing.

But I let it go. For one thing, I'm pretty sure the big, top-secret story that Aaron wanted to collab on a few months ago doesn't actually exist. He was promising dirt on some unnamed Hollywood agent, but I've seen the rest of his channel. All the videos have titles like "The Dark Truth About Your Favorite TV Shows" and "How Timothee Chalamet Stole My Career," except all Aaron ever does is make vague suggestions cut off by ads for acne cream or online therapy. Aaron Tyler Banks needs a win a lot more than I do right now. So, I let him have it.

When we make it back inside, everyone's already gathered up in the living room. Aaron speeds to the only open chair left, and I sigh, settling for the floor.

"All right, listen up for a sec," Tilly announces. She takes a careful breath. "So, there's a bit of a situation. Due to some unforeseen weather, the production team's flights were canceled."

"The weather?" I glance out the windows at the perfectly sunny sky. My vision isn't the best, but the lack of storm clouds is pretty hard to miss.

Tilly nods. "The storm isn't supposed to get here until tonight, but it's looking bad, especially near the airport. Our team was able to book another flight out, but unfortunately . . ." She steels herself with another breath, and then speeds through the rest. "They won't be able to get here until tomorrow morning."

Okay, I don't *love* where this is going, especially since we're so far from the nearest signs of civilization.

"Hang on," McKayleigh starts. "Now, I'd never try to tell anyone they're doing their job wrong, but I'm a little confused. Shouldn't the crew have gotten out here before we did?"

"To put it in less Southern-belle terms," Aaron adds snarkily, "this is totally unprofessional. I've been on sets my whole life, and this has never happened."

"Were you on a TV show or something?" Logan asks, feigning surprise.

Aaron's ever-present scowl somehow reaches a new level, and I've got to admit, I enjoy it.

"I know it's not ideal," Tilly says, "but it's the situation. And . . ." She swallows. "They need me to come back to the mainland. Tonight."

"Wait, tonight?" Corinne repeats. "Like, you want us to stay here alone?"

"There are some urgent things they need me to handle, so . . . unfortunately, yes."

"Dude." Cole grins, leaning back on the couch with his hands behind his head. "This is totally where the horror movie starts."

"Is this, like . . . legal, though?" Graham asks. "Just leaving us here?"

Elody rolls her eyes. "It's not like we need a babysitter, babe."

"Some of us, maybe," Corinne mutters, giving Cole a look.

Tilly ignores their quips, forging ahead in classic PA fashion. "I understand the concerns, but I'll be back first thing in the morning. The whole team will."

"What do we do if something happens?" Kira's standing behind the couch, bouncing on her heels like she might take off at any second. She glances at McKayleigh, and I start to wonder if there's something more than their old TV rivalry going on there. Just as it crosses my mind, Kira catches me watching her, and I look away, feeling weirdly like I'm back in tenth grade and handing a bouncer my McLovin-level-bad fake ID. Normally, I'm good at reading people, but there's something about Kira that I can't pin down.

One second, she seems nervous and shy, but the next, I'm pretty sure she can see into my soul.

"Rest assured, you guys will be totally safe here," Tilly says. "There's a first-aid kit in the closet, but if there's an emergency, I'll be leaving a phone behind, so don't hesitate to call. The cell service is pretty reliable, even this far out from the mainland."

Tilly reaches into her bag and takes one out. As she plugs it into the wall with a charger, I relax. It seems like everyone else does, too. At least we'll have *some* sort of connection to the real world.

When no one argues, Tilly sighs, looking just as relieved as we are.

"Think of it this way," she says. "Tonight's a chance for you guys to do what you came for—you know, unplug, get to know each other for real. And now, you get to do it without a whole camera crew in the way."

Right, what we came for. Looking around at this group, I can't say that *unplugging* is anyone's primary goal here.

"What time do we start shooting tomorrow?" McKayleigh asks. She glances up at a camera on the wall, fixing her hair and proving my point: supposedly, we're all here to get away from our phones, but this is a cast of influencers. They may act annoyed at my filming, but none of them would be here if it weren't for the cameras.

Well, maybe not all *of them,* I think, looking at Kira. For someone who grew up on reality TV, she seems about as uncomfortable with the cameras as I am.

"We're aiming to have everyone here and ready by eight," Tilly says. "And don't worry about food. We're fully stocked. Plus, we have a catered dinner for tonight, courtesy of our Sponsor."

She sweeps a hand toward the kitchen, where an array of covered trays sits on the counter.

"There's vegan options, right?" Zane asks. "Also, my manager should have mentioned, but I can't do nuts either. I have this—"

"We get it," Aaron grumbles, waving a hand at Zane's head. "The man-bun is pretty much a blaring 'I have annoying dietary restrictions' alarm."

Zane doesn't respond, but judging from his expression, I have a feeling the comeback brewing in his head is something along the lines of *At least I have enough hair to put in a bun, asshole.*

"Yes, of course," Tilly says. "We've taken all dietary restrictions into account. And as an added bonus . . ." She gives a mischievous smile. "Our Sponsor has thrown in a fully stocked bar."

"Noice!" Cole shouts.

"Now we're talking, babe," Elody says.

Tilly relaxes. "The legal drinking age *is* a bit fuzzy on international waters. But please, please, *please* be careful."

I'm pretty sure careful is the exact opposite of what production wants. Reality TV thrives on getting their casts as drunk as possible. Still, this isn't the worst thing. A private island, alcohol, and no supervision . . . maybe I'll be able to get some ideas for this doc.

Tilly's phone chimes, and she checks it.

"I should start heading out," she says, looking back up at us. "Thanks so much for understanding. We'll be back on track tomorrow, and I'm only a phone call away. Okay?"

"Okay," Elody says, when no one else will. She's lounging on the couch, legs stretched out on the coffee table like she owns the place, shorts riding dangerously high up her thighs. She catches my stare and grins, catlike. "We're big kids, right?"

My face gets hot, which makes her smile even more. *Jesus, Max. Pull it together.* Forget tenth grade—it's like I'm back in middle school, probably because Elody reminds me of all the girls I used to be too scared to even look at back then. I turn away from her and focus on the rest of the group, which, for the first time, has completely run out of arguments.

"Okay, then." Tilly clasps her hands like she's praying. "This is where I leave you."

LOGAN

I'm in hell. Actual, biblical hell. It's the only explanation I can scrounge up for why I'm here, trapped on an island with the three people who I specifically came here to get away from. The worst part is, it's my own fault. I know the cast list was supposed to be secret, or whatever, but I should have done something, anything. Like tell Tilly I'd refuse to work with anyone even a little bit associated with the Bounce House, or blackmail her for the cast list, or just yeet myself off the dock and swim for it as soon as I saw the three horsemen of the apocalypse—I mean, my former *friends*—coming toward me.

Oh well. If this is hell, at least the weather's nice.

For now.

"Wow." I flop onto my pillows, staring at my *hashtag-roomie.* "It's been twenty minutes since Tilly left and you haven't said a word. That's a new record."

Silently, McKayleigh lays out two dresses side by side on her bed, smoothing them out so roughly you'd think they personally attacked her entire family.

"Oh, cool. We're still doing the thing where you act like I died. Got it." I reach for a pillow and wave it around, making ghostly sounds. "Wooooooo. It's floating!"

"You're not as funny as you think you are."

I drop the pillow, trying to ignore the gutted feeling in my stomach. Objectively, I'm behaving like a two-year-old, but it still hurts, someone telling me I'm not funny. Especially when she used to think I was pretty goddamn hilarious, actually.

"Sorry," I say. "I guess I'm just trying to figure out how to be here without, like, impaling myself."

"That makes both of us, *hon*." McKayleigh says that last little pet name like she means something a lot nastier, and honestly, it would be better if she just called me a bitch. We both know she's not too prim to say it. But instead, she snatches a dress off of her bed and steps into the closet, closing the door on me and this subject. From inside, she adds, "You should change, too. There's cameras in the kitchen, so they're definitely getting footage of dinner."

I groan, looking down at my oversized *SNL* T-shirt. It's vintage, a gift from my dad for my thirteenth birthday, in honor of my childhood dream job. I guess it still is. Funny how some things never change: I still want to make people laugh for money, and my dad's still a deadbeat asshole. Last time I saw him, he'd flown in from New Jersey with his new girlfriend, Sheila, for some country-music festival. He forced me to have dinner with him, claiming he wanted to "reconnect," but really, he spent the whole time bragging about how famous I am before pretending he forgot his wallet. Maybe I should have burned the *SNL* shirt for catharsis or something, but whatever. It's a fucking cool shirt.

It *is* a little sweaty, though, and it smells like a boat, so I throw it over my head and unzip my suitcase, reaching for my second favorite item of comfort clothing: my XXL hoodie, #1 GRANDPA printed across the chest. I found it in a thrift store a few weeks after I moved to LA. Graham, McKayleigh, and Zane all teased me about it after I got it, but in a way where I knew they were only kidding. At least, I thought so. Maybe I was always their own little secret joke, a shiny new thing to bring home and then sledgehammer to pieces just because they could.

A few weeks after I got the grandpa hoodie, there was a shopping bag on my bed, stuffed with three different designer hoodies, the tags still on. Once I pulled my jaw up off the floor from the prices, I noticed the note scrawled in Zane's handwriting.

Thought you deserved a glow-up, grandpa.

I force down a hard lump in my throat as I pull my thrifted hoodie on over my jean shorts and bury my hands in the sleeves.

McKayleigh steps out of the closet, frowning at my outfit. "Not *that* thing again."

"That one of your Bless by Kaylz originals?" I ask, gesturing at her flowy sundress.

She glares at me. To be fair, I may have said the name of her clothing line like it's the most ridiculous thing I've ever heard, because it is.

"It's called marketing," McKayleigh says, fixing her hair in the mirror.

I laugh, and she whips around to stare at me.

"What's so funny?"

Oh, I don't know, McKayleigh—maybe how you think slapping your name on a clothing line that you only sort-of helped design makes you the Jeff Bezos of the gaslight-gatekeep-girlboss community. I almost say it, but then I remember that I'm trapped with her for the foreseeable future, so I keep my mouth shut.

McKayleigh huffs, checking her watch, the one our lovely

Sponsor is contractually forcing us to wear. "We should head down to dinner."

I look at my own watch, like it will give me a brilliant excuse for why I don't need to go down there and engage with my peers. If only the messaging app on here actually worked so that I could send an SOS to . . . I don't even know who. It's not like I have a bunch of friends fighting to be my emergency contact these days. Dad probably wouldn't pick up, and Mom, who's always taken it personally that I could leave New Jersey and survive without her, would "I told you so" me for the rest of my life. And Harper . . . hearing my little sister's voice would make me so homesick it would snap the last string that's been holding me upright.

In the end, my growling stomach wins out.

"Fine. Let's go."

I follow McKayleigh to the door, but her hand freezes on the handle. She turns back to me.

Something in her expression sends chills down my spine. The mean-girl look is gone—for once, she looks completely serious. Almost scared.

I've only seen that look once before.

McKayleigh flicks a glance up at the cameras, and then angles her body so they can't see her face.

"The rest of us talked about it, and we're all on the same page," she says. "We're not getting into any drama for the cameras."

I almost laugh, because it's such an understatement. *Drama,* like all we have between us is some kind of stupid fight. But then I realize: her forced casual tone, the vague wording. It's like she's afraid someone is listening.

I hug my arms around my ribs, suddenly cold.

"So if anyone asks," McKayleigh goes on," our mouths are shut. Okay?"

Like I have any other option. Like I'm not powerless in the face of them, *the rest of us,* my three former best friends. But I don't say any of that. I do what I've become an expert in over the past two months: I shut up and nod.

McKayleigh sighs. "Good. We don't need all that on TV. It's tacky."

"Don't worry." I tighten my hands to fists. "I'd hate to be tacky."

She opens the door with a glance at my hoodie, a cruel smile curving on her lips. "You haven't changed a bit, hon."

Dinner is another circle of hell, only with better food. The table can barely fit it all: trays of juicy shredded pork, soft tortillas, bowls of guac, chopped onions, and cilantro, all of it filling the room with spice and citrus that make my eyes and my mouth water. But no matter how much food I shove into my mouth, it can't distract me from what I've already learned over the past year: I don't like my friends. Or ex-friends, I guess, but who's keeping track?

Besides every single person in my DMs.

"Okay, y'all." McKayleigh holds up her glass, tapping the side with her knife like we're at a wedding. She's at the head of the table, because of course that's where she put herself. "I just want to make a little toast."

I slump into my chair, bracing myself for a monologue. In McKayleigh land, there's no such thing as *little* when it comes to public speaking.

"Now, I know tonight started out a little wild, but I just want to say that I'm so grateful to be sharing this opportunity with all of you, especially my two best friends."

She gives a dazzling smile to Graham and Zane, on either side of her, and I want to puke. I want to pretend it doesn't hurt as much as it does.

"But seriously, these past few months have been, like, so hard. Of course, it's been such a blessing, the work I'm getting to do with Bless by Kaylz—"

I shove a piece of pork in my mouth to keep from screaming.

"—but starting a business at twenty frickin' years old is hard work, you know? And I'm just . . ." McKayleigh gives an Oscar-winning sigh, hand on her heart. "I'm just so grateful to have a dang vacation, for once!"

"Cheers to that, babe," Elody drones, obviously wanting to shut McKayleigh up. I smile into my drink. At least someone has the balls to do it.

As everyone drinks, Zane stretches, showing off the black ink cobwebbing all over his arms. Looking at his tattoos now, I can't believe I ever thought they were cool. He has his star sign on his bicep, for fuck's sake. Leo, because what else would he be?

"For real, man," Zane says, laying an arm over the back of Graham's chair, like everything is his personal property. "You forget how screwed-up our brains are from looking at screens all the time."

A few seats away, Corinne makes a face. "I mean, that's not really a hot take anymore. But come on. We're all here because of socials, right?"

"Sorry," McKayleigh says. "Remind me what you do again?"

"Twitch, mostly. Working on world domination on the side."

"Aren't you the cutest." McKayleigh's smile gets tighter. "That video-game stuff is so violent, though. Like, don't take this the wrong way, but do you ever think about how you're exposing kids to that?"

"Not really." Corinne sets her fork down with a thoughtful look. "Completely unrelated question for you: how many guns did you have in your house growing up?"

McKayleigh's jaw drops, and I almost choke on my drink. I've never seen someone get right to the core of McKayleigh's bullshit so quickly. I almost want to give Corinne a standing ovation.

"Well, that's different," McKayleigh says, trying to recover. "It's not like my parents were teaching us how to use them on people. Daddy wouldn't even let Hunter shoot his first deer until he was—" She stops, turning pink. "Whatever. It's different."

Corinne smiles, victorious. "Right. So glad we cleared that up."

"I think gaming can be really good for kids," Kira jumps in. "My brother would kill me for saying this, but he's like your biggest fan." She smiles at Corinne, and a dimple curves in each of her tanned cheeks. "You actually inspired him to learn coding. He's even trying to teach me some stuff. I've gotten about as far as opening the program, but it seems really cool."

Corinne brightens. "That's awesome. I'm going to college for computer science in the fall. I want to get into game design, maybe teach kids how to code, too. It's such a huge skill, and so many communities just don't have the resources."

"Kira, I can *totally* see you as a coder," McKayleigh says, bulldozing past even the suggestion of a meaningful conversation. "You've always been such a little nerd. Y'all, just picture this tiny twelve-year-old doing her math worksheets backstage at competitions. No wonder she used to forget the choreo! Too much in that big brain of hers." She laughs, like it's the sweetest thing she's ever heard. "None of us were surprised when you left *Dance It Out.* Honestly, girl, I have so much respect for you. Staying in school, getting your degree. The second I hit a million followers, I was out of there. But you're just so . . . down to earth."

She says it like the name of a fatal disease, and Kira bites her cheek, looking down at her plate. I feel a pinch of guilt. If the McKayleigh I know is the "mature" version, I can't even imagine what she was like as a fourteen-year-old. Well, probably the same, only smaller and with a lot more bedazzled leotards.

And as cruel as she still is, I was friends with her.

"Hey, motion to stop talking about high school? Reliving my two years there gives me a rash," Graham says, using his familiar *let's change the subject before chaos erupts* tone. "Maybe we can all agree that it's nice to have a break and leave it there?"

"I don't know why everyone's so obsessed with taking a break." Elody examines her sharp acrylics. "It's not like our job is so hard."

"I don't know what you mean," McKayleigh says sweetly, pissed as hell.

"I mean I used to live in a trailer park and now I'm a literal homeowner, and all I had to do was post some pictures." Elody shrugs. "No offense, babe, but it's pretty easy."

I can't help but laugh. Elody has about as much substance as a Jell-O shot, but I like her. It's hard *not* to like other creators who grew up like I did, or something like it—creators who probably know what it's like to work a job after school instead of going to dance class or horse grooming or whatever the hell McKayleigh did before she was a reality-TV star. Who maybe even know what it's like to stick some of your pathetic barista paycheck under Mom's pillow because even at sixteen, you were scared we wouldn't make rent that month.

I almost say something to back Elody up, but oh god, McKayleigh's forehead vein is throbbing, and that only means one thing: we're about to get the bless-your-heart equivalent of a curb stomp.

She smiles, practiced and thin.

"Obviously, I've been very blessed to grow up the way I did. I have no idea what it was like for you, not having the same privileges."

McKayleigh sounds genuine enough that for half a second, I

think maybe I was wrong. Maybe she's actually grown as a person in the past two months.

"But if you think this job is easy, girl, you've got another thing coming."

Nope. Here we go.

"Maybe it's different when all you have to do is stand there and take pictures, but I work a full-time job. I mean, I've got my own content, Bounce House stuff, brand deals, and now running my own company . . . like, it's more than some people do at their 'real' jobs. That's honestly my biggest pet peeve. People thinking all I do is dance around and look pretty."

"And she's so *humble*," Graham says, giving an ironic Debby Ryan hair tuck.

It's a joke, but McKayleigh takes the cue to chill out. She fake-swats him.

"It's called confidence."

"Or delusion."

"Don't worry, Kaylz." Zane swings his arm over her shoulder, the three of them in a perfect best-friend tableau. "We love you *and* your very healthy ego."

And there it is. The ache in my chest, the truth I can't ignore, which is that I miss them. Even their little digs, the ones that go too deep. Even though they're not good people—because neither am I. That didn't matter. When I was with them, I was a part of something. It was shallow and stupid and self-involved, but it was *something*, and it was ours.

"You good?" Max asks, quietly enough that no one else can hear.

I turn to frown at him. "Why?"

"You're holding your fork like you want to wring its neck."

"Maybe I do." I put it down, deadpan. "You don't know how this fork has wronged me."

Max laughs. I don't. I'm not into his whole thing, the sickly Victorian-child vibe that some people find hot. Also, I can see his camera on the table, ready to start recording whatever drama he thinks he's about to get right now. He's so obvious, I'm starting to think Jared Sky confessed just to get Max off his ass.

I look away from Max and across the table, where Zane's launching into a Bounce House story that I'm not a part of, something about filling McKayleigh's bedroom with cardboard cutouts of herself as a prank.

"What's going on there, by the way?" Max asks, eyeing Zane. God, he's relentless. "Earlier, I saw you guys—"

"If you keep asking, I'm going to wring *your* neck," I tell him.

"Whoa!" Cole's laugh cuts from across the table like a dying seal. He gestures between me and Max. "Sounds like some kinky shit is going down over here. I want in."

I flip him off.

"Come on, y'all." McKayleigh laughs, but her green eyes flash a warning my way. "Can we not with the drama tonight?"

The *drama*. I remember McKayleigh's scared, robotic face earlier, the way she angled away from the cameras. When I glance up at the ones blinking down at us now, a chill prickles my neck.

Aaron snorts. "Yeah, good luck with that."

"What's that supposed to mean?" McKayleigh asks.

"I mean, look around," he says. "Obviously something happened with Logan leaving the Bounce House. And then there's your little *Dance It Out* rivalry, or whatever you want to call it." Aaron points between Kira and McKayleigh. "Sorry, but if you didn't want drama, you shouldn't have come on a reality show."

McKayleigh's hand tightens around her wineglass, and for the first time, I stop to really wonder: why *did* they come? Some people, it's obvious. Aaron's trying to get relevant again, Cole's trying to uncancel himself. But McKayleigh, Graham, and Zane . . .

since I left, it seems like things have been going well. So well, it's like I was never even there. But that's the thing: no one goes on reality TV because things are going *well* in their career. Just look at me.

"Is that why you came?" McKayleigh asks Aaron. "I'm sure you had *so* many opportunities to choose from. There must have been something that made you pick this one, right?"

Aaron flushes, his mouth hanging open.

"Hey, is anyone thinking about going swimming later?" Kira pipes up, clearly trying to take back control of the conversation. "Because I think swimming could be . . . nice."

"No comment on the *Dance It Out* thing, then," Aaron says.

Kira shrugs, fixing an imaginary fault in her ponytail. "I left the show almost four years ago. It's not exactly relevant."

"Thank you! I'm with you, girl. No drama." McKayleigh's stare lingers on me. "Can we all get behind that?"

I take a long pull of my drink, wishing I'd put way more rum in it than Coke. Or held off on the Coke entirely.

"For real, dude," Cole says, sucking pork juice off his fingers. "I'm so tired of people coming for me. A bunch of trolls egged my Tesla, like, two days before I came here. I literally had to turn off my DMs because this one girl who doesn't shave her pits sends me a paragraph about 'accountability,' like, every day."

This time, I catch myself trying to murder my fork before Max says anything. I loosen my grip.

"What's wrong with accountability?"

Cole holds up his hands like I'm going to shoot. "C'mon, Costello. I already got canceled once."

"Yeah," I mumble. "And it worked so well."

"Sorry, what was that?" Cole asks.

Feeling McKayleigh's silent *don't you dare, Logan,* I look down at my plate. "Nothing."

"No, seriously, bro," Cole says. "I'm open to feedback. I'm 'doing the work,' remember?"

"Cool." I stand up, taking my plate with me. Escaping isn't the most mature solution, but the longer I stay at this table, the more likely it is that I'll say something I can't take back. And as much as I hate it, McKayleigh has a point. We need to act normal, especially me. Because here's the ugly truth: I need to be here. After leaving the Bounce House, all I am is a walking failure. I don't even need my phone to have a pretty good idea of what people are saying about me right now.

> Wtf did she do to get kicked out of the Bounce House lol
>
> I heard Zane rejected her so she quit
>
> He would never date her thirsty ass, the BH just got tired of her being such a bitch
>
> Who cares? Her content sucked anyway

The DMs and comments have been flooding in ever since we released our "joint statement," the one that said there were "no hard feelings." Everyone knows it was bullshit—the Bounce House collectively unfollowing me made that pretty obvious. Still, it's always me and Zane they fixate on. The rumors, the "were they or weren't they" crap, like all I am is my connection to him. Like I'll fail without him.

I'm here because I'm afraid they're right. Because I can't let them be.

Because as much as I want to ignore the dwindling balance in my bank account, Harper needs me and my weekly Venmos for the things Mom can't swing on a nursing aide's pay.

By the time I make it to the kitchen, I'm starting to feel calmer. Maybe being the bigger person isn't the worst thing.

And then, I hear it.

Cole. Laughing.

"Damn, Zane. You dodged a bullet, my dude."

I freeze.

"Come on, man," Zane tells Cole. "We weren't—"

"Nah, fam, you *all* dodged a bullet." Cole snorts. "Like, sorry, but she's not hot enough to be that much of a bitch."

The plate flies out of my hand and across the room, shattering on the floor a few feet away from Cole.

"Shit!" He stands up, almost tripping over his chair. "Are you trying to kill me?"

I don't move, staring at the shards like I don't know how they got there. And then I see Zane's face. His amber eyes. The hard line of his jaw. It's not even anger anymore—it's like he knew exactly what would happen. Like he can see what we both know I am.

Weak.

So, I do what I'm best at: I run away without looking back.

ELODY

"Damn," I say, when the awkward silence has gone on for five full seconds. "First dramatic exit and it wasn't even me. I'm, like, kind of jealous."

McKayleigh puts her hands on her face, all freaked out, like Logan just threw a plate at *her*. "Cole, are you okay?"

"She's psycho," he says, running his hands over himself like he's looking for blood or something. "That was literally insane."

"Well, to be fair," Corinne says, "you kind of deserved it."

Kira chews her lip. "Maybe we should go check on her?"

"Check on *her*?" Cole snaps. "She just tried to kill me!"

I lean back in my chair, reaching for my champagne. Sue me, or whatever, but I'm entertained.

"We should leave her alone," Graham says. "Whenever she gets like this, she needs space."

"Sorry," Aaron interjects, "is Logan regularly throwing plates at people's heads?"

Graham rolls his eyes. "Obviously, that's not what I meant."

I turn to Max, who's sitting to my right, and bring my glass to my lips.

"Please tell me you're getting this, babe."

Max's mouth opens a little, caught, because he *is* getting it, camera in hand. Such a little journalist.

Noticing, Cole groans. "Can you put that thing away, dude?"

"Can *you* stop being such a dick?" Max asks. "And there's already cameras all over the place. I don't see what's wrong with trying to—"

Zane slams his beer down on the table so hard the plates shake. "What's wrong is we didn't sign up to be on *your* camera."

Everyone shuts up. For someone who likes to act all chill, Zane can be kind of scary, apparently.

He slumps, putting his face in his hands and then pushing his plate of specially made vegan tacos away. "This tofu was, like, nothing. My blood sugar's so low right now."

And just like that, all the scariness is gone. To be honest, I can't take him seriously ever since my sort-of friend Sasha told me that Zane has an avocado tattooed on his ass. A *literal* avocado. On his *literal* ass. Apparently, she saw it when they were hooking up at some party. She couldn't stop laughing, and he got so mad he kicked her out. I don't know if Logan and Zane ever actually hooked up, but if they did, she might be the one who dodged a bullet.

Aaron stares at the broken plate, hunched over in his chair like a grumpy little ginger elf. "Is anyone going to clean that up?"

McKayleigh stands up and brushes off her dress. "I'll do it."

I clap. "A full-time business owner *and* cleaning up other people's messes. You're, like, so brave."

McKayleigh glares at me, and I try not to giggle. Maybe it's the two glasses I've had so far, but I'm starting to really have fun.

Aaron squints up at one of the cameras. "I bet Tilly regrets ditching us now. First catfight, and all she gets is lame security footage."

"No offense, man," Zane says. "But shut up."

Aaron sinks into his chair, all pouty. Honestly, there's something kind of cute about him, in a sad way. The way he still tries so hard, even though his career ended a million years ago. It's like one of those puppies that has wheels. Like, because it lost its legs.

Corinne stands up. "Well, this has been fun, but I'm gonna call it a night. We have an early day tomorrow."

"Same," Zane says. "Graham, let's help Kaylz clean up."

Graham follows, and then Kira and Max, and oh my god, I guess I have to take charge here.

"Um, hold up." They stop, waiting for what I'm going to say, because let's be honest—I have that effect. "I don't know about you, but I didn't come here to be lame. We have a stocked bar and a *whole private island* to ourselves, and you're gonna just go to bed at literally eight PM like a bunch of old people?"

"I prefer world-weary and wise," Corinne says. "But I brought a really good book to read, so . . ."

"Hell no!" I grab the champagne bottle off the table and climb up onto my chair so I'm standing above everyone. I have their attention now, and I smile, because that's my favorite way to be. "We're not going to bed! We're a bunch of hot people on an island, and you know what we're gonna do?" I cover the bottle with my thumb and shake it up. Then, I let it go, champagne exploding out like a fountain, and yell over the fizz, "We're gonna get *fucked up!*"

KIRA

Elody Hart means business. We may be miles from civilization, but an hour after dinner, we're partying at the pool like we want the entire mainland to hear. And by we, I mean . . . not me, exactly. Bass thuds from the speakers someone found downstairs, laughter and shouts rising and falling like waves, and I'm in the pool, swimming slow laps just to feel busy. I'm not hiding in my room, though, so for all intents and purposes, my plan to get out of my comfort zone is off to an excellent start.

Something big and loud crashes into the pool behind me, sending up a wave that soaks my hair and sprays my shoulders.

Cole splashes to the surface, whooping.

"Ugh!" McKayleigh scowls from her lounge chair, wrapping her towel over her retro-style bikini—I'm guessing a Bless by Kaylz original. "You got me all wet."

"Broooo!" Cole gives a drunken snort. "That's what she said."

He takes a swig from one of the giant bottles taped to his hands, the dumb Edward Fortyhands thing people at my school do at parties. The bottles are probably filled with pool water, thanks to the plunge, but Cole doesn't seem to care. Anyway, he's probably ingested worse.

McKayleigh wrings out her barely wet hair, glaring at him. "You're lucky I have wine."

"Aren't we all." Graham is draped on his own lounge chair, rocking sunglasses and his beanie, even though it's still warm and the only light is coming from the house.

Cole cracks up, paddling away.

I pause in the shallow end and look over to the other side of the terrace, where Elody's trying to make Max dance with her. Aaron bobs awkwardly a few feet away, looking like my dad when he chaperones school dances. Max is clearly uncomfortable, but that doesn't make me feel better, or anything, because I definitely don't have a quickly developing crush on Max Overby.

"You can go talk to him, girl."

I spin around to find McKayleigh smirking at me.

"I see you looking," she says, eyeing Max.

"What? Who? I'm not—"

McKayleigh nudges Zane, who's in the chair to her right, chin tipped to the sky like he's meditating.

"Isn't she the cutest? Kira was always so shy."

Yeah, I want to tell her. Because you made me afraid to speak up.

"You're being condescending again," Zane says, eyes still closed. "Kira, is she being condescending?"

Before I can open my mouth, McKayleigh keeps talking.

"No, Kira knows I love her. Right, girl? Wait, oh my gosh." McKayleigh sits forward. "I totally forgot. I've been meaning to ask you. Corinne, too."

From her lounge chair—two away from the nearest Bounce House member—Corinne looks up from the book she's reading with a wary expression. "Yeah?"

"So, Bless by Kaylz has been looking for brand ambassadors, and I just think y'all would be perfect. I brought some samples with me, and if y'all wouldn't mind maybe wearing a few on camera—"

"Thanks," Corinne says sharply, looking back at her book. "But I'm good. Wouldn't want to let my violent video games corrupt the youths *and* your brand."

McKayleigh gives a fake laugh. "Stop, you're *so* funny. But come on. I bet once I show you the samples—"

"Look, it's nothing personal." Corinne stands and tucks her book under her arm, clearly over this disruption to her reading. "You got me at a bad time. I *just* bought a lifetime supply of floppy sun hats."

She gives McKayleigh a *bless your heart* smile to rival her own before making a completely badass exit to the house. I fight a grin. Even in the dark, I can tell McKayleigh's face is three shades redder with indignation.

Taking a sharp breath, she tosses her hair and sets her sights back on me, making my smile drop.

"Well, I don't know what *her* problem is, but I'm serious about you. You'd look killer in our swimsuits, Kir."

I flinch at the nickname, which I've always hated—the way it shapes her mouth into a sneer.

Before I realize what's happening, McKayleigh turns to the terrace and shouts, "Hey, Max! Don't you think Kira would look hot in a bikini like this?"

She stands and models for him, holding her wineglass high. Max's eyes meet mine, his mouth opening like he isn't sure how to respond. I don't wait to hear it. Face burning, I climb out of the pool and snatch my towel.

"Aw, wait," McKayleigh croons after me. "You've got to stop being so shy, Kir! Be proud of what the good Lord gave ya!"

She laughs, tipping her glass to her pouty lips. I wrap the towel tightly around me and march to the house, angry tears pricking my eyes.

My problem isn't that I'm not *proud of what the good Lord gave me.* I've worked hard to build confidence in who I am, both inside and out. What I didn't count on, what's making me so mad, is that a few hours with McKayleigh Hill are turning me back into the little girl who used to cry whenever she watched herself on TV and found even one imperfection—a missed triple pirouette, a smile that didn't seem quite convincing enough—until dancing started to feel less like breathing and more like a test she'd never pass.

"Can you stop staring?" McKayleigh's hushed voice stops me in my tracks.

For half a heart-pounding second, I think she's talking about me, but when I glance over my shoulder, I realize she's talking to Zane. They're both looking out into the dark, past the terrace and down toward the beach, where the moon shimmers on the water.

Straining through the shadows, I see someone on the sand, a slim, tall figure in a hoodie. Logan. She's walking along the water, following the curve of the island to the other side of the house.

"Why is she here?" Zane asks, an anxious edge to his voice that feels out of character.

"Why do you care?" McKayleigh leans back in her lounge chair, crossing one pedicured foot over the other. "She's not our problem anymore."

Graham looks over his shoulder, noticing me, and I speed back to the house.

In the kitchen, the mess from Logan's plate is gone, but I still get a shivering feeling. Because for the first time, I wonder if I was looking at this all wrong, the island and the solitude. Maybe it's not freedom. Maybe we're just trapped.

Okay. Calm down, Kira. I press the heels of my hands to my

eyes, breathing until the tears stop threatening to fall. I'm not about to let McKayleigh make me cry, and I'm *not* going to let myself fall into an anxious spiral. Everything's fine: Tilly left us a phone, and the crew will be here tomorrow. We're safe. And whatever's going on with Logan and the Bounce House, it's really none of my business.

I'm halfway to the stairs when I hear the front door open behind me.

"Hey." Max walks inside, that crooked smile on his face.

I forget my name and birthday and also a little bit how to breathe.

"Hey." Right. Speaking. That's a normal thing to do.

Max looks over his shoulder, shifting his camera bag. "Sorry, I'm kind of recalibrating. There's . . . a lot happening out there."

"Yeah." I glance out one of the big windows to the terrace, where Cole is currently taking a shot of Elody's bikini top. "A lot is . . . an understatement."

Max sees where I'm looking and laughs. "Oh god."

"Looks like you've been replaced, *camera dude.*"

Max runs a hand through his messy hair, blushing slightly, and it feels kind of nice to turn the tables after he so rudely made me forget my basic motor skills.

"You know, *fitness girl,* I think I'll survive." Another smile twitches on his lips. "Okay, so I could make up another excuse for why I came in here, but really, I just wanted to talk to you."

"Oh." I tighten my towel around my quickening heartbeat. So much for turning the tables. "About what?"

He cringes. "Sorry, that sounded ominous. I just mean—and totally stop me if this is overstepping, but—"

"This is you being *not* ominous?"

Max laughs, sitting on the couch. "Fair."

I sit next to him.

"Look," he says, "McKayleigh has been kind of a jerk to you all day, and I just wanted to make sure you were okay."

That was definitely not what I was expecting. And it *definitely* shouldn't be setting off a swarm of butterflies in my stomach.

I look down at my hands, my pool-pruned fingers. "Thanks. I'm really fine, though. I've learned how to tune her out." I meet his stare, intense and blue behind his frames, and my resolve starts to melt, morphing into frustration. "It's just . . . I really thought she would have changed. Or *I* would have changed. But maybe we don't, really. Maybe we're all just our middle-school selves, only taller and with better skin."

"Or worse vision, in my case," Max jokes.

I smile a little. "And not all that much taller in mine."

He laughs, prompting a return of the butterflies and a reminder that I am totally, 100 percent screwed.

A loud squeal interrupts my internal spiral, and I look out the window to watch as Zane and Graham grab McKayleigh by the arms and legs, swing her back and forth, and then toss her into the pool. She crashes up with a joyful shout, splashing water their way as they dodge it, whooping. It makes me uneasy, how quickly they went from their hushed, anxious conversation to their usual antics.

"There's something off with them, isn't there?"

Right away, I wonder if I shouldn't have said it, but Max nods quickly.

"No, I'm glad you see it, too," he says. "They've been . . ."

"Weird," I finish.

"Yeah." He glances out the window and then back to me. "Do you have any idea what's going on there?"

"I don't know. Just now . . ."

I pause, wondering if I should tell him. But there's something about the way he's looking at me, like he really needs to know. And you know what? I don't owe McKayleigh anything.

"Just now, I overheard them having this intense conversation about Logan. McKayleigh said she wasn't 'their problem anymore.'"

"What does that mean?" he asks.

"I don't know, I—" I stop short, because Max's hand is in his pocket, his long fingers closing around a shape. I catch a glimpse of something shiny and black, and then I realize. "Max, are you recording this right now?"

"What? No, I . . ." He deflates, taking out his recording device. It's small and rectangular, barely bigger than a lighter. "I never would have used the audio anywhere without your permission, I swear."

Of course. Max doesn't care about how I feel. He cares about getting whatever story he thinks I have.

I stand up. "I'm going to go shower."

"Wait, Kira. I—"

A scream cuts him off. We both freeze, my heart climbing into my throat. That definitely wasn't McKayleigh squealing again from the pool. It was someone else. Someone terrified.

I move toward the back patio, where the sound came from, and as soon as I slide the door open, there's Logan running up from the beach. She's breathing hard, her skin sickly white.

An icy feeling floods my veins.

"What's wrong?" I ask.

She sucks in a breath.

"A body," she says. "I saw a body."

LOGAN

Kira's eyes go wide. "What?"

I shove my hands in the front pocket of my hoodie, shivering even in the heat. It doesn't feel real. It can't be. But it was. The dark shape down by the water, the thing I thought was seaweed or driftwood, something discarded by the sea. Until I saw the legs.

"I was walking on the beach, at the back of the house." I squeeze my eyes shut. "And I saw a body."

"Are you sure?" Max asks quietly.

"Yes! I mean, I think. I—" I swallow, try to breathe. "I didn't, like, examine it. I just started running."

Kira turns and walks back inside, going straight to the closet. She throws it open and starts digging around.

"What are you doing?" I ask, sounding as small and helpless as I feel.

"Flashlights." Kira pulls a couple out. "Let's go."

There's no way in hell I'm going back out there. But then, as Kira and Max start walking, I realize there's no way in hell I'm staying here alone, either. I jog out after them, stopping on the patio and watching as they get farther from the house. It's like they disappear into complete darkness, nothing but the beams of their flashlights. Like we're floating at the edge of the world.

Footsteps sound behind me, and I jump.

"Logan?" Zane's voice is like cold hands down my back. He stands in the doorway, McKayleigh and Graham behind him. "What's going on? We heard someone scream."

My mouth goes dry.

Cole stumbles out with his stupid Fortyhands. "We boolin' out here now?"

Aaron's at his heels, and Elody steps out in front of both of them.

"Babe? You look like you're gonna vom."

Corinne's next, wearing her pajamas and a pair of tortoiseshell glasses. "What's happening?"

I take a breath, force it out. "I saw a body."

"*What?*" McKayleigh squeals.

But I can't deal with them right now. I run down the patio steps and out to the water, toward Kira's flashlight.

"Do you see it?" I call out, keeping my eyes on the sandy ground, because I don't know if I can look. The waves break against the sand, loud enough that it feels like they're inside my head, crashing against my skull.

"It's not a body," Max says. But his voice sounds like what it *is* isn't any better.

Finally, I look up to see what Kira's light and Max's camera are trained on.

A mannequin. Faceless, turned up to the inky sky. A message on its chest, painted the color of blood:

YOU'VE BEEN #CANCELED.

. . . .

"Okay, so, like . . . what the actual hell?" Elody asks.

"Was this supposed to be a joke?" Zane looks around the living room like he's searching for the culprit. "Because it's not funny."

His gaze lands on me, sharp and probing, like this is my fault. I glare back, clenching my teeth to keep them from chattering. Now, back in the living room with everyone, I'm embarrassed at my own freak-out, but Zane doesn't get to act like *I* did this.

Aaron shoots a look at Cole. "Why don't we ask our resident prankster?"

"C'mon, bro." He laughs, still drunk. "'You've been hashtag-canceled'? That's so cringe, dude. Not my style."

Corinne shifts her weight from one foot to the other. "To be fair, Cole's probably lacking the hand-eye coordination required to pull off a prank right now."

He gives a warrior cry, raising his Fortyhands.

"Then who was it?" McKayleigh's eyes snap around the room, landing on me. "If this is part of your little meltdown from earlier, then you need to grow the heck up."

"What?" My embarrassment morphs into anger, hardening my spine. "Where would I even find a mannequin and spray paint anyway?"

"I don't know!" She throws up her hands. "But we all saw what you did to Cole."

A harsh laugh cuts through me. What I *did*, like I'm some kind of criminal. Throwing a plate, like, six whole feet away from Cole Bryan might have been immature, fine, but it's hardly the worst thing I've ever done. McKayleigh should know that better than anyone.

"Logan's right," Kira says. "Why would any of us do this?"

"Well, someone did," Aaron mumbles.

"Maybe it was Tilly." Corinne rubs under her glasses like a tired librarian. "I don't know. Some kind of joke to set the mood."

"God, Millennial humor is so lame." Elody looks at Aaron. "No offense."

He glowers. "I'm not even the oldest one here."

"Okay, wait," Graham cuts in. "We're saying Tilly did this?" He wrings his beanie in his hands, black hair staticky. "When? We were with her the whole time."

"Not when we were moving into our rooms," Kira points out. "She could have snuck back there before she left. Did anyone go out to the beach between Tilly leaving and now?"

The room is silent.

"Just Logan," McKayleigh says, like the smuggest fake detective I've ever seen.

"Again," I say through clenched teeth, "*why* would I do this?"

"Why would Tilly?" she shoots back.

"I guess it could've been her." Graham is trying to keep his voice level, to keep the peace like he always does, but I hear it tremble. "Maybe she just has, like, a super weird sense of humor."

I laugh bitterly. "She *does* work in reality TV. Those people eat human suffering for breakfast."

As usual, no one seems to find me funny anymore. I throw my hood over my head and tighten the drawstrings, wishing it would eat me alive.

Corinne lets out a breath. "Look, I'm pretty exhausted, and this seems more like a whole lot of nonsense than an actual threat to anyone's safety, so . . . I'm going back to bed."

Kira nods. "Tilly said they'd all be here by eight tomorrow. We can get this all figured out then. I'm sure it's nothing."

Corinne and Kira start toward the stairs. Cole boos after them, cupping his bottles around his mouth.

Elody stands up from the couch. "Well, if anyone wants to *not* be super old and boring, I'm gonna keep getting drunk."

Cole cheers, and soon, everyone is trickling to the kitchen, where Elody rifles through the alcohol like a drunk-but-somehow-sexy raccoon. For half a second, I want to join them, but then I see them looking at me. McKayleigh, Zane, and Graham, their stony glances making it clear. I'm not one of them anymore. I'm not wanted.

I climb upstairs alone.

As I go back to our room, all I can think is that I wish I had my phone. I'm pretty sure I'd give my left ovary just for the distraction, even though I know what's waiting there: an endless parade of comments, mean and hateful, words that claw under my skin even though the people who left them probably think I'll never read them. Emails from brands explaining that, without the reach of the Bounce House, I'm not the partner that they're looking for.

But I'd take it all, if I could at least call Harper. Laugh with her about my shitty luck until it stops hurting so much.

I close the bedroom door behind me, shutting out the rest of the house. The truth is, if I had my phone, I know exactly what I'd be doing, the same ritual I've done at least once a week for months: scrolling through my old TikToks. The ones I posted before the Bounce House, the sketches and dumb jokes that made people laugh—made Zane laugh enough that he saw something in me, that he sent a DM that changed my life. I don't know why I've been watching them again. Maybe to remind myself that I used to be more than trends and lip syncs and sponsored videos. At least, I used to think I was.

But thinking about it is pointless, because my phone is fifteen miles away, and I chose this. Because I thought this would help me fix things, or at least tune them out for a while.

Voices float up from downstairs as I turn off the lights and crawl into bed. Closing my eyes, I try to focus on the crash and pull of the waves, to forget what I thought I saw down there. What I thought I'd run away from.

TRANSCRIPTION: NIGHT ONE, 3:47 AM
(RECORDING FROM WATCH #2)

[FOOTSTEPS. DOOR OPENING,
CLOSING. WAVES GET LOUDER.]

COLE

Shit. [Hushed laugh.]

[FOOTSTEPS. CREAKING SOUND. PAUSE.]

COLE

Hello?

MAX

I wake up sweating somewhere that isn't my bed. The couch, I realize as my brain starts to work again. We all must have passed out here last night. Sun cuts through the big windows, making my head throb. Sitting up, I cringe at the pain in my neck and feel for my phone before remembering I don't have it. Instead, I find my glasses, and the room comes into focus.

Elody's asleep at the other end of the sectional, her fists curled under her chin like a kitten, and Graham's between us, one arm dangling to the floor. Aaron's on one of the armchairs, sleeping in a seated position, which . . . checks out, I guess. Cole, McKayleigh, and Zane aren't here. They must have gone upstairs after we all fell asleep.

When I spot my camera bag on the floor, the strap drooping, disappointment hits. I only stayed up with everyone last night to try to get some more out of the Bounce House, but all I got is a cramp in my neck that's honestly a little concerning for an eighteen-year-old.

Quietly, I start to extract myself from the couch, glancing at the watch our Sponsor left in my drawer. 7:18. The sheer audacity of how early it is sends my head pounding again. Jesus, it's way too bright in here. Which is ironic, actually. All that stress, and Tilly's storm never even came.

And then it hits me: it's past seven. The production team should be here in less than an hour. We need to get up. But before I can rouse anyone on the couch, I hear the sink running in the downstairs bathroom. The faucet clicks off, and the door opens. Kira walks out in biker shorts and a workout top, looking like she's been awake for hours. Her hair's wavy, cut just above her shoulders, drawing my attention to her sharp collarbone. It's the first time I've seen her with her hair down, and it makes my breath hitch a little.

"Oh," I say. "Hey."

"Hi."

She's looking at me like she did last night, when she saw the recorder. Like she doesn't trust me. I know I need to make it up to her, but it's hard to think straight when she looks like that and I'm coming off of less than five hours' sleep on the couch.

"You going for a run?" I ask, nodding at her clothes. I can't help but notice the way they hug her waist, the hint of tanned stomach between the top and the shorts.

"Already did," Kira says, tying her hair up into a ponytail. "At, like, five. Couldn't sleep. I showered, though. Don't worry." She shakes herself slightly. "Not that you need that information. I just mean I'm not gross or anything. I'm . . . going to get breakfast."

She practically sprints toward the kitchen—god, did I screw up that badly?—but I follow her anyway.

"Kira, wait."

She stops, looking at me with that intense stare. I take a breath.

"Okay, let me preface this by saying you have every right to think I'm an asshole and to reject this apology completely, but—"

"This apology is off to a great and very concise start," she says flatly.

I feel my face heat. "Fair assessment."

"You were saying?"

"I shouldn't have recorded you without your permission. I know it's not an excuse, but I've been stressed about what I'm going to do next on my channel, and I guess I got a little overenthusiastic with this Bounce House stuff, but—" I stop myself, pulling a hand through my hair. "I'm making excuses. What I mean to say is that was wrong. I deleted the recording. And I'm sorry."

"Thanks." She crosses her arms, but her lips quirk with the hint of a smile. "But seriously, if I ever see that recorder again, I'm going to roundhouse it out of your hand."

A surprised grin works its way up to my cheeks. "Well, now I kind of want to see that."

Kira laughs, her mouth opening like she's about to say something else, but before she can, a door opens upstairs. Our attention snaps to McKayleigh as she struts out onto the indoor balcony, dressed and looking like she's already had four cups of coffee.

"Morning, y'all!" She stops at the railing like it's her own personal stage, looking down at our sleeping castmates, and checks her watch. "Oh my gosh, the crew's gonna be here soon. Why's everyone still sleeping?" She calls into her room, "Logan, get your booty up, girl. It's almost seven twenty!"

Kira escapes to the kitchen before I can finish my sentence. McKayleigh has a point, though. I should get ready.

But when I get to the third floor, I stop. Something's off. It's too warm in here, too muggy. I notice the French doors to the balcony are open. Weird. Closing them, I spot the other thing that's off: Cole's bed is empty. But then I clock the closed door to the bathroom, light shining from underneath, and groan. I could wait for him to finish, but I don't love the idea of going in there immediately after Cole, so I throw on fresh clothes, then grab my toothbrush and toothpaste to head to the second-floor bathroom.

By the time I get back downstairs, more people are up and moving. Kira sits at the table, slicing an apple, and Corinne's making coffee. Logan's slouched a few seats away, staring longingly at the coffee maker, her hoodie tight around her face.

The back door slides open, and Zane walks in with a yoga mat under his arm.

"Morning," he calls, cracking his neck as he checks his watch. "Man, I totally lost track of time out there."

Still in the chair where he slept, Aaron groans, rubbing his head. "Why is everyone so loud?"

"It's almost seven thirty," I tell him.

"So?" Aaron stretches his arms over his head, setting off pops and cracks all over the place. "I don't need half an hour to get ready."

Elody stirs on the couch. "Mmmph. Babe. Talking. Early. Why."

"Apparently Max here thinks we're doing a pageant and need thirty minutes to get camera-ready."

God, Aaron must have been a real treat to work with as an actor.

Elody picks up a pillow and throws it at Graham's head, his black hair sticking up like he got electrocuted. "Wake up. The producers are coming."

Graham groans, looking half-asleep, and slowly, the rest of the group gets moving. By a few minutes to eight, everyone's downstairs and at least sort-of ready for the day, gathered in the living room. Wait, actually . . . not everyone.

"I think Cole's still upstairs." I glance at my watch. Jesus, I don't even want to know what he's doing in there. "Should I go get him? The crew should be here soon."

"Can we not?" Logan asks, cradling the largest cup of coffee I've ever seen. "I need three of these before I can handle Cole."

No one argues.

"Cool," I say. "I guess we'll wait."

Something pings. And then again—it sounds like a text tone, dinging over and over. I don't realize what it is until my watch lights up on my wrist, the screen glowing with a text.

A message from your Sponsor

I look up, and everyone else is reading their screens, too. The watches ping again with a new message.

Hey influencers
Ready to get real?

Wait a second. How are we getting texts right now? I checked yesterday, and the app didn't work. Another message flies in.

Let's start off with a question...
What's the biggest lie you've ever told?
You have 5 minutes to share
Go

A timer appears on my watch screen, already counting down.

Intrigue jolts me out of my early-morning fog. This must be our first challenge of the show. It's a little heavy-handed with the influencer theme, maybe, but I have a feeling things are about to get interesting.

"Are we supposed to do this?" Graham asks.

Zane gives his kombucha a tired swish. "I guess so."

"But shouldn't we be waiting for Tilly, or whatever?" Graham says. "This is weird."

More pings fill the room.

I'm watching

Logan groans, leaning back into the couch cushions. "It's too early for this *Pretty Little Liars* shit."

"Maybe we should go with it?" Kira bites her lip, looking up at the cameras on the walls. "It's probably part of the show."

Another text:

If you don't play . . . you're canceled

Logan's scream flashes in my head, sending a nervous rush of energy through me. But that wasn't real, and neither is this. It's what I signed up for: reality TV and all of the drama that comes with it.

"'Canceled.'" Corinne sighs. "I mean, at least they're thematically consistent."

McKayleigh frowns. "Right, because that was *so* funny last night."

"Oh my god, can we just do the stupid question game?" Elody asks. "Like, this is so boring."

I start to unzip my camera bag but stop myself. If yesterday taught me anything, it's that leading with my camera isn't the way to go—counterintuitive, maybe, since everyone here makes a living being in front of cameras, but still. I'll have to be careful, wait for the right time to start recording.

"Who wants to go first?" I ask.

My question hangs in the air as the seconds drain from the timer.

"Ugh, fine. If no one else will . . ." Elody tosses her hair over her shoulder. "This is, like, definitely none of you guys' business, but whatever." She takes a deep breath, like she's steeling herself for a dramatic reveal. "My boobs are fake. I got them done when I was sixteen, after I got my first brand-deal money. I wanted it really bad and my mom signed off, which is totally legal, McKayleigh, so don't make that face. You'll get wrinkles."

McKayleigh rolls her eyes. She *was* just looking at Elody's chest like it had personally threatened violence upon her. Now I'm looking, too, and oh god. Elody notices, and she's grinning.

"Whatever," she says. "I'm not, like, ashamed, or anything. But the first time a follower asked me if they were real, I freaked out and said yeah. So, that's my 'biggest lie.'" Elody waits, looking around the room. "Oh my god, someone else go."

"Mine's easy," Aaron says. "Promised everyone on *Mag Millers* I would start 'behaving.' I didn't. You all read the articles." His beady eyes find me, and a thin smile stretches over his face. "What about you, Max? I'm dying to hear." He glances at my camera. "Seeing as though you're so committed to the *truth,* and everything."

Jesus, I'm really starting to wonder if it's humanly possible for Aaron to speak without that condescending tone, or if his voice is just stuck like that after years of using it to compensate for . . . well, everything else. Still, I let go of the camera bag. Now is not the time.

"Fine. I guess . . ." I pause. I hadn't thought about my answer, but here it is, wading to the front of my memory like an old password or address. "Mine happened in high school. Freshman year. Technically the summer before. I met this girl at camp, and we were friends. Pretty good friends, actually. But I guess she took it the wrong way. She had this crush on me, and . . ."

I trail off, remembering Lacey Warren, with her acne-dotted face and loud laugh, how she never toned it down, not even when people stared.

"I wasn't into her that way," I continue. "Like I said, we were just friends. So, a few months into freshman year, me and my school friends ran into her in the city. She wasn't from New York, so I was caught off guard. It was a new school for me, and the guys were new friends, so I just . . . I was a dick, honestly. I pretended I didn't know her, told my friends that she was just some crazy girl stalking me. I was embarrassed. But it wasn't cool of me."

Kira shifts, the corners of her mouth turning down, and I wish I hadn't said it. She was just starting to forgive my asshole behavior after last night, and I wonder if she's regretting it.

"That's your lie?" Aaron stares me down. "A girl threw herself at you and you shot her down?" He claps. "What a hero."

"I don't know what you want me to say," I tell him, face heating. "That's my answer."

"Can we keep it moving, guys?" Zane asks.

I sit back, relieved. "Go for it."

Zane blows air out of his cheeks. "Okay, so . . . you guys probably know I've been vegan for two years now. I mean, it's totally changed my life in a lot of ways, you know. I always say it's like a spiritual—"

"Can we get to the point, please?" Aaron interrupts.

Zane glares. "Fine. Yeah. So, my followers are really inspired by my vegan journey. But then a couple months ago, I was going through a rough time, and . . ." He takes a deep breath. "I ordered a pizza."

Someone laughs, sharp and dissonant.

"Sorry, Logan, do you think me sharing about a hard time in my life is funny?" Zane snaps.

She just takes another sip of her coffee.

He sighs and goes on. "I only ate a few bites before I realized how much of a mistake I was making, but I still did it. I feel like I lied to my followers, I guess." He gives Graham a clap on the back. "You're up, man."

As Graham shifts, Zane starts to fidget, tracing one of the

tattoos around his arm with one finger. He's obviously eager to change the focus from his vegan crisis—or whatever it is he's actually hiding, because I have a feeling this story is bullshit. My leg starts to bounce. What is Zane really lying about?

"Um, okay." Graham pulls on his earring. "So, I've been working on my EP, and I'm supposed to have songs ready to share with my team next month. I've told them everything's on track, but the truth is . . ." He lets out a shallow breath. "The songs aren't finished. Not even close. I just . . . I'm hitting a wall."

Huh. Graham's been talking up this EP on TikTok for months, like it's going to be the thing that launches him from being an influencer to an A-list artist. I guess I feel bad for him, but at the same time, I'm getting frustrated. If the only fodder I have for this documentary is Zane eating cheese and Graham having writer's block, then I'm in trouble.

Then again, it's not like I told them a real secret. Not all of it, anyway. I shove that out of my mind, tightening my jaw.

Graham looks to Corinne, who's sitting on the floor to the right of his chair.

"You want to go?" he asks.

"Fine. So . . ." She chews the inside of her cheek. "My little sister, Elyse, and I share clothes a lot. We're only a year and a few months apart, so our taste is annoyingly similar. Elyse designs her own stuff sometimes, and she let me borrow this top she knitted one night, but I accidentally got it caught on my jacket. I tried to unstick it, but it ripped a huge hole. Basically, it was ruined. So, I pretended our dog got to it." She reaches for her necklace. "I still haven't even told her. It's a tiny thing, but I've always felt terrible about it. Elyse didn't deserve that, and neither did Chewy. Our dog, not the Star Wars character. I swear he still gives me the eye sometimes, like he knows."

"I get it, girl," McKayleigh interjects. "My little sister Bronlynn always used to steal my stuff. But that's just sisters, right?"

Corinne looks annoyed, and I don't blame her. For one, of *course* McKayleigh's sister is named Bronlynn. But more importantly, something about her tone is off, like she's trying too hard. I get the feeling McKayleigh wants to steer this conversation to anything but the game.

"Do you want to go next?" I ask her.

"What, like, my lie?" McKayleigh presses her lips together. "I don't have one."

"You don't have one?" Corinne repeats doubtfully. "Like, at all?"

"I don't know what you want me to say. I'm an open book." She shrugs. "Kira, why don't you go next?"

Kira straightens, looking surprised to hear her name, and my curiosity spikes. She doesn't strike me as a liar, but then again, she's been about as easy to read as the tiniest letters at my eye exams before they shift the prescription lens in. Kira Lyons could be a trained assassin, for all I know. And for some reason, I can't stop looking at her.

"Okay, so I guess . . . sometimes I feel like I'm lying to my followers," Kira says. "Like, I have this mindset where I'm like, 'all it takes to be your happiest, healthiest self is committing to your goals,' but . . . I don't know. It's kind of bullshit?" Something in her loosens now, the words coming easier. "I've been an athlete my whole life. I have brands sending me meal-prep kits and workout equipment and it's just . . . not everyone can do that. I pretend it's easy, like they're the only ones standing in their own way, but it's not true. It's all a lie."

"So basically your lie is that you're too naturally hot?" Elody asks.

Kira's mouth falls open. "No, I just . . ."

"I get it," I say.

Elody smirks. "Don't tell me *you've* always been this hot, too, babe."

Jesus Christ. "No, I just mean . . . 'influencing' and everything. It's all a lie, isn't it? I think it's normal to feel that way."

Kira gives me a look that I can't quite read—still guarded, almost like she's trying to figure me out, too.

"Logan?" McKayleigh gestures to her. "I think you're the only person left."

"Maybe I'm hallucinating," she says, "but I don't remember you giving an answer."

"I already told you. I don't have one."

"It's just a game, babe," Elody says. "It's not, like, confession."

"I don't care," McKayleigh tells her, adopting a distinct *I need to speak to the manager* tone. "I shouldn't have to do something I'm not comfortable with on TV just because you say so. Like, maybe it was easier for y'all to come up with an answer, but I'm sorry. I'm not a liar."

"So, wait, which is it?" Logan asks. "You're not a liar, or you're not cool with admitting that you're a liar on TV?"

"I think we're still waiting on *your* answer, Logan," she snaps. "Since you're so high-and-mighty, why don't you tell us your lie?"

Logan's eyes flash, something dangerous behind them. She sets her coffee down on the table with a thud.

"Fine. You want to know my lie?" Logan's gaze tracks around the room. "I don't know if you guys saw my post, the one I made after leaving the Bounce House. I said there were *no hard feelings,* that I was so *grateful* for my time there." Her stare locks on McKayleigh. "Biggest fucking lie I've ever told."

McKayleigh visibly tenses, but then she breathes out, fixing on a calm expression.

"Sorry, but if this is how I'm going to be treated, I'm going to go ahead and set a healthy boundary. Y'all have fun with your little game. I'm out."

She stands and marches out the front door, shutting it behind her.

The timer on my screen ticks away to zero, an alarm sounding. At the same time, we all get a new message:

Time's up
Hope you told the truth . . . because I hate liars
—Your Sponsor

A bloodcurdling scream rips from outside. Everyone's heads whip toward the sound. Panic sends a cold sweat down my back.

"Oh, perfect," Aaron mumbles, like the scream didn't make him jump as much as the rest of us. "Wonder what the mannequin says this time."

But that scream didn't sound like Logan's, someone mistaking one thing for another in the dark. It sounded like something terrible in the early morning light. Something unmistakable.

I run to the door, but before I can get there, it swings open, and there's McKayleigh, all the color drained from her face.

"Cole," she whispers. "He's . . ."

I rush past her, out onto the terrace, and she doesn't have to finish, because even before I see him, I know. It's not a mannequin.

It's Cole, his body, crumpled on the terrace in a pool of dark blood.

ELODY

Blood. There's blood coming out of his head and into the cracks between the terrace stones. His eyes are open, his neck is all wrong, twisted, and I can't stop looking. My brain won't put it together. Last night, Cole was alive and doing a shot out of my boobs, and now . . .

Oh my god. Cole Bryan is *literally dead*.

My stomach drops, and I close my eyes, feeling like I might puke up all of last night's champagne.

"What happened?" Zane asks, panicked.

"I don't know. I walked out here, and he was just . . ." Mc-Kayleigh starts to sob.

"The balcony," Max says.

I open my eyes and look at him. Max is even paler than usual, staring up at the third floor.

"The door was open." He swallows. "He must have fallen."

Max might not have the best judgment—I mean, he didn't even try to make out with me last night—but he's right. Cole, or his body, *the* body, whatever we're supposed to say now that he's *dead*, is right under the balcony, like he just climbed right over the railing and jumped. Like he was just doing another one of his stupid cannonballs into the pool.

"Shit." Max's eyes go wide behind his glasses, like he's just now realizing what's actually happening. "Cole wasn't in his bed this morning. The bathroom door was shut, so I figured he was in there. But maybe . . . maybe he fell last night."

"Did anyone see anything?" Kira asks. "What happened after me and Corinne went to bed?"

I don't like the way she's looking at me, like she thinks this is somehow my fault. I cross my arms. "Um, I don't know? We were all pretty wasted."

Then I remember: early this morning, when I was sleeping on the couch, I woke up to the sound of the back door sliding open. It was still dark outside, but I could see Kira walking in all sweaty in her workout clothes.

"Weren't *you* out this morning?" I ask her.

Her Bambi eyes get bigger. "I just went for a run. I didn't . . ."

"You ran past a literal dead body and didn't even notice?"

"It was dark. I went out through the back and down along the beach. I didn't see him."

"I didn't either." Zane pulls at his man-bun. "When I was meditating this morning, I mean. I was on the back patio. I couldn't see the terrace."

Aaron sizes him up. "Defensive, aren't we?"

"Okay, hold on," Graham says. "We don't need to accuse each other. We just . . ." He looks at the body and flinches. "We need to figure out what happened."

"I don't think that's a mystery, Discount Troye Sivan," Aaron says.

Logan walks a few steps away from the group and puts her hands on her knees, like she's going to be sick.

"When did everyone see him last?" Kira asks.

"Zane and I went up to our rooms around two. Cole and everyone were still downstairs." McKayleigh grips her cross necklace like she's on the witness stand or something. "I went right to sleep."

Of course she did. Probably after brushing her hair a hundred times and reading her Bible, or whatever it is Christian Girl Autumn clichés do at night.

"Same," Zane says. "I didn't see anything, either."

"What about the people who slept downstairs?" Kira looks at me. "Was Cole there, too?"

I try not to roll my eyes. What is she, some kind of girl detective all of a sudden?

"Yeah," I tell her. "We all passed out a little after McKayleigh and Zane left. Cole was snoring a lot, and it woke me up, so I told him to shut up. Then he went upstairs. And I guess that's when he . . ."

Oh my god, did I accidentally send Cole Bryan to his literal *death*?

Kira looks between the rest of us. "But did he seem drunk enough to . . . to fall?"

"I don't know." Graham scrapes at his nails, chipping the black polish. "I mean, yeah, he was wasted, but people don't just fall off of balconies."

"What, you think he jumped?" Aaron asks.

"No!" Graham closes his eyes. "I don't know. This is so messed up."

"I saw him." Corinne's voice is so quiet that, for a second, I think I imagined it. "Around three thirty, maybe? I got up to go to the bathroom, and he . . ." She takes a breath. "Cole was coming up the stairs, and he looked . . . I mean, we all saw him last night, but he could barely even walk in a straight line. I thought he might have been on something besides alcohol. I asked him if he was okay, if he needed help, and he lashed out. Said no one even knows who I am, so why would he need my help. So, I just . . . let him go. I thought he was going up to his room."

God, this whole thing is so depressing. I try to imagine what it must have been like, just letting go of the balcony and flying into the air, but I can't. Like, actually can't. Even blackout or high, I don't think I'd be *that* reckless. I'm pretty sure my basic self-preservation instincts would stop me. There's no way I'd go over that railing unless . . .

Oh my god.

"Okay, but what if he didn't?" My heart starts to pound. "We were all drunk last night, but none of us, like, fell off the balcony. Graham's right. That doesn't just *happen*."

Max looks sick. "But why would he . . . why would he do that on purpose?"

"I don't know." My heart is going faster and faster, and my mind can't keep up. "Maybe he was, like, super depressed about getting canceled, or whatever. Or maybe . . ."

I stop. Because there's only one other option, but there's no way. There's no fucking way.

"Maybe someone pushed him," Aaron reads my mind, with a twisted little laugh.

"Oh my god," McKayleigh whimpers. "Oh my *god*."

"Okay, but who would do that?" Zane asks. "Like, why?"

"I don't know, because they're psycho?" I look at Logan, who's still standing away from the group. "I mean, we all saw what happened at dinner. Maybe you wanted to, like, finish the job."

She turns around. "Sorry, are you high?"

"Why not?" McKayleigh jumps in. "We all know how much you hated him."

"That doesn't mean I yeeted him off the third fucking story!"

McKayleigh takes a step toward her. "What's your alibi, then?"

"I was sleeping," Logan says. "In the same room as you, might I add."

"Okay, well, maybe you got up. I was asleep all night. How would I know?"

Logan backs up. "This is insane."

"You hated him!"

"Oh, like *you* two were so tight?" Logan laughs. "You wouldn't be caught dead near Cole if you weren't literally trapped on an island with him! He never got invited to Bounce House parties because you said, and I quote, 'Cole Bryan could make God go back on the whole no-more-flooding-the-earth thing.'"

McKayleigh opens her mouth, caught. "I—"

"Zane and Graham, too. You guys used to talk shit about him all the time. I mean, did anyone here actually *like* Cole?" Logan looks around the group.

No one says anything. Logan holds up her arms, like, *See?*

I mean, she's got me there. Cole was fun, I guess, but last night, he said four different things about my boobs that made me want to slap him in the face, even drunk. But that doesn't mean I wanted him *dead*.

"Okay, no." Kira shakes her head. "No, we're not going there. None of us had any reason to . . . to hurt Cole. He was really drunk, and this was just an accident."

The way she says it, it sounds so obvious. Because duh. Cole was wasted. Corinne says he could barely walk in a straight line. It's totally possible that he just lost his balance and fell, and we're all just freaked out and in shock. No one here is an actual murderer.

But then why do I feel like we all believed it just now?

"We need to call Tilly," Corinne says.

She starts walking back to the house, and as we follow her, I try to make myself calm the hell down. This was an accident. It was a sad, dumb accident. But I still can't get it out of my head. I don't know any of these people well enough to be, like, 100-percent sure they're not a murderer. Yeah, Cole probably fell, but then why does it seem so possible? One of us sneaking up behind him, just one quick shove . . .

I'm so caught up in my head that I run right into Max when he stops in the living room. Which would normally be, like, an exciting moment for me, but then I see his face. He's looking at the outlet by the TV, where Corinne's crouching, staring. Except . . .

"The phone," she says. "It's not here."

KIRA

"What do you mean it's not there?" McKayleigh demands. "Where is it?"

"I don't know." Corinne looks behind the TV, on the floor, and then stares helplessly at the empty outlet. "It's not there. Neither is the charger."

Elody laughs. "Oh my god. Love this for us."

"Sorry, is this funny to you?" McKayleigh snaps. "We're stuck here with a dead body and no way to get help!"

I count a slow breath, four seconds in through the nose, hold, four seconds out through the mouth. We can't afford to panic. Right now, we need a solution.

"The watches," I realize, relief flooding through me as I open my text app and type out an SOS message to our "Sponsor." I press SEND, but right away, there's that little exclamation point of doom: message failed to send. I hit RETRY, but it still won't go through. And then I remember what Corinne said yesterday, how it didn't work when she tried to message her family.

No, no, no . . .

"It's not sending." I try to contain the panic in my voice. "Can someone else try?"

Corinne taps at her watch, shaking her head. "I'm not getting service. I don't think we have a call function, either. Just the message app."

"We're screwed." Graham pulls out a vape and takes a long hit. He blows out smoke, coughing. "We're so screwed."

I take another slow breath, trying to stave off the fear that's quickly tightening its grip. "It has to be somewhere. A phone doesn't just disappear."

"Unless someone took it." McKayleigh stares at Logan.

"Seriously?" Logan says. "We're *seriously* still doing this?"

"Wait." I look up at the camera above us, still blinking its little red eye. "They're still recording. They'll realize what happened, and they'll have to come for us."

Just barely, the knot of tension in my chest starts to unspool. For once, I'm grateful for the cameras tracking our every move.

Max nods, looking as relieved as I am. "They're probably on the way. Maybe Tilly's tried to message us, but it didn't go through."

"That's all well and good, Spielberg," Aaron says, "but it doesn't change the fact that someone *took the phone.*"

The knot starts to tighten again. He's right. But there has to be some explanation, some logic . . .

"Cole," I realize. "He could have taken it last night and forgotten to put it back."

"And was that before or after he went splat off the balcony?" Aaron asks.

I breathe out, trying not to let my frustration show. Is this seriously the time to be a sarcastic jerk?

"Before, obviously," I tell him. "He was probably just trying to get on YouTube, or something."

"But what do we do?" Graham asks. "Just sit around and wait for Tilly? When he's still . . . lying out there?"

"Maybe we should move him," Zane says, looking out the window. "It doesn't feel right just leaving him there."

Graham sucks on his vape and breathes out again. "Where?"

My mind flashes back to my run from this morning. It was still dark, and the air was warm and heavy, almost electric. I was so close to his body, and I didn't even know.

"The pool house?" I suggest, remembering its solid shape in the distance as I ran down the beach.

McKayleigh looks terrified. "And have him, like, five feet away from the house?"

"The boathouse, then," I try. "We could take him there. It's not too far."

No one argues.

"We should split up," Corinne says. "Half of us stay and look for the phone, half of us . . ." She swallows. "Half of us take him down there."

Silence stretches out between us as we wait for someone to volunteer.

Zane gives in first. "I can help move him. Graham?"

Graham nods weakly, even though he looks like he might be sick. Max volunteers, too, and Zane looks to Aaron for a fourth person, but I step forward.

"I'll help."

I don't love the idea, but Aaron looks like he might pass out, and anyway, now is not the time for casual misogyny.

"Okay." Zane nods, letting out a tense breath. "Let's go."

The four of us file out to the terrace. Outside, we stand around him in silence, the sun warm on our skin. It briefly occurs to me that I'm wearing new running shoes, sent to me by one of my brand partners, and they'd be mad if I get blood on them before I make my sponsored post. Why is *that* where my mind goes? I shake off the thought and tighten my ponytail.

It's a slow process. Heavy. Zane calls out directions, and I try to think of good things, things besides the lifeless leg in my grip. Things I used to think of before competitions to calm down: dancing around the kitchen with my mom, both of us sliding in our socks. Dad guiding my hair into a tight bun, his palm soft on my forehead to protect my eyes before he hair-sprayed it. Me and Alex playing soccer in the backyard, dirt ground into our hands and knees.

I try to stay with those things as we move past the terrace, the beach, and down to the dock, slow and steady so we don't slip, until finally we walk him through the wide, open entrance and into the shade of the boathouse.

"Over here." Zane nods at an open stretch of the floor.

We set Cole down carefully, but his head thuds against the wooden planks below our feet. My stomach lurches.

Zane motions to a tarp bunched up against the wall, and Graham helps him lift it, the air puffing it out like a sail, and for an out-of-body second, I think of parachute day in elementary school. As they bring it down over Cole's body, I turn away and focus on the details of the boathouse. Wooden walls painted white and hung with life vests, rope, and some fishing tools. In the middle, the floor gives way to an open rectangle of water, where a motorboat bobs. It's small but expensive-looking, with cushioned seating that could probably fit a few people plus a driver.

Max walks over to the boat and looks inside.

"What are you doing?" Graham asks.

"If we can't get in touch with Tilly soon, we could try to get out to the mainland ourselves."

"Are you kidding?" Graham frowns. "That's, like, fifteen miles."

"I'm just saying, if nothing else works." Max starts to feel around inside. "There should be a key in . . . here."

He holds up a silver key, hanging off a ring. Through the haze of exhaustion and worry, I have a vague thought that Max doesn't seem like a guy who knows a lot about boats. But then I put two and two together: Jonathan Overby from *The Overview*. Max's dad. So his mom must be Eileen Hale, the movie producer. In other words, Max grew up super rich, probably with access to several boats. It makes a little more sense, all of a sudden: Max recording me without permission, feeling entitled to my words. Even though I accepted his apology, it doesn't change the way he grew up.

I clench my teeth, trying to stay focused on the problem in front of us, and not my increasingly complicated feelings about Max Overby.

"So we just need to . . ." Max twists the key in the ignition. He twists it again.

I try to count more breaths, but panic distorts my rhythm. The briny smell of the boathouse is too thick, making my head swim.

It's possible that Cole took the phone. It's possible that he accidentally fell off the balcony. It's possible that the producers are just running late, that the spotty watch connection is the result of being in the middle of the sea and not some other malicious force. But each new coincidence feels like one too many.

"Why won't it start?" Zane asks impatiently.

"Everything seems fine. I don't . . ." Max bends down and opens something up near the front of the boat. "Shit."

"What?" I ask.

His eyes dart back and forth, like he's willing them to be wrong. "The cables are cut."

LOGAN

I curse, throwing Cole's bag aside. "Where is it?"

"I'm telling you, babe, it's not in there." Elody's lounging on one of the beds like she's by the pool. "Can we just give up before we do something embarrassing like sweat?"

I chew on a hangnail, my head throbbing. We've already gone through all of Cole's luggage, opened his drawers, and checked under the mattress, but the phone is nowhere, like it finally wised up to the heinous vibes of this place and peaced the fuck out. At least someone had the right idea.

The door swings open, and Corinne walks in. She looks a little out of breath, like she just jogged up the stairs. Or maybe it's the same panic that's been dripping into my veins like a steady IV since the second I saw Cole's body on the terrace.

"Anything?" she asks.

I shake my head. "You?"

"Nothing downstairs." She pulls at her watch strap. "If anyone happened to sneak their phone in, now would be a really great time to come clean."

She's looking right at me, because I *would* be the one to break the rule, but I shake my head. I probably would have tried, if I could have afforded a decoy phone to give the producers. Which I couldn't. As if I need the reminder.

Aaron laughs sharply. "Classic. Suddenly we're a bunch of off-the-grid rule followers."

"They searched our bags like we were criminals," McKayleigh says. "It's not like it would have worked."

I bite my hangnail again, making my skin sting. A bad habit. I should stop. I also should have never come here in the first place, but clearly none of the decisions I've made in the past year have been stellar, have they?

"Let's look somewhere else," Corinne says.

"Where else could he have put it?" I ask, exhausted. "We've looked everywhere, unless Cole was purposefully hiding it, which . . . actually sounds like something he would do."

"Not to speak ill of the dead, but I don't think Cole was smart enough to hide stuff anywhere but in plain sight," Aaron says.

"Can you try to be less mean?" McKayleigh folds her arms. "He's *dead*."

Aaron laughs. "Yeah, and apparently you wished God would smite him."

McKayleigh glares at me. "That was taken out of context."

I want to snap right back at her, but Corinne's face changes, like she has an idea.

"We should check everyone else's bags," she says. "That's something Cole would do, right? Frame someone else as a prank or something?"

Even though we've basically progressed to the seventh circle of hell in the last three hours, I let out a genuine laugh. "Cole Bryan. The world's shittiest prankster even from beyond the grave."

"This isn't funny," McKayleigh says. "And no way. I'm not letting y'all go through my stuff like the freakin' TSA."

"Why?" Aaron asks. "You have something to hide?"

Her face goes red. "No, Aaron, I don't. But I value my privacy."

"Okay, how about a vote?" I say. "Who here is down to get their bags searched because they're not hiding anything and also they don't want to be stranded on this island with a dead person forever?"

I throw up my hand, and everyone but McKayleigh follows suit. She stares at me, her nostrils flaring, but finally, she gives up.

"Fine. Whatever you want."

We start with Max's and Graham's things, but that gets us nowhere. Even the bathroom is a bust. The only thing out of the ordinary is a giant box of Magnum condoms labeled with Cole's name. I cringe, shoving it back under the sink. Maybe it's awful of me, but I really wish he'd made it a little easier for us to be sad for him.

We go downstairs next, to Aaron and Zane's room, but it's more of the same. There's nothing in the girls' triple room, either. By the time we get to our room, I'm about ready to scream or cry or do a running leap out the nearest window.

"Go right ahead." McKayleigh flops down onto her bed. "Tear through my stuff. But it's not going to be in here."

"We did everyone else's," Corinne says. "Let's just finish what we started."

She takes one of my beat-up duffels and tosses the other in McKayleigh's direction, almost smacking her in the face. Actually, judging from Corinne's small smirk, I think that might have been the goal, and I immediately like her more than I already did.

Aaron turns to the door. "Sorry, I'm out. You guys go ahead, but this is pointless. I'm going to check downstairs again."

He leaves, thumping his way down the stairs with surprising volume for someone so elf-like.

"Oh my god, fun," Elody drones in a voice suggesting that it's anything but. "Girl time."

"Can we just get this over with?" McKayleigh huffs.

I ignore her evil stare and unzip her suitcase, finding a mountain of Bless by Kaylz designs: swimsuits, dresses, and I count at least three sun hats. Beneath those, I sort through self-help books written by rich white women and try not to get physically burned by the toxic positivity emitting from them.

And that's when I see it: a white cord, coiled under a pair of jean shorts like a viper. An iPhone charger with a label on the cube: PROPERTY OF IRL.

I start digging through the rest of the suitcase like a starving animal.

"Logan!" McKayleigh runs over. "What are you—"

I whirl around, the charger gripped in my hand. "Where's the phone, McKayleigh?"

Her eyes go wide. "I don't know."

"Tilly's charger is in your bag. Call me a skeptic, but I feel like it didn't grow legs and walk there itself."

"Cole must have put it there!" she yelps. "I swear, I didn't take it. I don't know how it got there."

"The phone's not in there?" Corinne asks me.

I do another dig, unzipping all the outer pockets, but I already know it's hopeless. I kick the bed frame.

Corinne leans against the wall like she's too tired to stay fully vertical.

"Okay, disrespectfully," she says, looking at McKayleigh, "what the hell?"

McKayleigh scoffs, dabbing at her eyes, even though she hasn't shed a single tear. "I can't believe y'all think I would steal the phone." Seeing that none of us are giving in to her little pity party, she drops the act, scowling at me. "You'd better at least clean my stuff up, if you're going to accuse me of *theft*."

Staring at the mess of her things on the floor, I want to laugh and cry at the same time. It's like the setup to a really bad joke. I can almost hear the long-haired, big-toothed vlogger on the cover of McKayleigh's books laughing at me.

Because I was right. This is hell, and I know exactly what I did to get here.

"Guys?" The door creaks open, and Aaron's standing there, face pale. "I found something."

"The phone?" Corinne asks hopefully.

But Aaron shakes his head and holds out a neat black case.

He clicks it open, revealing the gun inside.

MAX

"Finally." McKayleigh stands up from the living room couch as we walk inside, lasered on Zane and Graham. "Y'all need to talk some sense into everyone."

"About what?" Zane asks.

Corinne breathes out. "We found a gun."

The word itself is like a shot. *A gun.* Stepping deeper into the living room, I can see it sitting in an open case on the coffee table. It's small and black, the kind you can hold in one hand. I've never seen one up closer than in a subway cop's holster.

"Where'd you find it?" Kira asks.

Aaron nods at the storage closet near the front door. "In there. Must be the owners'."

That makes sense, at least. I've heard some of my parents' most tone-deaf one-percenter friends talking about guns like they're collector's items. But when you add a gun to everything else that's happened here . . .

"Did you guys find anything in the boathouse?" Corinne asks us.

I swallow, getting that buzzing feeling I always do when I'm just about to crack an interview subject. Except this time, it's not excitement. It's more like dread.

"There's a boat," I say. "But it looks like the cables are cut."

McKayleigh gapes. "See? This is why we need to keep the gun! To protect ourselves!"

"From what, shoddy boat cables?" Corinne asks.

"Literally name *one* time keeping a gun around has made people safer," Logan adds.

McKayleigh crosses her arms. "It's a constitutional right."

"Oh my *god,*" Logan groans.

"What? It is!"

"Did y'all find the phone?" Kira asks pointedly.

Elody rolls her eyes. "Does it *look* like we have help on the way, babe?"

"We didn't find the phone," Logan says. "But we found the charger. In McKayleigh's bag."

"Wait, what?" Graham's eyes widen.

"For the last time," she snaps, "I didn't put it there!"

Elody reaches down and picks up the gun.

McKayleigh jumps back. "What are you doing?"

She smiles, catlike, and pulls a small black rectangle out of the handle. "Safety first, babe. I'm just unloading it."

"Plot twist," Aaron mutters.

"What, that I care about people not blowing their heads off?"

"No, that you know how guns work."

Elody shrugs. "Grew up around them. Kind of comes with the whole trailer-trash thing."

With a swift motion, she aims the barrel at my chest. My blood rushes. I know it's unloaded, but still. She's kind of terrifying. Elody laughs, clearly amused by my reaction.

"Can we put it somewhere safe for now?" I ask, trying to recover from that distinctly uncool moment. "And, you know, stop pointing it at people?"

"Any objections?" Corinne looks around the room, waiting. "Okay, then that's settled. We put away the weapon of mass destruction."

"Ugh. You guys are no fun." Elody pouts, but she hands the gun over to Aaron, who puts it back where he found it in the closet.

Now that Elody's not actually brandishing a weapon, I process what she just said. *Trailer trash.* It's the second time she's mentioned her childhood. Just now, she said it like a self-deprecating joke, but the way she pointed that gun . . . I wonder if there's something darker there, some hurt she's hiding.

A chorus of pings sounds through the room, and everything stops. On my watch, there's one new message from our Sponsor:

Now, what did I say about lying . . .

"We must have service again." Corinne taps furiously at her watch.

Taking her cue, I type out a message to the Sponsor contact.

Where are you?

But when I press SEND, it fails. I hit RETRY, and then again. Nothing. I glance up to see a devastated look on Corinne's face, like a mirror.

"It should be working," she says. "I don't—"

More pings cut her off as a new message hits each of our watches.

Time to vote

Which one of you is the liar?

There's a link attached. I click on it, and it brings me to an app I don't recognize, just a plain black screen with a box for inputting text. Another message:

> Enter a name
> You have 1 minute

A timer appears at the top of the screen, the seconds already disappearing. I feel a cold sweat break out under my shirt.

"I don't think we should do this." Kira's eyes are dark with fear. "Something's really wrong."

"No shit," Logan mumbles, but even she can't muster her usual biting tone.

I look up at one of the cameras mounted on the wall. Are they watching us? But there's no way. Because then they would know that Cole is dead, and they still haven't sent help.

Another message whooshes in:

> If you don't vote, you're canceled

Aaron starts to type, tongue poking out from the side of his mouth in concentration.

"What are you doing?" I ask, embarrassed by the panic in my own voice.

"Voting." He gives a final tap. "I've seen horror movies. I don't feel like waiting to find out what 'canceled' means."

Corinne stands, walking closer to one of the cameras on the wall. She looks into the lens like she can see our anonymous Sponsor through it and asks slowly, "What does 'canceled' mean?"

I hold my breath, waiting for another ping to pierce the silence. But five seconds go by, then ten, and there's nothing.

"Maybe they can't hear us," I say, relaxing slightly. If the messages were prescheduled somehow, then maybe the producers don't know what happened yet. Maybe this is just the worst timing ever.

And then, a new message flashes. A screenshot of what looks like a computer desktop with ten folders, one with each of our names.

Let's just say none of you are very good at keeping
    secrets ;)

My mind is a film reel spinning to a stop.

Corinne looks up from her watch. "What the actual . . ."

"Is this supposed to be blackmail?" Logan erupts.

Graham drums his fingers on his thigh, frantic. "Thirty seconds. What do we do?"

"Vote, obviously," Elody says, and then, seeing Graham's shocked expression: "Do *you* want to wait and see what those folders are supposed to mean, babe?"

"We should do it." Zane's tone is calm, but there's fear in his eyes. "It's probably just another dumb challenge, anyway. I bet those folders are empty."

He starts to type, and Graham and McKayleigh follow his lead. Logan gnaws on a thumbnail, staring at her screen with a haunted look. I look down at my own, mind buzzing. Who do I vote for?

Twenty seconds.

When I look up again, I find Kira staring. My breath catches. She bites her lip, glancing quickly up at the cameras and then back down at her watch. Wait, she's not going to vote for me, is she? I thought we were starting to rebuild a shaky trust this morning, but now I'm not so sure.

Fifteen seconds.

People are starting to finish voting. I look around the group, the

Sponsor's question playing in my head on repeat. *Which one of you is the liar?* Most of them, probably. But . . .

McKayleigh catches me watching, her fingers freezing midtwist in her long red hair. I think of her refusal to answer the question earlier, her insistence that she's an open book. Then, I think of the way she looked at Kira last night, like she was some sad little creature on the side of the road, hurt and helpless. Like Kira was beneath her.

It's the exact same way that she's looking at me right now.

I type out McKayleigh's name as the timer hits ten seconds. I hesitate before pressing ENTER, gripped by the feeling that once I do, there's no turning back.

Five seconds.

Does McKayleigh deserve to get canceled—whatever that means?

Four, three . . .

And then another thought hits me, dark and twisted: if I don't vote for someone, the person getting canceled could be me.

Two . . .

I hit ENTER.

One. The timer goes off, sending a staticky feeling over my skin. My watch switches to a new screen, a graph with each of our names listed, bars growing as the votes get counted. Then, they stop, the results frozen.

My eyes go straight to my name in the middle of the page. Only one vote, thank god. I relax for half a second before anger starts to flare. One vote? I look at Kira, but she's looking down at her screen, her fingers pressed against her mouth.

I check the rest of the graph. Graham has one vote, then Logan has two, and at the very top is McKayleigh, her bar stretching out for four votes. Wait, that's only eight. Someone didn't vote.

"Seriously, y'all?"

McKayleigh's holier-than-thou tone confirms it right away: she's the abstainer.

"Is this because someone planted the charger in my bag?" she asks. "I said I didn't take it!"

Before anyone can argue with her, another message pings:

Time's up

Now, I promised secrets, didn't I?

Well bless your heart, McKayleigh, but it's time to spill
    yours

KIRA

In an instant, all of McKayleigh's righteousness floods away.

"What the hell?" Her eyes snap to the cameras. "Okay, listen. Tilly, or 'the Sponsor,' whoever you think you are, this needs to stop. Right now. My daddy's one of the most powerful lawyers in the country, and he'll sue the pants off your smug little—"

Another message cuts her off.

Let's play spot the difference

This time, the message has pictures, a series of Instagram screen-shots. Heart thudding, I open the first one. McKayleigh, posing in one of her Bless by Kaylz pieces, a white linen jumpsuit with a complicated strappy pattern on the back. I swipe to the second one and dread pools in my stomach.

Another girl, her face and Instagram handle blurred out. All we can see is the girl's braids, brown skin, and what she's wearing: a jumpsuit, practically identical to McKayleigh's. Except this girl posted the picture six months before McKayleigh did, and it got only a few hundred likes. McKayleigh's got five hundred thousand.

Something hard and angry takes shape inside of me, growing roots. I swipe through the rest of the pictures, and the pattern is clear. McKayleigh in the swimsuit she was wearing last night, then another girl in the same one, just a different shade. McKayleigh modeling a pair of dangly earrings, then a screenshot of those same earrings from a small Etsy shop.

And then, at the very end of the stream of pictures, there's a screenshot of a DM exchange.

> Hey McKayleigh. Since you've been deleting my comments idk what to do except DM you. The jumpsuit you just posted as part of your collection is really similar to one I posted last year. I designed it myself, and yours has an almost identical back and strap design. You seriously can't even give me credit for the inspo?

> Hey girl! I'm sorry you feel that way but I've literally never seen your account before? Hahaha like no offense, ur stuff is really cute!! But if u google linen jumpsuits you find so many that look like this?? So maybe don't go around claiming people stole stuff from you without doing ur research xoxo

> Sorry but the similarities are too much for me to think you've never seen my picture before. I'm not even asking you for anything

except credit. Even a tag would do so much
for me as a small creator

Ok honestly sorry girl but you sound so
thirsty rn. Please stop contacting me about
this or my lawyers will be getting involved

I look up from my screen to McKayleigh's face. Her jaw is clenched, nostrils flared. She doesn't look sorry, or even embarrassed. She looks *pissed.* And then, like she's just realized how bad this looks for her, she works her face into a calm expression.

"I don't know why y'all are looking at me that way."

"Because you *stole* from people and then threatened to *sue* them," Corinne says, her expression steel. "Do you seriously not see what's wrong with that?"

McKayleigh clamps her mouth shut.

Corinne laughs harshly. "Pleading the Fifth, then. Was that Daddy's advice?"

Aaron snorts. When McKayleigh glares at him, he shrugs. "I mean, it's kind of funny."

"I don't have to explain anything," McKayleigh spits.

"Seriously?" I ask, too disgusted to stay quiet. "You can't act like this isn't wrong." When she doesn't answer, I turn to Graham and Zane. "Did you know she was doing this?"

Zane shakes his head sharply. "Bless by Kaylz is her own thing. We didn't—"

McKayleigh cuts him off with a scoff. "Typical."

"What's *that* supposed to mean?" he asks.

"She means your number-one concern is always saving your own ass," Logan says.

McKayleigh looks almost surprised, but gives Zane a pointed look. "See? Even Logan gets it."

"Hold on, I'm not backing you up," Logan tells her. "To be super clear, I had no idea you were stealing from people, and I think it sucks. Like, a new low, even for you."

Before McKayleigh can say anything else, we get another message. The room goes silent. This time, it's a video. I press PLAY. It's a screen recording from Instagram, an account called @theIRLproject. I can feel us all collectively holding our breath as whoever's controlling the account navigates to their drafts and chooses one, a carousel of all the pictures we just saw. They type out a caption:

Looks like @mckayleighhill has some explaining to do. And I don't think Kaylz is #blessed enough to get away with this one...

The account hits post, and then it's done. Proof of McKayleigh's lies flies out into the world for everyone to see.

For half a second, all I can think is *good.* But one look at McKayleigh's terrified face, and it hits me, what's really at stake here. Those folders aren't empty. Tilly and whoever she's working with think they know our secrets, and they intend to share them.

"Delete this," McKayleigh hisses at the cameras. "Someone better delete this *right effing now.*"

She looks back at the group, her expression shifting from fear to disgust. Following her gaze, I realize why: Max has his camera out and pointed directly at her.

"What is your *problem?*" she blows up at him. "I don't know if you think this is cute, or something, but you need to get that thing out of everyone's faces or I'll—"

"Or you'll sue?" Max finishes, dripping with sarcasm.

Her jaw drops.

"Damn," Elody says. "No offense, babe, but this is getting kind of good."

McKayleigh huffs. "Maybe I *should* sue."

"Do you get off on legal action, or something?" Corinne asks, rage vibrating in her voice. "Because I'm still struggling to understand why you think it's okay to steal from smaller creators and creators of color and then threaten them with lawsuits when they finally call you out on it."

McKayleigh rolls her eyes. "What, so I'm a villain for being inspired by other people? There literally aren't any original ideas anymore. Everyone does this."

"That's bullshit," I tell her. "You know exactly what you're doing."

She shoots a look at Zane and Graham. "Aren't y'all going to back me up on this?"

Graham shifts. "I don't know, Kaylz. What you did is pretty messed up."

Zane just shakes his head.

"Fine. Go ahead and stab me in the back, then." She laughs bitterly. "I bet y'all even voted for me, too."

"That's ridiculous," Zane grumbles.

"Well, you're not denying it!"

"We didn't vote for you," Zane snaps. "Chill out."

"That!" McKayleigh stands, jabbing a finger at him. "That's what I'm *so freaking* tired of! It's like y'all think I'm some stupid Southern belle who can't do anything but look pretty and dance around. I'm one of the *founders* of the Bounce House, just as much as y'all are. I'm literally an entrepreneur, and y'all act like that's nothing!"

"You're not an entrepreneur."

It comes out of me before I can stop it, and now, everyone's eyes are on me. McKayleigh's face is dangerously still.

"What did you just say?" she asks slowly, like she doesn't think she heard me right.

"You're not an entrepreneur, McKayleigh," I say, louder now. And suddenly, it's like the floodgates are open, everything I've wanted to say for years spilling out in an unstoppable rush. "Your name is on a business. Fine. But you're not an entrepreneur. You stole those designs. You haven't worked for anything, ever. The only reason you have a platform at all is because you have rich parents who could pick up and move to Dallas when you got cast on a TV show, and then when you got on that TV show, you said awful things about me and everyone else on the team just to get more screen time. And for some reason people loved that, so here you are, acting like you're some kind of self-made success when all you ever do is knock people down just to get what you want. So maybe, for *once,* you can stop making this about yourself and own up to your bullshit."

For a second, McKayleigh stares in stunned silence. I'm breathing fast, my heart fluttering and my face flushed like I just finished a long run, and that's what this feels like—victory. Power.

Then, she smiles.

"You know what, Kir?" She gives the nickname extra venom. "You're right. Maybe I've done some things I shouldn't be proud of. Maybe I'm *privileged.* But if you think that hiding at home with your sweet little family and your normal little high school makes you better than me, then bless your heart, honey, but you've got it all wrong. You could be exactly where I am if you wanted to. But you know the difference between you and me?" She looks me up and down, her smile turning even more saccharine. "You don't have the guts."

I want to say something, to fight back, but my mouth is frozen with a mix of anger and disgust. McKayleigh knows exactly what she's doing. She isn't sorry, and she's never going to change. She has no reason to: this sweet-little-Southern-girl act has always worked for her, and it always will.

McKayleigh sniffs and grabs her sun hat, indicating the end of this conversation.

"Now, if we're all done berating me, I need some air." She sticks the hat sharply on her head and marches to the front door, giving me one last look before she goes. "Don't y'all have too much fun without me."

She slams the door behind her.

ELODY

I know I asked for drama, but this is, like, *so* on the nose, it's kind of boring.

"Okay, babes." I stand up from the chair, stretching. "This has been super fun, but I didn't eat breakfast, and I'm starving."

"Yeah, great plan," Aaron whines as I walk to the kitchen. "We'll just sit and wait for the grown-ups to come pick us up."

"Are we not even going to talk about what just happened?" Graham asks. "They're watching us. They know Cole's dead, and they're still trying to blackmail us!"

"We don't know that for sure. There has to be some other explanation for this," Kira says, like she didn't just give the most surprising comeback speech ever. Apparently, she's all business all the time.

"The messages could be on a timer," Max says.

"But they know we voted for McKayleigh," Corinne argues. "That couldn't have been prescheduled."

"And even if it was," Graham says, even more frantic, "are we just cool with the whole 'canceled' thing? Like, is *this* what *IRL* was always supposed to be?"

Corinne sighs. "It's definitely one take on the 'real life' theme."

It sounds like she's trying for sarcastic, but she mostly looks freaked out.

"They're going to ruin all of our lives," Graham continues. "Don't you guys see that?"

"Oh my god, can you just chill out?" I ask, but it comes out too panicked. I relax my face, fixing my hair. "Like, it's not helping."

"Then what *should* we do, Elody?" Zane demands.

I fight a smile. It's, like, totally the wrong reaction for me to be having right now, but there's something weirdly satisfying about watching an overconfident asshole like Zane lose his cool.

He wipes his face, taking a deep breath. "Sorry. I just— Tilly or whoever else is behind this might have just ruined McKayleigh's career. How are we not on the same page about this?"

"I don't know, babe." I shrug, walking to the kitchen. "Maybe because we don't all have, like, super dark secrets we don't want getting out."

It's a lie, but the thing is, I need to stop feeding into all this anxious energy or *I'll* start to lose my shit.

"We should look for the phone again," Kira says. "There's got to be somewhere we haven't checked."

I open the fridge and reach for the leftovers from last night.

"Do whatever you want." I take out the taco meat and a bag of kale and close the door with my hip. "But I'm not gonna be good at finding anything until I eat something."

Max blows out a breath.

"Elody's right," he says, because duh. Of course I am. "Our best bet is to stay calm and hope production gets here soon."

"They will," Kira decides. "They have to know something's wrong by now."

"Perfect." I set the tray of leftovers on the table with a loud smack. "Now, can we chill with all of the creepy talk, and eat?"

As usual, I'm a trendsetter. Everyone starts to follow me to the kitchen. Corinne makes a cup of coffee and heads upstairs, and Kira's right behind her with a protein bar. Logan sulks up to her room, too, but everyone else stays. Aaron's the only one who doesn't come to the kitchen. He just wanders around the living room, looking at the bookshelves and stuff like a weirdo.

Zane grabs his leftovers out of the fridge, and Graham comes up next to him, pulling his vape out of his pocket. Which, ew? I thought we were over vaping as a generation, like, a year ago.

"Should we go talk to her?" Graham asks, looking out the window.

"Nah, she needs to chill out first," Zane says.

Max sits down at the table and reaches for his camera bag. Zane shoots him a look, and Max stops, unwrapping his Pop-Tart instead.

Graham messes with his vape, like he's having withdrawals or something.

"I'm gonna go sit by the pool and try not to lose my mind," he tells Zane. "Wanna come?"

"Yeah, go ahead. I'll heat this up and meet you out there in a sec."

Graham leaves, which means that besides Zane microwaving his weird tofu and Aaron sulking around the living room, me and Max are, like, basically alone.

"So," I say, spooning kale into a bowl. "Fun first day, right?"

"Yeah." Max laughs a little, but it's the annoying, polite kind, where it seems like he doesn't want to talk to me. He breaks off a piece of Pop-Tart, but then just kind of stares at it. "I guess I'm not that hungry."

I put some taco meat on my salad, because Max may be hot and all, but I'm not about to let him make me feel weird about eating. I sit at the counter next to him and take a bite.

"Getting anything good, at least?"

Max blinks at me, all confused behind those nerdy glasses. "What?"

"For your little documentary." I flick his camera. "I don't know if you've noticed, but today has been, like, nonstop drama?"

Max glances at Zane. "Thought I'd give it a rest for now."

Zane gives him an annoyed look but doesn't say anything. Instead, he finally takes his food out to go meet Graham, and we're *really* alone. Finally. I get closer, bumping my knee against his.

"That was an interesting 'biggest lie' you told us about, with that girl you knew. She sounds thirsty as hell."

I lean in so he gets a good view of *my* biggest lie, but Max is staring out the window, distracted, and ugh. How hard is he going to make me work for this? I sit back in my chair, away from him, like I'm getting bored.

"What's your deal? You're being all weird."

He frowns. "Cole's dead and someone's trying to cancel all of us. I feel like that's a pretty solid reason to be 'weird'?"

I want to roll my eyes at how superior he's being. Like, obviously I know what's going on. I have eyes and ears and a brain, believe it or not. I just have a different way of dealing with stress—which honestly, he should maybe try out, because flirting is a hell of a lot more fun than sitting around and *thinking* yourself to death.

Instead, I say, "Okay, solid point. But I don't know. Seems like there's something else going on with you."

Max looks out the window again, and then back at me. He lowers his voice. "Something's up with the Bounce House."

I follow where his gaze just went, out to the pool. Zane and Graham are sitting on the lounge chairs, having some sort of tense conversation. I wonder what they're talking about, and then I remember that I'm going for hot and uninterested, so I shouldn't care.

"I mean, duh," I tell Max. "Like, it's pretty obvious they all hate each other?"

"Yeah, but . . ." He picks at his Pop-Tart wrapper. "I feel like there's something else there. Something deeper."

Deeper makes me think of a lot of things I want Max Overby to do to me, but I play along because I'm a good sport.

I smirk. "Like something you could make your documentary about?"

"Yeah, maybe."

Oh my god, he's actually committed to this whole documentary thing, isn't he? Like, what do I need to do, take off all my clothes at the kitchen counter?

Either that or make him jealous.

"Aaron Tyler Banks," I call over to the living room. Not my best option, but I'll take what I can get. "Want to stop creeping and hang with us, babe?"

Aaron looks over his shoulder, like he's not sure if I'm talking to him. "Uh, okay?"

Max shifts, and it's so obvious these two have some kind of drama going on, which is perfect. I smile as Aaron sits down.

"So, what are your thoughts on all this Bounce House drama?"

He scratches his freckly nose. "McKayleigh got what was coming to her, I guess."

"Damn." I laugh. "But you're not wrong. I would say I can't believe she stole all those designs, but, like, I kind of can."

A weird, almost evil look flashes on Aaron's face. "I can't wait to see what's in Max's folder."

Max stands up, his chair scraping the floor. He leaves his Pop-Tart on the counter and walks away without a word.

"Aw, come on, babe," I call after him. "Aaron's just messing with you. I bet he'll apologize. Right?"

Aaron breaks off a piece of Max's Pop-Tart and shoves it in his mouth. "No."

Max sulks upstairs.

Ugh. Literally, what is *wrong* with both of them?

"It's not worth it," Aaron says the second he's gone, mouth full. "Max is into Kira."

"Shut up." I take an angry bite of my salad. "You don't know that."

"Yeah, I do."

"How?"

"I'm good at noticing things. It tends to happen when people stop caring you exist." He shrugs, wiping crumbs off his mouth. "Also, it's obvious to anyone with eyes."

I think back to last night, when I looked through the window and saw Max and Kira talking on the couch. Max acted like a literal piece of cardboard when I was pulling my best moves on him, but then all of a sudden he was running off after Kira. Oh god, is Aaron *right*?

I slump back in my chair, trying not to let him see how much that thought makes me want to puke. "I don't get it. Like, she's pretty, or whatever, but she's so boring. Even when she was ripping McKayleigh apart, she was like . . . nice about it."

"Max is an asshole, anyway. And . . . ." He pauses. "Look, you don't need me to tell you, obviously, but you're really pretty. You could get anyone you want. Or whatever."

He goes all red, and there it is again, that sweet little legless puppy thing. I stand up and put my hand on Aaron's cheek. I can feel his pulse in my hand.

"That's sweet, babe." I lean closer. "But don't get any ideas. I still think you're, like, physically repulsive."

"Yeah." Aaron shoves another Pop-Tart piece into his mouth. "And you've got the personality to match."

I give his cheek a little pat. Okay, maybe it's more of, like, a light slap. "Have fun with your Pop-Tart."

I walk off toward the stairs, but Aaron calls after me.

"Word of advice? You might have a better shot with Max if you didn't try so hard."

Something rushes up inside of me, like a pot boiling over, but I clamp the lid back on, forcing it all down. I turn around and give Aaron my best I-don't-care face.

"You know what? It's a good thing acting didn't work out. You're, like, destined to be a therapist."

I turn and go up the stairs, keeping up the act until I get to the bathroom. Then I close the door behind me, and it all bubbles out.

Who the hell does Aaron Tyler Banks think he is, anyway? Telling me that *I* try too hard when he's the one making up fake stories on his sad YouTube channel to try to make people care about him again. I don't try hard. That's my whole *thing*. I went from nothing to everything overnight, and people hate me because I make it look so easy.

Sorry, El. Mom's cigarette rasp floats into my head. Her barely hidden smile. *Some things you just can't fix.*

The memory of it makes my skin sting, right where my birthmark is, the splotchy red shape like dried blood on the side of my left thigh. It's my least favorite part of my body, even worse than my boob job scars or the spidery stretch marks on my hips that showed up during puberty and faded after lots of trips to the dermatologist. The birthmark, though—the derm couldn't fix that. Mom took me to get it lasered off once, but like pretty much everything else she ever did as a parent, it didn't work. Just stung like hell.

I grip the countertop, stare at my reflection, and force it all down: Mom, her eight thousand crappy boyfriends and their wandering eyes. Her precious little guns that made me wonder what it would be like to take one and point it right at those boyfriends' gross, ogling faces. *Bang.* I let the thought fade like the sound of a shot.

When I'm sure I won't cry, I dab under my eyes with my fingers, and then use the tip of my nail to smooth out the lipstick at the corner of my mouth.

I take a breath and smile until I believe it.

LOGAN

Hot afternoon sun shines through the window and onto Mc-Kayleigh's empty, perfectly made bed. I have no idea where she is right now—probably moping around the beach, doing everything she can to make us feel bad for her, even though *she's* the one who should be apologizing.

I curl onto my side and sink deeper into my bed. If Harper were here, she'd jokingly quote one of the "inspirational" phrases we found when we stalked Dad's girlfriend on Instagram. *Smile, it's free therapy!* Or my personal least favorite, *Be like a pineapple: stand tall, wear a crown, and be sweet on the inside.* I'd throw a pillow at Harper and say, *only if my citric acid gives Sheila reflux.*

Right now, though, I'd even settle for McKayleigh's company. At least I'd have something to distract me from this shit show of a day.

There's a knock on the door, like I summoned her. With a groan, I roll out of bed and open the door, but it's not McKayleigh. It's Graham.

"Um, hey?"

"Can we talk?"

I make a show of looking out into the empty hallway. "Huh. Didn't realize you could do that without Zane's hand up your ass."

Graham rolls his eyes and walks into the room, closing the door behind him. "Now, Logan, you'll never find a husband with that attitude. So vulgar."

It's an echo of our old friendship, and it thaws my icy heart by a few degrees.

"Good. Maybe I want to be alone forever. I'll become an elderly spinster with, like, a pet parrot that I teach all my favorite curse words."

He laughs, sitting on the edge of McKayleigh's bed. "You looking for roommates? Because that sounds low-key better than my current living arrangement."

I sit on my own bed, nervous again at the mention of the Bounce House. "Okay, as much as we all love discussing my marriage prospects, I get a vibe that's not why you're here."

Graham picks at his nail polish, staring down at his hands, and then looks up at me. "You can't keep making a scene."

Ice hardens again in my chest. *Making a scene,* like I always do. Poor, dramatic Logan who can't keep her stupid emotions in check.

"Logan . . ."

"No," I tell him. "Fine. Whatever."

"Come on. Just—throwing the plate at Cole last night, and then earlier, telling everyone your statement was a lie . . . something really messed up is happening here. We have to keep it together."

Graham's eyes are wide and pleading under his thick eyelashes. The worst part is, he looks like he's actually worried about me.

I look away. "I mean, if we're talking about making a scene, I'm pretty sure McKayleigh won the Oscar today."

He laughs humorlessly. "Well, yeah, but . . ."

"Cool. Then are we done here?"

Graham's quiet for a second, collecting himself. "Look, this 'Sponsor' stuff. The folders. Maybe it's all some kind of elaborate joke, but I don't think so anymore. They exposed McKayleigh on Instagram. Her career might be literally ending as we speak, and she can't do anything about it."

"Are you saying she didn't deserve that? Because no offense, but I think that's bullshit."

"No, she definitely deserved it. But that doesn't change what it means for the rest of us." Graham looks at me, desperate. "Cole's *dead*, and—"

"You think I don't know there's a body out there?"

A body. The word tastes vile in my mouth, poisonous.

"I know," Graham breathes. "But we need to remember we're in this together."

A shot of nervous energy jolts through me, coming out as a sharp laugh. Because it's so obvious that we're not. What we are now feels so far away from *in this together,* it's on a whole different planet. We're light-years away from the Graham who used to be my best friend, who never failed to surprise me—Graham, who could be so quiet one second and then, two shots later, tearing up the dance floor with his flawless rendition of Lady Gaga's "Judas" choreography. Graham, who I really thought would at least answer my late-night calls after I left, when I missed my friends and the world felt too heavy. Graham, who blocked me just like the rest of them.

"Logan, please."

I clench my teeth. "Fine. I won't make a scene anymore. Promise."

Graham watches me for a second, and then stands, brushing himself off like McKayleigh's bed wasn't totally pristine. He starts toward the door, but then stops.

"What?" I ask.

"I don't want to sound like I'm accusing you, or—"

"Graham, *what?*"

He takes a breath. "Did you tell anyone?"

It's like a kick in my stomach, but I force out an answer. "No."

"Okay. Sorry. I just . . ." Graham looks up at the camera on the wall and lowers his voice. "If Tilly, or whoever this Sponsor person is—if they know, then how did they find out?"

"I don't know," I tell him, my throat burning. "Why don't you go ask one of your *friends?*"

Graham looks at me like he's going to say something else. Like maybe he's even hurt. But instead, he dips his head and leaves without a word. I lock the door behind him.

Tears sting my eyes. Just as I'm about to climb into bed and give into them, my watch dings with a new message.

Want to make a real scene?

Shock roots me to the floor. A scene. Wait, were they listening to me and Graham just now? I look up at one of the cameras on the wall, the blinking red dot. Adrenaline shoots through my veins. Did everyone else get this message? What the hell do I—

Another message.

Let's keep this one between us for now, Logan
But check your backpack
There's something in there you'll want to see

KIRA

"You going out?"

I tense, but it's just Corinne. She's sitting at the table, looking up from her watch.

"Yeah," I say, tightening my shoelace. "I was just going to walk around for a bit. Get some air."

That's one way to put it. Really, I need to escape. My head is pounding, my nerves tight. If I have to stay in this house with my thoughts for another minute, I'm going to snap.

"Mind if I crash?" Corinne asks.

On instinct, I want to say I'd rather go by myself, but as she stands, I feel the panic start to ebb. It would be nice to not be alone, to have someone to distract me from the whirlpool of thoughts in my head. Plus, I like Corinne. She's one of the few people here who seems to have at least one foot in reality, so as far as panic-walking buddies go, she's the ideal choice.

I give her a small smile. "Let's go."

It's hotter out than it was this morning, the air damp and thick with saltwater. The mannequin is still lying by the shore, face up to the cloudless blue sky. It looks so much less scary in the daylight, like a theater after a horror movie when they turn the lights on and you remember the half-empty soda cups, the popcorn crunching under your feet.

"Which way?" she asks.

"We could make the loop around. See if there's any boats passing by."

Even as I say it, I know there won't be, but still, it feels good to have a task. We walk down to the shore in silence, the damp sand squeaking under our feet. Then, Corinne takes a breath.

"I think there's something off with the watches." It comes out of her in a rush of air, like she's been holding on to it since we stepped outside.

"What?" I stop. The tide reaches out, foam curling close to my shoes.

She holds up her watch. "Look at the message app. Notice anything weird?"

As far as I can tell, it's the standard message app—green square, white message bubble. But then, I notice that it's ever so slightly off: the green is the wrong shade, the message bubble more square than circular.

"It's not the normal app," I realize.

Corinne nods, pulling on her necklace pendant, gold and clover-shaped. Looking closer, I realize it's the four buttons of a video game controller, a different shape etched into each prong.

"At first, I figured maybe this was a different app that works better in remote locations, or something. But . . ." She looks over her shoulder one more time before facing me again. "I'm starting to think they specifically coded this app so that we could receive messages but not send them."

Suddenly, the strap of my watch feels too tight. "What does that mean? Like, why would they do that?"

I stare at her, waiting for her to give me some other explanation, some computer logic that stops this from being so sinister. But the phones, the boat, the gun, the messages, *Cole* . . .

"They planned this, Kira," she says. "They were never going to let us have contact with the outside."

It's like a terrible equation, all the numbers falling into place. I turn and start for the house.

"Wait, where are you going?" she asks.

"We have to tell everyone. We should take these watches off."

"No."

The severity of her tone stops me. I turn to find her still standing close to the shore, water crawling up behind her.

"Why?"

"For one, watches may not let us reach help, but they let us have contact with Tilly—or our 'Sponsor,' whoever that is. Even if we can't respond to their messages, it's our only link to them. And two . . ." She sighs. "I don't trust them."

"The Sponsor? I don't think any of us—"

"No, *them*. The others." She looks at the house, where sun glints off the big front windows. We can see right into the living room, and for the first time, all that natural light seems menacing, like we're living in a big glass cage.

When Corinne speaks again, it's quiet, like she's scared they'll hear us from all the way out here.

"I don't trust them enough to know that one of them isn't . . . involved in this somehow."

A chill races through me. Corinne's right. I don't think there's a single person in that house who I trust—not even Max, not fully.

My next question comes out small. "But you trust me?"

Corinne nods, her hand finding her necklace again. "You're the only one who seems like you're here for the right reasons." She makes a face. "Not to sound like I'm on *The Bachelor*. I just mean . . . you're in school. You didn't move to LA to live in a giant TikTok mansion on the corner of Delusion Street and Asshole Avenue. You still have a connection to the real world, and I get the sense that unlike everyone else, you're actually here to take a break from everything."

I know she's at least sort of joking, but a nervous feeling prickles at the back of my neck. McKayleigh's clothing line, Max's documentary, whatever is going on with the Bounce House and Logan . . . Corinne's right. It seems like everyone came here with an ulterior motive.

Corinne gives a half smirk. "Also, anyone who gives McKayleigh Hill an epic takedown speech is immediately a friend of mine."

I grimace. "Okay, that was a first for me. I'm not usually an epic-takedown-speech kind of girl."

"All I'm saying is, it had to be done." Corinne's tone warms, and for the first time, I really register what she said just now. She trusts me. Corinne, with her cool energy and coding brain and outfits that shouldn't work but do, thinks of me as a friend. I didn't realize how much I needed that right now. The sudden flush of comfort reminds me of home, where Alex is probably hunched over a video game or another Twitch stream, pizza rolls in the oven.

"Okay, this might not be any of my business," I start, "but my brother would never forgive me if I didn't ask why you haven't been streaming."

Corinne looks away quickly, something I can't read flickering on her face. "Things have been busy, getting ready to start college in the fall and everything. I guess I needed a break, too." She looks back at me with a weak smile. "Some vacation, right?"

It hangs between us, weighty and thick, and for the first time, I feel like I can say the thing that's been on my mind for months.

"I'm thinking about quitting," I tell her. "Instagram, YouTube. All of it."

She raises her eyebrows. "Oh."

"My manager is always trying to get me to leave school and do the LA thing, but . . ."

"Everyone else who does that kind of sucks?" Corinne nods at the house with a small smirk.

I laugh, but it fades quickly. "Yeah."

Corinne shifts. "I've actually thought about it. Not necessarily moving to LA, but trying to make Twitch a full-time thing. I mean, supporting myself with something I love—something creative and flexible, instead of some soul-sucking tech job . . . that's the dream, right?"

"Yeah," I echo, barely even scratching the surface of the countless nights I've spent turning this same idea over in my mind. The pros are impossible to ignore, and money's at the top of the list. I've seen people my age, like Elody, buy their own houses with what they make influencing. Growing up, we always had everything we needed, but my parents are both teachers. It's not like they're . . . well, Max's parents, with boats and New York City real estate. And the thought of having my own space, being able to take care of my family . . .

"I guess I can't get past the risk," I say. "You know? One slipup, and it could all go away."

Or there's the even worse and more likely option, the one I don't say aloud: people just losing interest. And what would happen then, if I left everything behind and moved to LA, if my family came with me, and it all fell apart?

"I get it," Corinne says. For a moment, it looks like she's going to say something else, something serious, but then her tone shifts, lightening. "Also, I'm a Chicago girl. I could never do LA. Any place with weather that *isn't* inhospitable to human life for half the year is not a place I trust."

I laugh, and for a second, it feels normal. Good. Then I remember where we are, what's happening, and tension floods through me again. I hug my ribs.

"Those folders," I say. "Do you think they really have something on all of us? Something as bad as what McKayleigh did?"

Suspicion shadows her face. "Is there something you're worried about them knowing?"

"No, I just . . ." I breathe in, out. "Clearly, Tilly or whoever's doing this is out to get us."

And there it is, the real source of my panic. I know I haven't done anything truly worthy of being canceled, no buried tweets or drunken mistakes, but somehow, this is worse. Because there's still a folder with my name. I'm still not safe. Anyone could sift through the pieces of me that I've shared online and hold them under a microscope until they find the crack. Until they broadcast my flaws before I've even thought to hide them.

Suddenly, I need to ask the question I've been holding on to since I first saw the folders, maybe even longer.

"Do you think they're doing this just because of who we are? Like, being 'influencers' and everything—" I fight the urge to put air quotes around the word. Even after all these years of being one, I still don't feel comfortable claiming it. "Does that make us bad people?"

Corinne presses her lips together, quiet for a few seconds.

"I don't think it's inherently bad to want a platform," she says finally. "And I sure as hell don't think we've all done something like what McKayleigh did. But we're all capable of doing bad things, I guess. It's easy to lose yourself, once you start feeling like a product instead of a person."

The truth of it is like a stab, sharp and quick. All the workout videos and vlogs, the carefully curated pictures . . . maybe there was a time when I did them for me. But now, there isn't a single thing I post without considering my brand or the algorithm first. Sometimes, I'm not sure if I'm the creator or the content. If all I am is something to consume.

I wonder if Corinne feels the same way. Something in her expression pulls at me, her faraway look.

"Is that why you came here?" I ask.

But she's not looking at me anymore. Her attention is fixed on something behind me, and the look melting over her face sends goose bumps crawling on my arms. I turn, but there's nothing there.

"Do you see a boat?" I ask, hopeful in spite of the empty horizon.

"No. There."

She points, and I see it: a sun hat riding the breeze, tumbling over the rocks and onto the sand like a wounded seagull. All of my muscles tighten, like armor trying to protect me from what my instinct tells me this could mean.

Corinne starts to walk faster, toward the rocks, and no. That's not what this is. This is only leftover adrenaline from this morning, too much sun and fear—and now Corinne's running, and I'm behind her, the panic closing up in my chest until we're close enough to the rocks to smell the waves beneath them, and then we're standing at the edge.

The rocks lead down to a small patch of sand, no more than a six-foot drop. And there, lying at the bottom, is McKayleigh. Her eyes staring lifelessly at the sky. A puddle of blood, sticky in her red hair.

LOGAN

The room is dead silent. Dead, like McKayleigh out on the rocks, blood like a halo. As soon as Kira and Corinne came inside, before they even told us, I knew, maybe just from the looks on their faces, and I ran. I shouldn't have. Now I'll never be able to forget what she looked like. Eyes open, but not just blank and dead.

She looked afraid.

"This is our fault." A strangled sob comes out of Graham's throat. "We shouldn't have let her go off alone when she was so upset. We should have checked on her."

"It's not our fault." Zane puts a big hand on Graham's shoulder, like a caring friend, but I know what it really means. *Shut up.* I know because I've felt it. Those hands gripping my arms, hard. *We're going to fix this.*

Reaching into my hoodie pocket, I brush the papers inside, still creased from the envelope that someone—our "generous Sponsor"— left in my backpack.

Want to make a real scene?

I start to shiver.

"Not to be that guy," Aaron says, "but we have two dead bodies, and no one's come to get us. So I'm starting to think—"

"No." Kira shakes her head sharply. "No. We're not going back to that."

"Okay, then what happened?" Aaron asks. "She just slipped off the rocks like Cole slipped off the balcony? Some slippery island we have here."

"Stop it, man," Zane says. "That's not helping."

"Well, neither is crying about it."

"Our friend just *died*," Graham hisses, moving toward Aaron. "What the fuck is your—"

Zane tugs him back. "It's okay."

Graham glares at Aaron, like he might rush forward, but then he slumps into an empty chair, pulling out his vape and taking a long inhale. The mist curls out with his breath in slow motion, like the thought creeping into my head.

When I ask, it comes out at almost a whisper.

"What if this is what they meant by 'canceled'?"

Somehow, the room gets even quieter, like all the air's been sucked out.

"Wait, like they want us to *die*?" Elody lets out a humorless laugh. "Oh my god, if *IRL* was a cover for an actual *murder* plot, I'm going to kill my manager."

"*That's* where your mind is going?" Aaron asks.

"I don't know, babe, I'm freaking out!"

"Okay, stop," Kira cuts in. "Don't go there. This could still be an accident."

Corinne shakes her head. "I don't think so anymore."

Kira looks at her, and something passes between them. Corinne runs her hands over her face and then looks at the rest of us.

"I think Tilly or whoever's in charge here messed with the watches so that we can't send messages. As in, they planned for us to be stranded like this."

A shocked laugh bubbles out of me. It's not funny, but I can't help it. This whole thing is so over-the-top ridiculous, like every shitty event from the past few months is culminating in the perfect storm of—well, shit.

"Okay, yes," Kira says. "But even if they messed with the watches, that doesn't mean this was definitely . . . *murder.*"

She lowers her voice for the last word, like if she says it too loudly it'll come true. A little late for that, I think. I reach for the papers in my pocket again, the Sponsor's messages ringing in my head.

"Again," Aaron says through gritted teeth, "we have two dead bodies. What else could this possibly be?"

Kira starts to pace. "McKayleigh said she was going for a walk, right? Did anyone see her after that?"

"Wait, Graham and Zane." Max leans forward. "You both went outside after McKayleigh left. You didn't see anything?"

"Are you really asking us for an alibi?" Zane snaps. "She was our best friend. What's *your* alibi?"

Typical. I can almost hear McKayleigh's voice in my head, just like when she said it earlier. And she was right. It feels like we're on a time loop from hell, every version with the same ending: Zane puts himself first, even if it means throwing someone else to the wolves. Even if it means taking us all down with him.

"We're just trying to figure out what happened," Kira says carefully.

Zane pulls at his golden hair, hanging loose and damp around his shoulders like he just showered. I'm not close enough to smell it, but his vegan shampoo is seared into my sense memory, earthy and sweet. Now, the thought of it makes me sick.

"Fine," he says. "We were out by the pool for maybe twenty minutes, but we didn't see her. Then we came back inside."

"Convenient," Aaron says.

Elody presses her hands to her temples. "No offense, babe, but the sound of your voice is literally making my hangover worse."

That makes two of us. Although maybe my sick feeling has less to do with Aaron and more to do with the evidence burning a hole in my pocket. The bomb I could throw to send Zane and his innocent act up in flames.

"McKayleigh was upset." Kira puts her hands out like she's trying to placate a bunch of asshole kids. "Maybe she wasn't looking where she was going."

Aaron frowns. "Interesting, coming from you."

She falters. "Why?"

"Well, you *did* just tear her to shreds in front of everyone right before she died, so . . ." Elody shrugs.

"That doesn't mean I *killed* her."

"I think we can all agree that McKayleigh deserved that," Corinne says. And then, off Graham's tortured look: "Not *death*. I'm just saying, we all agree that what McKayleigh did was bad. We were right to put her in check."

"I'd love to hear from Logan." Aaron's weaselly eyes bore into mine. "I mean, you tried to smash a plate on Cole's head. You hated McKayleigh. What do *you* think could have happened?"

"I didn't hate her." It comes out on autopilot, but I don't even know if it's true. McKayleigh was cruel, self-centered, and ignorant. She was a bad friend and probably a bad person. But there were moments.

Like that night at the Bounce House. I was curled in my bed, sobbing for so long it felt like my new way of breathing, when McKayleigh knocked on my door. She didn't try to talk about it or tell me to stop. She just asked if she could braid my hair. I still re-member how it felt, her manicured nails on my scalp, firm but gen-tle, practiced over years of dance competitions. I'd done Harper's hair plenty of times, brushing through tangles of the same stick-straight, almost-black color as mine, but this was the first time I'd ever let anyone do my own.

Want to make a real scene?

It's what Zane was so afraid of that night: that I'd lose control, ruin everything because I was weak and afraid. If he knew what I'm holding in pocket right now . . .

Across the room, Zane has that familiar look in his eyes, fear disguised as a warning. And suddenly, I know what I have to do. I reach for the papers again, but as my fingers brush them, a new message sounds on my watch.

Just when I thought you'd learned your lesson . . .

Panic sparks under my skin, but looking around the room, I realize I'm not the only one who got the message. The Sponsor has something to say to all of us, and I hold my breath as the rest of it comes in.

Looks like we have another liar on our hands
So, I think it's time for another vote
Who gets canceled next?

There's another link to the voting app, and this time, it doesn't feel so much like a threat. It feels like a sign. Because now I know what's at stake: Zane could finally get exposed for what he's done. I don't care who the Sponsor is, why they've given me this ammuni-tion. If they want a scene, I'll fucking give it to them.

I pull out the papers.

"Wait," I say, glancing at the timer ticking down on my screen. "Stop the clock."

It stops. A shiver runs down my spine, and I straighten. No going back now. I stare at Zane.

"There's something everyone should know before we vote."

KIRA

When the timer stops, I feel half a second of relief before I understand what this really means: they're listening. Logan asked them to stop the clock, and they did. I don't know who—Tilly, the Sponsor, whoever else might be behind this—but someone's watching. They can hear us, they can see us, and they still haven't sent help.

"What are you doing?" Zane asks slowly. Carefully. Like Logan is a land mine that might go off if he steps the wrong way.

She holds up the papers she pulled from her pocket, her eyes locked on him. "I found these in my bags earlier. Do you want to tell them, or should I?"

"What are you talking about?"

"I'm talking about Madison." Logan unfolds the first paper. "And Bella." She opens the next one. "And Abby." She opens the last one and holds them all up.

Zane moves toward her. "Whoa, okay. Can we take a step back?"

"Why? If we're gonna vote, we should have all the facts." Logan starts to pass the papers around, handing one to me.

It's a printed screenshot of some DMs from last December, six months ago. The messages are between Zane and a girl named Madison.

DECEMBER 11, 2:02 PM
ZANE: Hey what kind of alc are you and your friends
feeling for tn?
MADISON: omg haha you don't have to do that
ZANE: you're the guests!! I've gotta
ZANE: plus I'm the only legal one here lol
MADISON: okie whatever you want! Surprise me ;)
ZANE: yes ma'am

DECEMBER 12, 3:18 PM
MADISON: hey . . . soooo last night was fun ☺
MADISON: would you wanna hang out again some time?

DECEMBER 14, 9:42 PM
MADISON: omg my friends literally won't stop telling
everyone how they went to a bounce house party lol
why is high school so annoyingggg

DECEMBER 16, 2:01 AM
MADISON: sorry if I'm being annoying haha but idk after
the other night I thought maybe you felt something?

DECEMBER 17, 3:45 PM
MADISON: hello???

My stomach drops when I see the bottom of the page. It's an Instagram post from Madison's account, dated the same week.

In the picture, Madison is posing in front of a HAPPY BIRTHDAY banner and holding two silver balloons shaped like the number sixteen.

Oh my god. Zane, a twenty-two-year-old adult, did this to a sixteen-year-old girl. A *newly* sixteen-year-old girl.

Corinne looks up from the paper she's holding. "Zane, what the hell is this?"

He reaches for it, but she shifts away and reads the messages out loud.

"Zane to seventeen-year-old Bella: 'what are you doing?' Bella: 'about to shower.' Zane: 'without me, frowny face?'"

Aaron laughs. "Holy shit."

"Ew," Elody says.

"It's the same thing with Abby," Max says, reading the third paper. "You sent her flirty messages for days, bought her alcohol, paid for her Uber to get to the Bounce House, and then ghosted her after the party. She's sixteen, too." His face darkens. "And this was only last month."

Zane makes a garbled noise. "I didn't—"

"Go ahead." Logan's eyes are blazing. "Talk your way out of this one."

Zane sidesteps, snatching the paper from my hand.

"Hey," Max interjects. "Don't—"

"Let me see." Zane's eyes dart back and forth over the page, a vein bulging in his temple. Then, suddenly, a calm look comes over his face. "Fine. You made some fake texts and printed them out. Nice, Logan." He tosses the paper on the ground with a dry laugh. "Sorry, but I've never seen or heard of these girls in my life."

"Bullshit," she says.

"We all know you have anger issues, but this is beyond crazy. I didn't touch those girls. I don't touch *any* underage girls."

"You didn't touch them?" I ask, heart pounding. "Or you've never heard of them?"

Zane stares at me, caught, and turns to glare at Logan. "Do you see what you're doing here? Like, do you want to ruin my life? I didn't do this!"

"Yes, you did."

"Logan, you lived in the Bounce House when I *supposedly* sent some of this stuff. Are you saying that you knew this was happening all along and waited until now to bring it up? Because that would be pretty messed up." At her silence, he laughs. "See? She doesn't know shit."

"Fine," Logan spits. "Maybe I was too stupid or naive to realize what was going on back then. But I know now. I know what you've been doing."

Zane stares her down, almost daring her. "How? What actual proof do you have?"

"I know," Logan repeats, hard and unrelenting even through the tears in her hazel eyes, "because you did the same thing to me."

Zane's face goes slack, mouth hanging slightly open, and for a moment, I forget to be afraid. All I feel is anger reaching out from my center, growing roots and thorns. Because I've been in this industry since I was twelve, and that's more than enough time to learn what men in power think they can do to girls whose biggest crime is believing they're special. I know, because my parents have done all they can to make sure it doesn't happen to me—but that doesn't mean I haven't seen them, the sleazy "managers" in my DMs promising me everything I've ever wanted in my career, if only I do what they say. The adult men who thought they had every right to tell me how my fourteen-year-old body looked in a leotard.

Next to me, Max starts to reach for his camera, but then Zane laughs. Hard, like this is all a hilarious joke.

"I'm sorry, you guys know I believe women, but come *on*. That's insane."

"You started DMing me a few months after I turned seventeen," Logan says. "You were twenty-one."

"What kind of DMs?" I ask.

A smug, superior look washes over his face. "DMs asking Logan to join the Bounce House because I liked her work. Strictly professional." He looks at Max and adds icily, "I appreciate the concern, man, but you can put away the camera."

"You lured me there," Logan says. "You told me you'd make my career."

"Yeah, and I'm pretty sure I did exactly that. I didn't *lure* you anywhere. I gave you an opportunity."

"And then I wouldn't fuck you and you made my life a living hell!"

The room goes silent, a held breath. Zane and Logan stare each other down, poised like they might lunge, and I know. I know right away that Logan is telling the truth, and Zane's about to do whatever he can to twist it against her.

"What are you even talking about?" he asks.

"My birthday," she says. "Don't try to gaslight me right now."

Zane laughs weakly. "Where'd you get that from, an Instagram infographic? Don't throw words around when you don't understand them. Gaslighting is a real issue."

His superior tone shoots disgust through my veins like poison, and I can't contain it anymore.

"It seems a lot like what you're doing right now."

Zane gives me a dismissive sigh. "I know you're trying to be supportive, Kira, and I respect that. But honestly, you met both of us yesterday. You don't know anything about this."

"Then let Logan tell us," Corinne says.

Zane holds up his hands in a *go ahead* gesture, like she needs his permission.

Logan takes a breath.

"As soon as I got to LA, it started. You know, little touches. Flirting. Never anything big enough for me to be sure it was real, that I wasn't just reading into things. But then . . ."

Zane starts to speak, but Logan gets louder.

"Don't fucking interrupt me," she says.

"I'm just—"

"Let her finish," I tell him.

Zane shuts his mouth.

"Things escalated slowly. Little touches turned into cuddling when no one was around. Eventually, he told me he was into me, but we had to wait until . . ." Logan closes her eyes for a moment, like she's steeling herself. "On my eighteenth birthday, we kissed. And then . . . he wanted to have sex. I wasn't ready. I told him that, and—" She stops, wiping away a tear with her fist, but she doesn't look broken. She looks like she's ready to burn it all down. "He got mad. Throwing shit, screaming. Telling me I led him on. I was fucking terrified. Eventually, he just slammed the door and left, but that wasn't the end of it. He started icing me out of everything. Tried to turn everyone against me." Logan looks at Graham. "Why aren't you backing me up on this? You know I'm telling the truth."

Graham looks genuinely confused. "I—I don't know if I can get into this right now."

"Get into it," Logan demands.

"Logan, I don't know what happened. You wouldn't tell any of us. All I could see from my perspective was that you were into Zane. And obviously that doesn't mean you owe him anything. But Zane told us . . ."

Graham looks to Zane, whose jaw tightens, but he nods for Graham to go on.

"Zane told us that you tried to hook up on your birthday, but he shut it down, and that's why you were acting weird. He said you needed space, so that's why we kept our distance."

Logan blinks fast, and I can see the anger vibrating inside her, like she's seconds away from exploding.

"That's not what happened," she says. "He lied."

Graham swallows and looks at Zane. When he speaks again, it's quiet, like he already knows the answer but needs it not to be true. "Those girls you've been bringing to our parties. You always say they're in college. Was that a lie?"

Zane's jaw tightens.

"*Shit,*" Graham hisses into his palms. "I've seen you take some of them into your room, Zane. That's—"

"Fine," Zane cuts him off. "Maybe a few of them tried to hook up, or whatever. I don't see why that's such a huge deal. It's not like I had sex with any of them."

That look on Zane's face. I've seen it before on Ms. Tammy, on McKayleigh. It's a look that refuses blame, that reflects it back on you like blinding light in a mirror. Just like them, Zane thinks he can get away with anything because he can. Because life hasn't taught him anything different.

"The reason it's a *huge deal,*" I spit, "is because you're clearly taking advantage of a screwed-up power dynamic. I don't care what happened. It's wrong. It's disgusting. And *illegal,* by the way."

"Oh my god, that isn't—" Zane's eyes dart to Elody, who's slouched on the couch, picking at her nails. "How old was the oldest guy you've ever dated?"

She shifts, almost surprised, and then shrugs. "Like, thirty, I think?"

"And how old were you?"

Elody rolls her eyes. "Seventeen. But don't drag me into this."

"What does that have to do with anything?" Corinne asks. "You're still trying to make excuses for an inexcusable thing."

"I'm just saying," Zane argues. "Logan's eighteen. Even if we *did* hook up, which we didn't, it's not—she's not some helpless kid!"

"Sorry, Zane, but that's bullshit," Max says. "You're older than her, just like you're older than all of those girls. You have a huge following. They're still in *high school.* You're a full-fledged adult."

A small part of me loosens. Finally, one of the guys in the room is actually calling Zane out. The bar for men is truly underground, but I'm glad Max is backing the rest of us up.

Zane groans, covering his ears like the little kid he insists Logan wasn't. "Those messages aren't real!"

"Funny," Corinne says sharply. "You didn't say that about the designs McKayleigh stole."

"There were pictures," Zane argues. "Actual proof. It's not the same thing."

"I think we all know what the Sponsor had on McKayleigh was real," I tell him. "And I sure as hell believe this, too."

Quiet settles over the room, heavy and solid. No one argues, because by now, it's clear: we all know Zane is lying. Even Graham—head hanging, kneading the beanie in his hands. His silence is an answer.

"So that's it?" Zane's nostrils flare. "You all believe Logan, but not me? Do you see how messed up that is? You're going to vote for me. You're going to vote to leak all this stuff, to ruin my *life,* and all you have to prove it is some stupid DMs and one half of the story!"

"To be fair, that's not exactly how the legal system works in this country," Aaron says.

"See?" Zane grumbles. "At least *someone* here isn't batshit."

"Sorry, to clarify, I still think you're probably a perv."

"Two people are *dead*!" Graham's face is skeletal and panicked. "For all we know, that's what 'canceled' means here. Do we really want to keep playing this game?"

For a second, I let myself consider it. Two people are dead. McKayleigh died right after we voted for her. How do we know that whoever we vote for next won't end up dead, too? What if that's the real game here?

But no. That's not what this is. There has to be some shred of logic here, some explanation. There always is, if you look hard enough.

I shake my head sharply. "What happened to Cole and Mc-Kayleigh was an accident."

"Then why haven't they shut this down?" Graham asks.

I don't know. The words die in my throat, useless. None of this makes sense. But there has to be something we can do besides play this terrible game, dancing like puppets on the Sponsor's strings.

"What if we don't vote?" I realize, feeling the slightest trickle of hope. "They can't keep doing this if we all refuse."

"Yeah, right," Zane scoffs. "How do we know they won't leak all this stuff anyway?"

"Interesting." Max raises an eyebrow. "I thought those DMs were 'fake.'"

"Get that smug look off your face, man. There's a folder with your name, too. All of you."

As much as I'm starting to hate him, I know Zane's right. But whatever's in my folder, there's no way it's as bad as what they had on McKayleigh and Zane. It can't be, because I haven't *done* anything like that. Still, the thought is enough to send fear crackling through me.

"I think we should vote," Logan says.

"But what if they—"

"Leak our shit?" she cuts Graham off. "Exactly. If we *don't* vote, they might leak everything. If we vote, at least we're not just sitting back and watching it all go to hell." She looks, fearless, at Zane. "We get to decide whose stuff gets leaked."

Corinne takes a deep breath. "I want to vote."

I stare, surprised. "But . . ."

"They're listening to us," Corinne says. "Logan asked them to stop the timer, and they did it. They stranded us on purpose. Something seriously bad is going on here, and Logan has a point. I . . . I think the safest thing is to follow their rules."

Elody twists a lock of hair tightly around her finger. "To be honest, I don't really want to find out what happens if we don't."

Seeing the others' faces, I know the decision has been made. I want to argue, beg them to hear reason, but I'm starting to wonder if they're right. We're trapped here. Powerless.

Well, maybe not completely. Because there's still *one* thing we have the power to do, and looking at Zane, his slow, spiteful nod, I can tell he knows it, too.

"Seems like your minds are made up, then. You want to vote?" He looks at the camera, and fear twitches in his face, like he's staring into the mouth of a beast. "Let's vote."

MAX

The timer springs back to life just as a new message hits our watches:

Go

My heart picks up, and I glance at Kira, the dimple creasing on her cheek as she focuses on her watch. I wonder if she was right. If we'd just refused to keep doing this, could they stop us? But it's too late. Time is ticking down, and someone else is going to be canceled. Survival instinct kicks in like a raspy whisper in my ear: *Are you going to let it be you?*

I type in Zane's name without hesitating. When the timer sounds and our watches show the results, I get a wave of anxiety, even though I know exactly what they'll say.

Zane wins by a landslide with six votes. There's one for Logan, I'm assuming from Zane, and . . .

Shit. There's still one for me.

Another message sounds. A screen recording. I think we all knew this was coming, but still, it's chilling to watch the @theIRLProject Instagram add the DMs Logan showed us to a carousel post and type out the caption:

Thought the Bounce House was big already?
Well, @zanerivers, I have a feeling you're about to make
    headlines

They share the post, and the video ends.

In the silence that follows, Zane nods, looking like he's trying to be brave in the face of a fatal diagnosis. Is that what this is? *No.* If there's one thing I know, it's the difference between reality and fiction, and the idea that someone brought us here to kill us? That's not real. It's a goddamn slasher film. We didn't vote for Zane to die—only to get what he deserves.

He stands, locking eyes with Logan. "I hope that felt good."

Without another word, Zane turns and marches up to his room. Once he's gone, Logan gets up, too, hunching as she storms away.

"Wait, Logan . . ." Graham starts, but she's stomping upstairs before he can finish, veering toward her own room and slamming the door.

Graham takes a hit of his vape, breathing out shakily. For a moment, there's silence. Then, he addresses the rest of us.

"I really hope there isn't anything in those folders that you guys don't want getting out. Because it's coming. One way or another, this is blowing up in all our faces."

He sucks on the vape again, but nothing comes out. Cursing, Graham takes one last look at the rest of us and then shuffles upstairs.

"You know, babe," Elody calls after him, "maybe it's a good

thing your vape is out. Like, this could be a sign to find a less nasty coping skill."

Her voice is its usual unbothered rasp, but the spark of humor is gone. When Graham slams the door on the third floor, she flinches like a gun went off.

"God," she mumbles. "Dramatic, much?"

In the silence, Graham's voice replays in my head. *One way or another, this is blowing up in all our faces.*

I bob my foot, keeping time with my racing thoughts. The Bounce House crew is hiding something. I know they are. And maybe it's just this mess about Zane, but it doesn't add up. Because why the hell is Graham so freaked out? His name isn't anywhere in those messages, and it didn't seem like he knew what Zane was really doing to those girls.

There has to be something more. And this time, I'm not going to sit by and watch things happen.

I stand up and grab my camera bag.

"Where are you going, Spielberg?" Aaron snorts. "Grabbing your next Oscar?"

I ignore his increasingly unoriginal insults and walk to the stairs. As I do, I catch Kira looking at me. Something flashes in her face, suspicious, like she knows what I'm about to do.

But I can't have any doubts about this. I reach into my pocket and feel the smooth rectangle of my voice recorder.

Up on the third floor, I stop in front of our door and switch on the recorder. Then, I knock.

"Graham?"

He doesn't answer, so I come inside. The balcony doors are open, and he's leaning against the railing, staring out at the sea. The waves seem louder, slamming against each other as they fight their way to the shore, like they're trying to escape something we can't see coming.

Graham looks back at me, his expression changing from fear to irritation. "What?"

"I just wanted to make sure you were good."

He clocks my camera bag. "Yeah, right."

"I'm not filming."

It's not technically a lie. And anyway, sometimes you need to bend the truth to get the truth.

"Good. 'Cause this isn't an interview." Graham shoves his way past me and back inside.

"I just want to hear your side of things."

"Yeah, well, I'm not in a sharing mood."

Okay, so offering to be an objective ear isn't working. I need to change tactics.

"You voted for Zane, didn't you?"

Graham stops.

Yes. I press him. "Only one person voted for Logan, and I'm assuming that was him."

"What about the person who voted for you?"

The question knocks me off balance, even though I should have been prepared for it. It's the same one I've been asking myself. It had to be Aaron, right? He's the only person here who hates me enough to be that petty, but . . .

"That's not the point," I say, both to Graham and myself. "Look, I think we both know that what happened back there looks pretty bad for you, too. Unless you speak up now. Clarify your version of what happened."

Graham looks at me, something moving behind his stare, like a machine clicking into gear, and for a second, I think I've got him. But then he speeds to his bed, grabbing his guitar bag and slinging it over his shoulder.

"I'm going to go write," he mumbles, pushing past me.

Shit. I knew he wouldn't talk to me right off the bat, but I thought I'd be better at this. I'm usually better at this. I just need to find the way in.

And then, I notice the front pocket of his guitar case, slightly unzipped.

I mean, it's a bit literal, but I'll take it.

"Wait, Graham."

He stops, exasperated. "What?"

"I'm pretty sure Cole had some pods in his bag, if yours are out."

Graham's jaw tenses. He looks toward Cole's luggage, and then back at me, probably fighting an internal battle between how much he hates me and how much he needs nicotine.

The nicotine wins. "Where?"

"Front pocket of his backpack, I think."

Graham bends down to dig through Cole's bag, his guitar still hanging over his shoulder, and this is it. I take a few steps toward him, leaning over like I'm looking for the pods, too.

"I could have sworn he had some." I close the recorder in my fist, slowly reaching for the open guitar-case pocket, and then, carefully—

Graham stands up, and I shove my fist back into my pocket. Apparently, I made a lucky guess: Graham holds a fresh pod in his hand. But I shouldn't be surprised that vaping is among Cole's many vices.

Was.

Graham shoves the pod into his pocket, shooting me an annoyed look. "If you think I'm giving you some kind of sound bite in exchange for this, I'm not."

He puts his empty vape between his teeth and starts for the door.

"What's in your folder, Graham?"

He stops, turning to look at me. "What's in yours?"

I don't answer. A spiteful smirk curves on Graham's mouth, and he stomps out of the room, slamming the door behind him.

I breathe out, opening my empty fist.

I've got him bugged. Now, I just have to hope that he's about to do what I think he is.

[KNOCK.]

GRAHAM

Hey, you in there?

[DOOR OPENS.]

ZANE

Yeah?

GRAHAM

[Hushed.] Someone knows.

ZANE

Whoa, chill out. What's—

GRAHAM

Someone knows what we did to her.

ELODY

"Babe?" I knock on the door again. "Come on, I'm literally aging out here."

I shift the wine bottle under my arm, waiting a few more seconds. Then, just when I'm about to give up on this whole being-nice thing, I hear footsteps, and Logan opens the door.

"Oh." I can't even hide my shock at her red, puffy face, her hood so tight around it that I'm pretty sure she wants to move in. All the lights are off. "You look . . ."

"Is that wine?" Her eyes go straight to the bottle.

"Yeah. Thought you could use some."

I hold it out. She unscrews the cap and takes the longest sip I've ever seen.

"Damn," I say. "Guess I thought right."

She takes the wine and crawls back into her bed, cradling the bottle like a baby doll. I flick on the light.

"No," she begs. "Off."

Oh my god. I'm starting to remember why I don't normally try to be nice to people.

"Nope. I'm not gonna let you just, like, lie here and feel sorry for yourself."

She sits up, wrapping the covers around her head. "Why are you here?"

"I don't know. You've been locked up here for, like, two hours. I thought someone should make sure you're alive."

She stares into the bottle. "Are they all talking about me? Saying I'm a bitch who ruined Zane's life?"

"No, narcissist. Everyone's just, like, sitting around and being freaked out. It's literally so boring I could scream." I roll my eyes. "Also, I'm pretty sure everyone's with you on the whole 'Zane deserved to get canceled' thing."

Logan gulps down more wine.

"Whoa, okay." I hold out my hand for the bottle. "I was thinking more like we'd share it? I'm not trying to watch you black out and die."

She makes a pissed-off face, but hands it over, and then throws herself back onto the pillows. I take a sip to fill the awkward silence. If she doesn't start talking soon, I might have to give up on this little project and go get drunk by myself.

"Why are *you* checking on me?" she asks. "Female friendship doesn't seem like your thing."

"Um, rude? But you're not wrong, I guess." I pick at the wine label. It's a cheap Moscato, because apparently Tilly couldn't be bothered to get us wine that won't make me feel like crap tomorrow, but whatever. Some nights you've just got to drink bad screw-top wine. "Look, I've been in your whole situation before."

"What, with the thirty-year-old you dated? You seemed pretty proud of that when Zane asked."

Okay, I know Logan's been through some stuff, but she could at least *try* to not have such a gross personality.

"I wasn't proud of it. Zane just put me on the spot. Like, to be honest . . ." I take another sip, preparing myself. "That guy kind of did the same thing to me. What Zane did to you."

She sits up. "Wait, he groomed you?"

"Yeah. Whatever you want to call it." *Grooming* sounds more like what you do to a fancy dog than what it actually is, how it feels, but I push that thought down. "I guess I kind of knew it was happening, but also . . . I don't know. I didn't realize how bad it was until I was in too deep, if that makes sense?"

I down more of the wine, and I almost want to laugh, because Derek would literally die if he knew I was drinking something so cheap. For him, it was top-shelf only.

"Who was he?" Logan asks.

"A photographer. But, like, one of those fancy high-fashion ones." I take another drink, trying to forget how exciting it felt to walk into his studio, down the hallway with all those famous people framed on the bright white walls. "He slid into my DMs and asked if we could do a shoot. I thought he was a catfish at first, but then I saw it was his verified account. I literally almost died."

Logan pulls a pillow close to her. "What happened?"

"It was all pretty basic at first. We did the shoot. I looked hot."

"Ethereal" was the word that Derek used, actually. I had to Google that one in the Uber home, the one he ordered for me.

"We did some more shoots. He was totally obsessed with me. And then he started talking about how he had this huge opportunity for me. The cover of a big magazine. I won't even say which, because it's so embarrassing that I actually believed him." I laugh, but it's hard in my throat. "I don't know why. Like, he also kept telling me that he was going to post our shots on Instagram, but he never actually did that, either. He kept saying he hadn't found the perfect one yet. And I believed him."

"Dickhead," Logan says.

I laugh. "Yeah. For real. So maybe I should have known. I don't know. But whatever. He told me that to get the cover, we'd have to do something that really got their attention." I shudder and take another pull from the bottle, the alcohol starting to warm my cheeks. "It started with some kind of sexy poses, and then all of a sudden I was just in my bra and underwear, and then . . ."

I hold the bottle tighter. The worst part is, even as I realized what was happening, I only felt excited. Derek's hand on my back, undoing my bra like he'd done it a million times, not like all the guys my age who acted like they'd never seen one in their lives. His breath on my neck, waiting. Because that's what Derek did. He wouldn't kiss me first. It had to be me. I had to decide. Back then, I thought it was him being careful, not wanting to pressure me or whatever, but now, I know what it really was: plausible deniability.

Logan curls tighter around her pillow. We're the same age, but right now, she feels so much younger than me.

"What happened after that?" she asks.

"We hooked up for, like, two months. In secret. I thought the whole thing was super hot. All the running around and stuff. But then he broke it off. Got bored, I guess."

"Fuck him," Logan whispers.

A weird feeling starts up in my chest. A good one. Like, I didn't realize how good it would feel to hear someone else say it, what I've been thinking for years.

"Yeah. Fuck him." I nod, letting myself feel it. "Don't worry, though. I wasn't just going to sit there and take it." I grin over the mouth of the bottle. "I got revenge."

"How?"

"Leaked his nudes."

Logan snorts a laugh. "You're lying."

"No, babe, I'm so serious. They were bad, too. So cringe. But he couldn't report me or anything, because then he'd have to tell everyone why he sent those pictures to a minor."

"Damn," Logan says. "That's kind of badass."

"Yeah." I bring the bottle to my lips, stopping before taking a sip. "I wish I would've done more, though."

"What do you mean?"

"I don't know. Like, obviously he was super pissed, but he got over it. It didn't hurt his career at all, and he probably found another girl. I just wish I could've done something to really make him feel it, you know? Because guys like Derek and Zane . . . they always get away with it."

Logan lets out a shaky breath, and her voice comes out soft. "I'm really sorry that happened to you, Elody."

"Thanks." I roll my shoulders, shaking off the serious energy. "Sorry. Not to be, like, a huge downer. I just wanted to let you know that you're not alone."

I hand Logan the bottle.

"Thanks." She takes a sip and then looks at me. "You know, you're a lot nicer than people give you credit for."

"If you tell anyone that, I swear to god I'll kill you."

Logan laughs. "Yikes. Not the best choice of words."

"Oh." I lean back on my elbows. "Yeah, guess not."

"Noted, though." Logan looks sad all of a sudden, and I realize she's staring at the empty bed across from us. "McKayleigh would do this sometimes. Like, come check on me when no one else would. She could be surprisingly nice, when she wasn't, you know . . ."

"Being a total bitch?"

"Yeah, I guess." Logan's eyes look foggy and definitely a little drunk, which . . . duh. The girl might be tall, but she's bony as hell, and also majorly going through it. Lightweight central.

God, it just hit me how depressing this is. Logan has to sleep in this room when, just last night, her dead ex-friend was sleeping here, too. McKayleigh's hairbrush is still on the nightstand, her long red hair all tangled up in its bristles.

I hold up the wine bottle in a toast, because someone needs to cheer up this sad-girl energy, like, real quick.

"To McKayleigh Hill," I say. "Who was sometimes a bitch, but also sometimes a good friend. And that's how all the realest ones are."

I take a long pull, and hand it over to Logan.

"To McKayleigh Hill." She kills the bottle.

It gets quiet again, and I stand up. "We need more wine."

"I don't want to go down there."

"Sorry, babe." I snatch the empty bottle from her hands. "You want wine, you're coming with me. I'll give you five minutes to make yourself look"—I wave my hand at her—"not like this, and then you're meeting me downstairs."

Logan groans, climbing back under the covers.

"Okay, fine. If wine isn't enough, then think of it like this." I pull the covers down so she has to look at me. "If you stay up here and hide, then you're just letting Zane win. Do you want to let that happen?"

Logan turns onto her side. "Ten minutes?"

"Five. That's my last offer, babe." I take the empty bottle and turn toward the door. "Now, get your ass up!"

Out on the landing, I look down to the living room. Max, Kira, Corinne, and Aaron are having an intense-looking conversation.

"There's got to be something we can do with the watches, right?" Max asks, looking at Corinne. "Undo whatever programming is stopping us from sending messages?"

Corinne shakes her head. "We can't fix that on our end without the right tech. This isn't a movie where I just type really quickly on a keyboard and go, 'I'm in.'" She slouches. "But a keyboard would be nice."

"Oh my god," I say, walking down to the first floor. "Can we take a break from this techy stuff? It's boring."

Kira looks at me like I grew a third boob. "We're trying to find a way out of here."

"Unsuccessfully," Aaron adds.

"Sounds like we need a break, then." I point at Aaron with my empty bottle, and it gives me the perfect idea. "Spin the bottle. We're playing."

"Seriously?" He frowns. "We're on a death island and you want to play spin the bottle?"

The patio door opens, and Graham and Zane walk in.

"Spin the bottle," I tell them. "Anyone who doesn't play is lame."

"Yeah, I don't really know if we're in the mood," Zane answers for them both.

"Okay, seriously?" I put the bottle down on the coffee table with a loud thud. "What have you two been doing all day? Having some kind of e-boy jam sesh?" I gesture at Graham's guitar and turn back to the rest of the group. "And you guys have been trying to find a way out of here for, what? Two hours? So, what's the brilliant, amazing plan you came up with?"

"Two hours." Kira looks at her watch and frowns. "Has it been that long?"

Max slumps. "She's right. We're not getting anywhere."

For once, he knows what he's talking about.

"I don't know about you guys," I say, "but if we have to spend the rest of the night, like, sitting and talking and *thinking* about all of the shit that's happening today, then I might lose it, okay? Like, actually."

Kira shifts her weight, crossing one arm over the other. "A distraction might be . . . kind of nice."

Definitely not who I expected to back me up, but I'll take it.

"Hell yeah! That's the kind of energy I'm looking for."

Zane sighs. "Fine."

A door opens upstairs, and Logan comes out of her cave and onto the landing.

"Spin the bottle," I call up. "You in?"

She groans. "Seriously?"

"There'll be wine."

"Fine."

I smile. Maybe it's wrong to be excited right now, but whatever. This day has been a lot, to say the literal least, and we all need to do *something* to forget it.

We move the coffee table so there's enough space for everyone on the floor. Logan goes to the kitchen to grab another bottle of wine, and everyone circles up. Everyone except for Max, who hangs back, staring at Graham's guitar case.

"You coming, babe?" I ask.

Max looks at me, his eyes dipping down to my chest. When he realizes I noticed, his face goes tomato-red. I grin. This is definitely going to be fun.

"Yeah," he says, fixing his hair. And then fixing it again. "Sure."

Max sits down on the floor next to Kira. Of *course*. But you know what? I love a challenge.

I hold up the bottle. "Who's first?"

KIRA

"I'll go."

Elody grins at me, surprised. "Damn. Miss Kira Lyons is coming out of her shell."

Heat rushes to my face. She's not the only one who's shocked here, because the top of that list would be me. I hate spin the bottle. There are too many variables, too many potential disasters, just like, well . . . anything that could get into make-out territory.

But maybe it's the way Elody was looking at Max just now, like she wanted to eat him whole, or the way Max was looking back, like he wanted to be eaten. Maybe it's everything that's happened today, the slowly suffocating vise of panic in my chest, or maybe . . . you know what? Maybe I just want Elody to wipe that shocked look off her face.

Tonight, I'm choosing chaos.

I reach for the bottle. For a second, Elody tightens her grip, both of us holding on before she lets go, and the bottle gives way.

She smiles. "All you, babe."

I smile back at her, like a girl whose heart isn't hammering against her ribs, and set the bottle on the floor.

"Okay, before we start," I say, "I feel like we should make sure we all give consent."

We go around, and everyone says they're cool with standard spin the bottle kissing. But when we get to Zane, he rolls his eyes.

"Come on, man." He smiles, lopsided. "I'm all for consent, don't get me wrong, but it's just spin the bottle. It doesn't have to be so intense."

The same disgust I felt earlier today sizzles inside of me.

"Pretty fitting statement for someone who's trying to convince us he's not a predator," I snap.

"Oh my god." Elody puts a hand on her heart, her jaw open in exaggerated surprise. "Who *is* she?"

Corinne looks to Logan and asks gently, "Are you okay with playing this game if he's here?"

She shrugs. "Fine with me."

Still, an uneasy feeling starts to brew.

"Maybe this is a bad idea," I say.

"I said it's fine," Logan insists.

"See?" Zane smiles at me, so calm and normal, it's unnerving. "It's just a game, right? I consent."

I glare back. "Fine."

Swallowing my anger, I give the bottle a twist. It spins, and spins, and . . .

Graham takes his vape out of his mouth. "Uh, that's me, I guess."

I can't ignore the little dip in my heart, because physics has failed me. One more shift to the left, and it would have been Max. As soon as I have the thought, I want to crawl right back into the carefully constructed shell I've just started to creep out of. There are so many more immediate, terrible things to worry about than how I feel about a boy. But I can't ignore the war of feelings deep in my stomach, fear fighting my need to release it, overthinking at odds with how badly I want not to think.

So stop thinking, I tell myself.

I look at Graham. He doesn't seem all that excited about this game or the prospect of kissing me, so we might as well just get it over with. I lean across the circle, give Graham a quick peck, and hand him the bottle, forcing myself not to glance at Max.

Graham spins, and it lands on Aaron. Elody "oohs" excitedly as the guys glower.

"Seriously?" Aaron mutters.

"Hate to tell you, dude, but you're not my type," Graham deadpans.

Zane gives him a shove, a little too hard. "Come on, guys. Lighten up."

He holds out a hand for Graham's vape.

"Fine." Graham passes it to Zane, leans across the circle, and gives Aaron the quickest, least enthusiastic kiss I've ever seen. Aaron spins, and when it stops, he groans like the entire universe is against him.

"Sorry, Logan, but I'm twenty-one years old. I'm not kissing a high schooler." He looks pointedly at Zane, who's hitting the vape, mist swirling from his lips.

Logan laughs. "You're a good man, Aaron Tyler Banks. But technically, I'm a dropout." She takes a messy swig from her wine.

Zane grabs the bottle out of her hands.

A sharp, sober look cuts through her tipsiness. "What the hell?"

"I think you've had enough," he tells her.

Logan glares, and suddenly *if looks could kill* feels less hyperbolic. And I don't blame her. But it seems like she wants to move on. Logan sets her half-full bottle down between them and grabs the empty one, spinning it. It lands on Elody, and Logan gives her a quick, sloppy kiss.

My heart beats faster as Elody lets the bottle fly. I know exactly who she's hoping it lands on. When it's Zane, she doesn't even try to hide her disappointment.

And then I see Max watching her. A sick feeling spreads through me. I hate thinking of other women as competition—I had more than enough of that during *Dance It Out*—but it's hard not to compare myself to Elody. It's not even that I'm insecure. I like the body I'm in, the person I try to be. It's just that Elody's whole *thing* is that she's everything I'm not: loud, fun, and fearless. It's hard not to focus on that.

Elody sighs and gestures at Zane. "Come here, babe."

She gives him a reluctant little kiss, and then he takes his turn. The bottle goes around weakly until it wobbles to a stop.

Corinne looks down the bottle pointed right at her. "So actually, I'm gonna pass."

"All good." Zane reaches for Logan's wine bottle, the half-full one. "I might tap out. I'm a little old for this game, anyway."

He takes a long swallow before Logan snatches the bottle back.

"I think you've had enough," she snaps, throwing his own words back at him.

Zane laughs, wiping his mouth with the back of his hand. "Don't worry. It's all yours."

"I think Max should go," Elody says, *totally* casual and inconspicuous. "He hasn't had a turn yet."

Max gets red, and I clench my teeth. I don't care about this boy. I am immune to his messy hair and crooked smile, and the disarming effects of his blue eyes. I am definitely not noticing the little freckle on his hand as he reaches for the bottle, or the way my heartbeat is kicking up again as he spins it around. It spins, and spins, and—

Elody stops the bottle with her hand, a wicked smile spreading on her face. "Oh, look. Me again."

"That's not how you play," Aaron says.

"Sorry, babe." Her stare is locked on Max. "Can't argue with the bottle. It's the rules."

It's not the rules and she knows it, but that's why she's already won—because it *is* just a game, and it doesn't really matter. I can't argue without making it embarrassingly obvious that I like Max.

Elody crawls forward and pulls off his glasses. His face flushes.

"What?" she asks, low and raspy. "You scared?"

Elody inches close enough that there's barely a breath between them, but she won't close the gap. Instead, she dares him with her eyes, waiting. Max starts to lean in with a blank look on his face, like he's just caught in her gravitational pull. Then, with a swallow, he shuts his eyes, and I swear, in the millisecond before their mouths meet, Elody looks at me out of the corner of her eye and smiles.

And then they're kissing.

At first, Max barely moves, mouth closed, but then Elody digs her fingers into his hair, and I can see the exact moment his resolve breaks. Her pink acrylics scratch down his neck, and he kisses her harder, his hands finding her hips, the small of her back. She bites his lip, hard, and this low sound comes out of his throat, and I can't watch this. I can't believe I'm letting myself feel like this over a boy who never even liked me to begin with. A boy who I already knew I couldn't trust.

"You guys want to get a room?"

For the first time ever, I'm grateful for Aaron's interjection. Like his voice broke them out of a spell, Max and Elody pull away. Max laughs like he isn't sure what came over him, her lipstick shining around his mouth. She grins, wiping a finger across her bottom lip, eyes on fire.

Elody's gaze slides from Max to Zane. "Damn, babe. Are you that much of a prude? You look like you're going to be sick."

For once, Elody isn't being dramatic. Zane's pale, almost green, and there's this distant look in his eyes. He reaches for the full wine bottle and takes a sip, and then another. He swallows. Swallows again.

"Zane?" Graham asks.

The bottle slips out of his hand, gurgling onto the floor.

"Oh my god." The dazed look falls from Max's face. "Are you—?"

Zane claws at his throat, wheezing.

"Peanuts." Graham's eyes get big. "He's allergic to peanuts. Did anyone . . ."

"There shouldn't be any in the house," I say. "Tilly said so, didn't she?"

But even as it comes out of my mouth, I'm not sure. I remember Tilly saying everyone's dietary restrictions had been considered, but I don't know if she said there weren't any peanuts in the house. Zane gasps, falling onto his side.

"Do you have an EpiPen?" Corinne asks him.

Graham jumps up. "It's in his bag."

"Go," Corinne orders.

Graham runs for the stairs, almost slipping as he goes.

I shake my head, like it might reset my brain, make it find the logic. "But Zane didn't even eat anything. Where would he have . . ."

And then my eyes land on the wine bottle. Logan's bottle. Her gaze locks on mine, and the look in her eyes is pure shock, terror.

"I didn't . . . I don't know how he . . ."

"It's not there." Graham calls down from the second floor, running out and gripping the balcony railing. "It's normally in his front backpack pocket, but it's not there."

Zane's face is swollen, his throat rattling, and his lips look blue. Oh my god, his lips are blue.

"Did you look everywhere?" Corinne asks.

"It's not there!" Graham screams.

This can't be happening. Tilly said . . .

The first-aid kit. I jump to my feet and run, throwing the closet door open. There are cleaning supplies, some old raincoats, and—there, on the top shelf. A plastic red box. I reach up and grab it, throwing it open. There's an EpiPen box inside. I could cry with relief. I drop the first-aid kit and open the box, reaching for—nothing. I turn the box over and look inside. It's empty.

"Kira?" Corinne calls. "Is there an EpiPen in there?"

I turn, feeling like I'm moving through water. Zane is lying on his back now, still. Way too still.

"He's not breathing," Logan says. "Oh my god, he's not . . ."

Corinne bends down and starts CPR. She goes through the motions, steady and sure, and time is an island. We're hovering in the middle of the sea, watching, waiting, I don't know for how long—maybe two minutes, maybe twenty.

I still don't know how long it's been when Corinne sits up. Shakes her head.

Gone.

Zane is gone.

For the second time today, the person we voted for is dead.

LOGAN

The room tilts, and I'm on my hands and knees.

Someone grips my arm, trying to help me up.

Elody. I throw her off. I don't want her stupid sisterly touch. I don't want anyone's hands on me.

The wine fog is clearing, everything sharpening to one point: Zane, lying on the floor. Zane's body. Zane isn't a person anymore, and all I can think is that this is my fault. If I hadn't brought up those DMs, if I hadn't been so set on making him pay for it . . .

"I don't understand," Kira says. "How did he get exposed to peanuts?"

Peanuts. I take a shuddering breath. Peanuts are what killed Zane, not me. It's almost ironic: Zane Rivers, the untouchable king of TikTok, was brought down by a legume. I would laugh, if I didn't think I was about to throw up or pass out.

"Was he allergic to anything else?" Corinne asks.

"No." Graham's voice is thick and raw with tears.

"Just spitballing here," Aaron says, "but what if someone slipped them in?"

My stomach drops.

"Why would someone do that?" Kira asks, terror flooding her expression.

"Because this is what they want!" Graham yells. He thrusts out his watch. "Tilly. The Sponsor. Whoever the hell they are, they want to expose us and kill us one by one. I told you guys this would all blow up at us, and no one listened!"

"Hold on," Max says. "Are we talking about one of *us* slipping peanuts to Zane? Because that's—"

"Exactly what happened," Graham snaps.

I can't make myself look at him, but I can feel his eyes, the accusation searing into me. It's exactly how Kira looked at me, her eyes shifting slowly from the wine bottle to my face.

"But how would they even do that?" Max pulls a hand through his hair. "Peanuts have a pretty recognizable taste."

"Peanut oil," Kira says quietly. "If you mixed it with the right thing, you wouldn't be able to tell."

"Like wine," Graham says.

Finally, I look at him. He's ghost-pale, except for the red around his nose, his eyes. His eyes, telling me that he's already made up his mind. That he knows exactly what I am.

"I didn't poison Zane," I tell him.

"Then how do you explain him dying five minutes after he drank your wine?"

"Yeah, *my* wine," I repeat. "He took it from me. It's not like I shoved it down his throat."

Graham takes a step toward me, and his fury sends me crawling backward.

"*You* got the bottle from the kitchen. *You* let him drink it. *You're* the one who had those DMs printed out and ready to show everyone. Who else could have done this?"

"Okay, wait." Elody walks over to the bottle, fully spilled on the floor next to Zane, and picks it up, wincing as she gets close to his body. "It's a cheap-ass screw-top. Anyone could have opened it and put something in there, like, anytime today." Her eyes dart around the room. "It could have been any of you."

"It could have been Tilly, too," Corinne adds. "Or anyone who was here before us."

Max walks over and takes the bottle from Elody. Adjusting his glasses, he holds it up to the light.

"I don't think I see any oil in here. It's hard to tell."

"Oh my god, *obviously* it's in there," Elody says. "Like, he didn't just inhale peanut oil in the air!"

Max flushes. "Unless it was on someone's mouth."

Elody laughs wryly. "Right. So, I ate some peanuts and then kissed Zane? Why the hell would I do that?"

"It could have been on Graham's vape," I realize. "Zane used it, too."

"Are you serious?" he growls.

"Everyone stop it!"

We all freeze, staring at Kira. Rational, calm Kira. Something about her freaking out makes this even scarier.

"No one killed Zane," she says. "That doesn't make any sense."

"Sorry, babe, but three people are dead," Elody says. "*Nothing* makes sense."

Kira starts to pace. "Think about it. If their plan is to expose us with these Instagram posts, then why would they kill us, too? Wouldn't they want us to . . . to suffer the consequences?"

"I'm starting to think whoever we're dealing with isn't exactly a rational individual," Aaron says.

"Unless this is their version of making us suffer the consequences." Horror warps Corinne's face. "Unless they want the rest of us to watch as they pick us off one by one."

Kira shakes her head. "Why would anyone—"

"Bring us all here to kill us?" Elody interrupts, more frantic by the second. "I don't know. All I know is we're stranded, the phone is gone, and now three people are dead. Two of those people died after we voted for them to get 'canceled.' Like, if you think that's a coincidence, then sorry, babe, but you're living on another planet." She stops, pressing her nails against her mouth, still bruised from sucking Max's face. "Oh my god. We're supposed to be here for three weeks. We could literally all die and no one would even know!"

A sound bubbles out of me, somewhere between a dark laugh and a cry. She's right. We could all die, and no one would know. And once they did, when it was too late, what would they have to say about us? Clickbait headlines calling us TikTokers and Instagrammers and *influencers*. That stupid word. And what would they call me? *Ex–Bounce House member Logan Costello.* Just like all the other articles, the ones about me leaving. Because even when I try to leave, I can't. Even now, with Zane lying dead on the floor, I can't get out of his grip.

Nausea lurches in my stomach, and I squeeze my eyes shut.

"We should look through the kitchen," Corinne says, launching into clear-eyed focus. "The peanuts had to come from somewhere."

She leads everyone to start the search, and I follow like the dust hanging in the golden glow of the windows, floating there, feeling like I'm watching all of this from above, from one of the cameras on the wall. Watching as they open every last drawer and cabinet in the kitchen. As Kira unscrews the olive oil and sniffs it. As Max digs through the trash. As Corinne and Aaron open the fridge, sifting through everything inside.

Nothing. There's nothing.

And I know I should be panicking, but I'm just tired. So tired of looking for things when we know they won't turn up. Of the world speeding along when all I want is just a few minutes of stillness, of giving in to my heavy bones and lying on the ground.

What would Harper think if she could see me right now? I came here for her, so I could get my career back on track and be the older sister she needs me to be. I came here for *me,* so I could prove to Zane and everyone else that I didn't need him. And now . . .

My heartbeat kicks up, sweat prickling at the back of my neck and my palms. Zane's still lying there with that horrible look frozen on his face. We can't just keep going when there's a *body* in the living room.

I turn away from the kitchen and walk to the living room. There has to be a blanket, something to cover him up. But I don't see anything. This isn't the type of cozy house I always dreamed about when I was little, with throw blankets flung over the couch for whenever you get cold. It's like the Bounce House: all looks, no comfort.

"Logan?" Graham sees me first. "What are you doing?"

I don't answer him, just go to the storage closet and throw it open. There has to be something in here. But I don't see anything. Except . . .

I stop. Something's different. Wrong. I scan the old rain jackets, the empty hangers, the cleaning supplies, until I land on the box, the one Aaron found the gun in. It's slightly open, the latch popped.

My heart hammers as I reach out and take it, opening the lid all the way. Inside, there's nothing but gray foam and a gun-shaped indentation.

"What the hell are you—"

Graham stops a few feet behind me. The rest of them are watching me now, too, waiting.

"The gun," I tell them. "It's gone."

ELODY

Oh my god. Literally, this day is trying to send me over the edge.

"Okay, somebody better start talking," I say. "Like, right now."

"I knew we shouldn't have kept it," Logan barks. "I *told* you guys!"

"Yeah, well, you didn't exactly guess that one of us was going to be a *murderer*, did you, babe?"

"No one here is a murderer," Kira says. "Whoever took the gun, just . . . put it back. You're not protecting yourself or anyone else."

"Oh, sure." I laugh. "Yeah, whoever stole it, just put it back real quick. None of us will be mad. Promise."

Corinne takes a sharp breath. "We need to go through everyone's bags."

"Come on," I say. "Do you actually think whoever took the gun is dumb enough to keep it in their own stuff?"

"Can we just look through everyone's bags?" Corinne's voice wobbles. Losing control. Maybe she's finally realizing that life isn't some video game with rules and goals, something you can beat.

But I don't have the energy to argue with her. And I don't have any better ideas.

"Fine," I say. "Whatever you want, babe."

We start with Aaron and Zane's room. I turn bags over and dump them all out, even get on my knees and look under mattresses and on the floor, but it's just like it is with every other thing that goes missing on this island. Like it fully ghosted, disappeared right into the air. Same with Logan and McKayleigh's room.

When we get to my room, I sit on the bed. "Go crazy."

While everyone tears through our stuff, Logan stands at the window with this blank look on her face, her hand in the pocket of her jean shorts. God, I really feel bad for her. Like, no matter how much someone hurt you, how much you want to hurt *them,* it's a different thing, watching them die for real.

Wait, Logan's hand in her pocket. My heart starts to beat loud in my chest. Does she have the gun? She's angry enough. Maybe—

Logan takes her hand out of her pocket, and it's empty. I breathe out, because duh. She's wearing jean shorts designed for women. Those pockets can barely hold a phone, forget a gun. I need to pull it together.

Kira closes my suitcase, all frustrated. "It's not here."

"Shocker," I say, but my heart's not even in it anymore. We only have one more room to look in, the third floor, and I have a pretty good feeling we're not finding anything there, either.

But we go anyway, marching up the stairs in a single-file line like a bunch of kindergartners. I check behind me, half-worried someone's going to pull the gun on me right here, but all I see is Max messing with his camera bag.

"You know, babe, you made a really good call with this whole documentary thing," I tell him, trying to sound calm. "If we get out of here, people are going to eat this up."

He just looks at the floor, like he didn't have his tongue in my mouth an hour ago. Like he wasn't losing his mind at my fingers in his hair. When he looks up again, it's still not at me. It's over my shoulder, at Kira, who's leading the way up the stairs.

No way. No *fucking* way.

That's it. I'm done. I'm not going to make myself look like an idiot over a skinny-ass guy whose priorities are clearly screwed the hell up, because I'm so out of his league it's not even funny.

I'm going to find this stupid gun.

I walk into the room and go straight for Max's stuff. I dig through his suitcase, tossing everything onto the floor until I get all the way to the bottom. When it's not there, I unball all of his stupid crew socks one by one: stripes, polka dots, waves, palm trees, ducks. Ugh. Ducks aren't even, like, island-themed.

The gun isn't in any of the socks, but whatever. Maybe I just wanted to remind him in front of everyone that he wears really stupid socks. From the embarrassed look on his face as he stands by the door, watching me, I'm pretty sure I did my job.

I'm about to move on to his second bag when I hear Graham.

"Logan, wait."

She's unzipping the front of his guitar bag, reaching inside the pocket.

"Stop," Graham says. "I don't like anyone touching my—"

Logan pulls something out, her eyes wide.

Graham freezes.

"What is this?" Logan asks.

"What? I don't . . ."

She opens her fist and shows us what she's holding.

A little bottle, the size of a travel hand sanitizer. At first, it looks empty, but then I see the ring of yellowish oil on the bottom.

Holy shit.

Logan moves slowly toward him. "Why is there peanut oil in your stuff, Graham?"

He shakes his head. "I don't know."

"Bullshit," Aaron says.

Graham backs up. "This is just like the charger in McKayleigh's bags. Someone's trying to screw me over!" He points at Logan. "You're the only one here with an actual reason to kill Zane. You're telling me that you just *found* that in my bag?"

"I didn't kill him," Logan says.

Max reaches into the guitar bag.

Graham rushes toward him. "What are you—"

"Two choices," Max says, pulling something out, a little rectangle. "You tell us what you and Zane were talking about out there, or I play it for everyone to hear."

Wait, oh my god. It's a recorder. Max Overby, you gorgeous, smart idiot.

Graham's face crumples like he's about to cry.

"Which is it?" Max asks.

Graham lunges, but Kira pulls him back. He tries to shake her off, but Graham weighs about a hundred pounds and Kira's, like, ripped. She holds on until Graham stops fighting.

"What were you and Zane talking about?" Max demands, and god, I hate how hot he looks when he's being bossy.

"I didn't kill him," Graham whimpers.

A buzzing feeling travels up from my toes to my chest. I look at Max, the recorder.

"Play it," I tell him.

Max presses a button. Sound comes out of the recorder, crackly white noise. Max fast-forwards through a lot of nothing, until there's voices, squeaky and high like a bunch of chipmunks. He presses another button, and the chipmunks turn into people.

"*Someone knows.*" Graham.

"*Whoa, chill out.*" Zane. It makes me shiver, like we're hearing his ghost. "*What's—*"

"I didn't do anything," Graham begs in real time, even as the Graham on the recording makes him sound guilty as hell:

"*Someone knows what we did to her.*"

Everyone's frozen as the voices on the recording go quiet, long enough that I wonder if it stops there. But then, recording-Zane talks again:

"*You need to pull it together, man. No one knows.*"

"*I don't think I can do this anymore. We have to tell someone. We can't just—*"

"*Pull it together.*" It's a threat, slow and clear. Zane's voice gets even lower, almost so I can't even hear it. "*There's cameras all over the place, so if I were you, I'd shut up.*"

There's a few seconds of silence, and then:

"*Okay.*"

The recorder goes back to white noise. Max stops it.

"What was that about, Graham?" he asks.

Graham jolts, like he's waking up from a bad dream. "Nothing."

Aaron laughs. "I'm gonna go out on a limb here and call BS."

"Fine," Graham snaps. "We were . . ." He glances over at Logan, and then at the floor. "We were talking about Logan."

She leans back against the wall, clutching the peanut-oil bottle with a weird, faraway look on her face.

"Wait." I give Graham a suspicious look. "I thought you said you didn't know what Zane did to Logan. I'm not a genius, or anything, but doesn't that make it *his* fault? Like, why are you talking about what 'we' did to her?"

Graham falters. "I—"

"Elody's right," Corinne says—which *duh*, even if I don't really love how surprised she looks about it. "You said 'we.' What did you mean, 'what *we* did to her'?"

Graham's eyes are going back and forth between us and Logan so quickly, I think they might roll out of his head. Just as he takes a breath to say something else, our watches ping with a message:

Things aren't looking too good for our resident e-boy,
    are they?
Well, I may be cruel, but I'm not a monster...
I think everyone deserves a fair trial

Seeing the voting link, I almost laugh out loud. Perfect timing, once again.

Graham's shoulders start to shake, and at first, I think he's crying, but then I realize he's laughing silently.

"Vote for me, then." He throws up his hands. "I'm sure we'll get a cute little *Gossip Girl* post with everything you want to hear. In fact, I'll do it for you." He taps theatrically on his watch, then flings his wrist out to show the rest of us that he just voted for himself. Another weird laugh comes out of him, this time more like a sob. "I don't even care anymore. Cancel me. Do whatever you want. My two best friends are *dead,* and I'm obviously next, so if I'm going to die here . . ." His eyes go to his guitar case. "Then I'm at least going to finish a song first."

Graham picks up the guitar, throws the strap over his shoulder, and starts walking to the door.

Aaron blocks his path. "No way. That recording and the bottle are proof. You don't get to kill a bunch of people and walk away!"

"I didn't kill anyone," Graham says through clenched teeth. "Zane was my best friend."

"Sure didn't seem like it."

Graham gets up close to him, like a challenge. "Go post about it on your channel, then. I'm sure some premature-hair-loss brand is dying to pay you for an ad."

Aaron punches him in the face.

Well, he tries. He swings his freckly little arm out, but Graham ducks, and Aaron stumbles forward.

"Pathetic." Graham walks out of the room, mumbling as he goes. "Fucking pathetic."

As the door slams, Aaron straightens, fire-truck red. He wipes sweat from his shiny forehead, looking at the rest of us.

"Well? Are we voting for him, or what?"

"He voted for himself." Logan's voice drops to a murmur. "I don't think it even matters anymore."

Like a confirmation, the timer on my watch hits zero, and nothing happens. I wait a few seconds, and then a few more. Nothing. I close the voting app, because apparently, Logan's right. There are no rules anymore.

Aaron gives a frustrated grunt. "He obviously killed Zane. We can't just let him go!"

"He didn't—" Kira falters. "No one killed Zane."

"Okay, I'm loving the positivity," I tell her, "but also, you sound delusional, babe."

She crosses her arms like she's about to make me do jump squats, or something. "If we tell ourselves that someone here is doing this, then we're going to fall apart."

Corinne shakes her head. "I don't want to believe it either, but . . ." She takes a breath, like it's hard to get the words out. "Three people are gone now. We know they're watching us. We found the peanut oil. Maybe it was Tilly who slipped it into the wine, or maybe . . ."

She doesn't have to say it. We're all thinking it now, feeling the truth of it like someone breathing down our necks. Maybe it was one of us.

"Either way, this wasn't an accident," Corinne says. "And I think we need to accept what's really happening here."

A shiver rocks through me, and I cross my arms tight to stop it. The light from the windows seems darker, all of a sudden, and looking closer, I realize why. Big gray storm clouds are rolling in, wind whipping the palm trees. I want to laugh, because it's so perfect, but I don't, because I would sound insane. I feel insane.

"It still doesn't make sense, though." Max stares at his little recorder like he's getting an idea. "Why would Graham kill Zane? Whatever they were talking about, it seems like Graham was the one who wanted to come clean. Zane wanted him quiet." He looks over at Logan. "Do you have any idea what that was about?"

Logan shrugs. "Not sure if anyone's noticed, but I'm kind of Bounce House public enemy number one these days. I'm not really up to date."

"Wait, Graham *did* have a point." Aaron sizes her up. "You were the one who found the peanut oil in his bag. You could have slipped it in there when no one was looking. Planted it so we thought it was Graham's."

"Yeah, well, I didn't. So."

"You were the only one who was digging around in there," Aaron argues. "Who else could've done it?"

"Max was in there, too," Kira says. "When he slipped the recorder."

Max looks at her like she actually just took out a knife and stabbed him in the heart, which would be really entertaining to me, if there wasn't the whole issue where one of us is probably an actual murderer with a literal gun.

"I didn't," Max says. "I swear."

Logan flings out her arms. "Well, then, we've reached a bit of an impasse, haven't we?"

For a second, we're all quiet.

Kira looks at Max. "Was the peanut oil already in there when you put the recorder in?"

"No." He pauses. "I don't know. Maybe. I just dropped it in when he wasn't looking. I didn't have time to feel around in there."

Thunder cracks outside, and all of our heads snap to the window at the same time.

I can't keep the laugh in anymore, because once again, the timing is perfect, and of *course* this is happening. Mom basically predicted it.

When I first hit ten thousand followers, she lit a cigarette and told me, *Soak it in while you can, El. You think these people love you now, but they won't. None of it lasts. Not beauty, and especially not love.* Smoke floated around her red mouth, settling into my hair. *You want my advice? Never let them see you weak. Because the second you do,* she said, her lips curling into a cruel smile, *they'll take that little crack and press until you shatter.*

Every milestone after that felt like a win, like spitting in her face. Because they *did* love me. And sure, there were mean comments, but the ones who wanted me—they weren't going away, only growing. After so many months of nonstop success, I was sure that Mom was wrong and bitter. Just because you climb high doesn't mean you have to fall.

But now here it is, the fall she promised: hurtling fast and thrilling to the ground, waiting for the crash. Eyes open. Blood leaking on the terrace stones below.

LOGAN

When they lift Zane's body, his arm lolls to the side, the one with the tattoo of the I Ching hexagrams that I used to think were a sign of how wise he was. *An old soul.* Both of us. That's what he used to say, when his hand lingered a little too long on the small of my back, blurring the line between thrilling and wrong.

Wise. I almost laugh. Zane's tattoos never made him wise. Just a culture-appropriating dickhead.

As they move him to the back patio, I don't watch. I sit on the floor, hugging my knees to my chest and staring at the spot where he died. I stay that way until everyone comes back in.

"Where is he?" I ask.

"Under the awning," Kira says. "Out of the rain."

The room is heavy and silent except for thunder rumbling overhead. What is there to say for someone who may not deserve mourning?

"I think we should keep looking for the gun," Corinne says.

We're not going to find it. Already, I know. Still, we turn the house upside down. We go through all the bags again, searching every room, every drawer, under every cushion. We search until night falls, the storm clouds rolling over us as the whole island turns from purple-gray to blue-black, like a bruise in reverse. We search and search until we do what we should have done hours ago: give up and make dinner.

As the rest of us sit with our sad plain pasta at the kitchen table, Aaron stares out the window, watching Graham. He's been out on the front terrace since before they moved Zane, bent over his guitar. Rain falls, just a drizzle for now, but the clouds threaten worse.

"Where the hell is he hiding it?" Aaron wonders. "There's no way it's not him."

Graham's voice floats through the window, raspy and thin. It's the kind of singing voice that isn't necessarily good, but hard to stop listening to, emotion rubbing it raw. Back at the Bounce House, it annoyed me so much, his nonstop singing. Now, though, it feels like an old nostalgic song, the kind you sing along to, drunk and warm.

"We already looked through his stuff," I say. "He didn't have it."

"Neither did anyone else," Aaron argues. "But the gun's still missing, isn't it?"

I try to imagine Graham sneaking into the closet, stashing the gun. The thing is, I can believe it. Even before everything went to shit, Graham has always been anxious, the kind of guy who likes to know the earthquake-safety plan and where all the emergency exits are. But if Graham has the gun, then we can relax. Because as scared as he may be, I don't think he has it in him to actually shoot.

But then I never knew my friends as well as I thought, did I?

Thunder rips through the sky, and the rain starts to pick up, wind whistling against the window.

The front door swings open, and we all jump. Graham walks in, his guitar case strapped to his back.

"Got a Grammy winner already?" Aaron sneers. "Let's hear it."

Graham doesn't answer. He just shakes out his hair, wipes his pale face with his hands, and walks to the stairs, humming and tapping out chords on his thigh. Ophelia flashes through my head, like from *Hamlet,* one of the last things I read in English class before dropping out. Ophelia with her mad songs and flowers, sinking to the bottom of that shallow river, like she doesn't even care enough to stop what's coming for her.

I stand and move toward him. "Graham."

He doesn't turn around.

"You shouldn't be alone right now," I almost beg.

He stops, finally, and looks at me. I try to remember the last time we hung out for real, before everything went wrong. There were so many nights curled up around a video on his phone, sharing headphones and laughing so hard we cried. Nights of drunk dancing, spinning and spinning under disco lights until it felt like the glow was coming from us. But I don't remember the last thing we did together before everything happened. Before Graham started to hate me like the rest of them.

I think I see his eyes start to water, but he blinks, and any feeling there hardens to nothing.

He shakes his head. "I can't trust anyone but myself."

With that, he turns and stomps up the stairs, leaving me at the bottom. There's nothing else to do but drift back to the table like a ghost and sit. The rain pummels the windows now, dripping down the glass like blood.

"We need to keep thinking of other ways out of here," Corinne says, always in plan mode. Maybe it should be comforting, that determination, but it's starting to feel pointless, like this thing is so twisted that even the best plan couldn't untangle it.

"What are we gonna do?" Aaron asks sarcastically. "Swim for it?"

"We could signal for help," Kira says. "An SOS. Maybe a fire, or something."

Elody makes a face. "What is this, Girl Scouts?"

"It's a good idea," Max says.

Elody smiles at him, an icy look in her eyes. "Of course it is, babe."

God, it's so obvious how bad Elody has it. How jealous she is. I still don't get it, why *Max*, but I recognize the look on her face. That hunger. Like she'd kneel at his feet for scraps, eat out of his hand. Like she isn't so far out of his league, it's ridiculous. Like she'd kill for any touch at all, as long as it says *I see you.*

"We just have to get through the next couple of weeks, right?" Kira says, clearly trying for encouraging. "That's how long filming was supposed to take. That's how long my parents are expecting me to be gone without my phone."

Max nods. "Same."

"People will start to notice something's off soon, won't they?"

"Yeah," Aaron says, "assuming we survive that long."

Fear claws at my stomach. "That's not funny."

Aaron shrugs. "Wasn't supposed to be."

Except it is. It's pretty fucking hilarious, actually, now that I think about it: that I'm here, and this is happening. That even Elody Hart, unrealistic male fantasy made flesh, is still letting a skinny, kind-of-attractive white guy make her feel like shit. That I could be home with Harper watching old seasons of *Drag Race* but instead I decided to come here, so far away, without even telling Mom and Dad where I am, because it's not like they'd care anyway.

"Logan?" Kira asks. "Are you okay?"

She's probably concerned because I'm currently laughing my ass off, so hard it hurts and tears blur my vision.

I suck in a breath. "It's just funny."

"We have to stay calm," Kira says softly. "Someone's going to realize something's wrong. They have to."

"What about your followers?" Corinne points her fork at Kira. "Elody, Max, and Logan, too. You guys have huge followings."

Aaron is visibly pissed to be excluded from that, which sends another snorting laugh through me. Of all the times and places to be butthurt about followers.

"And they can be pretty intense, right?" Corinne goes on. "Someone will notice you're not posting."

"I mean, yeah, I have a few stalkers, or whatever," Elody says. "But I have posts scheduled for the next three weeks. People won't know until then."

Kira slumps. "I have scheduled posts, too."

"And my followers don't exactly give a shit lately," I mumble.

Corinne drops her fork into her bowl, defeated. I don't blame her. Our followers might literally be our only hope. People who don't even know us. People who can turn on us like a summer storm.

"It's kind of brilliant, honestly," Aaron says. "A remote island, no phones, no telling anyone where we are . . . they got us all to sign a contract for the perfect setup for murder."

"Okay, but you could say that about all reality TV," Kira says. "My *Dance It Out* contract gave the producers the right to do basically whatever they wanted, and we wouldn't be allowed to sue."

Aaron scoffs. "Yeah, sure. This is all normal reality-TV stuff. Except for the three dead people."

I don't feel like laughing anymore. Actually, I feel like screaming, like I can't be at this table for one more second or I'll explode. I stand, scraping my chair back, and everyone's heads whip toward me.

Like they think I have a gun.

Tightening my jaw, I walk to the trash can and empty my bowl. I stare at the mess inside, meat and garbage and empty bottles, the smell sickly sweet. Like death. Closing the can, I rush to the sink, grip the counter. Count my breaths, like my therapist told me to, when I could still afford therapy. When I wasted all of my sessions, tossing my new influencer money at my problems and hoping they'd just go away without me trying. My therapist always told me to go easy on myself, but she wouldn't say that if she knew any of the real stuff. The things I never told her.

"We haven't gotten any more messages." Kira looks at her watch. "We also didn't vote last time, and they haven't said anything. That's a good sign, right? Tilly and whoever else could be on their way as soon as the storm passes. Maybe they're done playing this game."

"Yeah, if Tilly's even the one behind this," Aaron says. "Because like it or not, someone slipped Zane the peanut oil, and my money's on vampire Shawn Mendes." Aaron juts his chin over to where Graham was, and then looks at me. "Or *you*."

I don't even have the energy to fight him anymore.

"Someone will come soon," Kira says again, less convinced.

"We shouldn't get our hopes up." Corinne's quiet certainty feels like fingers on the back of my neck.

"Why not?" I ask.

She stares up at one of the cameras, the red blinking light in its black void. "Games don't end until somebody wins."

[KNOCK.]

GRAHAM

[Whispering.] Logan.

[LOUDER KNOCK. DOORKNOB RATTLES.]

GRAHAM

[Louder.] Logan, come on.

[DOOR OPENS. SMALL SILENCE.]

LOGAN

I thought you were only associating with guitars now.
[Pause.] Wait, are you okay? You look—

GRAHAM

Who did you tell?

[FOOTSTEPS. DOOR CLOSING.]

LOGAN

Okay, first of all, don't say that so loud. And we already
talked about this. I didn't tell anyone.

GRAHAM

Yeah, but that's the thing. I've been thinking about it, and it doesn't make sense. [Lowers voice.] Because someone knows. Someone wants to kill us for it. So either you told someone, or . . .

LOGAN

Or what?

GRAHAM

Or it's one of us.

MAX

Sleep is a lost cause. Even without the storm raging outside, there would still be Graham—sitting on his bed with the guitar like he's in a trance, playing, humming, scratching something down in his notebook and doing it all over again. He's been at it ever since he sulked back into our room from who knows where.

Rolling onto my side, I reach for my glasses and check my watch. Eleven thirty. Jesus, I've been in bed for over an hour, and I'm still wide awake.

I sit up, trying my best to sound calm and friendly. "Hey, man, I'm trying to sleep. Would you mind—"

Graham sets his guitar down next to him, harder than he should. "You really think you're more important than everyone else, don't you?"

My brain short-circuits for half a second. "Too tired for this" has never been a more accurate statement.

"I don't see how wanting to go to sleep makes me—"

"No, that's not what I mean." Graham works his jaw. "You

think you're this, like, moral figure because you make documentaries, but all you're really doing is profiting off of people who *are* doing things."

Even dead tired, I'm not going to let that slide without pushing back.

"It's not about the profit," I tell him. "It's about—"

"Exposing people. Telling the truth. Whatever. But you make money off it, don't you? With Jared Sky, your big catfishing reveal. How much money did you make from the ads on that one?"

An uneasy feeling comes over me, slow and crawling.

"I don't know the exact number," I say. "But I get it, okay? I'm not an artist. I'm not trying to be. I make documentaries. You make music. But you really don't have to prove that point, like, right now."

Graham shoots to his feet, and I shrink back. The missing gun flashes in my head.

"Yes, I do," he says. "I have to finish this song. I don't have time."

I wish that comment didn't freak me out so much.

"Come on," I tell him. "You're not going to *die*."

"My friends are dead!" Graham snaps, and there it is—the complete lack of logic in my own argument, loud and undeniable. "The only people who ever made me feel like I belong anywhere are *dead*, and Logan—" His voice breaks. He takes off his beanie, digging his hands through his hair. "The point is, if someone's next, it's going to be me."

I want to ask him what he means about Logan, if anything happened after their fight earlier, but I'm worried any more questions might send him over the edge.

"Maybe if you try to just go to sleep—"

"You don't get it." He sits back on his bed. "We're running out of time. Even before all this, people were already getting bored of the Bounce House. Like, yeah, we were big for a while, but even now, people are over it. The whole TikTok house thing. Why the hell do you think we all came here?" He wrings his beanie in his hands. "And they all knew their next move. Zane. McKayleigh. Even Logan. It's all about the next move. I mean, you should know. You need your next story. That's why you're shoving that camera at everyone all the time, right?"

I don't answer. He's right again, and I don't like it.

Graham tosses the hat aside, burying his face in his hands. "I spent so much time letting Zane tell me what to do instead of just making music. And now I might die here. I might actually . . ." His head snaps back up. He grabs his guitar. "I need to finish the songs."

Thunder claps, making me tense up.

"Okay, but you're nineteen," I tell him. "You don't have to have your whole life figured out. And honestly, there are more important things to deal with right now."

The gun, for example. And the fact that someone here might actually be killing people. It's ridiculous, now, that I thought I'd ever be able to sleep tonight.

Graham laughs humorlessly. "Thanks, but you still don't get it." He starts to strum again, but then stops. "I have three million followers. And I'm not trying to be a jerk, I'm just—that's where I'm at. I can only go down from here. And if I'm not putting out something new, I'm over. There's a hundred other sixteen-year-olds on TikTok with fresher faces and better songs who could steal my whole career in the next two years. Just watch."

I stare, dumbstruck. In a way, I know how it feels. I've been posting documentaries for years, but until the Jared Sky one, none of them got more than a couple thousand views. And then everything changed overnight—and not in that hyperbolic way people always say. I mean literally, I posted the video, and the next morning, my phone was blowing up with follows and interview requests and gratitude.

But then, once the glow of all that faded, there was the panic, rising like a flood. Because the truth is, as much as I hate it when people like Aaron tell me I'm only riding off my parents' success, I know they're sort of right. I never would have been able to get that interview with Jared, the one where I laid out my evidence and cracked him open, if he hadn't been a guest on my dad's show first. If Dad hadn't set up the interview, claiming I was an aspiring You-Tuber who wanted advice. Since then, I've had this itching need to prove that I can do this on my own. That I know what's next. And the longer it takes me, the closer I feel to drowning.

"And once that happens," Graham goes on, "once we're done, then we turn into Aaron. Over at *twenty-one*. Making a sad You-Tube channel and doing hair-loss ads for the rest of our lives." His face crumples. "I'd rather die. I'd literally rather die than be that."

"I think . . ." I start, but I don't know what I think. I don't know anything except that I can't sleep, can't just lie here when something this big and terrifying is happening. Someone brought us here to expose us, maybe even to kill us, and I need to do what I do best: get to the bottom of it.

I climb out of bed. "I'm going to go get some water. Just—try to chill out. Okay? It'll be fine."

I don't wait for him to answer, because we both know that was a bullshit thing to say. We don't know if it'll be fine. We don't know if we'll wake up in the morning, if there will be more messages or another body, but I'm not going to wait here until that happens. I grab my camera bag and open the door.

Footsteps thud down the stairs. I grip the banister. Someone was just here, turning the corner. I can't see who, but someone was listening.

Thunder booms, and I scramble downstairs. Shadows of palm trees wave on the wall like fingers, warped by lightning. I stop at the second floor, my heart hammering. Tightening my grip on the strap of my bag, I look down over the balcony at the first floor. We left all the lights on, so I can see it all: the living room, the kitchen, the rain slamming against the windows.

A hooded figure sliding the back doors open and running out onto the patio.

Turn around. My basic human survival instinct screams at me to go back, take my chances with Graham. I've seen enough movies to know that nothing good happens on stormy islands at night, or to the idiots who follow mysterious figures out into the dark.

But I can't make myself turn around. Instead, I unzip my bag and take out the camera, brushing off the waterproof surface. If what's happening on this island is more than a series of bad co-incidences, if there's really someone behind it, one of *us* . . . then this is my chance to turn this documentary into something huge. Something that changes everything.

I creep down the stairs, stopping at the storage closet to find a flashlight, and then out onto the patio. Adrenaline pulses through me as I step past Zane's body, trying to forget it's there, and click on the light. All I can see is the water shifting, crashing against the sand—and then there: something moving again, a figure running from the patio to the other side of the house.

I break into a sprint. They're fast, smaller than me, but the rain's a blinding sheet. I pull off my useless glasses, shove them in my pocket, and press RECORD. The figure runs faster, veering around the house and toward the terrace.

"Hey!" I yell.

They skid to a stop and spin around, the hood flying off to reveal a tight ponytail and wide brown eyes.

Kira, a knife glinting in her hand. One from the kitchen, the kind you use for raw meat.

I hold up my hands, the camera still gripped and filming in my right one.

"What are you doing out here?" she asks.

"I'm—"

Her stare locks on my camera bag, fear flashing in her eyes, and I understand.

"I don't have the gun," I say. "You can go through my bag. You can even look through my pockets. I just—it's pouring. Can we go inside?"

Lightning flashes, turning the sky a sickly purple. For a few seconds, she watches me. Then, she lowers the knife.

"The pool house," she says, glancing behind her. "Not the main one. And turn off your camera."

Before I can answer, Kira sprints off, and there's nothing for me to do but follow her orders. Inside, I shut the door behind us, locking the storm out. Kira takes off her rain jacket and grabs two towels from a rack by the door. She wraps hers around her shoulders and stops short of handing me the other, staring suspiciously. She's still gripping the knife.

"What were you doing out there?" she asks again.

"I'm . . ." I swallow, looking at the knife. "I'm having a hard time focusing with that thing, you know, brandished."

She blinks like she'd forgotten it was there. "Sorry." She sets it on the table. "I saw someone moving outside, and with the gun missing . . . it freaked me out. This whole thing is really freaking me out, which I guess is the biggest understatement of all time."

"Here." I hold out my camera bag. "You can go through it, if it'll make you feel better."

She takes the bag, unzips it, and looks around inside. It hurts that she still doesn't trust me, but I can't stand seeing her so scared. I didn't realize it until now, but seeing how calm Kira has been through all of this might be the only thing that's keeping me from breaking down.

When she's done looking, Kira hands me the bag and the other towel. She's close enough that I can smell her hair—something sweet, maybe coconut. Heat flushes through me, and I'm suddenly aware of my own heartbeat. We haven't been alone together since this morning, when I apologized for recording her without permission.

"Thanks," she says, when I'm still standing here like I forgot how to talk. "I don't have it either, if you want to check."

"No, I trust you." I wrap the towel around my wet shoulders, wondering why my heart hasn't calmed down yet, if I have some kind of medical issue. And then I remember what she said before. "Wait, you saw someone outside?"

"Yeah, I thought maybe . . ." She shakes her head. "But it was only you, I guess."

"Wait, let me get my facts straight. You thought you saw a murderer, so you followed them outside with a knife?" I crack a smile. "That's pretty badass, Lyons."

"The knife was a panic decision." She crosses her arms, looking up at me with that tough expression of hers. "And weren't you doing the same thing? Running after a potential murderer with . . . a camera?"

"Okay, yeah. Clearly also a panic decision." But then it hits me. My smile drops. "I wasn't outside, though. I followed *you* out here." She looks confused, which makes me even more uneasy. "You were outside of my room, weren't you? I heard someone going down the stairs."

Kira shakes her head, a line crinkling between her eyebrows. "I was downstairs when I thought I saw someone."

Lightning flashes. Kira runs to the window. I look over her shoulder, but all I see is the pool, the water looking alien from the pool lights. The terrace, where Cole's blood is drying between the stones. No one thought to clean it. I get a feeling like ice water trickling down my spine.

"Did you see someone?" I ask.

"No, I just thought . . ." She pulls the towel tighter around herself. "I think I'm starting to lose it."

"It's okay." I move closer. "I mean, if there was ever a situation that merits losing it, it's probably this one. Although I'd really appreciate it if you didn't lose it, because . . ." I breathe out, my face getting warm. "You're kind of the only person who's been keeping *me* from losing it, and I have a cool tough-guy image to protect. You know, for the fans."

A laugh softens her face, deepening the dimple in her cheek.

I pretend to look offended. "Wait, do you think I'm *not* a cool tough guy? Ouch."

"Don't worry. You have other redeeming qualities."

"Like what?"

Kira looks up at me. She takes a breath, her dark lashes fluttering, and I can't stop staring at her mouth, the soft curve of her lip.

Then, she goes back to the couch, picking at the arm of it like it's the most interesting thing she's ever seen. "Ask Elody. I bet she's got a very long list."

The warmth in my face turns into a full-on furnace. I look down at my shoes. "Yeah, like my sad, skinny arms. She made a huge deal about those when we got here."

"She seemed pretty into them earlier." Kira shrugs, starting to pull her wet hair out of her ponytail. It falls to her shoulders, brushing the edges of her collarbone, curling around her face, and I forget everything about kissing Elody.

I swallow. "I mean, she kind of trapped me into it."

"You didn't seem all that trapped."

"I didn't want to kiss her." I falter. "I mean, maybe I did for a second, but it wasn't—"

"Max, it's fine." She unwraps the towel and uses it to dry her hair. "I'm not judging you."

"No, I . . ." I walk toward her, and she freezes, her dark eyes on me, and I think about what she said before, how we're all just our middle-school selves, because that's how I feel now—scrawny and scared, always tripping over my words. "I wanted the bottle to land on someone else."

She's quiet for too long.

"Oh."

"Sorry," I start. "I—"

Kira moves so quickly, I barely have time to register it. One second, she's over there, and then her hand is on the back of my neck, and her mouth is on mine. The kiss is fast, too, small and soft, and for a second, I don't know if that just happened or if this island is actually getting to me, *Cast Away* style.

"Sorry." Kira steps back, touching her lips. "Was that—"

I take her free hand and pull her back to me, kissing her, and this isn't a volleyball with a bloody face. It's Kira, warm and real, with her careful fingers in my hair, mine tracing the back of her neck, the curve of her waist, wanting to feel all of her, to take my time, and this is different. So different. Elody kissed like she wanted to fight, pulling my hair and biting my lip so hard it almost hurt, but this is slow, like something unfolding, and I could keep doing this for I don't even know how long.

Kira pulls away, her arms still locked around my shoulders. She bites her bottom lip, and Jesus Christ, I want to bite it, too. Instead, I brush my lips to her ear, looking at the knife on the couch.

"This wasn't just an elaborate plan to get me alone and kill me, was it?" I ask.

She lets go.

"Shit," I say. "Did I . . . ?"

"No, no, you're fine. It's just . . ." She covers her face with her hands and makes this adorable sound, halfway between a groan and a laugh. "So, I liked that. A lot. But I haven't ever, you know, done that before. Outside of spin the bottle, I guess."

I raise my eyebrows, confused and a little honored but mostly shocked. "Oh."

"Yeah. Not to be weird about it, but I've just never . . . gotten around to it."

"It's not weird." I brush a drop of rain from her temple with my thumb. "I guess I'm just surprised. I mean, you're . . ."

"Eighteen? Practically an old maid?"

"I was going to say beautiful."

I feel her face get warm under my hand. She looks down, her thick eyelashes shadowing her face.

"I've always had to be careful. Growing up on TV, it's so hard for things to be private, you know? So I guess it's always been easier to just stay inside myself. Not do anything that could go wrong."

I bring my other palm to her cheek, and she looks up at me.

"What makes you so sure things will go wrong?" I ask.

Gently, she covers my hands with her own and lifts them off of her face. My heart sinks a little. Her gaze shifts to the window.

"Look where we are," she says. "This place is basically Murphy's Law in island form."

I laugh softly to fight through the fear jumping into my chest. "Okay, but this feels like a pretty extreme example."

"I know, I just . . ."

I move closer. "What?"

She looks up at me, and everything blurs except for her eyes, my heart, and the anxious thought underscoring it all: Kira was running around outside with a knife. She could be a murderer, and for some reason, I don't think I care.

"I don't know if I want to go back out there," Kira says. "To the house."

"Me neither."

"We could stay here."

I suck air through my teeth. "Well, actually, I was *really* looking forward to falling asleep to Graham's creepy guitar-playing tonight."

She punches my shoulder. "Asshole."

"Ow!" I make a show of rubbing my arm even though I kind of mean it. The girl's got an arm. I laugh and kiss her softly. "Yes, fitness girl. There is literally nothing I would like more than to sleep in this pool house with you."

The couch isn't big enough for both of us, so we put some of the cushions on the floor and find a blanket in a wicker basket next to the TV. Thunder claps overhead, deafening, and Kira curls into my side, warm and smelling like something sweet and beachy.

It hits me that I've never done this before. Sleep with a girl, in the most innocent sense of the word—just sleeping, without anything more than kissing first, without expecting anything else after. Somehow, this has my heart beating even faster than if we were doing all of the other things. Just lying here, breathing, with the rain on the roof and the wind in the windows, the darkness outside making it feel like the pool house is its own world, like nothing else on the island can touch us—not the messages, the folders, the gun, or Graham's words still ringing in my head.

One way or another, this is blowing up in all our faces.

I pull her closer and try to hold on to it. The hope that maybe Graham was wrong.

VIDEO FOOTAGE: NIGHT TWO, 2:03 AM
THIRD-FLOOR BEDROOM, CAMERA #2

[A HOODED FIGURE OPENS THE DOOR AND LOOKS
AROUND THE EMPTY ROOM, PAUSING TO OBSERVE
THE LIGHT EMANATING FROM THE LOCKED BATHROOM
DOOR. THEY MOVE QUICKLY BUT CAREFULLY, CREEPING
OVER TO A BED, CLIMBING ONTO IT, AND REACHING UP
TO CAMERA #1 TO COVER THE LENS WITH A RAG. THEY
APPROACH CAMERA #2, LOOKING UP INTO THE LENS.
THEIR FACE IS OBSCURED BY THE HOOD, SUNGLASSES,
AND A PIECE OF FABRIC WRAPPED AROUND THEIR
MOUTH AND NOSE. THEY REACH UP WITH A RAG, AND
THE CAMERA GOES DARK.]

KIRA

I wake up to gray morning light spilling into the pool house, casting a stormy glow on the empty space next to me. For half of an embarrassing second that I'll never speak of again, I bring my hand to my lips, my stupid smile. I kissed a boy. I kissed *Max*.

Max, who isn't here.

And just like that, the spell breaks. I scan the room, alert now. Max's camera bag is gone. The knife, too. Panic jumps through me, and I stand, telling myself that everything's fine. Max probably just brought it back to the house. For all I know, a boat will be here to take us home any minute, and the knife won't even matter.

But I can't shake the fear gnawing inside of me. My jog out of the pool house turns into a run, my shoes pounding the terrace in a quickening rhythm as light rain mists my face. *Calm down. Calm down. Calm down. Breathe.*

I throw open the front door.

"Morning, sunshine." Elody stands at the kitchen counter with a cup of coffee. "God, that storm was literally insane. I couldn't sleep." She smiles slowly, baring teeth. "Seems like you didn't, either."

Heat floods my cheeks, but I push down the embarrassment and walk toward the kitchen, scanning the second floor as I go.

"Is anyone else up yet?" I ask.

Elody shrugs. "Don't know. Not a morning person. I don't go looking for friends before I get caffeine."

I glance at the knife block on the counter, and my breath catches. A knife is still missing. But no—it's in a different spot. Last night, I took the knife out of the top left corner, but now, there's an empty slot in the bottom right. At least, I thought I took it out of the top left corner. My tired brain strains to make sense of it, like those logic problems we used to do in math class. *If Kira took the knife out of slot A, but Max put it back into slot B . . .*

Elody sets her coffee down with a thud. "No offense, but your whole energy is freaking me out right now. What's your deal?"

"Sorry, I just . . ." I chew my lip, wondering if I should tell Elody about the knife. "I don't know. I guess I'm a little on edge."

Upstairs, a door opens. Fear shoots through me, but it's Corinne, walking to the bathroom with her toothbrush in hand. She gives a small wave, glancing between us with a dash of suspicion.

"Oh, wait, I forgot," Elody says. "Max is in the shower." Her eyes flash with something I can't read as she nods to the downstairs bathroom door. "If that's who you're looking for."

"Wait, why?"

"I don't know, babe, because he wanted to shower?"

"No, I mean—" I swallow, reminding myself that I am totally fine and not at all losing my mind. "Why the downstairs shower? Doesn't he have one in his room?"

"I think he said Graham was in theirs, or something?" She laughs. "Huh. I guess I did know who else was up. I swear, my brain is, like, totally useless when I don't sleep."

The bathroom door opens, and Max walks out, a towel wrapped around his waist.

"Morning, babe," Elody calls.

"Hey." He runs a hand through his hair, damp and curling at his forehead, and looks at me with a hint of his crooked smile.

There's a fluttering feeling in my chest, which I'm sure I can reasonably attribute to fear about the missing knife or relief that he's not dead—definitely not anything more embarrassing than that.

He flushes, nodding at the stairs. "I'm going to go . . . clothe myself."

"Aw." Elody brings her mug to her lips. "Who told you to do that?"

Max laughs awkwardly and heads upstairs, shooting another look my way before he goes.

Elody leans forward onto the kitchen counter. "He's in a weird-ass mood today, right?"

I try my best to look calm and casual. "I guess."

"He probably didn't sleep last night either." She glances at me like she's waiting for me to confirm, and wait, does she know?

Oh my god, of course she does. Corinne, too. Because, as I finally break through my fog of Max weirdness and knife panic, I realize: they're my roommates. It's pretty hard to ignore the fact that my bed was empty all night.

Still, I play dumb. "I don't think anyone slept last night. The storm kind of freaked me out. I had to take a walk around the house to calm down."

"Oh my god, by yourself?"

"Yeah." I chew the inside of my cheek, not sure if she believes me or not.

"Wow. I was too scared to even leave the room to pee," she says. "I literally convinced myself that I heard someone scream in the middle of the night. Like a movie, or something. My dreams are totally messed up right now." Elody sizes me up. "You know, you had me worried, babe. You weren't in our room when I woke up."

"Oh." I look away, heart jumping. "Must've been when I was up walking."

"Yeah, sure. But don't worry. I went back to sleep. I wasn't, like, *that* worried about you." Elody laughs. "I think I'm just paranoid. It's such a gross look for me."

I stare at the knife block again. Maybe I'm just imagining things. Maybe it didn't move at all. Max must have put it back, so unless someone else happened to take a knife last night . . . wait, a scream. Elody heard a scream. But she said it was nothing, just a bad dream. That's all it was.

"Okay, if you're gonna vom, can you like, let me know? Because I can't do puking."

"No, I'm just . . ." I stop, mentally ticking off the people I've seen today. Me, Elody, Max, Corinne, Graham's in the shower . . . "Have you seen Logan and Aaron?"

"I think they're in their rooms, why?" Elody white-knuckles her mug. "Seriously, you're freaking me out."

"When you thought you heard a scream last night, where was it coming from?"

"I don't really remember. I'm pretty sure it was just a dream, though. What are you—"

Max scrambles down from the third floor, looking like he threw his clothes on in a panic, shirt backward.

"Something's wrong," he says. "I think the bathroom's flooding, but Graham won't open the door. He—he's not . . ."

I run to the stairs, fear building with each step. *Calm down. Calm down. Calm down.* The door to the third-floor bedroom is already open, and right away, it feels wrong. Inside, the air is too warm and thick.

Calm down. Breathe.

A puddle of water leaks out from under the bathroom door. The shower's still running inside.

"Graham?" I pound on the door. "Graham, are you in there?"

No answer. I step back, my shoes squishing in the puddle, and that's when I notice. The water looks off. Pink.

I grab Max's arm, my nails digging into his skin.

He looks down. "Oh my god."

"Guys, what's . . ." Corinne stops in the doorway, fear washing over her face. "Is Graham in there?"

Elody runs up after her, breathing hard. Corinne speeds toward us as we pull on the door. It won't budge.

"It's locked," Max says.

I pull harder on the knob, my hands slipping on the metal, until it moves toward us an inch.

"No," I say. "It's stuck."

Max's hands close around mine, and we pull until the door swings open, sending us both stumbling back.

Water seeps out from the shower, pooling between the floor tiles. The mirrors are all steamed up, and so are the glass shower walls, so I can't see through.

Except for a dark shape slumped inside. A vein of red spreading through the water like the branches of a river.

"No." The word slips out, and I cover my mouth, like I can take it back, make it go away.

Corinne flies past me, her bare feet splashing in the water, and opens the shower door. A strangled gasp chokes out of her. I don't want to look, but I can't stop myself. I follow her deeper into the room and see it.

Graham's body on the shower floor.

A kitchen knife next to him, red with his blood.

ELODY

I step back, away from the bathroom and what's inside. I was right. I was *right,* and I convinced myself it wasn't actually a scream, just another nightmare like the ones that used to make me run down the hall before Mom shoved me back to bed, telling me I'd ruined her sleep.

Corinne turns the shower off, and all of a sudden it's creepily silent.

"We need to find Aaron and Logan," she says.

Kira takes a towel and covers Graham up, looking away as she does. Like she's so nice and good that she can't handle it. Then, she looks at me.

"You only heard one scream last night?"

"I don't know, I thought I was dreaming! And you—" I stop when it hits me. "Maybe we should talk about how you weren't in the room with me and Corinne when I heard the scream. What's that all about, babe?"

A nervous look washes over Kira's little cartoon-deer face, and

I'm being petty, but there's a part of me that likes it. Seeing her squirm.

But Corinne speaks before Kira can answer.

"Guys?" Her eyes are trained on the corner of the wall, and looking up, I realize what she's looking at.

"What the hell?" I breathe.

Both of the security cameras are wrapped with dishrags from the kitchen.

"We need to find Aaron and Logan," Corinne repeats, starting down the stairs.

Obviously, none of us wants to be stuck here with Graham's literal body, so we follow. On the second floor, Kira runs down to Logan's door while Corinne bangs on Aaron's, calling his name.

He cracks it open, looking like he just woke up. "What?"

"Graham's dead," I tell him. "Someone stabbed him in the shower."

Aaron frowns. "Very funny."

When he realizes I'm not joking, he drops the stupid sarcastic look.

"Oh my god."

Logan's door opens, and she sticks her head out, hidden in her hoodie. "What's . . ."

"Graham got stabbed. Keep up, babe."

Kira shoots me an offended look, and I glare at her. It's not my fault I'm trying to act chill as a coping mechanism, or whatever. Also, I'm definitely not the girl she wants to mess with today. Not when I could get her in big trouble.

Because here's a secret: I lied to Kira earlier. Well, not lied—I just didn't tell her the whole truth, which is that after I woke up and saw that she wasn't in our room, I didn't go back to sleep. I waited, like, twenty minutes for her to come back, wondering if I should, you know, make sure she wasn't *dead,* because I'm a nice roommate. But she didn't come back. So I went looking.

And then I saw the light in the pool house. I saw them kissing in the window like they didn't even care who saw.

"No." Logan pulls off her hood like maybe it made her hear me wrong. "No. That's . . ."

"Proof that one of us is an actual murderer?" I dig my nails into my palms. "Yeah. Pretty much."

Corinne walks to the staircase. "We need to search the island. Now."

"There's no one else here," Max says.

"Well, there's only one other alternative, isn't there?" Corinne turns around and lets that hang over everyone like a giant, terrifying storm cloud, just as thunder booms outside. The timing is so perfect, it's stupid.

"We need to search the island," she says again.

"What exactly do you think we're going to find?" Aaron's voice gets higher. "Sorry, but four people are dead. Graham was *stabbed.* What about that seems unclear to you? One of us is killing people!"

"Can we just—" Corinne's voice breaks, finally losing it. "Can we search the island?"

Kira starts to pace, like she needs to be moving at literally all times—or maybe, I don't know, like she just *stabbed someone* and she's feeling a little guilty. Just a thought.

"Okay," she says. "If someone else were hiding out here, where would they go?"

"The boathouse," Max says. "Or . . ."

"Or the pool house." I stare at him, watching his face for a sign of, like, anything.

I could do it. I could tell everyone about their little pool-house hookup and have people going after them like a real-life Twitter mob. I don't know if sneaking around and making out in the pool house makes them murderers, but it's enough to make people suspicious. But there's this tiny little part of me that wants them to tell everyone themselves. I want to hear them say it to my face.

Or maybe I just want to watch them panic.

A sick, angry feeling twists around inside of me, and I start for the stairs. "Okay, so let's go to the pool house, then."

Max doesn't say anything. Neither does Kira. They just look at each other, like guilty little liars. The angry feeling in my stomach gets even sharper, like it's growing teeth or something, and I'm not going to stand here anymore and watch them. I walk down the stairs, and everyone follows me. Outside, thunder cracks over us, and the rain starts up again, light and misty.

When I open the pool-house door, we all see it. Max and Kira's little hideout. Pillows and a blanket on the floor, like a sleepover. Like summer camp.

I want to scream.

Aaron steps inside. "Oh my god."

"Someone's been staying here," Corinne says.

"Wait." Kira steps to the front of the group. "It was me. I slept in here last night."

Max is getting so red, I can't even help myself.

"Alone?" I ask. "That's, like, so dangerous. And also weird, no offense."

Max coughs. "I was, uh . . . I was here, too."

Forget screaming. I want to stab him.

Actually, I guess I shouldn't say that, even if it's just for dramatic effect.

Aaron looks between them and cracks up. "Oh, perfect. That's great. What is this, some kind of Bonnie-and-Clyde situation?"

"What? That doesn't even make sense," Max says. "Why would we—"

"There was no one here last night but us," Kira says. "Let's keep looking."

Looking at her now, I try to imagine her really doing it, taking a knife and shoving it into Graham's back. Sure, Kira can be intense, but I don't know if she's capable of anything worse than forcing people to do cardio. But Max . . . there's something dark in him, under all the messy hair and glasses.

Something like what's inside of me.

"We should check the boathouse, too," Corinne says, turning and leading the way outside.

We walk past the terrace, down the beach, and onto the dock, stopping when we get to the boathouse door. Because I think we all just remembered what—*who* else is in here. The water sloshes at the dock underneath us, and the rain is getting heavier again, probably making my hair look like a frizzy mess. I run my fingers through it, and then I remember that I probably shouldn't give a crap, because there's a literal murderer on the loose.

I dig my nails into my thigh, to the birthmark just under the hem of my shorts, and try to focus on the dull sting.

"I don't think I want to go in," I say.

"Me neither," Logan echoes.

Kira steps forward. "I'll go."

"Me, too," Max says.

Of course. I could shove them both into the water.

Not in a murdery way, because again, I'm not the one *literally killing people*.

"Okay." Corinne takes a sharp breath. "Let's go."

The three of them walk into the boathouse, leaving the rest of us out on the dock. Holding my breath, I peek inside, but there's nothing except for the useless boat, other random boat crap, and the tarp in the corner. The shape underneath it.

I step back onto the dock, closing my eyes and forcing myself to calm down.

Max comes back out. "There's no one in there."

"No shit, Spielberg," Aaron mumbles.

"We can try the house again," Kira says, aimed at Corinne. Clearly, she's trying to be supportive, but at this point, she sounds like a human version of the worst kind of toxically positive Instagram post. *Good vibes only! Murderers only win if you let them kill your shine!*

"What's the point?" Logan says. "We can see the whole island from the house. Unless someone's been hiding up in a palm tree for two days, we're not finding shit."

Corinne breathes out shakily. "She's right. There's no one else here."

"Let's just do another loop around the island," Kira tries.

"There's no one else here!" Corinne erupts, her voice breaking. She sinks to a crouch like she can't stand anymore, and says again, quieter, "There's no one else here."

For a few seconds, we're silent, no sounds except our breathing and the water under our feet. Water for literal miles, like it's going out to the end of the earth, or something. Like there's literally nothing else in the entire world except for this island and us.

"So that's it, then," Max says. "We're alone."

I can see it on everyone's faces, like when you first realize you're a little too drunk. When you stand up, and suddenly it goes from a warm, bubbly feeling to the floor wobbling under your feet, like you're moving through water, everything hitting you in the same second.

One of us is a murderer.

And one of us still has the missing gun.

KIRA

Thunder shakes the house like it wants to come in. We're all in the living room, gathered like we were on the first day, when Tilly told us she was leaving, when I should have listened to my gut and followed her out of here, except now, everyone's quiet. Eyes darting around the room, smelling like rain and fear, the same thought beating through us all: one of us is a killer.

"Okay." Corinne steps in front of the TV. "Okay, this is how it's going to work. We're all going to stay together. No one goes off by themselves."

I have to work to keep my breath steady, like I'm on a long run. I'm too aware of Max next to me on the couch. Everything good about last night is twisting, all tangled up with the only thing I can think of: Max took the knife. Max found Graham. Max didn't kill me, but maybe my instincts were right all along. I can't trust him.

"Hold up," Elody says. "We're all going to stay in one room, like, with the person who's killing people?"

She glances at me and Max. Does she really think *we* did this?

Aaron's whole Bonnie-and-Clyde idea? I tense, crossing my arms over my stomach.

"I'm with Corinne," I say. "We should stay together. If they wanted to kill everyone, they would have done it already."

I can't believe those words are coming out of my mouth, that it's an applicable piece of logic. I can't believe this is real.

Corinne nods. "It's not just about killing us. It's about exposing us one by one. Making us pay. Whoever the 'Sponsor' is—" She stops, glancing around the room as we're all reminded that the 'Sponsor' isn't just some shadowy figure anymore, or Tilly hiding behind the watches. Only one of us could have killed Graham. Only one of us could have taken the gun. And right now, one of us is pretending they're not planning to kill again.

"This is their twisted game," Corinne continues. "They make the rules, and they want us to follow."

"So how do we stop it?" Max asks, foot bobbing. "We can't just sit here and wait for whoever it is to come forward. That's—"

"Not what we're going to do," Corinne says, something just short of excitement in her eyes. "We're going to beat them at their own game."

"How?" Aaron's face bunches up. "This isn't a Twitch stream."

A half smile flickers on Corinne's face, almost sarcastic. "You guys ever played *Among Us*?"

I did once, with Alex and some of our cousins. It was like a fun puzzle, trying to figure out whose cartoon avatar was a killer. Now, the idea that we're living in a real-life version of the game makes me sick to my stomach. But I can't focus on that now. Corinne has a point: maybe seeing this as a game to beat is the only way through it.

"We have to find the impostor," I say.

She nods. "And the first rule is, we stay together. If we stay together, no one gets killed."

Max's eyes meet mine, and I look away, heart thudding. It could be him. He could have killed *four* people, and I let him hold me while we slept.

"Next step," Corinne says. "We talk it out. Look for suspicious behavior."

"Oh, I get it." Elody eyes me. "Like sneaking around at night, right? That's pretty sus."

"Sure," Corinne says, with a hint of irritation. "Things like that." Her gaze settles on me and Max for a moment, and my heart sinks as I wonder if she suspects us, too. "We also need to build a timeline. Figure out when we last saw Graham. When it could have happened."

Max shifts. "I saw him last night in our room, around eleven thirty. Before I went downstairs."

"Why'd you go downstairs?" Aaron asks, dripping with suspicion.

"I heard someone on the stairs, like they'd been listening at the door. They were moving down the steps, but I couldn't see who. And then, when I went down . . ."

"I was going outside," I jump in. "He followed me out."

"What were you doing out there?" Corinne asks.

"I thought I saw someone." I try to conjure it up again, the flash of movement I caught in the shadows beyond the patio. Can I be positive it wasn't just the waves or the trees shifting in the storm? I swallow. "But now I'm not sure."

Aaron slow-claps, the sharp sound making me jump.

"Amazing," he says. "Great alibi. You both heard mysterious people go bump in the night while you just *happened* to be creeping around the house."

"We were in the pool house all night," Max says. "We can vouch for each other."

He looks at me, and the truth starts to creep in. Max can vouch for me, but I woke up alone. I woke up to a missing knife.

"Hold on." Aaron has this look of sick delight on his face, and I know I messed up. My face gave me away. He looks from Max to me. "Kira doesn't look so sure."

I search Max's expression, my mind feeling like the blank chaos of TV static. "I . . ."

"Okay, fine. There's one more thing." Max takes a breath. "I had a knife."

I open my mouth to tell him I don't need him to lie for me, but the look in his eyes stuns me into silence. It's a warning.

"Kira knows, obviously, but yeah," he says. "I had a knife. I took it with me outside in case I needed to protect myself. It was with us in the pool house all night, and then I took it back to the house this morning. But when I went to put it back in the block, there was another knife missing."

Wait, I was right. The knife *was* in a different spot. Someone else took a knife last night, too. But why would Max tell everyone we had a knife with us at all? They didn't need to know. He didn't need to lie for me. Unless . . .

Unless that's not what he's doing. Max could be bluffing, trying to look less suspicious by laying his cards on the table. Maybe Max isn't lying for me. Maybe he's covering for himself.

For a second, Aaron's forehead is lined in confusion, like he's trying to do the math. Then, he breaks out into a laugh. "Oh, so now we have *two* people running around the house with knives last night? Makes sense."

"I don't know what to tell you," Max says. "I'm not lying."

Corinne furrows her brows. "Maybe we're going down the wrong path. I mean, we were all asleep or separated last night, so it's not like anyone has a real alibi. What happened to Graham . . .

any of us could have done it." She starts to pace. "Same with Zane. We were all in the room, right? Anyone could have had access to the peanut oil."

"It was in Graham's bag," Logan argues.

"Yeah, but Graham didn't stab himself, did he?" Elody says. "That kind of rules him out as the murderer, babe."

Corinne stops pacing. "With McKayleigh, there was what—an hour between the last time anyone saw her and when we found her? So, again . . ."

My stomach clenches as I think of the sun hat floating through the wind. McKayleigh on the rocks, eyes open, like she was scared. Of *someone*.

"It could have been any of us," I finish. "Same with Cole."

"Wait, Cole," Corinne says. "We never voted for him. And we never saw an Instagram post exposing him."

Logan picks nervously at her cuticles. "Yeah, but he was canceled already. Everyone already knew about his shit."

"We didn't really vote for Graham either," Max points out. "He just voted for himself."

Corinne sinks into a chair, her hand closing around her necklace. "They're changing up the rules."

"Wait, let's go back to the alibis," Aaron says. "Not to be a downer, but if any of us could have killed anyone, then doesn't that make this, I don't know—impossible to figure out?"

"We have to think about the motive," Corinne says. "That's what we're missing."

Elody rolls her eyes. "We already have it, babe. Whoever brought us here clearly has something against influencers. I think murder is, like, probably a little far, but what do I know?"

"But it's not just influencers." My mind starts to race, thoughts coming together faster than I can keep up with them. "It's us. The ten of us who came here. Nine, if you don't include whoever . . . whoever's doing this." I glance around the room, at these five faces, and it's in my head again like an awful refrain: *one of us.* "They picked us for a reason, right? They want to expose us for something. Whatever's in those folders. Something specific for each of us."

I stand up and walk to the storage closet. I need to organize my thoughts, get them out of my head and onto paper.

"What are you doing?" Aaron asks, his sarcasm replaced with distrust.

"I just need to . . ." I stop, spotting a stack of printer paper. Some pens, too. I take them back to the coffee table.

Aaron groans, back to his usual charming self. "What is this, an art project?"

"We're getting organized," I say, counting out pieces of paper. When I have ten, I write one of our names on each.

Elody leans forward to see. "Sorry, but how is this helping?"

"We need to think about why we're here," I say. "So far, two people got 'canceled,' right? McKayleigh for stealing the designs . . ."

I grab the paper with her name and write *designs* on it.

Corinne reaches for another paper and another pen. "And Zane, for . . ."

"For what he did to me," Logan says. "To those girls."

Corinne writes it under Zane's name. "Cole had the tweets."

I add it to Cole's paper.

"But what about Graham?" Max asks. "It's the same as Cole. We didn't see an Instagram post exposing him."

"But he's connected to McKayleigh and Zane." I take Graham's paper and slide it next to theirs, making a little triangle. "Maybe he's guilty by association."

Corinne taps her pen on the table. "There's also the conversation Max recorded. Something was definitely going on there."

"Right," Max says. "But we still don't know what that was about. Unless Logan has any idea."

He looks at her, but she just shrugs.

"Whatever," Aaron jumps in. "Logan's still connected."

He takes Logan's paper and turns the Bounce House triangle into a square.

Logan frowns at the table. "This is a murder board. We're making a fucking murder board."

"Um, what's a murder board?" Elody asks.

"Like in murder investigations on TV," I say, realizing Logan's kind of right. "With the index cards and the string connecting things."

"Wait. Hold on." Corinne walks to the kitchen, where she starts opening drawers. She comes back with a roll of tape and picks up the four Bounce House papers, sticking them to a bare spot on the wall next to the TV.

"Might as well commit." She squints at the wall. "I'm guessing no one has string or something we could use to connect them, so we can visualize?"

Elody reaches into her pocket and pulls out a tube of lipstick. "Like, close enough?"

She tosses it over and Corinne catches it. "Guess we're vandalizing, then."

Uncapping the lipstick, Corinne draws lines on the wall, connecting all four of their names. The peach-pink shade looks way too upbeat for the purpose it's currently serving, but it does help to visualize it, the web of links.

"How else do we connect?" I ask.

"Well, you and McKayleigh were on *Dance It Out* together." Corinne picks up my name and sticks it to the wall.

"And you totally boss-ass-bitched her right before she died," Elody adds.

Suddenly, it's a lot harder to be into the murder-board idea. Until now, I forgot I'm technically a suspect, too.

"Right," I say, trying to sound normal, "but I was twelve. She was fourteen. I was mad at her, but that doesn't mean I—"

"Draw the line, babe," Elody tells Corinne, shrugging at me. "It's not personal."

She does, and then steps back to look at the interweaving lines, giving me an apologetic look. "We can't count anyone out."

"Well, I think you're forgetting something pretty big." Aaron snatches Cole's paper from the table and slaps it onto the wall with a jagged piece of tape. He holds out a hand for the lipstick, which Corinne warily hands over, and draws a messy line from Logan to Cole.

"Wait," Logan starts. "Why are you—"

"You threw a plate at Cole's head, like, twelve hours before he ended up dead." Aaron steps back, admiring his work. "And would you look at that? Now, Logan's got a line to all four dead people. Boom. Murder board over."

Aaron drops the lipstick like a mic, and Corinne catches it, scowling at him.

"That's not fair," Logan says.

"Sorry," Aaron shrugs. "But you're the only person here with a reason to kill all four of them. It's obvious. I don't know why we're even doing this."

I bite my lip and look at Logan's lines, harsh against the white wall. As obnoxious as he's being, Aaron has a point. Logan's face when Zane was choking flashes through my mind again, but in a new, warped light. When she shook her head at me after I looked at the bottle, I thought it was denial. Pure shock. But maybe it was more than that. Maybe she was asking me not to tell.

Logan's hand darts out, and I tense, but she's only snatching another name off the table. She slaps Aaron's paper onto the wall, takes the lipstick, and draws angry lines between his name and the rest of the Bounce House.

Aaron sputters. "What—?"

"Graham told us. Don't act like you don't know what I mean. You're connected, too."

Adrenaline jolts through me as I remember Aaron's fist swinging at Graham. *Pathetic,* Graham called him.

"What are you talking about?" I ask Logan.

"Aaron was up in Graham's DMs, like, constantly."

His neck starts to blotch. "That's not true."

"I've seen the messages." Logan turns to the rest of us. "Aaron was basically begging Graham to let him into the Bounce House. It was really fucking sad."

"I wasn't—" Aaron stops and almost growls, running his hands over his face. "Yeah, whatever. I tried to get into a couple Bounce House parties. But if you think I actually gave a shit about hanging out with you guys, you're insane."

Logan folds her arms. "Yeah? Then why'd you want to so bad?"

"Because I wanted to get something for my channel. Give my subscribers an inside look at all of your crap."

"Sure." Logan laughs.

"Whatever. You know what's *really* sad?" Aaron takes a step toward her. "You acting all superior, like your career isn't totally failing without the Bounce House to back you up."

Logan surges forward and shoves him in the chest. Aaron reels back into the murder board, knocking a few of the names so they drift to the floor like leaves. With a grunt, she lunges again, but Max pulls her back. She doesn't fight him—just goes limp, like she doesn't have the energy.

Aaron winces, rubbing his collarbone. Corinne sticks the fallen names back up on the wall, and he shoots her a smug look.

"Appreciate the effort, but we don't need the murder board anymore. I don't know what other proof you need." He waves a hand at Logan. "She's clearly psychotic."

"No, she's not," I tell him, even though I'm not sure if it's true. All I know is that I can't stand back and watch everyone call Logan a murderer just because she's an angry girl.

"Let me *go*," Logan says, pulling out of Max's grip.

Aaron squints at me. "What's your diagnosis, then?"

"My diagnosis is you're a jerk," I tell him.

He snorts at that, and my face goes hot.

"She's right," Max says. "You're being an asshole."

I shoot Max a look to tell him that I don't need him to be my knight in shining armor.

Aaron grins at Max. "Your little girlfriend doesn't look so interested in what you have to say."

Anger flashes through Max's face. He reaches for the lipstick.

"What now?" Aaron rolls his eyes.

"Aaron has this whole vendetta against me because I wouldn't collab on his channel," Max tells us.

"Sure," Aaron says, sarcastic. "Because you're the peak of filmmaking talent and everyone is just *dying* to collaborate with you."

"You seemed pretty insistent," Max tells him, turning back to us. "Aaron was acting like he had this huge story that would change everything, but it's just like the rest of his channel. Bullshit."

I tense at the rough edge to Max's voice, a side of him I've never seen before. The side of him that could pick up a knife and creak open the bathroom door . . .

"What was the story?" I ask Aaron, pushing those other thoughts down.

"Dirt on some big Hollywood agent," Max answers for him.

"Wait, who?" Logan asks.

Aaron looks away. "Doesn't matter."

"We're on the same page, for once." Max shrugs. "I'm pretty sure it was fake anyway."

Something comes over Logan's face, a slow realization. "Scott West."

Aaron makes a noise like something's caught in his throat.

"Holy shit," Logan breathes. "It's Scott West, isn't it?"

"Who's Scott West?" Corinne asks.

"A big Hollywood agent," Logan says. "More importantly, Graham's dad."

Oh my god. Looking at Aaron's face, I know Logan's right. Aaron's eyes dart back and forth, frantic, until finally it bursts out of him.

"He's a piece of shit! All he cares about is turning a profit. Drops clients left and right for no reason. And I don't have proof yet, but I'm pretty sure he's been covering up some really shady stuff."

Max reaches for his camera. "Let me guess. You happen to be one of those dropped clients."

"Can you put that thing away?" Aaron hisses.

"I'm right, aren't I?"

Aaron growls. "Fine. Yes. But I didn't do anything!"

I take a step toward him. Aaron flinches.

"You have a motive." My heart pounds. "We're not attacking you. We're just trying to—"

"Why the hell would I kill *four* people just to get back at Graham's dad?"

"I don't know," I admit. But I can't ignore the adrenaline surging through me, the possibility that Aaron did this.

Aaron's hand flies out. I jump. He grabs Max's name, slapping it on the wall.

"I don't know why you're all looking at me when Max literally makes his living exposing people. He had a knife!"

Aaron snatches the lipstick away from Max and scrawls lines

between Max's name and everyone else's. As theatrical as Aaron's being, I know he's right. Exposing people is Max's MO.

Max reaches for the lipstick, and Aaron pulls away. Max grabs his hand and wrestles it back, leaving a gash of pink on the wall that leads nowhere.

Aaron wipes sweat from his forehead, breathing hard. He smiles. "Why so defensive, Max?"

"It wasn't me," he insists. "I put the knife back. Someone else took it."

"Yeah, but, like . . . did they?" Elody grimaces. "No offense, but it just kind of seems like you're a liar, babe. *Two* people taking knives is a little convenient, right?"

"Kira knows I didn't do anything." Max looks at me, pleading, and I freeze.

I want to believe Max. I do. But . . .

"I don't know," I say. "I'm sorry. All I know is that the knife was gone when I woke up."

Elody raises an eyebrow at Max. "Ouch."

Max looks at me, hurt coloring his face. Then he marches over to the murder board, jabbing a finger at Elody's name so forcefully I jump.

"Where are all of *your* lines, then?" Max asks her.

Elody blinks. "Um, I don't know?"

"And Corinne." Max's tone softens, and he steps back, running a hand along the angle of his jaw. "Everyone's so connected, but you guys don't fit."

It's true. There's at least one line coming from everyone else's name, but so far, Elody and Corinne don't have any. I look back and forth between their two papers, like it's one of those optical illusions where you look long enough and one thing turns into another, two faces into a skull.

Max turns to Corinne and Elody. "Why are you here?"

"I don't know." Corinne's eyes track over the murder board. "That's what I don't understand."

Aaron takes a step toward her. "You have the least followers of anyone here, right? Maybe this was your plan to, like—"

"What?" Corinne gives him a disgusted look. "Get followers? Organized murder is kind of a weird way to try to accomplish that goal, isn't it?"

Aaron shrugs. "Still. You were the last one to see Cole alive, too. It's weird."

"That doesn't prove anything," Corinne fires back.

"What about Elody?" Logan asks.

She folds her arms. "Um, excuse you?"

"You're the one who supposedly heard Graham scream, right?" Logan says. "You could've made that up to cover your tracks."

"Okay, but why would I do that?"

Logan throws up her hands. "I don't know, why would anyone do *any* of this?"

"The murder board doesn't lie," Aaron says. "Elody and Corinne are the odd ones out."

I press my hands to my temples, the names and lines blurring together. *Think.* It's like a math test: focus on what I know. Underline the undeniable. Three names, and the crimes written below them.

"But we still don't know why the rest of us are here," I say. "I mean, we know how we're connected, but we don't know why we're *here*. Why we're 'canceled.'" I look around the room, meeting Max's eyes. "Unless we've all been keeping some pretty huge secrets."

Thunder claps outside, and all six of our heads turn as rain starts to slam the windows again.

"It still doesn't make sense," Corinne says. "Why wasn't there an Instagram post for Graham? They broke the rules of the game."

"Maybe there aren't any rules." Elody's getting agitated now, losing her cool demeanor. "Like, maybe the murderer was just super jealous of all of us. I don't know. Does there have to be some big plan? Maybe they're just crazy."

"Well, they're here, aren't they? Let's ask." Aaron clears his throat. "Hey, murderer. Want to just clear this all up for us really fast?" He looks around the room, an overexaggerated performance of waiting. "No? Well, darn. Guess we'll just have to wait for the next body then."

"Shut up!" Elody stifles a whimper with her hand. "Can you just, like, shut up? You're freaking me out."

"Yeah, well, I'm pretty sure that's exactly what one of us wants."

Lightning flashes. We all jump again, our heads darting toward the door. I look around the room, trying to catch any hints, any cracks in the exterior that would give the killer away. The impostor. But it's just like the mess we made on the wall. Nothing except the feeling that the answers are staring us right in the face, if only we could make sense of them.

On the wall, the cameras blink their steady rhythm, watching.

LOGAN

The storm is back with a vengeance. Rain slams the roof and wind shakes the windows, whipping the palms around so they scrape the glass like witchy fingernails.

We decide to leave the murder board and make breakfast, because what else is there to do? Not that any of us is hungry. I pass on the eggs that Kira made and go for a Pop-Tart, but even the promise of brown sugar–cinnamon makes my stomach turn.

On my way from the pantry to the dining table, I stop, a fresh panic digging its teeth in as I look at the open seats. It's like the hell of lunch period at a new school, only so much worse. Because half of the people here think I'm a murderer.

And one of them is trying to kill me.

My heart kicks up as they all look at me. I go for the empty chair next to Kira, who, besides Corinne, is probably the only person here who hasn't outright called me a killer. The downside of this seat is that Elody is on my left, inching away from me like she might catch poison fumes of death. I try to ignore her as I open the wrapper.

Across from us, Corinne looks through the window and past the terrace, out to the choppy waves.

"It's getting bad," she says.

"No shit," Aaron answers, mouth full.

Lightning flashes outside. When me and Harper were kids, we used to count the seconds between lightning and thunder. There's some kind of math we did to figure out how far away the storm was, but I'm shit at numbers. Harper's the smart one.

One Mississippi, two Mississippi . . .

Thunder booms.

"We could lose power," Max says nervously.

Kira sets her fork down. "Can we not . . . you know, speak that into existence?"

"You afraid of the dark, babe?" Elody smiles, but even she can't keep her cool anymore. I can see the fear in her eyes.

A tree screeches on the window, and Elody drops her fork. "Shit."

"I don't see why you don't just get this over with." Aaron's looking right at me. "Just whip out the gun and kill the rest of us, right?"

I shove a piece of Pop-Tart in my mouth. It tastes like dust.

Aaron leans back in his chair with a nasty smile on his face. "Or maybe you'll pick a different method. What haven't you tried yet? Strangling? Drowning? Or you could always fall back on an old classic." He puts his elbows on the table and leans toward me. "I'm not allergic to anything, but good ol' poison should get the job done."

I open my mouth to speak, but I can't. I can't swallow. My mouth is dry and my throat doesn't work.

"Logan?" Kira's voice sounds like it's underwater. "Are you okay?"

Poison. Someone poisoned me. I don't know how, because I'm not allergic to peanuts, but my tongue is swelling, my throat closing . . .

Her hand touches my back. "Can you breathe?"

"No," I force out.

"You're breathing," Kira tells me. "You're talking."

She's right. I'm breathing, but everything's moving too fast, my heart in my ears, a feeling in my chest like I sucked in helium. "Yeah, I'm fine. I just . . . I can't . . ."

"You're okay," Kira says. "You're having a panic attack."

A panic attack. I've been anxious my whole life, but I've never had a full-blown panic attack before. Somehow, naming it calms me down. Makes the breath come easier. It comes back in sobs, hot tears down my cheeks. I'm okay, I'm alive, but only for now.

McKayleigh, Zane, and Graham, all of them falling like dominoes, and I'm next. Because I'm the only one left who knows what we did.

I stand up. I don't know where I'm going, just that I have to get out of here. My feet take me toward the patio, but then I remember that that's where we left Zane, so I spin around and go out the front door, to the terrace, straight into the rain. It hits my back like tiny pebbles, and I open my mouth to it, letting it run down my face, my neck.

"Logan." Kira stands halfway outside. "Come back in."

I shake my head. "I can't."

Kira glances back inside. "Okay. Can we go to the pool house?"

I nod, wiping snot from under my nose like a kid. Kira runs toward the pool house, and I follow her, thinking vaguely that this would be a great way to murder me, getting me alone like this, but I don't think Kira's a murderer, and even if she is, I don't know if I care anymore. It hits me like a shot burning down my throat: if someone wants to kill us all, they will. One by one, they'll take us down, and we can't do anything. We can't escape.

Stepping into the pool house, I close the door, shutting us both in as the rain hammers on the roof. The pillows that Kira and Max slept on are still on the floor, and it makes my throat ache. It's been so long, but I still remember exactly how it felt when Zane wrapped his arms around me from behind, the way he did sometimes when we watched movies in his bed: pulling me close, making me feel small for once, his warm breath on my neck feeling more intimate than if we'd been doing any of the other things he always said we couldn't do, not yet, not until the night that everything started to fall apart. The night he decided to break his own boundary.

"Are you okay?" Kira asks me again.

I nod. It's a lie, but at least I don't feel like I'm dying anymore. She sits on the couch and motions for me to come next to her.

I do, wiping my eyes. "I need to get it together."

"You're allowed to lose it sometimes."

Lightning flashes through the window, lighting up her expression, deep and full of something I can't read.

"Why are you being so nice to me?" I whimper. What I really mean—what I don't say—is that I don't deserve it.

"I used to get panic attacks all the time," she says. "Before competitions. They just started randomly happening one day and wouldn't stop. I'd be fine until I got backstage, but then I'd think about Ms. Tammy and McKayleigh and what everyone would say if I messed up, and then my heart would be pounding and I couldn't remember the choreo or how to breathe and . . ." Kira exhales, flexing her hands. "There was a really bad one that they got on camera for *Dance It Out*. That was when my parents decided to pull me out of the show."

As she talks, a memory floats into my brain: an episode of *Dance It Out* where fourteen-year-old Kira was crying, almost hyperventilating backstage while McKayleigh danced a solo for the judges. The way they edited it, it looked like Kira was crying because she was jealous. It was part of this whole dramatic multiepisode story-line leading up to Kira leaving the team. Now, it seems insane to me—grown people doing that, taking a little girl's fear and turning it into entertainment. Something to consume.

"Do you still get them?" I ask. "The panic attacks?"

"Not really. Leaving the show was good for me. I started therapy, too. That helped. Plus starting my channel, doing my own content . . . I don't know. It made me feel like I had control again. Of what I was putting out there. How people were seeing me. And that felt good for a while, until I realized you can't ever really control that."

Kira takes a sharp breath, tears welling, and my chest cracks open a little. I know we're the same age, but right now, all I can see is Harper, the way she tries to stop herself from crying whenever Mom gets in one of her moods or Dad forgets a birthday. So, I do what I would if Kira were my sister: I wrap my arms tightly around her. She leans into me.

"Thanks," she says. "Sorry. I'm just . . ."

"Trapped on a murder island and really going through it?"

She laughs. "Yeah."

Thunder claps, and both of us snap our heads toward the window. Suddenly, I have to tell her. I need to get the words out.

"Graham came to talk to me last night."

Her eyes get wide. "What? When?"

"A little before eleven, I think."

"What did you talk about?" Kira asks.

I shake my head, remembering Graham's haunted look as he stood in my doorway.

Who did you tell?

"He wasn't making any sense." I swallow.

Someone here knows. Someone wants to kill us for it. So either you told, or . . .

"What?"

Or it's one of us.

I run my thumb over the raw spot on my pointer finger, where I've been nervously picking at the cuticle, and suck in a breath.

"He told me that Zane might have killed McKayleigh."

Kira shakes her head quickly. "But that—"

"Doesn't make any sense? Yeah, pretty much." I pull on the skin again, a sharp sting followed by more blood. I wince.

"Why did he think that?"

"He didn't have any proof. He just . . ." I press my thumb to my cuticle to stop the bleeding, forcing myself to breathe. "Zane told everyone that he and Graham were together before we found Mc-Kayleigh, right? He said they were outside, like, hanging out, and then they went back inside together. But Graham told me that Zane was lying. Graham went inside, but Zane stayed out by himself. As in, Zane was unaccounted for when McKayleigh died."

A shadow of something passes over Kira's face, confusion or disbelief. "Why didn't Graham say something before?"

"I don't know," I tell her. "Graham always just went along with whatever Zane said. Zane had this way of making you feel like he was right, even when he wasn't."

His voice floats into my memory like a storm on the air: *We can fix this.*

Kira stands up. "But if Zane killed McKayleigh, then why— that doesn't—he can't be dead *and* be the killer."

"I know. I think Graham was just losing it."

"Come on." She starts for the door. "We need to tell everyone else."

"Wait."

"Why?"

"I don't want them to know that I saw Graham."

Kira lets out a frustrated breath. "Logan, you just told me that Zane might have killed McKayleigh. I can't keep that to myself."

"I know, but I don't think he did. It doesn't make sense. Because then who . . . who did that to Graham?"

I shiver, wrapping my arms around myself as more tears threaten. Graham. I was so mad at him for not backing me up earlier with Zane, but all he wanted was to keep the peace. To mourn our friend. Sometimes, I think Graham was the only one who actually understood me, and now he's gone. He'll never finish his stupid songs.

"Logan . . ."

I choke on another sob. "If you tell them I saw Graham, they won't even listen. They'll just think I did it."

Kira's expression changes, fear creeping in. She takes a step back, toward the door. "But you didn't, right?"

"What?" My throat squeezes. "That's—"

"I'm sorry. I just—if there's more than one killer, then it has to be two people who would have a reason to work together."

It hits me like a slap in the face. "So you think it's me and Zane?"

"I don't know. I'm just trying to make this make sense."

"Well, good luck. It doesn't."

Kira takes a careful breath. "You had the wine."

"So?" I blink fast, trying to stop more tears from coming. "You think I was in on this whole murder thing with Zane, and then I turned around and killed him? Why would I team up with him in the first place? After what he did to me, I wouldn't . . ."

Kira's face softens. "I know. I'm sorry. I shouldn't have—"

"No. Don't worry about it." I push past her and throw open the door, walking into the rain. My feet slap on the storm-slicked terrace, the rain shouting in my ears like a voice saying, *See? Even Kira thinks you're a monster. Even she can see right through you.*

"Logan, wait."

I walk faster, shoving my hands into my hoodie pocket. My fingers brush against something metal, sending an electric feeling all over my skin. I close my fist around it and pull it out.

A black choker, with a silver *J* hanging from the center.

I shove the necklace back into my pocket, sucking air into my lungs and wiping rain from my eyes. It's not hers. It can't be hers. There has to be some reasonable explanation for how this necklace appeared out of thin air and landed in my pocket.

Someone here knows. Someone wants to kill us for it.

Lightning splits the sky, forking down into the violent waves. So many miles of water all around us, churning, getting closer, like the sea wants to suck us all in with the tide.

And maybe it should. Because Kira's right, and so are the rest of them. I am a monster. And if everyone here is hiding something as big as I am, then maybe we all fucking deserve it.

ELODY

The door swings open, making me flinch, but it's just Logan stomping inside, Kira right behind her. Both of them are soaked, standing in the doorway like little wet rats. Logan's definitely been crying.

"Everything okay?" Corinne asks.

Obviously not, but Kira nods, glancing at Logan.

"Yeah," she says. "I think so."

Logan doesn't say anything. She just marches on over to the stairs, her hand shoved deep into her hoodie pocket.

"Wait, I'm serious about staying together," Corinne says.

Logan stops. "Yeah, well, I'm kind of soaking wet, so."

Solid point. Corinne sighs, pulling at her necklace.

"Okay. Maybe we should all take five minutes to get our stuff from upstairs and bring it down here."

"Wait, why?" I ask.

"We should camp out in the living room for now," Corinne says. "It'll be safer."

I make a face, but don't argue. Because actually, I don't love the idea of sleeping alone in a locked room with Kira. And fine. Maybe

I want to know if she and Max are going to do any more sneaking around. Like, for murder reasons.

"Whatever," I say. "Let's have a sleepover, then."

We clear up breakfast and start heading upstairs, but Aaron doesn't follow us. I catch him in the living room, squinting at the bookshelf.

"Um, what are you doing?" I ask.

He turns around quick, ears going red, like he got caught doing something bad. "Nothing. Just thought I saw something."

I make a face. "Okay, creep."

Maybe I should ask more questions, but honestly, I don't want to spend any more time talking to Aaron than I have to. I go upstairs, leaving him behind.

When I get to my room, Kira and Corinne are almost ready, their bags at their feet and their bedcovers folded. God. This is about to be, like, the most depressing sleepover ever. Their faces look like they're at a funeral.

And then I realize that Corinne has something in her hand.

"What's that?" I ask.

"A DVD," she says. "It's from our 'Sponsor.' And it was in your stuff."

"Wait, you went through my stuff?"

"Not on purpose," Kira says. "It was on top, kind of sticking out."

Yeah, right, I want to say. Sweet little Kira would never *ever* go through somebody's stuff. I'm so pissed at her that I almost forget what's actually happening. The Sponsor put a DVD in my bag. Wait, why the hell did the Sponsor put a DVD in my bag?

I put a hand on my hip, trying to keep it together.

"Okay, and? I haven't seen a DVD since I was like four. What even is it?"

Corinne turns the case around to show me the front: ELODY EVER AFTER, PILOT.

I forget to breathe. And then I see the message, scrawled on a piece of paper and stuck to the cover:

> *THOUGHT YOU HAD US FOOLED?*
> *THINK AGAIN, BABE.*
> *—YOUR SPONSOR*

Everything slows down. Stops.

"No," I tell them. "No. We're not watching that."

Kira takes a step toward me. "Elody—"

"No!"

I reach out to grab the DVD from Corinne's hands, but she dodges me.

She looks at me like I'm crazed. "What's on this DVD?"

"Nothing." I shake my head, my throat closing like I'm going to cry. I'm not going to cry in front of them. "Whatever. Just put it away."

Corinne nods. Then she tosses the DVD to Kira.

"Go," she says.

Kira's out the door so fast, I don't even have time to try to stop her. All I can do is look at Corinne, stunned. Hurt.

"I'm sorry," Corinne says. "But if the Sponsor planted this, then we need to watch it. It could give us another clue about who they are."

Suddenly, I remember how to move. I run after Kira, the panic building up like a scream that gets cut off by someone's hand over your mouth. Like Mom's voice in my head. *Never let them see you weak.*

"Elody?" Max is coming down from the third floor with all his stuff. "What's going on?"

Like he even cares. Max looks away from me and down to the living room, where Aaron's on the couch, staring up at us.

Logan appears in her doorway. "What's happening?"

"Everyone downstairs," Corinne says, coming out of our room. "Now."

When she sees my face, Logan looks like she's going to say something, but I don't wait to hear it, because she doesn't give a shit about me. None of them do. I run downstairs, trying to think of how I can stop this. Anything to keep me from having to watch that DVD. But when I get to the living room, the TV's all set up, and Kira's about to press PLAY.

I want to scream, but I'm too tired. All I can do is sit on the couch and close my eyes, waiting, thinking I should have known this would happen. It was all too easy. The lie. Getting away with it. I trace the spot of my birthmark, and I know it's probably just in my head, but I can still feel it. The pain there.

Sorry, El. Some things you just can't fix.

Kira presses PLAY.

TRANSCRIPTION: *ELODY EVER AFTER*
SEASON 1, PILOT

[INTRO-SEQUENCE MUSIC.]

MONICA

Elody? [Knocking.] El, what are you doing in there, honey?

ELODY

Oh my god, Monica. What.

MONICA

Come out here for a second.

[FOOTSTEPS. DOOR OPENS.]

MONICA

What's going on in there?

ELODY

Um, I'm taking pictures?

MONICA

Oh good, for the sponsored post with—?

ELODY

Literally none of your business.

[PAUSE.]

MONICA

Okay, well, do you think you should change into your new shorts?

ELODY

Why?

MONICA

Those old ones make your legs look big.

[DOOR SLAMS.]
[MUSICAL TRANSITION.]

ELODY

Hey. My name is Elody, and I'm sixteen.

MONICA

And I'm Monica, better known as Elody's mom. Although some people think we're sisters.

ELODY

Um, no?

[CUT.]

ELODY

How many followers do I have? Um . . .

MONICA

Just over five hundred thousand as of yesterday, right, baby?

ELODY

On Instagram, yeah. Three hundred K on TikTok.

MONICA

The growth over the past year has just been amazing, you know? It's unprecedented.

ELODY

. . . Sure?

MONICA

But I wouldn't call it an overnight success. Obviously, luck and timing are important, too, but there's so much work you don't see.

[CUT.]

MONICA

As a mother, of course I worry about so much of her life being online. But I like to think of it this way: in our circle, a lot of girls Elody's age—you know, girls who've grown up with a certain amount of privilege—

ELODY

Ugh, Mom.

MONICA

Well, honey, it's true! We're so blessed to come from our kind of family. And plenty of girls in our situation, like the girls from Elody's boarding school . . . they'd be thrilled to just sit back and be waited on for the rest of their lives.

But Elody . . . she's created something. She's got this gift people want to see, and it's like—

[OFF-SCREEN KNOCK.]

V.O.

Ms. Elody? Your smoothie is ready.

MONICA

We're in the middle of recording.

V.O.

Oh! I'm so sorry, Ms. Monica. I didn't—

MONICA

What did you think we were doing here with all of the cameras, Sonia? [Pause. Door closes.] I'm sorry. Sonia has been with us forever. She's like family.

[CHAIR SHIFTING.]

MONICA

Elody, we're—

ELODY

Whatever. This is boring.

MONICA

[Trying to cover mic.] Are you [censored] serious, Elody? Come back here right—

[FOOTSTEPS. DOOR SHUTTING.]

MONICA

[Laughs.] Teenagers, right?

[PAUSE.]

MONICA

We can—we can edit that out, can't we?

MAX

Elody marches forward and pauses the video. The screen freezes on a shot of her sixteen-year-old self in the kitchen of a classic California mansion, white marble and huge windows framing rolling hills. A woman—Sonia, probably—is cleaning up a blender while Elody sits at the spotless counter, drinking a smoothie and staring at her phone, looking completely at home because it *is* her home. It always has been.

"Well, that's the nicest trailer park I've ever seen," Corinne says sarcastically.

I shake my head in disbelief. "Why would you lie about that?"

Elody's ice-blue eyes lock on mine, and she smiles in a way that makes me feel like she can see directly into my internal organs. "You're probably loving this, babe. So perfect for your little movie."

My *little movie.* I know she's doing it on purpose, trying to turn this around so *I* feel like a fraud instead of her, but it still puts me on the defensive.

"Why did you lie?" I ask again.

She turns to look at the TV, tracing a pensive finger over her bee-stung lips like it's the first time she's really thought about it.

"You want to know why this pilot never aired?" she says finally. "Because production didn't think we were *relatable* enough. No one cares about a hot rich girl getting even richer. Been there, done that. I wasn't *likeable*."

"So you pretended to be poor?" Kira asks, disgusted.

Logan laughs. "Yeah. I've 'been there, done that,' and trust me, it's not as glamorous as it seems."

Elody rolls her eyes. "Oh, boo-freaking-hoo, Logan. You literally lived in a TikTok mansion, like, two months ago."

"You profited off of a lie," I say. "How is that any different from what McKayleigh did?"

Elody laughs. "That's so fun coming from you, babe. Where did *you* grow up? A New York City penthouse?"

"It wasn't a penthouse," I mumble, stopping before I can correct her. It was still a luxury condo building, and I know how that's going to sound. "But who cares if it was? I didn't lie about it."

"Fine!" The sharp turn in Elody's voice makes me tense. "Whatever. It wasn't even my idea. It was *Mom's*." She spits out the word like it's rotten. "We rebranded, sprinkled in some lame posts about how far I've come and how *grateful* I am, and boom. Suddenly, I was likeable. No one wants an influencer who actually tried to become one, but when the whole thing is, like, a totally lucky coincidence that happened to some average girl? People eat that shit up. So, there. You got me. I'm a terrible person. But you know what?" She gives that same catlike grin. "It worked. Who cares how I got here?"

Aaron leans back smugly in his seat. "So you're totally fine with this getting out, then?"

"Shut up."

"I'm just asking." He shrugs. "Since you acted so *normal* when we found this DVD."

"I said shut *up*."

"Wait, this doesn't make sense either." Corinne glances at her watch. "Why would the Sponsor expose Elody's stuff without a vote? And why isn't this being posted?"

Elody rolls her eyes. "Why is any of this happening, like, at all?"

"You know what I think?" Aaron looks at the rest of us. "I think there's something else Elody's not telling us. Because if you ask me, the way she freaked out at this video doesn't line up." A slow smile creeps across his face. "You'd think she was about to be caught for murder."

Elody glares, her mouth twitching.

"Come on. We're all dying to know." The humor leaves Aaron's face. "Why did you freak out so much at that video?"

"I don't know."

"Bullshit. *Why?*"

"Because my mom's dead!"

Elody's shout reverberates through the room, underscored by a crack of thunder. She slumps into the nearest chair, crossing her arms over her middle like she needs to hold herself together.

"It was six months ago. A freak asthma thing, 'cause I know you're all wondering. Her doctor was always telling her she had to stop smoking, but she didn't listen. Said she needed it to ease the *stress* of her life. Meaning me. As if she wasn't obsessed with the attention and everything else we got out of my career." Elody laughs, but there's something sad in it. "Classic, right? I was a bitch to her, she was a bitch to me, and now we'll never get our sweet little kiss-and-make-up moment."

Looking at her, I see a hint of the girl she was when she aimed the gun at my chest, the way her smile seemed to be hiding something dark and broken. Elody may have lied about who she is, but I think I understand her now. Her mean jabs, the bored-party-girl act, even the way she dared me to kiss her—I thought it was just evidence of how shallow she is, but really, it's armor.

"I'm sorry," Kira says softly.

"I don't really need your pity, babe, but thanks."

Elody's eyes shift to me, glossy with tears that haven't fallen, and I get a feeling like static electricity on the back of my neck. Because as much as I believe what she just told us, I also can't shake the feeling there's more to it. She's hiding something.

Elody blinks, and all that vulnerability is gone as quickly as it appeared, her face morphing into its usual bored look.

"Let's get it over with," she says. "Kill me. That's the next step, right? I just got voted off the island?"

There's no answer except the rain on the windows. It's louder now, stronger. I stare at my watch, waiting for another message, but nothing comes.

Elody stands. "Whatever. If I might die, I'm at least getting drunk first."

She goes to the kitchen.

Logan pushes her hands deeper into her hoodie pocket, watching the camera on the wall. "We're so fucked."

"Don't say that," Kira says quietly.

I want to believe her, to let her sureness ground me, but it's starting to seem like Kira doesn't even believe herself anymore. With a sharp stab, I remember what she said earlier: *All I know is that the knife was gone when I woke up.* She doesn't trust me. And I can't ignore this gut instinct I have, stronger every time I look at the mess of a murder board—that all the pieces are there, if I could just slot them into place. That I might not have enough time.

Corinne stands, the sudden movement making me flinch.

"We should finish setting up." She gestures at all of the things we brought downstairs. "Figure out where we're going to sleep."

Thunder cracks, making me tense. I don't think anyone's going to be sleeping anytime soon.

"Um, babes?"

We all turn to the kitchen, where Elody is rising from the cabinet under the sink. All of her armor is gone now, replaced by blank shock. The stormy light through the window gives her face a sickly glow.

"I think I found something."

KIRA

Elody stands back, angling away from the cabinet like whatever's in there might explode.

"What is it?" I ask.

"A safe, I think?"

Running over to the kitchen, I crouch and look into the cabinet. My breath catches. A safe. It's small, maybe the size of a toaster, dark and sleek with a number keypad on the front.

"This wasn't here before, right?" Max asks.

"I don't think so," Elody says.

Logan frowns. "Okay, so what is it, then?"

In answer, a new message pings on each of our watches.

A gift from your generous Sponsor

I look up at the nearest camera, its little red eye blinking down at us. Heart thudding, I reach inside the cabinet and lift out the safe. It's surprisingly light, and something slides around on the inside. Something small that feels a lot like . . .

"A phone," I breathe. "I think there's a phone in here."
Another message lights up our screens.

Not so fast—every gift comes with some conditions:
1. Figure out who I am, and you get in

In spite of all that's happened so far, I feel hope washing over me. We could get out of here. Maybe the Sponsor has changed their mind, realized this entire plan is too evil, even for them.

2. You have until sundown. If you get in, you get out

I hold my breath as the next message chimes:

3. If you don't . . . you're all canceled

Canceled. The word is so pervasive, it's almost a joke, but now, it sends a chill through me. Because now, four bodies later, we all know what it really means.

"Cool," Aaron says, panic cutting through his sarcasm. "So if we don't figure this out, we all die? That's what this is, right?"
Another message:

Stumped already? Don't worry. By now, each of you has
    received a clue about why you're here. Let's just hope
    you're smart enough to put it together in time.

A clue? I haven't gotten a clue. At least, I don't think I have. I look around the group for any signs of recognition. Aaron tightens his jaw, and Elody twists a strand of hair tightly around her finger. Do they look a little nervous? And Max . . . Max looks just as confused as I do.

"I didn't get a clue," he says.

Corinne shakes her head. "Me neither."

"Same," I add, knowing it sounds like a lie, even if it's the truth.

Elody laughs. "Right. Because you're all so nice and perfect."

"Yeah, I don't buy it," Aaron says.

Elody cuts him a look. "Okay, so what was *your* clue, then?"

"What was yours?"

"Obviously the DVD." She rolls her eyes. "Now, can the rest of you stop being all weird and just, like, tell the truth?"

Aaron sighs. "Fine. I found something earlier. It was some script pages from *The Magnificent Millers,* like, shoved into my bedroom drawer. I don't know what that was about, though."

Elody claps sarcastically. "See, babe? That wasn't so hard. Now, who else?"

Silence. Uneasiness creeps up like a shadow behind me.

"Seriously?" Her jaw drops. "Wow. Two seconds ago, everyone was on my ass about being a liar, but I guess you were all just projecting."

"I don't know what to tell you," Max snaps. "I haven't gotten a clue."

"Well, Spielberg, maybe you missed something," Aaron shoots back.

Corinne lets out a small breath. "Okay, crotchetiness aside, I think Aaron has a point. Maybe we missed something. We just need to think harder. Logan, what about you? Have you found anything?"

Logan's eyes flick to mine, and I wonder if she's still worried that I'll tell them what she told me about Zane in the pool house. Why *was* she so worried?

"Logan," I say softly. "Maybe they should know."

She looks from me to the others, like she's making some invisible calculation, and then breathes out. "Graham thought Zane killed McKayleigh."

"What?" Max asks. "That doesn't make any sense."

"Yeah, I know."

Corinne narrows her eyes. "Why didn't you tell us before?"

"Because she knows it's bullshit."

"Aaron—"

"Sorry," he cuts me off. "But what kind of made-up crap is that? Logan's just trying to cover her own ass." He laughs. "Zane's *dead*, and Logan probably killed him. I can't believe she told you that and you just believed her."

Aaron's smug tone brings an angry flush to my cheeks, but I can't ignore his logic. Zane died after drinking from Logan's bottle. She's the only person here with a clear reason to want all three Bounce House members gone, and she hated Cole, too.

"See?" Logan looks at me with so much hurt in her eyes that all of my logic dissipates. "I told you. They think I did it." Her stare drops to the ground. "You probably do, too."

"Okay, but, like . . ." Elody takes a step back, scanning the room like she's looking for something to protect herself. "Did you?"

"Wait. Let's just take a second to—" I move forward, freezing when Logan's hand shoots back into her pocket. Everything in my head shuts off except for the frantic pounding in my ears. *The gun.*

When I look up from Logan's hand to her eyes, they're wide, wild, but it doesn't look like she's about to attack. It looks like she's the one who's been cornered.

I take a breath and ask, in the steadiest voice I can manage, "What's in your pocket?"

She pulls her hand out. "Nothing."

"Wait, no," Max says. "There's something in there."

Logan shakes her head quickly, ponytail whipping.

Max takes a careful step toward her. "Can we just—"

"No!" Logan jerks away, her hand diving back into her pocket.

"Get it," Aaron orders. "Someone grab her!"

Max moves forward, reaching for Logan, but she shoves him away.

"Stop it! Don't touch me!"

Aaron lunges at Logan from the side, and with a yelp, she pulls away from him, her hand shooting out of her pocket again, this time with something in her fist. Max grabs for it, his hands closing around her wrists, pulling, but she fights him, and I can't watch this.

"Stop!" I shout.

Max and Logan both turn to me.

My throat burns as I lock eyes with Max. "Just—don't grab at her like that. Let her show us herself."

Max's shoulders slump, shame darkening his face, and Logan stares at me, something like gratitude or relief or just exhaustion filling her eyes. Slowly, she unfurls her fingers, revealing what looks like a choker necklace, a black cord with a silver *J* charm.

"What is it?" I ask her.

"It was my friend Jenna's." Logan squeezes her eyes shut. "She died."

Something cold and tingling starts to crawl up my spine.

"How?"

She shakes her head, begging.

"You can tell us," I say.

A tear falls from her cheek and into her open palm.

"Logan," I plead. "This might be the only way we can get out of here."

She takes a shaky breath, and finally says it, so small I can barely hear:

"We killed her."

LOGAN

I thought I was the ghost, but I should have known: I'm the one being haunted. And the parade of ghosts keeps getting bigger. Graham. Zane. McKayleigh.

Jenna.

I met her a few weeks after my eighteenth birthday in April—the same birthday when Zane and I first kissed, the night that pushed the first domino that sent all the rest of them tumbling. Happy fucking birthday to me.

In a cosmic turn of events, Jenna and I had the exact same birthday. *Aries queens,* she said, because like Zane, she believed in astrology. Maybe she was onto something, some star-crossed bullshit, but besides being born on the same day, we were totally different.

Jenna Hyatt barely cleared five feet. She had the kind of curves that I used to cry about wanting, when I would buy push-up bras to turn the skin around my clavicle into something people would want. She had strawberry-blond hair cut to her chin, and normally, McKayleigh couldn't stand someone else being the redhead, but

Jenna was the exception—because Jenna was hard not to like. She was bubbly and feminine and easygoing. None of that anger I carried around like sharp stones in my pockets, like scales on my skin.

But there were two ways Jenna and I were the same. First: no one was looking out for us. And second: Zane chose us, probably for that exact reason.

I look up from the necklace in my hand to everyone staring at me, waiting.

"Jenna ran away from home," I tell them. "She'd been living on her own in LA since she was sixteen. Pretending she was older. She wanted to be an actor or a writer or something like that. She was never that specific. Mostly, she worked at a bar. That's how Zane met her."

I shiver, thinking of the way he talked about her when he came home that night, scrolling through her socials for all of us to see. Her TikToks were mostly of her dancing or lip-syncing along to whatever sound was going around that week, but Zane's whole face had lit up.

She has It, he'd said. "It," capital *I*. The same "It" that he used to think I had.

"He started bringing her around the house, but it was this big top-secret thing. He didn't want to make anything official until we were all on board with making her a member."

That was how it worked: we were a team. Our decisions were unanimous, at least on paper. And they all got on board quick. Graham decided that Jenna was cool because they both liked this one underground punk band and hate-watching *The Real Housewives.* McKayleigh warmed up to Jenna after the first night she drank with us—probably because they spent a good hour of it together in the bathroom, Jenna gently touching McKayleigh's face and telling her she was so beautiful it should be illegal, in that way that only drunk girls and especially drunk Jenna love to do, just spilling over with love for everything.

Meanwhile, I sat on the sink counter, staring at Jenna and wondering what it was about her that had Zane so obsessed. Jenna was pretty, prettier than me, but she wasn't, like, *Elody* hot, the kind that stops every person who's ever been even a little attracted to women in their tracks. Jenna, as far as I could tell, was just a normal girl.

But as much as I wanted to hate her, I couldn't. Because there was a part of me that wished she'd brush her fingers over my cheeks and tell me stupid crap about how pretty I am, too. More than that, I wanted Zane to stop looking at me, through me, like I ceased to matter the second I wouldn't give him what he wanted. I wanted Graham and McKayleigh to stop ignoring me. I wanted to be a girl who, for once, didn't make a scene. So, when Zane finally sat me down and asked me what my problem was, I told him I didn't have one. I voted yes. We took Jenna in with open arms and open bottles.

"It happened in May," I tell them. "The night before we were going to officially announce her as a member." I close my fist around her necklace, feeling the cool metal of the *J* press into my palm. "We had a party."

It was one of my favorite kind of nights: cold enough for a hoodie, but warm enough to hang out outside. We were by the pool, the hills sloping down from our house like we lived in some annoyingly perfect mythological kingdom in the sky.

Normally, the house was full, other creators coming in and out in a never-ending parade that I used to think was exciting, until it got exhausting, not knowing whose hair that was in the shower, whose toothpaste left in the sink. But that night, it was just the five of us: Zane, Graham, McKayleigh, Jenna, and me. It was the first time in weeks that they didn't act suddenly busy the second I walked in, that they didn't treat me like I was invisible. Deep down, I knew it was because Zane wanted everyone on their best behavior for Jenna, to make us seem like the best of friends, but it felt good anyway. For a few minutes, at least.

I can still picture the exact moment in my head. Zane leaning in, brushing his mouth against Jenna's ear so I could practically feel the ghost of his stubble on my own skin. His hand on the small of her back, her laugh, the two of them going back into the house. The drop of a stone in my stomach, the glitch in the simulation. I'd been lying to myself all night, telling myself it wasn't going to happen, and then it was right there in front of me, bright and twisted.

Well, Graham said, once they were gone, *looks like that's finally happening.*

McKayleigh laughed. *Thank goodness. He needs to get it out of his system.*

Out of his system, like Jenna was a stomach bug and not a girl. Is that what Zane thought of me? That once he got what he wanted, he'd discard me like the out-of-season clothes he pretended to donate?

Is that what he was going to do to Jenna?

I took a long pull of my drink, letting it burn all the way down. Then I stood up and stormed away.

What's your deal? McKayleigh quipped behind me, but there was something fearful in it. Of course. She was probably worried I was about to do something stupid and overdramatic, just to ruin the whole night. Maybe I was. To be honest, *I* didn't know what I was going to do yet—only that I couldn't let Zane do to Jenna what he did to me. Not again.

So, I mumbled something about getting a drink and trudged back to the house. Someone's footsteps followed.

You okay? Graham, his voice soft.

Back then, I thought he was afraid, like McKayleigh was, that

I'd ruin everything with Jenna. Now, I wish I'd told him the truth: I wasn't okay, and I didn't know if I would be. Maybe if I had told him what really happened on my birthday, he would have realized that Zane had twisted the story. We could have put the pieces together and figured out that Zane was the real villain all along. Maybe then, none of this would have happened. Maybe Graham would still be here.

But instead, I told him, *Yeah. Fine.*

Now, tears blur my vision again. I swipe them away with my fist, Jenna's necklace going warm in my sweaty palm.

"Zane and Jenna went off together, and I was worried about what he might do, so I followed them."

I don't know what made me do it, what gave me the courage. Maybe the shot I knocked back before going upstairs. Maybe the pure rage blazing through my veins as I marched to his locked bedroom door.

But when I got there, I was frozen by a too-familiar sound. Voices, getting louder and angrier. Breath shuddering, I pressed my ear to the door and listened.

What the fuck, Jenna? Echoes of the way he'd yelled at me, the absolute disgust and disbelief when I wouldn't give him what he felt entitled to. *Did you think you would get away with this shit?*

And then Jenna, quiet but strong, so much stronger than him: *Did you?*

"She found out that Zane had been grooming girls," I say. "Jenna was going to expose him."

It wasn't until I heard it in Jenna's own words that I really understood what had been happening to me. To the other girls. I'd seen them—pretty and shining, showing up to our parties flushed with excitement and the drinks Zane pressed into their hands before taking them into his room. Most of the girls came during my early months at the Bounce House, and I was too drunk on the glamour of it all to see what was so clearly wrong. I assumed the girls were older than me. I was even *jealous* of them—the way Zane gently touched their hips, guiding them through his door, to the hidden part of him I thought I'd never see. Until I did. Until I realized he hid it for a reason.

"When they went off to his room, Jenna was secretly recording him. She pretended to be into him just to get a confession or something, but he caught her. And then . . ."

I wasn't really afraid until the fighting stopped.

Jenna wouldn't back down. She was going to do it, she told him. She had the proof and he couldn't stop her—she was only giving him a chance to come clean on his own. Her voice was building and building, not stopping even as Zane told her to shut up, until suddenly, she made this startled noise. Then, nothing. In the quiet, I could hear my heart pounding. I strained until I heard it: Zane grunting, and something muffled and terrifying. Something that sounded like a girl trying to scream.

My grip flew to the doorknob as I shouted her name. Locked. I yelled again, pulling and pulling, my hands slipping, until the door finally swung open.

Zane, red-faced and breathing heavily, his hair falling out of his bun and around his face. In every other way, he looked like he just did one of his workouts, except for the look in his eyes. Not even feral or wild. Just cold. Calm.

Zane, what the fuck did you—

I stopped when I saw her. On the bed, limp like a doll, one of Zane's stupid sustainable luxury pillows covering her face.

Before I could speak through the startled tightness of my throat, I heard the door open downstairs, footsteps coming inside.

Logan, you better not be cockblocking right now! McKayleigh giggled, the cursing a telltale sign that she was drunk.

Graham shushed her. Their footsteps neared the stairs, my mind swimming as Zane just stared at me with that cool, unbothered expression.

I'm serious! McKayleigh called. *What are you—*

She and Graham came into view then, stopping cold at the bottom of the stairs.

What's going on? Graham asked, looking frantically between me and Zane.

Something about it snapped me back into my senses. I pushed forward, but Zane was a concrete wall, holding me in place with his giant hands.

She's hurt, I told him stupidly, like I didn't know he'd done this to her. *We have to do something. We have to—*

The slap was sharp and hot, leaving me stunned, hand on my cheek.

For the first time, Zane looked afraid.

She was going to ruin everything, he said. *I had to make her stop. Logan, she was going to destroy us.*

Now, I'm still too afraid to look into everyone's eyes as I tell them the truth. "He killed her."

Even then, when the undeniable proof was lying motionless on the bed, Zane tried to spin things. He gave us all of his best excuses: Jenna was threatening him. She was going to get us canceled, arrested. When she lunged at him, he was just acting out of self-defense. For all of us. As Zane droned on, I finally broke out of the stupor his slap had put me in and pulled my phone out of my pocket, fingers hovering over the screen.

We could still call for help, I said. *We could come up with something. We don't have to tell them that you—*

They can't help her, Zane decided. *And we're not bringing anyone else into this.*

It didn't really hit me until then. Jenna was dead. Zane killed her while I listened, helpless. No, not helpless. I could have done something. Kicked down the door, called for help, but I didn't. I couldn't save her.

Graham reached for his phone. *No fucking way.*

Zane lunged forward, pulling at the phone as Graham clutched it tighter.

You killed her! Graham screamed.

And you're an accomplice. Zane finally wrestled the phone out of Graham's hand, breathing hard as he looked around the room. *All of you.*

Like hell we are, McKayleigh snapped. *This is your mess. Not ours.*

Zane came closer, making her shrink.

You think anyone will ever work with us again if this gets out? We're dead. All of us.

Reaching through the fear, my stunned silence, I found my voice again. *But you killed her.*

Zane spun to me, and I flinched. He was going to hit me again, I thought. But instead, he pulled me into a hug, his breath hot on my neck.

You know what happens if we tell someone about this, right? This is over. Everything we've built together. He squeezed tighter and then let go, leaving me cold as something like clarity flashed in his eyes. *But we can fix this.*

"It was Zane's idea to move her," I tell everyone now. "She was gone, and we couldn't . . . we didn't . . ."

Corinne nods, her stare searing into me. "Right. Because murder would be pretty bad for the brand, wouldn't it?"

"It was *him*," I argue. "He killed her. Not us."

Even as I say it, I know it's bullshit. We didn't have to let him get away with this. But we were all under his spell.

"What did you do next?" Kira asks, her face hard.

I swallow. "Zane had a boat. We drove her out to the marina, went out a bit into the water, and . . ."

Staring at the necklace again, I realize for the first time that this probably isn't even Jenna's. That one went with her. Jenna told us she bought it from some cheap stand at the Santa Monica Pier when she first came to California.

"And that was it." I sniff, wiping at my nose. "The next day, I packed my shit and left."

The thing I still can't say aloud: that day, as I closed the Bounce House door behind me for the last time, I wasn't sure if it was the right thing to do. Six months as a full-time influencer makes you money, sure, but not the kind you can live off of for years, especially when you don't even have a high-school diploma. It's not the kind of money that can buy you a new apartment, a car, and still leave you enough to help your mom out. To send money to Harper, for the things Mom can't give her.

Walking down the long Bounce House driveway was the start of a free fall that hasn't ended until now, this moment like a final crash against hard ground.

"That was it," Corinne repeats, cold. "No one ever came looking for her? No one had any idea?"

I shake my head, more tears spilling out. "None of us really knew where she came from, but it didn't seem like . . . I don't think she had anyone looking for her. I don't know if Jenna was even her real name." I shove the necklace back in my pocket and look at them, tears stinging. "But I swear I'm not the one doing this. I'm not the Sponsor."

Max looks like he doesn't believe a word I've said. "Logan, you're the only one here with a motive to—"

"I know. But I didn't kill them. I wanted to get as far from them as possible, forget it ever happened. I just—" I close my eyes, wiping the mess of tears from my face. "I need you guys to believe me."

It hangs there. The silence is like a kick in my stomach. They think I did this. And I don't think I blame them.

Aaron clears his throat. "Okay, not to be a jerk, but I'm starting to think this is all a little unfair. I mean, the Sponsor's clearly after Logan and the rest of the Bounce House for actual murder, and whatever the rest of us did, there's no way it's on that level." He pauses, his lips pressing into a thin white line. "Unless anyone has anything they want to clear up?"

No one talks.

"We're going to die." Elody laughs, shaky and scared. "Oh my god, we're literally all going to die."

"We're not going to die," Kira says softly, but even she doesn't sound convinced anymore.

I run my hands over Jenna's necklace, or whoever's necklace this really is, thinking that I don't feel any different. Finally, I told the truth, let go of the thing I've been dragging around for months, but I just feel heavier, like the air of this room is too thick and warm, and even with all the space, these high ceilings, I'm trapped in a tiny box and I can't breathe.

Max reaches into his pocket, glancing down as he does, and I catch a flash of something black and shiny.

And then I snap.

"What the fuck is that?"

He looks at me, eyes glazed. "I . . ."

"You recorded that!"

Max doesn't even try to deny it this time.

I manage a bitter laugh. "We might all get murdered, and all you care about is getting it on tape." And then the thought leaks into my mind like bile. "But maybe that's the whole point." I gesture at the cameras around us. "This would be a pretty messed-up way to get your documentary content, but I'm starting to think you don't give a shit."

"Are you kidding me?" Max erupts. "You're not about to accuse *me* of murder when you just confessed to dumping a girl's body in the ocean. I didn't do anything. I don't even know why I'm here!"

He says it so genuinely, like he believes it. Like he's perfect. Just like Zane. And then all I can think of is Max's hands around my wrist, trying to take Jenna's necklace from me, and I don't think they're that different at all, actually. Him and Zane.

I march over and grab his camera bag from where it's sitting on the ground.

Max reaches for me, but I jerk away.

"This is what you want, right?" I pull the zipper hard and take out the camera. "Might as well get video, too, while you're at it."

I throw the camera, and he lunges, catching it just before it hits the ground. Too bad. Maybe it's wrong, but all I want right now is destruction, shattered pieces.

And then I notice the crumpled-up papers inside the camera bag. I grab and unfold them.

Shock jolts through his expression, and then panic.

"Wait," he starts. "I don't know what—"

And then I see what's on the page. It takes me a second to compute, to really understand what's happening here. When I do, I try to laugh, but it comes out as more of a rattle.

"Max Overby, you fucking hypocrite."

KIRA

Max grabs the papers from Logan's hand. As he reads, the look on his face isn't fear or confusion or shame at whatever's there. It's even more terrifying—behind his glasses, Max's eyes are totally blank.

"I can explain," he tries. "Let me just—"

Logan glares at him. "Go ahead. Spin this in a way that makes it not entirely fucked."

"I was fifteen."

"You're disgusting."

"Is someone going to tell us what's going on right now?" Aaron asks.

"Yeah. I'll let Max do it, actually." Logan bunches up the paper and throws it his way. "Since he seems to have an explanation for everything."

Before he can grab it, I run and pick it up, backing a few paces away from him.

"Kira," Max says, and there are the eyes I've seen before, bright and gentle. I want to believe them. "Please."

I open the paper, and the air hisses out of my lungs.

It's a screenshot of a Snapchat group named Da Boyz. The first message is dated around three years ago, from an account called @maxamillion13.

Guys she sent it holy shit

Max had sent a screenshot of an Instagram DM chat. At the top is a picture of a girl from the chin down, mousy brown hair obscuring her face. She's completely naked. It's a mirror selfie, so I can see her phone case in the reflection, one of those rubber ones shaped like a pink bunny. In the background is the girl's bedroom. An oversized teddy bear in the corner, a bright purple backpack spilling school supplies onto her bed.

The photo was sent by an account called @lacey_w to an account called @jake_hardin.

Lacey wrote: only for you.

Jake wrote back: beautiful.

"Okay, seriously, someone tell the rest of us what's happening right now," Elody demands.

"Max was a catfish." I look up at him, something boiling inside me. "That's what this is, right? 'Jake Hardin'?"

Max just looks at the floor. "It wasn't like that."

Elody makes a face. "That's it? I mean, it's a little messed up, but come on. It's not, like, *murder*."

"He got a nude from an underage girl," Logan says.

Elody's mouth hangs open.

Aaron claps. "Oh, this is perfect. This is excellent."

Max shakes his head. "It wasn't—"

"Read the rest of it." Logan looks at me. "Out loud."

I don't want to, but part of me needs to see Max's face, needs to watch him hear it, so I read through the rest of the Snapchat conversation with Max and the boys.

> CHASE: ahahahahahahah Max is the MVP!!
> AUSTIN: dude holy shit I can't believe she sent a nude
> KENNY: me looking for the tits 🔎🔎🔎
> CHASE: I'm so dead
> MAX: lol what can I say? Jake Hardin's a beast
> AUSTIN: "jake hardin" lmao I can't believe she hasn't
>   figured out it's fake yet

When I look up again, Max's stare hasn't moved from the floor. He takes his glasses off and rubs his eyes like he's tired.

"We were all fifteen. So was she. It's not like . . ."

"You catfished a girl and made her send a nude that you shared with your friends," Corinne says, enunciating every word. "And now, your career is based on exposing someone else for doing this *exact* thing. No part of this looks good for you, Max, so I think you should just stop."

He swallows. "I know."

"Lacey," I realize. "Was that the girl from summer camp? The one from your 'biggest lie' who you said you blew off in New York?"

Logan laughs. "Understatement of the fucking year."

"You don't understand," Max says. "Middle school sucked for me. I was the scrawny film nerd who couldn't even talk in class without feeling like I was going to puke. My parents literally tried to buy me friends by inviting kids to tapings and expensive birthday parties because it was so obvious that none of them wanted to be around me. It was the worst time of my life."

"I was bullied on national TV for two years," I tell him, fighting the shake in my voice as I hold up the paper. "I went to therapy. I didn't turn around and do *this* to someone else."

"Kira, I've literally been punched in the face before. Like, yeah, McKayleigh was a dick to you, but it's not the same."

And there it is. Maybe I could give him the benefit of the doubt, decide that this Lacey thing was three years ago and Max was fifteen. But here he is, still recording people without consent, like he has some divine right to share our secrets with the world. He thinks he's this beacon of truth and morality, but when I look at him now, all I can see is every guy who ever made a comment about my body or sent the kind of DMs a fifteen-year-old should never have to see. The kind of men who made me wonder if the comments were right. If all I am is something to look at.

"Don't tell me it's not the same," I say. "You don't know me."

"Wait, I didn't—"

"Sorry," Corinne interjects, "but I'm still not seeing how you getting bullied turns into *this*." She gestures at the paper in my hand.

"I know. I know. I just . . ." Max lets out a desperate breath. "I started a new school freshman year, and when these guys came along and they weren't trying to kick my ass . . . I would have done anything to keep it that way. So, when we saw Lacey that day in New York and I blew her off, told the guys that she was stalking me, one of them said maybe Lacey would leave me alone if she just found someone else, and I wanted them to like me, so I just . . . as a joke, I said . . ."

"It was your idea." I want to laugh, but I can't. "You made the account, right? This was all you."

"The guys were in on it, too," Max says, too quickly. He pauses, wincing. "I mean, yeah, I was the one who sent the messages and everything."

"How long did it go on?" I ask.

"Few months, maybe."

"Oh my god," Aaron says, delighted.

"I know," Max almost begs. "I know. But I was *fifteen*."

"So was she," Corinne says.

It hangs in the air for a few seconds, thick and heavy like the island air, and I have to ask. Because maybe, *maybe* there's a chance this tight anger I feel can start to uncurl.

"After all this, what happened? Did you ever reach out to her to apologize? Tell her it was you?"

Max lets out a long breath. "No. I ghosted her, I guess."

Logan makes a disgusted noise, and I feel it in my chest, in my whole body.

"I don't get it," I say. "What did you even get out of this? And don't say it was for those guys, because you didn't have to do *this*."

"I know." His face crumples, and he starts to cry.

"Don't." The word feels like acid in my throat.

He sniffs. "I think maybe I liked talking to Lacey like that. I was embarrassed by her at camp, but . . . as Jake, it felt different."

I toss the paper down onto the counter, because I don't even want to touch it anymore. I don't want to be anywhere near this part of Max or the feelings he's still dredging up in me, the part of me that knows I've done exactly what I was afraid of: I trusted someone I shouldn't have.

"I know it was wrong," Max goes on. "Everything I did with the Jared Sky doc, everything I'm doing with my whole channel, it's all to—"

"To clear your conscience?" I snap.

"I guess," Max says, getting smaller. "No, it's more like . . . I wanted to make things right. Or better."

"But you never apologized to Lacey," I say. "You never made it better with her."

He deflates. "She deleted all of her social media after everything. So I haven't . . ."

"You have no idea where she is," Corinne finishes.

Max shakes his head.

"Sorry to burst this little self-reflective bubble, but what now?" Aaron picks up the paper. "Max is a catfish, Elody lied about being poor, Logan's a sort-of murderer, and one of us is an actual murderer, who, by the way, still wants to kill the rest of us. Where the hell does that leave us with the safe?"

Elody leans back against the fridge, an empty look on her face. "Nowhere."

Aaron starts to read the DMs, his forehead wrinkling with concentration or disgust or both.

Corinne takes a deep breath. "Okay. As messed up as this is, we need to set it aside. Right now, we need to focus on the safe." She checks her watch. "It's almost three. They said we have until tonight, so there's time. We need to figure out the other clues."

"Why can't we just try everyone's names as the code?" Logan asks.

Corinne shakes her head. "Because we don't know if—"

"I just want to get out of here!"

"Yeah, babe," Elody tells Logan quietly. "No offense, but you're not special."

Wind whips against the windows, making my whole body clench. In the quiet, the truth slips in again. One of us is a killer. Someone in this room wants me dead, maybe even tonight, and we're trapped. Panic branches out from my middle to my toes and fingers, making them itch to move, to run, to get the hell out of here, but I can't. We're stuck, and nothing makes sense.

"What if there's no answer?" The thoughts come faster than I can stop them, a panicked flood. "What if the Sponsor isn't actually going to let us leave? What if—"

An earsplitting boom of thunder shakes the house. Then, there's a buzzing noise, and the room goes black. In that first second of darkness, the terror zips between us like molecules, heartbeats and breath and sweat. When my eyes adjust to the stormy light still filtering in through the windows, I make my way to the wall and flick the light switch back and forth. Nothing.

Aaron laughs in the shadows. "Here we go."

ELODY

"No one panic," Corinne says.

"Babe, that's literally the worst thing to tell people when they're about to panic."

As usual, she ignores me.

"Let's just wait a few minutes," Corinne says. "It might come back on."

"It's not coming back on," Aaron snaps. "We're fifteen miles from the mainland. Where do we even get power from, anyway?"

Max marches toward the closet, fists clenched.

"What are you doing?" I ask.

He throws open the door.

"I'm assuming there's a generator out there." Max digs out a flashlight and a rain jacket, tugging it on even though it's way too small. "I'm going to find it."

"Oh, so you're some kind of electricity expert who's going to save the day?"

"Do you have a better idea?" he asks sharply.

I clamp my mouth shut. I don't know why he's being such a dick. It's not like *I'm* the one who just exposed him in front of everyone.

Max starts for the patio door, but Logan blocks his path.

"No way are we letting you go off by yourself."

"We can't split up," Corinne says.

"If you guys want to come, fine." He pushes past them. "But I'm not just going to sit here in the dark."

"I think it's a great idea, actually," Aaron says. "Every man for himself now, right? It's a big house. We have enough rooms for everyone to lock themselves up alone."

Kira shakes her head. "I'm with Corinne. No one splits up."

After how she just reacted to those DMs, you'd think Kira would be fine sending Max off alone to get nabbed by a psycho killer, but I guess she's too nice for that. Or maybe she's afraid of what he'll do if she lets him out of her sight.

"Like I said: invitation still stands." Max slides the door open and walks out into the storm.

Corinne curses under her breath and heads to the closet. "We can't let him go off alone."

Kira follows her. Of course she does. Even after all that, the big game Kira was talking just now, she's still going to chase Max into the rain like a lost little puppy.

Well, not me. Not anymore. I start walking toward the stairs.

"Elody, wait."

"Sorry, babe," I tell Corinne. "But my hair looks good right now. I'm not going out there."

She blows out a breath, all frustrated. "Fine. Meet us back here in ten minutes."

I don't answer her, just keep walking up the stairs. Behind me, a door slams shut. When I look back, Aaron's gone, the downstairs bathroom door closed. Corinne gives Kira a tired look and shrugs. They pull up their hoods, click on their flashlights, and run out into the rain, Logan trailing after them.

At the top of the stairs, I open the door to my room and step in quickly, clicking the lock behind me. God, my heart is going crazy. I need to pull it together. Taking a deep breath, I climb onto my bed and reach for my pillow. I need to scream or something, get all of this out of my system, and then—

There's something under my pillow. What the hell? I feel for the smooth rectangle stuck to the back of it and pull it off. I have to angle it toward the window to see what it is in the dark. When I do, my blood rushes, beating in my ears.

A picture of me and Mom from four years ago, when I was fourteen. My birthday. We're at the table at some expensive restaurant I don't even remember except that it was freezing and dark, and she picked it because Instagram said it was the place to be. I'm sitting in front of a giant slab of chocolate raspberry cake that they brought us but I never ate. She's behind me, her hand on my shoulder like a claw, white-knuckled.

I flip the photo over, and there, written in the same serial-killer scrawl as the note on the DVD:

THINK I DON'T SEE RIGHT THROUGH YOU, BABE?

I drop the picture on the bed, panic jumping up and choking me. Someone knows. Someone knows everything.

Mom's Botoxed, smiling face stares up at me from the picture, but all I can see is the way she looked when she was dying. On the floor, looking up at me. Begging with her eyes for me to get the inhaler and call 911, save her life. Telling me she needed me.

I would have done it. I was going to. But it felt so good, I just wanted a few more seconds of it. Being the one with all the power.

Someone knocks on the door, and my skin starts to buzz.

They knock again, and I swallow, my mouth dry.

"Yeah?"

"It's Aaron. Can we talk?"

I stare at the door like it might turn see-through if I look long enough, wondering if it was him who did this. If he knows.

"I thought it was every man for himself," I say, trying to keep the panic out of my voice.

"Elody, come on." He gets quieter. "I think I know who the Sponsor is."

I go cold. "What?"

"Just—can we talk? I need to do this before they get back."

This is a bad idea. I know it is. But Aaron sounds genuinely freaked out. And the thing is, he's never been that great of an actor. He got away with it on *The Magnificent Millers,* but it's not as easy to fool everyone when you're not twelve and adorable. If he really knows something . . .

I take a breath, wipe my face, and open the door. "Let's talk, babe."

Aaron steps inside, looking over his shoulder.

"Lock it," he says.

"But—"

"Please. Just do it."

I click the lock.

"Okay," I start. "What's—?"

Aaron's hand flies over my mouth, pushing me back against the door.

"Don't scream," he says.

I try to push him, bite his clammy palm, but he's stronger than he looks. I freeze, my heart pulsing.

When he speaks again, it's calm and slow, almost a whisper.

"I said don't scream." Something hard and metal presses into my chest. Aaron smiles, tightening his hand around the gun, his breath hot and sour on my face. "It's time for us to have a chat, *babe*."

He clicks off the safety.

MAX

Corinne shouts my name.

I push wet hair out of my eyes, squinting to see without my glasses, which are stowed in my pocket. Kira and Logan are behind her, all three fighting their way through the rain.

My jaw tightens. I don't know why I'm annoyed that they followed me, but I am. It's like I haven't had a second to breathe since I stepped off the boat, except for last night with Kira. Kira, who won't even look at me.

Corinne catches up first. "Have you seen anything?"

I shrug. "Haven't gotten very far."

"Should we do a loop around the house?" Kira asks. She's still not looking at me.

I know whatever we had is probably over, and maybe it should be, but it still gives me this hollow feeling in my chest. The truth is, I'm pissed. At myself. At her, for giving me exactly what I deserve.

"Fine," I say. "Let's go."

We start a half walk, half jog around the house, straining our eyes through the rain for anything that looks like a generator. It's not until we get to the back patio that I realize I don't even know what I'm looking for. Elody was right. I'm no expert. Even if we found one, what would I do? Electrocute myself, probably.

Lightning splits over the sea, lighting up the mannequin still lying on the beach, that stupid message dripping across its chest. YOU'VE BEEN #CANCELED, like a goddamn joke. It's idiotic, and still, I know whoever dragged it out here must have been so satisfied with themselves, what they knew was in store for us.

Rage rushes through me, hot and fast. I stop and rake my soaked hair out of my face, a growl dying in my throat.

"Max?"

Kira. She's standing a few feet away from me, looking at me in a way I can't read, but maybe—maybe there's a hint of concern there. Of the Kira who doesn't hate me.

"Do you see anything?" she asks, and all at once, it's gone, a trick of the light. Now, there's nothing but distrust in her eyes.

Corinne and Logan are behind her, pulling their hoods tight around their faces.

I look away. "We should go inside. This is pointless."

"Seriously?" Kira says, annoyed now. "This was *your*—"

"Do *you* know how to fix the power on an entire private island?"

She blinks at me, her lips parting like she wants to say something. Instead, she presses them together, looking hurt. Angry. She wipes the rain from her eyes and turns to march away.

Wait, no. Jesus, why do I keep making this worse?

I call her name, but she doesn't answer, so I run after her and reach for her hand. Kira flinches and steps back, glancing at her palm like I shocked it.

"I'm sorry." The words spill out, desperate. "I don't know what's wrong with me. I—"

I take a breath, lost for words. Corinne and Logan can probably hear me floundering right now, but I don't care. I need Kira to know that I'm not who she thinks I am. I can fix this. I step closer and lower my voice.

"Kira, I know I look like a hypocrite right now. And a jerk, and an ass, and any of the things you can think of to call me, and maybe I am, but . . . but I'm not like the rest of them. Jared Sky. Everyone else here." I reach out, but I'm not sure what for. My arm falls to my side again. "I want to be better. I'm doing everything I can to fix this, because *you* make me want to be better. Because you're not like them, either. You're different."

Something changes in her expression. Hardens.

"I'm different?" she repeats.

I don't know how, but I screwed up. "You're . . ."

"'Not like other girls,' right? I'm better?" Kira laughs drily.

"No, wait. That's not what I meant."

"But you did." Her mouth twitches like she wants to laugh again but can't. "That's your problem, Max. You want to be better than everyone. Different. You came here to make a documentary exposing the rest of us, but you forget that you're one of us. And so am I." Something passes through her eyes, maybe surprise. Doubt. Then, they're fiery again, her words coming sharp and certain. "We're not different from everyone else. Every single person here turned content creation into a career. And it doesn't matter if it's fitness or thirst traps or *hard-hitting journalism*. We all need followers to survive. Sure, you call people on their bullshit, but that doesn't excuse your own. It doesn't make you above us just because you're better at lying to yourself."

I want to say something else, but I'm rooted to the ground, my tongue thick and unmovable. Kira's stare is unrelenting, her shoulders moving up and down with quick breaths, and she's right. Here I was, trying to figure her out, while she's seen right through to my dark, twisted center and pulled it out to analyze in high definition.

Kira turns back to the other two, who stand stunned. Equally disgusted with me.

"Let's go." Kira starts walking, and Logan follows, but Corinne stays put.

"We all go together." From the way she looks at me, it's clear she isn't worried about my well-being. Corinne's gaze flicks to my pocket, and I realize. She's afraid of me. She thinks I *did* this.

Logan gives me a dark look over her shoulder. "Let him stay out here if he wants. He won't kill anyone until he's got his camera to take it all in."

Corinne relents, following the others, and I watch them go, letting the rain soak through my jacket. Anger shoots through me, making my teeth chatter. Logan, of all people, thinks *I'm* the bad guy. They all do. They don't care if I follow them back to the house. They might as well be leaving me for dead, all because of one mistake I made three years ago. One mistake that I didn't even get to defend myself for, because . . .

Because instead of trying to fix it, I did nothing. I let Lacey disappear.

Thunder booms overhead, and it shocks me into my senses. I jog to catch up with the rest of them, and we sink back into the shadows of the house.

As Corinne and Logan go deeper inside, Kira stays by the door, locking it behind us with a little click that feels final.

"Kira," I beg. "I . . ."

I need you to forgive me, I think. *I need you to tell me I'm not un-salvageable.* It's what I want to say, but I can't make the words come out, not when she's looking at me with those eyes. I take a breath.

"I just—"

The gun goes off before I can finish.

KIRA

Our heads all snap to the sound of the gunshot. My room. Our room, where Elody went alone. And Aaron . . .

I run, and their footsteps are behind me, all of us synced to the same rhythm: *the gun the gun the gun*. At the top of the stairs, I freeze, breathing hard and staring at the closed door. Fear settles into my bones. Aaron and Elody. Behind that door, one of them could be dead.

And one of them has the gun.

Max gets to the top of the stairs last, a kitchen knife gripped in his hand. Graham's limp body flashes through my mind, and a fresh wave of fear pumps through me. But Max has the right idea. We may need to protect ourselves.

I look at Corinne, and she nods, her flashlight casting shadows that shift like flames on the wall.

I knock on the door.

"Elody? Aaron?" I'm surprised at how calmly my voice comes out.

For a second, nothing. And then, footsteps. The door creaking open.

Elody stands with the gun in her shaking hand, a blank look on her face. Then she breaks, sobs racking through her.

With a jolt of adrenaline, I push the door open, and in the beam of Corinne's flashlight, I see him: Aaron lying on his back, blood blooming through his shirt around his chest. His eyes are wide open, lifelessly staring up at the ceiling. There's a red trickle at the corner of his mouth.

"I didn't mean to." Elody's voice is wet and thick from tears. "He had the gun on me, and then—"

"Wait, Aaron had the gun?" Max moves toward her.

Elody's hand tightens around the gun, and he freezes, hands half-raised like she might shoot again.

Then, the gun thuds to the floor. Empty-handed, Elody holds her arms tightly around her ribs, shaking with tears until Max puts the knife in his pocket and cautiously wraps his arms around her. It's an unexpected flash of the boy he was last night, gentle and safe, but I can't forget the version of him I just saw outside: desperate, believing he deserves to be forgiven even though he still hasn't apologized, at least not for the right things.

Corinne grabs the fallen gun and turns on the safety.

"It was him," she says, staring at the weapon like it might not be real. "Aaron was the Sponsor."

Elody nods, pulling away from Max and wiping her face.

"What happened?" I ask.

"He came up here and told me he knew who the Sponsor was. But then . . ." Elody winces. "It happened so fast. He just pushed me up against the wall and told me not to scream. And then he had the gun out of nowhere."

Thunder cracks, and Logan takes a sharp breath, leaning against the wall like she can't stand up on her own.

"But why?" I keep my gaze on Aaron's feet. His boat shoes, the faded leather toes pointed at the ceiling. "Why did he do this?"

"Because he was insane?" Elody wipes her face, sounding more like her usual self. "Like, I didn't really ask. Once the gun was out, I wasn't about to let him do a whole speech, or whatever."

Max is still standing awkwardly at Elody's side. For half a second, I'm sorry that I ever thought he was capable of murder, but when he glances at me, the anger starts to boil again. Max may not be a killer, but he's still a hypocrite. He's still a liar.

"I still don't get it," Corinne says. "Why would he do all this? Just to get back at Graham's dad?"

Elody bites her lip and sits on the foot of her bed, looking like she's not sure if she should tell us.

"What?" I ask.

"There was more. Just before . . ." She flinches, shutting her eyes. "Before anything happened with the gun, he told me what really happened with Graham. Apparently, they were, like, friends when they were kids, which is how Aaron got signed by Graham's dad. They were both going to the same auditions and stuff, but Aaron was doing better. Then, he got *The Magnificent Millers,* and when it started blowing up, Graham got jealous that Aaron was getting famous first, or whatever, so he ratted Aaron out for drinking on set. That's why Aaron got fired. Graham's dad dropped him as a client, got him blackballed, and then . . . you know. Aaron spiraled. Got a DUI, let his whole life go to shit."

A sick feeling starts to gnaw at me.

"But why would he bring the rest of us here?" I ask.

"I wasn't making up that stuff about Aaron trying to get into the Bounce House," Logan says. "I had no idea he and Graham had a history, but he obviously hated us."

"But why the *rest* of us?" I ask. "We don't have anything to do with the Bounce House."

"Does it matter?" Elody asks. "Like, he's dead. Can't we just . . ."

A new wave of tears chokes her up before she can finish.

"We should have known," Max says. "This whole thing is like Aaron's channel on steroids. He always wanted to expose people, but he never had any real ammo. Until now, I guess."

It all sounds so logical, but something still feels off, like walking into a room and finding the furniture slightly rearranged. Aaron killed *four* people. It had to be something more than just jealousy or anger or hating Graham that made him do this. But maybe there wasn't. Maybe this isn't like the crimes you hear about on a podcast, something to dissect and digest in an hour. Maybe there's no explanation.

Logan rests her head against the wall, closing her eyes. Tears start to spill quietly down her cheeks, and it's not until now that it really hits me: the Sponsor's dead. It's over. Now all we have to do is get home.

Lightning strobes the relieved, exhausted faces around me before hiding them again in shadow. Corinne's the only one who doesn't look any calmer. Her eyes are dark, haunted.

"We need to get into the safe," she says, standing. "Come on."

Following her flashlight, we make our way back downstairs and to the kitchen, where the safe still sits on the counter.

"How should we do this?" she asks. "The keypad's just numbers."

We settle on the basic alphabet conversion: *A* is one, *B* is two, and so on. After writing out the list, Corinne starts punching in numbers, starting with Aaron's first name. But when she presses ENTER, the safe flashes red. She tries again with his full name, but still nothing.

"Does anyone know his birthday?" Corinne asks.

No one does.

"Seriously? No one has, like, *any* idea?" Elody looks around. "God. No wonder he wanted to kill us."

It's a half-hearted joke, trailing away into the heavy silence of the room.

"Can't we get in another way?" Max asks. "Like break the lock, or something?"

An idea jumps into my head. "Aaron was hiding the gun somewhere, right?"

"I mean, yeah," Elody says, looking sick at the mention of it. "Probably. But, like, what does that have to do . . . ?"

"He must have had a hiding spot somewhere. If we find it, maybe we'll find a phone or something, too." I look at Elody. "Do you remember where Aaron was right before he came up to your room?"

She scrunches up her face. "Um . . ."

"The bathroom," Corinne says. "The downstairs one. That's where he went when we were all going outside, right?"

"Ew. Why would he hide it there?" Elody asks.

"Let's just look." Corinne walks to the bathroom, and we all follow.

Inside, she kneels to open the cabinets beneath the sink, while Max looks behind the shower curtain. I go for the other cabinets, aiming my light inside, but they're empty aside from basic bathroom stuff: extra hand soap, lotion, old rusty rings made by the bottoms of old bottles and jars.

Corinne looks up at me. "Nothing?"

"Nothing," I say.

She stands up, her focus shifting to a frame on the wall. It's a watercolor painting of the island, the house. Corinne's eyes narrow, and she moves closer, reaching her fingers around the edge of the frame. For a moment, she hesitates. Then, she pulls. With a small sucking sound, the frame hinges away from the wall like a door.

Oh my god. It *is* a door, opening to a little hidey-hole the size of the frame. But it's empty. I lean against the sink, limp with disappointment.

A laugh bubbles from just outside of the open bathroom door.

"What?" Elody asks Logan, frowning.

"Nothing. It's just . . ." She wipes under her eyes, laughing so hard they're watering. "You just killed the only person who actually knows how to get us out of here."

ELODY

Max groans, burying his face in his hands.

"Let me guess," I say from my chair. "It didn't work. Again."

"I don't get it." Kira aims her flashlight at the keypad, staring at the safe with her Bambi eyes like it just shot her mom or something. "We've tried everything."

Believe me, babe, I want to tell her, *I know.* It's been, like, an hour of this crap. We've literally tried the number version of every single person's name, dead ones and Tilly included. Kira and Corinne even went upstairs to go through Aaron's pockets and his bags. They found his passport, but guess what happened when they typed in his birthday? Here's a hint: the exact same thing that happened just now, AKA nothing.

Corinne sighs. "Maybe we should try just breaking it."

She and Kira start to talk pros and cons or whatever it is responsible people do, and I turn to the window and close my eyes. Dig my nails into my thighs. Try to tune them out. Try to breathe.

Except when I close my eyes, all I can see is Aaron's face as he went down. The big eyes. The shock. And the worst part is that under all that, he just looked *hurt*. Not in the way where he just got shot, but like I hurt *him,* the part of him that's more than his body and blood.

It's the exact same way Mom looked at me when she died.

I stand up. "Anyone want a drink?"

Kira blinks at me. "I don't know if this is a good time for that."

"I'm kind of having a day right now, babe, so I'd love it if you don't, like, attack my choices."

Rolling my eyes, I go to the kitchen and crack open a spiked seltzer. Everyone probably thinks I'm an alcoholic or something, but I don't care. Actually, I think I'm the only person who's handling this the right way.

I take a long sip, letting the carbonation burn, and look out the window. The storm is letting up now, but it's still gray outside. In a few hours, it'll be too dark to see anything. The thought makes me take another long gulp.

Logan groans. "Let's just break it. What do we have to lose?"

"Fair enough," Corinne says. "Brute force it is."

"How should we do it?" Max asks.

"My sister taught me how to unlock stuff with a bobby pin once, if anyone has one."

I frown at Logan's suggestion. "Ew. Who uses bobby pins?"

Kira reaches into her pocket and pulls one out, and I have to fight a laugh, because of course she has one, little miss competition-dance Girl Scout. She hands it to Logan, who straightens it out so it's almost a line. Kira and Corinne shine flashlights on the lock while Logan messes around with the pin, jiggling it around like a criminal. After another couple minutes, she curses and sits back. "Okay, a concept: we throw it off the balcony and hope for the best."

"I don't know," Kira says. "If there's a phone in there, that might break it."

Corinne shrugs. "I don't think we have a better option right now."

So, we take the safe upstairs. As we pass the second floor, I catch a glimpse of our bedroom door, still shut, and it's like the echo of the gunshot comes back into my head, bouncing against my brain. I suck in air, gripping the railing.

Max looks back at me. "You okay?"

I give him my best bored smile. "Yeah, babe. Perfect."

Like he gives a shit.

We take the safe into the third-floor bedroom, where Graham's body is still behind the closed bathroom door. I try to picture Aaron sneaking through the room, knife in hand, covering up the cameras like some kind of criminal mastermind. He did that. Aaron was a murderer. It should make me feel better, but all I can think of is how sad he looked when he told me why he killed Graham. His whole *life* seemed so sad, which should make me feel better, too, but I just feel like I might pass out.

God, why did I leave my seltzer downstairs?

"Okay," Corinne says, out on the balcony. "We ready?"

For a second, we all stand there, looking out at the rest of the island. The rain is light, misting our faces. It's spooky everywhere, dark but still loud, the waves crashing. I look down at the terrace, and my whole body clenches up. This is how Cole must have felt, standing here. I wonder if he knew what would happen. If he thought about what it would be like to fall.

"Ready," Kira says, helping Corinne lift the safe. "Three . . . two . . . one."

They throw the safe over the balcony, and it crashes to the ground with a sound that makes me jump, like the pop of a gun. They both lean over the railing. Right away, I can tell from their sad droopy shoulders that it didn't work.

Corinne steps away from the railing. "It looks kind of dented, but I think it's still locked."

"Let's at least go see," Kira says. "Maybe we can force it open."

I don't think anyone even has the energy to argue with her anymore.

When we get down to the terrace, Kira jogs to the safe.

"Anything?" Max asks.

She shakes her head. "Locked."

"Shit." Max stares out at the water, pulling a hand through his hair. "*Shit.*"

A warm breeze comes through, smelling like the sea, and I close my eyes, wishing the rain felt nicer. But it's too muggy, almost suffocating.

"So, what now?" I ask Kira, maybe a little too mean, but I don't care. "Any big ideas, babe?"

She chews on her lip. "I don't know."

"Love that. Amazing." I laugh, sounding more anxious than I want to, but I can't help it. I thought I was in control. Sure, they all think I'm some scared girl who talked a big game about her mom's guns and then fell apart the second she had to pull a trigger, but it shouldn't matter. I'm Elody Hart, and I don't give a shit what people think about me. Except apparently, I do. *Never let them see you weak,* Mom said. But I did, and I am. And we're still stuck here.

Corinne stares at the safe in that weird way of hers, like she's taking it apart with her eyes.

"We can figure this out," she says, like everything is just a video game to her. Like we can always just *figure it out.* "We're missing something. We just need to look at it the right way."

Logan gestures angrily at the safe. "We don't even know if there's a phone in there. Maybe this is Aaron's last 'screw you.' We open it, and it's nothing."

"There's something in there," Corinne insists. "We heard it."

Logan shifts, picking at her nail. "Maybe we shouldn't be in such a rush to get out of here."

Max looks at Logan like she just shit-talked some movie that film nerds get horny for.

"Are you serious? We're stranded on an island with five dead bodies!"

"Yeah, exactly," Logan says. "How are we going to explain that when someone shows up to save us?"

My stomach flips. I hug my arms around myself, suddenly wishing I'd packed something besides crop tops.

"The cameras," Kira says, pointing at the ones on top of the house. "We'll have proof that Aaron did this. Even if he covered the ones on the third floor, there's still the others."

"Yeah, exactly. He's been filming us this whole time. Everything we've admitted." Logan's stare lands on Max. "Don't tell me you're psyched to go back to a world that knows what you did to that girl."

Max clenches his jaw, silent.

"What about you, Elody?" Logan asks. "You just killed someone."

A defensive feeling jolts me out of my panic.

"And?" I snap. "It was self-defense. He was going to kill *us*. You should all be thanking me."

I wish I felt more convinced. I wish Aaron's confused face wasn't flashing through my memory again. The blood coming so fast . . .

Something crashes behind us, and I spin around, my skin feeling electric, thinking *gun*. But it's just the waves slamming against the rocks. The rocks, where McKayleigh's body is still lying, probably soaked from the storm.

I brush the corner of my eye with my finger, and it comes away smudged with cried-off mascara. I can feel them looking at me, judging me, and suddenly, I don't want to be anywhere near them.

"Whatever," I say. "Play with the safe all you want. I'm going swimming."

"Elody," Corinne warns, except it's so half-assed, it's barely even a warning.

I ignore her and walk to the beach, pulling my shirt over my head, shrugging out of my shorts, and unstrapping my lame fitness watch. I toss them all on the sand, wearing nothing but my bra and underwear now, but I don't care. I don't want those clothes on my body anymore. I don't want to think about the way Aaron looked at me when he was dying, the things he knew about what I've done. I just want to *breathe*. To let the waves drown out all of the thoughts in my head.

When I get to the shore, I turn back. No one's trying to stop me. Of course not. I could drown, for all they care. The only one who's looking at me is Corinne, her eyebrows bunched together like she feels bad for me or something. When she realizes I caught her, she glances away.

Whatever. Let her look at me. Let them all look. It's the only thing I've ever been good for anyway.

I walk into the water, letting the waves wash over me. Wishing they would shut up the voice in my head. The one that sounds like Mom. Like she's laughing all the way from hell.

TRANSCRIPTION: DAY THREE, 7:38 PM
(RECORDING FROM WATCH #6)

[FEET HITTING THE SAND. BREATHING. FOOTSTEPS
SLOW DOWN. SILENCE. THEN, A GASP.]

WATCH GOES DEAD AT 7:39 PM.

LOGAN

The sun sets fast. One second, gray light filters through the windows, but by the time I come downstairs, the room is pitch-dark, the windows as black and empty as the camera lenses. Max sits on the couch, his face lit up by the blue glow of his camera screen.

I stop at the bottom of the stairs, casting my flashlight around the dark room. "Where is everyone?"

Max looks up, startled. "Not sure. I just came down here a few minutes ago."

I walk into the living room and settle into a chair, checking the time on my watch. A little after eight thirty. After Elody stormed off to the beach, we spent another hour trying to get the safe open, but that didn't really get us anywhere besides wanting to claw each other's eyes out. So, we decided to take a break, which has now become several hours long, but it doesn't matter. Aaron's deadline is pointless now. The sun is down, we figured him out, and we're still trapped here.

Max goes back to his camera, eyes tracking over the screen.

"Get anything good?" It comes out meaner than I meant it to, but I'm not sorry.

"What?"

"For your documentary. I mean, look on the bright side. Still a hot opportunity to get into the true-crime genre."

"We caught Aaron. I don't know why you're still making me out to be the bad guy." Max puts his camera down next to him and leans back into the couch, pulling off his glasses and rubbing his eyes. "But not really. Besides the vague conversation between Graham and Zane, and—"

He stops himself, but we both know what he was about to say. My confession about Jenna. Maybe I should be begging him to delete it, but at this point, I don't know if I can bring myself to grovel. Besides, Max already knows that if he releases what I said, there's nothing stopping me from sharing his little secret with the world, too.

"Basically, all I've got is a bunch of shitty B-roll," he says. "We probably don't even have Aaron's confession to Elody." He gestures at the cameras. "I bet they stopped recording as soon as the power went out."

I laugh, dark and sharp.

"What?" he asks.

"Just—you actually care about this documentary."

"Yeah, I do." Max is defensive now, chest forward. "We've been victims of probably one of the most insane crimes of this century. This story is huge, and we have the chance to share it with people. You don't care about that?"

"What I care about is—"

The sudden longing is so piercing, I can't finish. What I care about is what I should have from the beginning: getting home. *Home* home, not LA. Picking up the most nutritionally deficient snacks I can find and knocking on Harper's bedroom door, turning off all the lights and crawling into her bed together to binge the *Twilight* movies for the fourth time. And then, when we've finally caught our breath from sob-laughing at the CGI vampire baby, I'll tell her I'm sorry. For leaving her, even though I thought it would be better for her. For taking who I was, who I wanted to be, and squeezing them into the little box I thought they needed to fit inside to be worth something. For everything I've done since.

"What I care about is getting the fuck out of here," I say, almost a whisper.

For a few beats, Max is quiet. When he speaks again, the genuine desperation in his voice surprises me.

"Do you think I'm a bad person?"

I stare at him, his eyes so hurt behind his glasses, and all I feel is disgust. That after everything, all Max cares about is what people think of him. But then I remember the truth hanging over us like a storm cloud, thick and ominous: when we get out of here, the world won't be the same. People will know what we did. People will hate us. And the thought of Harper knowing what I've done, how disappointed she'll be . . .

Tears threaten, and I fight them back. *Am I a bad person?* It's the same question I ask myself every day, and the longer I'm here, the more sure I am.

"I'm not one to talk," I manage.

"I think I might be." His mouth twitches. "A bad person."

I shrug and tell him flatly, "If it makes you feel any better, I think I am, too."

Outside, the island is a shifting black shadow. I think of the bodies still out there. So many bodies—in the boathouse, on the terrace, behind closed doors, their faces up to the rain. I think of Jenna lying on the bed like a broken doll, silenced. None of them peaceful. None of them at rest.

"I think maybe that's the whole point." It comes out before I can really think it through, a half-formed idea. "Knowing you've done shit that people shouldn't forgive. Figuring out how to live with that. How to be better anyway."

"Yeah," Max says quietly. "I think maybe you're right."

There's a ping, and a bright spot of light makes Max's face glow in the dark. It takes my body a second to register the fear in his eyes. What it means.

I look down at my own watch to find the message staring back at me, two words that send every part of me buzzing with panic.

Time's up

Right on cue, a door swings open upstairs.

"Guys?" Corinne, her voice laced with terror. "Did you just get this message?"

I nod, but I can't make myself speak.

"Okay, what the hell?" Elody comes out onto the landing next, dressed again after her dip in the sea. "Did you guys see this?"

Corinne speeds down the stairs. "It could be prescheduled. Aaron could have planned this before—"

"Where's Kira?" Max asks.

Corinne stops on the first floor, her face ghostly in the light of her watch screen. "She said she was going for a run."

"When was that?" Desperation cuts through Max's voice.

"An hour ago, maybe?"

My panic calcifies into a hard stone in my stomach, heavy and unmistakable, as I remember the Sponsor's rules when we found the safe.

You have until sundown. If you get in, you get out. If you don't . . .

Grabbing my flashlight, I run to the door, throw it open, and step out into the thick darkness.

"Kira!"

The waves swallow up my shout. Footsteps follow as the rest of them catch up with me.

"Why are we freaking out?" Elody asks, out of breath. "Aaron's dead!"

"We'll stop freaking out when we find her," Corinne says.

We run, calling her name, following the beams of our flashlights as the sand turns from soft to hard and wet, the water hissing at the shore. My foot hits something big and rubbery, and fear races through my veins. Skin. A body. A garbled sound comes out of my throat as I swing my light to the sand.

The mannequin. It's just the stupid mannequin, still lying where we left it. I suck down a breath, the smell of salt and seaweed so thick I can taste it.

And then I see it. A few steps away from the mannequin, half-shadowed. Something small and shiny. Blue.

"Logan?" Corinne asks. "What is it?"

Shaking, I bend down and pick it up from the sand.

Kira's watch, the screen shattered. Dead.

MAX

"No." It comes out like a breath, like a gut punch. I look up at the three people around me, our stares shifting among one another.

"Maybe it just fell off," Corinne says. "Maybe—"

"It didn't fucking fall off," Logan snaps. She stares at the watch in her palm like it's a wounded bird.

"Kira!" I shout her name, my voice lost in the roar of the sea. I shout it again and start to run blindly down the beach.

The others follow me, all of us calling her name.

But nothing. No answer. My chest constricts, my breath coming high and tight.

"Aaron's dead," Elody whimpers. "Kira can't be . . ."

"Why should we believe you?" I turn to her, my voice raw.

She blinks. "What?"

"Why should we believe that Aaron was the Sponsor? We walked in on you with a smoking gun and we just believed you!"

I feel like an idiot. Like I'm losing it. I don't even know what to feel except fear and panic, like I'm grasping at blurry images and trying to shove them together into a coherent story.

"I wouldn't have . . . I mean, if I didn't think . . ." Elody presses her nails to her lips. "It was him! Don't try to gaslight me!"

"I'm not gaslighting you! I just . . ." I stop, raking my hands through my hair. Jesus, I sound like Zane. I can't let myself turn into that. "Did Aaron confess to being the Sponsor? Yes or no?"

"I . . ."

"*Yes or no,* Elody?"

"I mean, he didn't confess to every single murder!" She throws up her arms, walking a few steps away from us. "He told me he killed Graham. He told me why. He had a literal *gun* on my chest. I just, like—I don't know. I used context clues!"

The tide sucks out from under me, shifting the sand and making the ground unsteady, like the world is crumbling under my feet.

"It wasn't him." Corinne closes her eyes, taking a slow breath. "Aaron was just taking advantage of the situation when he killed Graham."

No. No, no, no . . .

"Oh my god," Logan says. "Oh my god, then . . ."

"It's one of us." I look up. "One of us is the Sponsor."

For a few seconds, the realization hangs in the air, all of us staring. Shifting. Suspecting.

Logan moves first, angling herself away from Elody. "Max is right. You killed Aaron. All we have is your word for it. How are we supposed to believe he killed Graham?"

"Um, because he did?"

"Prove it," Logan says.

Elody groans, frustrated. "I can't, okay? But I swear, I wouldn't have killed him if I didn't think . . ." Her eyes go wide. "Oh my god. Do you think it was *me*?"

"Can you prove it wasn't?" Logan asks.

"No," Elody snaps. "Can you?"

I watch Logan, her hands fidgeting, and her words from the

living room creep back into my head. *Knowing you've done shit that people shouldn't forgive. Figuring out how to live with that.*

"Logan's the only one here with a reason to kill everyone," I say hoarsely.

She stares at me, and the naked hurt on her face makes me want to take it back. Almost.

"Why the hell would I kill Kira?" Logan growls.

"I don't know, babe," Elody cuts in, "maybe you're just a literal psycho!"

Logan whirls around, her ponytail flying like a whip.

Elody cowers. "Don't touch me."

"I think we should all be a little more worried about Max," Logan says.

My face burns. "What? Why?"

"I still haven't let go of my theory. This whole thing would make a killer documentary."

"Are you insane?"

"I don't know, babe." Elody looks me up and down. "She's got a point."

Anger gathers in my chest and spreads, growing roots, so fast it scares me. I don't know what I'm going to do with it. I'm afraid of what I'm going to do with it.

I turn and walk away.

"Max, wait," Corinne calls. "We have to stay together."

I keep walking into the night, fighting through the sand.

"Max!" Elody shouts.

I turn around, a wild laugh burning through me. "I'm not staying with any of you."

"Then where are you going?" Elody asks.

I don't know, I want to shout. Away. Anywhere but here.

"We need to stay together," Corinne repeats, unrelenting.

She's not wrong. It's not safe. But I can't trust her, either. I can't trust anything but the fear working its way through me like a virus.

I should have taken a flashlight. Or better—the gun. I could go inside and get it, but stepping back into that house feels like more than I can handle. Scanning the sand, I see a sharp-edged rock a little bigger than my hand. Bending down, I pick it up, shove it in my pocket, and keep walking.

"Where are you going?" Elody asks again.

"To find her," I say without looking back.

"Maybe we should all go," Corinne says, moving toward me. "Max has a point. If all we have is the watch, then maybe Kira isn't really—"

I spin around, and she goes silent.

"I'm going alone," I tell her. "Don't follow me."

I walk away, not sure exactly where I'm going. Not sure of anything except for the weight of the rock in my pocket. The sound of the waves and my heartbeat.

LOGAN

"It's him," I tell them. "It's obviously him!"

Corinne watches as Max's tall shape disappears into the dark. "I don't know."

"Okay, then who do you think it is? Me or Elody? Or a fucking ghost?" I wait, watching Corinne's chest rise and fall with anxious breaths. "Who is it, Corinne?"

"I don't know!" she explodes. "I just—I need time to think."

My throat stings like I just got a mouthful of saltwater. "Yeah, well, ticktock. Because I have a feeling one of us is about to be next."

Without a word, Elody walks away from us, following her flashlight beam into the night.

"Elody, wait," Corinne tries.

But she doesn't stop walking.

"Great," I call. "Run after him, like always."

Elody snaps her head back over her shoulder. "Maybe I'm running away from *you*. Ever think of that, babe?"

It washes over me like alcohol on broken skin.

As Elody disappears into the darkness, Corinne holds her neck-lace pendant so tightly she could break it.

"This is bad," she says. "This is really bad."

"Oh, really? 'Cause I'm having a pretty great time."

"Logan—"

"Go. Chase after them if you want. Stay in a group, or whatever. Since you're so sure Max couldn't possibly kill anyone."

"I didn't say that." Corinne takes a small step away from me, the water swirling around her heels.

She didn't say it, but she doesn't have to. The way she's backing away from me, the fear in her eyes . . . it's all I need to know. But I still need to hear it, to dig my fingers into the wound.

"Tell me you believe me," I say. "Tell me you don't think I'm a murderer."

Corinne falters, her mouth opening slightly. Her hands still gripping the necklace, the flashlight. Holding on for dear life.

I turn around and start back to the house.

"Logan, wait!"

My walk turns into a run, like a little kid trying to outpace a nightmare, half tripping over mounds of sand, feeling my way through the dark until sand turns into terrace, until the tight pain in my throat turns into hot tears down my face. I run until the shadows of the house swallow me up. When I stop to catch my breath, fear prickles my skin as I start to wonder what might be hiding in the shadows.

Shakily, I cast my flashlight around the room. The beam spills over the murder board, the lipstick lines bright like blood, and then the cameras, their dark glassy eyes. Powerless. Dead. Shadows dance over the empty living room, bending with the trees and the waves. Finally, I bring my light to the kitchen, and that's when I see it. The empty counter.

The safe is gone. The safe, which was here when we went outside.

Adrenaline shocks through me, every instinct screaming what I already knew: I'm a target, and someone's here. Someone's hunting me.

I run to the first place I see, the downstairs bathroom, shutting the door behind me and pressing my back against it, my breath rattling in my throat. I can feel another panic attack starting, cold sweat and thick tongue, and I try to breathe through it. Focus on surviving.

As my head starts to clear, I curse myself for not grabbing something to protect myself. There must be something here I can use. I search the shower for a razor, but there's nothing. Then, I remember the frame, Aaron's hiding place. Could I break it? Use the glass?

Wait, the frame. Blood rushes in my ears as I realize: it was open. We left it open, but now it's closed. I pull on the edge, but it won't move. I pull harder. Nothing. I feel around the edges of the frame for some kind of key, but I can't find anything. My hands are exactly where Corinne's were when she pulled it open, but it won't budge.

"What the hell?" I whisper to myself. The door opened for Corinne. It should open for me.

I lean closer, running my hands over the border between the drawing and the frame. And that's when I see it: a tiny, barely there circle, where the black looks slightly different, shinier, almost like . . .

Holy shit.

Like a camera. But why would there be a camera? Unless . . .

Facial recognition.

Oh my god. But no, because that would mean—

"Logan."

I whirl around to see Corinne standing in the doorway like a ghost.

ELODY

I find him sitting on the beach, staring out at the water.

"Max!"

He doesn't turn around, and my hand starts to shake. I hold my flashlight tighter, walking toward him.

"*Max.*" I say it like a demand, and this time, he looks at me with this blank sort of expression, like I'm just a shadow or the wind. Then, he looks back out at the sea.

"I said don't follow me."

"Sorry, babe. But you're kind of not the boss of me." I sit next to him, holding my flashlight between my knees so it shines out at the water, making it look all purple and spooky.

For a few seconds, we don't talk. Max watches the waves, and I watch them reflecting in his glasses.

"Why'd you come after me?" he asks.

"Because I'm pretty sure Logan's a murderer and I don't really want to hang out with her."

Max turns to me with a look on his face that I've never seen before. Sadness mixed with something else. Something scarier.

"What makes you so sure it's not me?" he asks.

My heart starts to beat faster. Those DMs, the way he exploded when he got caught . . . I've always known there's something dark about Max Overby. And maybe that should make me turn and run, but I can't. Because his darkness goes perfectly with mine.

I smile. "No offense, babe, but I don't think you're the murdering type."

He makes a sound that's kind of a laugh, but kind of not. For a minute, he doesn't say anything, just digs his fingers into the sand, making tiny circles. When he talks again, it's so quiet, I almost don't hear him.

"It's my fault."

My heart skips a beat. I look at him, the sharp lines of his face in the dark.

"What?"

"Kira," he says, his voice all low and thick, like he's going to cry.

"No, it isn't."

He looks at me, a movie-perfect tear rolling down his cheek. "Yes, it is."

"Why are you so obsessed with her?"

Max blinks. "What?"

I spit it out like poison. "You're so obsessed with her and she never even liked you. I mean, look at how she reacted when she saw those DMs."

His face changes so quickly, it scares me. All that sadness disappears until it's just anger. I hold my breath, my heart beating against my ribs, but I don't look away. I stare into his eyes like I'm daring him to come at me. For a second, I think he will.

He stands and starts walking to the water.

"Max—"

"She could still be out there." He takes off his shoes and his glasses, tosses them away, and wades into the waves.

"Stop it." I get up. "She's not . . ." He doesn't stop. He goes until the water's up to his waist. "Max!"

He dives under, and my heart starts to beat faster. Farther out, he splashes back up to the surface for air, and then goes back down again. But it's too long. I count ten, twenty seconds, and then, letting out every curse word I can think of, I take off my shoes and go into the water, farther and farther until the sand disappears from under my feet.

The sea is warm and so dark that I can't see the bottom. I pump my arms, trying to stay afloat, to figure out what the hell to do, because Max might literally be drowning.

But then he crashes through the surface, gasping, a few feet away. I kick over to him just as he starts swimming back to shore. I swim after him, the waves breaking against my shoulders, pushing me forward, until we're both climbing out onto the sand. We stand with our hands on our knees, catching our breath, our bodies heavy.

He takes a deep breath, and then turns around like he's going back in.

"Wait." I grab his hand.

He fights me, but weakly. I pull him back, away from the water, until finally, he looks me in the eyes, both of us breathing hard.

There's nothing special about Max Overby. He's just a dumb boy. A hot, dumb boy who cares too much about stupid things. He's the kind of boy I like to chew up and spit right out, the kind of boy I could totally break, but for some reason, it's always been the opposite with us.

Now, I know why. It's this look, the one on his face right now. The determination. This totally obvious, doomed need to find this girl in the sea. And that's what I've always wanted: for that look to be for me.

He pulls away from me again, and I tug him back.

"Wait."

"Let me go." Max tries to fight me off, but I pull harder. "Elody."

"Just wait!"

He stops. I reach up for his shoulders, holding him there, my breath shallow and my heart going crazy.

"You need to let her go," I tell him. "Okay?"

"But I need to—"

"You need to let her go."

For a second, he stares at me. Then, his face breaks. When he talks, his voice is thick and quiet, so low I almost can't hear. "I know."

Slowly, I reach out and brush his wet hair behind his ears, his skin hot under my hand.

"You know what your problem is?" I tell him. "You tell yourself stories."

Max looks at me with this empty, confused look, but he doesn't say anything, so I keep going.

"I get it. It's why you do the documentaries, right? You're obsessed. You need to go and go until it's finished. Until it's perfect. But the thing is, you're trying to control it, and that never works. You tell yourself stories. And they're not real, babe."

I trace my hand down from the small space behind his ear to his neck, his pulse beating against my palm.

"Do you know how I know that?" I ask him.

He just shakes his head.

I lean in and whisper, "Because I do the same thing."

Max closes his eyes. "Why do you like me so much?"

I get this feeling in my skin like I'm growing spikes, and step back. "Um, okay. Someone has a bit of an ego."

His eyes open. "Elody."

I swallow, heat rushing to my face, because he's right. So was Logan, with her stupid, smug face. I always run after him. It's sad as hell, but I keep doing it. But it's also funny, all of a sudden. I laugh, a smile warming my lips.

"Because," I tell him, taking his chin in my hand, soft but firm, making him look at me. *Look at me.* "We're the same kind of fucked up."

When I kiss him, he doesn't fight it. Max melts into me, until we're melting together, down to the sand, me on top of him, and it's so much better this way, the two of us alone, without everyone watching. It's everything I've ever wanted, but it's not, because Max is opening his eyes, putting a hand gently on my shoulder. Pushing me away.

"Why do you like me so much?" he asks again, more firmly.

I laugh, tracing a finger over his bottom lip. "Come on, babe. I've wanted you since the day I met you."

And that's when I see the rock in his hand.

LOGAN

Corinne comes into the bathroom, and I step back.

"You opened it," I breathe. "Why did it open for you?"

"Let me explain."

I shake my head. "You're the Sponsor, aren't you?"

"No."

"Then why did it open for you?"

"Logan, I swear. It's not me. I'm not going to hurt you, and I don't think you want to hurt me. I just need you to trust me."

Trust me. It's such a stupid phrase, so small and basic, one no one should ever believe, but we do it anyway. I unclench my fists.

"Why are you here?" I ask her.

She takes a shaky breath. "I was working with Tilly. The *IRL* team. I'm . . . sort of their plant."

"You're *helping* them? Corinne, what the—"

She steps toward me, and I back away, the sink jutting into my spine.

"I need you to listen to me," Corinne says quickly. "I didn't know that anyone was going to die. I swear, Logan. I didn't know."

"Six people are fucking dead!"

Corinne sinks to the ground next to me, resting against the sink cabinet, like she's too exhausted to stand anymore. "I know."

"Corinne, what the hell is going on?"

"It was just supposed to be an experiment." Her face tenses at the word. "That's what Tilly called it. We were going to show everyone what this industry is really like. Expose the dark side of people like—"

"People like me." It burns in my throat.

Corinne looks up at me, anger flashing in her expression. "Yeah. People like you."

Suddenly, I feel too heavy to stand, too. I sit next to her. "Fine. Maybe we deserved that. But an *experiment*? People are dead, Corinne."

"I know," she says, her voice thick with sadness. "But I swear, this wasn't supposed to happen. That's not why I'm here."

"Then why? How did you even—I mean, you're a creator, too. You're one of us."

Her face hardens. "Yeah, I used to think so." She reaches up to her necklace, rubbing her thumb over the pendant. "My sister's a designer. One of the ones who McKayleigh stole from."

It hits me like a shock of ice water.

"Shit. I'm so sorry."

Her hand falls to her lap, my apology fading between us like the weak thing it was.

"After Elyse found out McKayleigh stole her jumpsuit, she sent a DM, but you saw what happened," Corinne says. "Elyse is a smaller creator, so McKayleigh thought she could walk all over her. But I thought maybe if I stepped in, since I have more of a platform . . ." She gives a small eye roll at the idea. "It didn't matter. McKayleigh never answered. I even reached out to her reps, but nothing. So, I sent one last DM saying I'd call her out in a live stream if she didn't start responding." Anger tightens her features, her mouth pressing into a straight line. "The next morning, my Twitch account was suspended. And I got an email from McKayleigh's legal team. If I posted anything about the whole thing, they'd sue. For 'what little I was worth.' That was the exact phrase they used."

I lean my head back against the sink, wishing I felt more surprised.

"I was ready to keep fighting, but Elyse . . ." Corinne closes her eyes. "She asked me not to do anything else. She thought I'd already lost enough for her sake. So, I didn't do anything. I tried to let it go, but I was just so *mad*."

"Yeah," I whisper. "I know what that feels like."

"No, you don't." Her stare cuts into me. "I mean, maybe you do. But you don't know what it's like to be a Black creator and watch this happen over and over again. Elyse and I have had to work twice as hard to get where we are, and then someone like McKayleigh Hill can just walk in and pull it all out from under us because she felt like it." Corinne presses her temples, taking a breath. "Look, I know the Bounce House treated you like shit, too. No one deserves what Zane did to you, but the thing is, you were still their friend. You got the money and the followers and that was enough. You knew exactly what kind of people they were, and it still took what you did to Jenna for you to finally wake up and leave."

I look down at the floor, my hands hanging limp between my knees. She's right. I know she's right, and it still hurts.

"After what McKayleigh did, I felt like I was out of options. But then I got a DM," Corinne says. "I'd posted something a while back, a subtweet about the whole thing. I didn't mention Mc-Kayleigh, just influencers in general, and I deleted it pretty quickly in case she could use it against me. But I guess Tilly saw the post before it was gone. She messaged me to say she was working on a project that she wanted me to be a part of. Something that would force people like McKayleigh to be held accountable. She said the Bounce House would be there, and other influencers, too. People who'd done bad things."

Something cracks inside me. "Did you know about Jenna?"

Corinne looks away. "Tilly had suspicions. She didn't give me details, but she thought the Bounce House had something to do with her best friend disappearing."

Her best friend. Oh god. Tilly was Jenna's best friend. This whole time, behind her chipper smile, Tilly was suspecting us. Wanting us dead. Would I do the same thing, if someone took Harper from me? It slices through me like a blade, the certainty. I would. I would in a second.

"I should've known she'd been playing me this whole time. I should've pressed Tilly for the whole story. I'm normally more careful than this. I just—" Corinne presses the heels of her hands to her eyes. "I wanted McKayleigh and the rest of you to look at what you've done. Clearly. Without running away." She breathes out, dropping her hands. "All Tilly told me was that I would come to the island, pretend to be one of the cast, and follow the Sponsor's instructions. Keep everything running smoothly. She told me I'd find a phone in there." She points at the hidden door. "But when I checked on the first night, there was nothing. And then after we found Cole, I got a bunch of messages saying to keep following instructions, or . . ." Her face twitches. "Or I'd be next."

She starts to shudder, a tear falling onto her freckled cheek, and I lean over to wrap my arms around her. She tenses away from my touch, but then reaches for my hand, lets me squeeze it.

"I wanted to come clean," she says. "I just—I didn't know who I could trust. I didn't know who Tilly was working with. I was so scared, and I didn't—"

"Corinne, it's okay. This isn't your fault."

"I know," she says, eyes blazing. "But I still want to fucking *end* it."

I swallow down the lump in my throat, forcing myself not to cry. I don't deserve tears, not now. And then, for the first time, I realize.

"But Tilly isn't here. Who the fuck is—"

"The Sponsor?" Corinne finishes, glancing at the door. "I don't have proof yet, but I think I figured it out."

And then I remember, fear radiating through me. "The safe is gone. Someone took it."

"I know."

"Wait, what?"

"I have a plan." Corinne gives a small, frustrated sigh. "This is why I needed everyone to stay together. We just need to—"

Footsteps sound in the hallway, getting closer until they stop just in front of the door. I take a breath, but Corinne shakes her head sharply, covering my mouth with her hand.

On the other side, someone knocks.

MAX

Her eyes land on the rock, its ridges pressing into my sweaty palm, and the look on her face isn't fear. It's hurt. And then anger.

"Go ahead." Her eyes water, glowing blue. "Do it, Max. Bash my head in. Is that what you're going to do?"

I falter, my grip loosening, and it's a moment too long. She lunges, grabbing my wrist so quickly that I drop the rock. I reach for it, but she knees me in the stomach, holding down my wrists while I writhe from the pain. I look up at her, breathing hard, the ends of her long hair brushing my neck.

She laughs. "That's the thing with you. You've always been too scared."

That laugh. There's something about it. It's too loud. Too messy. It reaches down under my skin, pulling up what I've been pushing down this whole time, and now I see. Underneath the dyed hair, the lip filler, and the blue contacts, it's all there. Her face is slimmer, but I know the slope of her cheeks, the small brown mole at the nape of her neck. It was all there, but I just couldn't see it.

"Lacey," I breathe.

She smiles, leaning in close, and says against my mouth: "Took you long enough."

And before I can ask any of the thousands of questions on the tip of my tongue, she's biting it, her mouth covering mine as she pins me down.

"Wait—"

Something cold and sharp presses into my neck, bringing me back to my senses.

A knife.

She grins, perfect teeth glowing in the moonlight. Those teeth that used to be crooked, one bottom tooth crowding over another.

"Wait," I beg. "Please."

"Oh my god, chill. I'm not going to kill you." She traces the knife from my neck to my jaw, her eyes flashing. "Yet."

My pulse beats against the blade. "It was you. You did this."

"Shh." Lacey puts a finger to my lips. The knife still hovers, centimeters away from lethal. "It's my turn to talk now, babe."

She brushes my hair from my forehead, gentle even with the knife against my neck, and when did she start calling everyone *babe*? I know so much about the girl pinning me to the ground, but I don't know anything. I don't know who this girl has become.

"You know, I really thought you'd recognize me sooner," she says. "I had this dumb little hope that the first time we kissed, you'd know. Like, boom. Fireworks. If you did, maybe this all could have been different. But it's like I said: I tell myself stories. We both do. And I guess that was just another one."

Her smile is so sad that I want to do something to make it go away, but I'm frozen to the ground.

"It was supposed to be different," she says. "I didn't plan for anyone to die, just so you know. I'm not an actual psycho. But then Cole happened, and everything started to fall apart."

"Cole?" I choke out. "What do you . . ."

"Oh, yeah. Total accident. He was drunk off his ass and trying to sit on the balcony railing. I wasn't sure at first, but then I went back and listened to the recording." Lacey bites her lip, tracing the line of my eyebrow with the knife point. "I really did think about calling the whole thing off after that. But then I had this crazy idea. When we first found him and we were all scared . . . for a second, like, I just *knew* we were all thinking the same thing. We actually thought one of us might have killed him."

Her eyes sparkle with the same excitement they used to have when she would talk about her favorite Broadway shows, childlike and unashamed.

"So I started to wonder . . . what would happen if I ran with it? If I made everyone think there was really a murderer on the island." She laughs, trailing the knife from my brow to my cheek, pausing at the corner of my mouth. "That would make for some pretty good TV."

The anger boils over, and I forget my fear. "What kind of TV network would air a show where people get *murdered*?"

"Oh, babe," Lacey croons. "You probably should've figured out by now that this was never really for TV. Honestly, I'm surprised none of you caught on. '*IRL*,' the whole 'hashtag-canceled' bit . . . like, ew. It was literally so cliché. But what can I say? I've always been a little *dramatic*."

She moves the knife against my throat, sending shivers through my whole body. I dredge up enough courage to ask:

"Why did you do it?"

She laughs. "You're not the only one who can make documentaries, babe. Actually, you kind of inspired me. When I first saw your

Jared Sky doc, I was pissed as hell, but then I realized . . . it's kind of poetic, isn't it?" The knife presses harder. "Catfish exposes a catfish. So I thought, how perfect would it be if I could do the same thing to you? And then I started thinking of all the people who deserve to get exposed. How maybe it was time to show everyone what kind of people their favorite *influencers* actually are."

So many questions flood my head, but I can't think with the knife pushing on my throat, almost breaking the skin.

"Lacey, please," I beg, ashamed of the desperation in my own voice. "I'm sorry. I'm so sorry for what I did to you. I should have told you I was Jake. You deserved someone better."

She laughs, throwing her head up to the sky, and there it is again—an echo of the old Lacey, the girl who didn't care that people thought her laugh was annoying. The girl with the laugh that grew on you, like vines climbing up an old building until they're part of the architecture.

"Do you really think I didn't know it was you?"

Cold leaches into my bones. "You knew?"

"Of course I did. Like, 'Jake *Hardin*'? Are you kidding? Also, I'm pretty sure the picture you used was a guy from an old Disney movie." She laughs again. "Yeah, I knew it was you. But I went along with it anyway. It's just like you said before. You were always so embarrassed of me, but I thought maybe if you just got to know me, *really* know me, then you'd know: it's me and you. Always was." She runs her thumb along my bottom lip, the knife jutting from her fist. "Honestly, I thought you knew that I knew. I figured you were just too embarrassed to admit how much you liked me."

She knew. It should feel like a weight off of my shoulders, but it only feels heavier, pushing me deeper into the sand. Because the truth is, she's right. I didn't have to keep it up for as long as I did.

I didn't have to stay up late, going blue-light blind in my bed, my heart pounding when I saw her start to type another message.

And then it hits me. What else this means.

"The picture," I say.

"It was for you." Her lip twitches, her eyes filling. She curses and wipes the tears, smudging her makeup. "You'd think by now I'd be done letting you make me cry. But I guess it's my own fault." Her hand tightens around the knife. "I should have known it was over when you ghosted me again, but I kept hoping it was only because you were afraid. But then, I heard from a camp friend that there was a picture of me going around. A friend who didn't even go to your school, by the way. That thing got *around*."

Lacey looks at me with so much pain in her eyes that logic fades. I know she brought us here, that she's done terrible things, but I still feel bad for her. Because it was me. I did this to her.

"It broke me, Max." Tears fall now, quiet and flowing. "And it wasn't just the picture. It was you. The fact that it was *you* who did that to me. But then I realized that I had an opportunity. You didn't want me as Lacey, so I'd become someone new. Someone you'd want. I'd make you see what you could've had."

She laughs, snorting a little. "Obviously, that got a little easier when I started getting hot. Because actually, that year after you dumped me, between fifteen and sixteen? I finally had my glow-up. Hips, boobs, the works. It was like magic. Well, magic plus some trips to Mom's favorite doctor." Her face darkens. "No, you know what? It wasn't magic. It was *work*. And it wasn't easy. It hurt."

She traces the knife over my lip, pressing just hard enough that I feel blood wetting my skin. Seeing it, her breath catches. She runs her thumb over the blood, smearing it across my chin, her teeth flashing.

"But it was all worth it because I got to be Elody Hart. And she was the best thing that's ever happened to me." She smiles, almost looking like the girl I knew. "Even better than you."

"Lacey, please," I whisper. Her name. I have to keep saying her name, remind her who she is. "You don't have to do this."

"I do, though." Her face crumples. "That's the thing. I had everything, but it wasn't any better."

"Lacey—"

"Stop calling me that."

I search her eyes for the scared girl behind all this anger. "What do you mean, it wasn't any better?"

"My life." Her voice is raw and thick. "People look at me now, and all they see is something to fuck or a way to sell their stupid shampoo. My own *mom* only ever wanted me when she realized what I could do for her." Her lip quivers. "Do you know what that's like, Max? To be a product?"

I shake my head.

"Well, Mom finally got what was coming to her. Since we're sharing secrets . . ." Her knee digs into my rib, and I wheeze. "I was there when it happened. I could have saved her. But I didn't. Because when she was lying there on the ground, gasping for air . . . I realized I had another opportunity. A chance to break free of her. Of all this shit."

My head spins, struggling to keep up. Lacey let her mom die. Lacey, who has a knife pressed to my throat.

She smiles, like she's loving this. "Monica may have been a bitch, but she came through with the will. Gramps was loaded. He left her the family island a few years ago, and she left it to me." Lacey gestures around us with a weak flick of her hand, almost sarcastic. "So, I started making a plan. Doing my research. I found Tilly on this weird online forum, telling everyone the Bounce House did something to her friend. Turns out she wasn't just some clout chaser making things up. After that, everything started coming together. We dug up secrets, figured out who we wanted to punish. I would stay on the island, and Tilly would be on the mainland, controlling the messages and the Instagram account. It was perfect. The only thing I was worried about was that you wouldn't come. But it's like fate, isn't it?" Her fingers brush my forehead, combing through my hair, a sad smile curving on her lips. "And here we are." The smile falls, her eyes turning desperate. "But you get why I had to do it, don't you? I mean, don't you ever feel sick, knowing that none of it is *real*?"

My heart hammers in my throat, mixing with the crash of the waves, the thrum of my blood against her blade.

I take a breath, knowing that it could be one of my last.

"I get it," I whisper. "I do. But do you know what *is* real?" I swallow, my neck moving against the cool metal. "I love you. I still love you, and I was always too stupid and scared to show it."

She blinks, her lips parting.

I reach for her wrist, and gently move her hand and the knife away from my neck, cupping her face with my free hand, searching her eyes.

"It can still be us," I tell her. "It always was."

When I kiss her, she gasps softly, tensing and then relaxing into me, kissing me back. I bury my hands in her hair and trace my fingers down her neck, her spine, rolling on top of her. When my mouth finds her neck, she sighs, arching underneath me, her fingers loosening around the knife.

And that's when I grab it from her hand.

Her eyes fly open.

"No!" Lacey grips my wrist, wrenching the knife toward her with a growl.

She pulls hard, the blade slicing across my arm. The pain shocks the wind out of me, giving her time to roll out from under me, the knife in her hand. I crawl backward, hot blood slicking my palm as she lunges toward me.

I catch her wrist, pushing her back, but she grabs my arm, pressing her fingers into the wound, and I cry out in pain. She shoves me back to the ground, and with one hand, she squeezes her bloodied fingers around my throat. With the other, she raises the knife. The blade glints in the moonlight.

I claw at her, but my throat is burning. She's so much stronger than I thought.

"I really wish it didn't have to happen like this," Lacey says, tears shimmering. "But, babe . . . you kind of asked for it."

She brings the knife higher, and I close my eyes, bracing for the flash of pain, for death.

"Put the knife down, Lacey."

That voice. I turn my head, because I'm not sure I really heard it, and for a second, I don't think I'm seeing right, either. But no, she's there. She's real.

Kira, leading Corinne and Logan down the beach like a movie hero, the gun in her hand.

ELODY

I climb to my feet, tightening my grip on the knife. Max crawls away from me and toward his saviors, one hand pressed to his arm like it might actually fall off, even though I barely grazed him. And *I'm* the dramatic one. He looks at me with terror in his eyes, like I'm a monster, and it hurts. All of this hurts.

But here's another secret: ever since things started to fall apart today, I wasn't sure if I had it in me to do this anymore. To keep playing this game, waiting around for everyone to realize it's been me the whole time. Dying for them to finally *see* me. I've been lost, stalling as I try to decide how this story ends, but now I know what I have to do.

This is my island, and I'm taking back the fucking control.

I paint on a smile.

"The classic fake-your-own-death bit," I say, turning to Kira, alive and well. With a gun aimed at my chest. "You really had me confused for a minute there." I clock Corinne and Logan. "Oh, but you had help, didn't you? Corinne got everyone outside to be your little search party while you snuck back in and snatched the safe right out from under me. So *clever*."

One look at Corinne's face tells me I've got them completely, and I laugh.

"I bet this was your idea, wasn't it? Ouch. I really thought we were a team, babe."

"We're not a team," Corinne snaps.

I wince, sucking air through my teeth. "Ooh. Pretty sure the contract you signed would disagree."

"Put the knife down, Lacey," Kira repeats, her knuckles white around the gun.

I hold up my hands, letting the knife fall to the sand. "Okay. God. I mean, *you're* the one with a gun in my face." I wait, my heart thudding, but she doesn't move. I smile. "Well, come on. I'm dying here. How'd you figure it out?"

"Your birthmark," Corinne says. "After I saw the picture from Max's DMs . . . it took me a while, but I saw it when you went out to swim, and I realized."

I fight a pulse of shame, remembering the way she looked at me when I was walking down to the beach. I thought she was embarrassed or sad for me, but really she was watching. Thinking. God, I can't believe I was that careless. I didn't even try that hard to cover the birthmark up. I guess I didn't count on anyone who makes a living as an *influencer* being clever enough to figure it out, even one smart enough to be on my team.

"So you went to Kira with your little fake-death idea." I look back and forth between them. "A little dramatic, but I get it."

Standing a few steps behind them, Logan shifts, her jaw clenched.

"Oh, sad." I pout at her. "They didn't trust you enough for their little plan, did they?"

"I don't give a shit about the plan," Logan says. "We got you. That's all that matters."

I grin now, because I realize they don't know everything. I still have the upper hand. "Actually, you don't, though."

"We caught you with a knife two inches from Max," Kira says. "I'm pretty sure your own cameras will prove the rest."

For the first time, I see Max's camera in Corinne's hand. My heart shudders, but I keep calm. If there's one thing I know, it's how to work a camera.

I look right into the lens.

"Oh, but that's the thing, babe. I only ever kill in self-defense."

Corinne scoffs. "Right. Because everyone else you killed just happened to have a gun on you, too?"

My smile gets even wider. "So even my little assistant didn't figure it out."

Max gives Corinne a confused look.

"Ugh, catch up, babe," I tell him. "Corinne's been helping me out this whole time."

"I didn't know I was helping *you*," Corinne says. "I didn't know you were going to do *this*!"

Okay, now I'm pissed. Corinne didn't know I was behind this, fine. And she didn't know anyone would die, but she knew what she signed up for. Tilly made that clear enough, as per my instructions. All I did was what I said I would, what we *agreed* on: I made these assholes pay. So what if I went a little off-script?

"First of all, I didn't kill anyone," I tell her. "Well, except Aaron, but that's different. Second, you should be thanking me. Like, maybe I had to scare you a little with those messages saying to keep following instructions or you'd be next, but come on. We both know there was never going to be an Instagram post exposing you, so you had nothing to worry about. And McKayleigh can never screw anyone over again. Isn't that what you wanted?"

"What I *wanted*," Corinne says through gritted teeth, "was for her to live with the consequences of what she did. You took that away from me."

"Sure, babe. Be a victim if that makes it easier for you." I take a step toward them, and Kira shifts the gun. I hold up my hands, trying to keep them steady. "I never would have killed you, by the way. Any of you. Not unless you made me. I meant it: only self-defense."

Kira lowers the gun a little. "What does that mean?"

"Um, exactly what I said? I only killed Aaron. And that was kind of a life-or-death moment for me, babe."

Another flash in my memory of the look on Aaron's face as he held the gun to my chest. So smug, like for the first time ever, he was one step ahead. *Nice to meet you, Lacey.* His breath hot on my skin.

Kira's face gets this haunted look. "Then who killed everyone else?"

I watch her for a few seconds, making her wait. Even Corinne doesn't answer, and I realize she must not know either. I smile, letting the tension build, because even though the masks are off now, I live for a performance.

"Now, that's where this gets interesting, doesn't it?"

"Lacey said Cole was an accident," Max jumps in. "He got drunk and fell."

Ugh. I know he's trying to be the smart one, but it would be a lot more convincing if he wasn't literally cowering on the ground right now.

"I don't believe you," Kira tells me.

I shrug. "Believe me or don't. But the cameras will prove it."

Corinne takes a breath. "The way Cole looked when I saw him going upstairs . . . I believe it."

Finally. I mean, how hard is it for my literal assistant to back me up for once?

"After Cole, I messaged Tilly that the plan was still on—just a little *revised*," I say with a smirk. "We'd go ahead with the votes and the Instagram posts, only now, we'd let everyone think there might be a killer running around the island. See how far we could really push you."

Watching the confused horror flood their faces, I laugh out loud. I'm having a literal supervillain monologue moment, and maybe it's cliché, but it's also fun as hell.

"And it was even easier than I thought," I tell them. "All it took was a dead body and a few threatening messages for Zane to crack."

Logan deflates.

"Graham was right," she breathes. "Zane killed McKayleigh."

"Ironic, right? Graham started to figure out what was going on just in time to get knifed in the shower by his old bestie Aaron."

"Prove it." Kira takes a step forward. "I don't believe anything that comes out of your mouth."

"You know what? Fine. But only because you asked so *nicely*." Tapping on my watch, I open my voice recordings, and flash Max a smile. "It's funny. We had the same idea. But I guess I did it a little better."

I press PLAY, and the sound of the waves comes through the speaker. Then, McKayleigh's annoying accent, high and panicked.

"I swear, Zane, I'll tell everyone what you did."

"Yeah? And how's that gonna go for you?"

"I'm not the one who killed Jenna."

I watch as Jenna's name hits Logan. Her eyes widen.

"Well, you sure as hell went along with it," Zane says.

"I'll tell the truth. Graham and Logan, too. All three of us. They'll be happy to let you take the fall. And honestly, wouldn't that be better for you anyway?"

Zane breathes through the speaker. *"What?"*

"I mean, what do you really have going for you outside of the Bounce House? Face it. We'd be just fine without you. Honestly, we'd be better, 'cause that crap you've been pulling with all those girls? That's a liability, hon."

"Shut up."

Footsteps, and then running. Zane grunts, and McKayleigh squeals.

"Get off me! What are you—"

"SHUT UP!"

A sickening crack, rock against bone. Everyone on the beach freezes, the blood draining from their faces when they realize what they just heard. If I were a nice girl, I'd stop it here. But I'm not a nice girl, and I want them to hear it. Zane breathing, cursing, calling her name. I want them to hear him realize what he's done. When they all look good and sick, I press PAUSE.

"Believe me now?" I ask.

They're all silent.

"But no. That doesn't . . ." Kira's eyes shift like she's doing math. "If Cole was an accident, and Zane killed McKayleigh, and Aaron killed Graham, then who . . . what happened to Zane?"

I sigh, because this part makes me sad. It really does. I know she deserved to be punished like the rest of them, but still, I see so much of myself in her. All that anger. The spark that just might burn it all down. So, I decide to give her a small mercy: a choice. A chance to say it in her own words.

I turn to Logan. "Do you want to tell them, babe, or should I?"

LOGAN

Everything stops. The crash of the waves, the warm breeze blowing, everyone breathing next to me—all of it washes away so there's nothing but her, waiting.

Lacey Warren, the girl standing in front of us. The girl who was so desperate for someone to recognize her that she made her own name the password to her safe. That's what Kira told us after she knocked on the bathroom door, the safe successfully stolen while we were all looking for her body. Back from the dead.

The dead. There's so many dead. The waves lap against the shore, and I can almost hear Jenna's laugh, all mixed in with her muffled screams that night. The night I couldn't save her.

I look up at the sky, scanning the dark. Lacey follows my gaze.

"They're not here yet." Seeing my surprise, her eyes sparkle. "I'm not dumb. If you figured me out, I'm guessing you got into the safe and called for help, too, right?"

Cold fear snakes through me. Caught.

Lacey smirks.

"But see, that's the beauty of a private island. It takes time to get out here, especially with a storm moving through. We've got, what, ten minutes? Five?" She looks at Kira's gun, her smile stretching wider. "Anything can happen in five minutes." Her gaze shifts to me, suddenly sad. "I can tell them if you want. I just thought you might want a chance to get your story straight."

And something about her sadness, her pity, is all it takes for the dam to break, for my voice to come hurtling back to me.

"This is your fault," I tell her. "You gave me the peanut oil."

Everyone else draws in a sharp breath, and I wince. Now they know. Now they'll never look at me the same way again.

Lacey just shrugs. "I didn't make you use it. I just gave you the idea."

The idea. It all clicks into place, and oh my god, how did it take me so long to see? Her kind words, the wine, our bonding over the shitty ways we've been treated by older men and the world.

"But you wanted me to," I tell her, my chest burning. "That whole conversation in my room, when you said guys like Zane always get away with it . . . and spin the bottle. You only wanted to play because you wanted me to do what I did. There was never even a Derek, or whatever his name was, was there?"

Lacey's face falls, looking genuinely hurt. "Everything I told you was true."

Hot tears wet my cheeks, and my chest feels like it's caving in.

"You were the first person who made me feel like I wasn't so alone with all this," I force out. "But you're just like everyone else. Like *him.*"

"No, I'm not." Lacey shakes her head sharply. "Logan, I wanted to give you your power back. I meant what I said. Zane would have gotten away with it. Like, yeah, he might have gotten canceled once people found out, but he would have found his way back. He'd find a lawyer good enough to get him a reduced sentence or even get him off completely. He would have been fine, and so will Max." She shoots him a vicious look, and then turns it back to me. "I wasn't sure if you'd do it, but I'm glad you did. Zane got what was coming to him."

"He didn't deserve to die!"

Even as it comes out, I don't know if I believe it. Zane had taken advantage of countless girls and killed *two* people just to save his own ass, and he hadn't shown one shred of remorse. And looking at Lacey, that same sad look on her face, I get the feeling she knows exactly what I'm thinking.

"Then why'd you put the peanut oil in the wine, Logan?"

"I didn't even know if it would work." My words come out panicked, matching time with the frantic beat of my heart. I look at the rest of them, begging them to understand. "I didn't think he'd drink so much. I didn't even know if he'd take it from me. But once he did, I couldn't stop it. I . . ."

I didn't *want* to stop it. The truth is like the flash of a blade. I let Zane die because I wanted him to. Because Lacey's right: even if Zane got exposed for everything he did, it wouldn't be enough. His career would be ruined, maybe he'd even rot in jail, but all of those girls would still be scarred from how he treated them. Jenna and McKayleigh would still be dead. And Zane *still* wouldn't be sorry. Everyone always talks about holding people accountable, letting them own up to their shit and live with the consequences, but what happens when people like Zane don't keep their end of the deal? Isn't there a point where we stop waiting for them to take accountability and *do* something instead?

The sad smile on Lacey's face turns up into a full-on grin.

"See, babe? We're not that different."

And that's when I start to snap. Because I never would have done this if it weren't for Lacey. *She's* the one who slipped poison into my pocket and whispered venom in my ear, letting me get blood on my hands so hers would stay clean. Lacey turned me into a killer just like Zane, and as good as revenge felt, it didn't come without one last victim. Me. The person I thought I could be.

"I am *not* like you," I snarl. "*You* did this. You took Zane's EpiPen, didn't you? We could have saved him if you hadn't taken it."

"Yeah, and he would still be alive if you hadn't poisoned him."

"This is your fault!" My voice rips out of me like its own creature, sharp-toothed and clawed, adrenaline pushing me toward her. "Who the fuck do you think you are, bringing us all here? Making us kill each other!"

"I didn't make you do anything," Lacey says calmly. "It was your choice."

"But you brought us here," Corrine cuts in. "You manipulated us. You knew what you were doing."

"So did you." Lacey's eyes flash. "You couldn't wait to bring McKayleigh down, could you?" Her gaze tracks from Corinne to the rest of us. "You *all* knew what you were doing. I didn't make you come here. I didn't make you choose this career. I didn't make you kill people or hide their bodies or ruin their lives!"

"Fine." Max stumbles toward her, dropping his hand from his arm, his palm slick with blood. "We all made shitty decisions. We all did bad things. But not Kira. What did Kira do to deserve this?"

Lacey smiles, but her eyes shoot daggers. "Goddamn it. You really are obsessed."

Kira steps forward, her arms outstretched, her grip firm on the gun.

Lacey's smile drops, leaving her bare with hatred. "Fine. You want to know whose life perfect little Kira ruined? *Mine.* And you want to know the worst part?" Her face twitches, a crack in the armor. "You don't even know you did it."

KIRA

"What?" The gun goes slick under my hands. "I don't even know you."

A small, spiteful smirk twitches on Lacey's face. "It's embarrassing, but I used to be one of your most loyal followers."

My mouth goes dry. Obviously, I know anyone can have access to the things I post, but the thought of someone like Lacey scrolling through my life, always watching . . . it makes my skin crawl.

Lacey glances at Max. "I still have no idea what he sees in you, but I'll give it to you: your videos really got me into shape, babe. My favorite was the Dance Boot-Camp Challenge." Something flashes in her stare. "Remember that one?"

Of course I do. I posted it on YouTube a little over two years ago, and it was my first set of videos to hit a million views each. I framed it as a two-week challenge with a different set of videos to do each day, all based on the kind of workouts I did as a competitive dancer, a mix of technique and conditioning. I even pulled out my old pointe shoes for a barre workout, and it felt so good to do the thing I used to love so much, the thing I'm still not always comfortable doing anymore: just dancing, but on my own terms.

Wait, the shoes in my drawer. Was *that* my clue? Something so insignificant, so . . .

But no. Looking at Lacey's face, I know—it wasn't insignificant to her. Something about that challenge was monumental to her, bad enough that she brought me here. That she wanted me to suffer, maybe even die.

I swallow, tightening my grip on the gun. "I remember."

"Do you remember what you said at the end of the ballet video?"

My mind stutters. What did I say? It was so long ago. "I . . ."

"Think harder."

And then it's there, bobbing up like I'd been trying to hold it underwater. "I think I said something like . . . 'I know you're tired, but ballet is all about discipline. You have to keep going even when it's hard, because—'"

"'Because it *is* hard,'" Lacey finishes, nodding like an approving teacher. "'But all the best dancers make it look easy.' That's what you said. Right?"

"I don't understand," I tell her. "What's wrong with that?"

Her lip curls. "You were right. You made it seem *easy*. So easy, I thought, well, if a two-week challenge is all it takes to look like Kira Lyons, then maybe I can do it, too." She laughs bitterly. "And I did. All two weeks of it. Only when I got to the end, I didn't look any different. But I remembered what you said about discipline. I figured I just needed to work harder. Make it look easy. So, I did another two weeks. And when that still didn't work, I went harder. Did each video twice, back-to-back. I worked so hard I passed out. It was kind of a nasty spill, too. Had to get stitches."

Lacey taps the faint scar on her chin, a vicious half smile quirking on her lips, and it's like a nightmare slowly taking shape, the shadowy monster revealing a face more terrifying than any I could have imagined.

"That isn't what I meant." The words come out weak. "I never would have told you to do that. You can't go that hard. No fitness goal is worth sacrificing your health or well-being. Ever."

"That's sweet, babe." She comes closer, unafraid of the gun. "But the thing is, it wasn't the videos that made me hate you. They even worked, eventually. Well, the videos *and* some top-tier plastic surgery." She laughs, taking another step. "No, what really did it for me, Kira, the reason I had to bring you here . . ." Another step, only a foot between the barrel and her chest. "It's because you made me hate myself. Every single picture, every toxic-positive mantra . . . you live to make other girls feel like they're not enough. You get off on it. You wouldn't sell products without all that self-hate."

It's what I've been afraid of this whole time, what I've been wrestling with for years, but hearing it out loud is like a punch in the gut. I started making my content because I wanted to be in control again. Because I wanted to stop letting people like Mc-Kayleigh, Ms. Tammy, and the strangers in my comments make me feel like I wasn't enough. But in the process, that's exactly how I made Lacey feel. I was too focused on the good stuff—the love and the gratitude, followers telling me I'm helping them feel happier and healthier. I clung to their support, too relieved to wonder about the hurt radiating behind those smiles.

The same hurt that I see now, so clearly, on Lacey's face.

"But do you want to know the *worst* part about you, Kira? What makes you so unforgiveable?" Her eyes are blue as ice, and I feel like I'm falling through them, the ground cracking underneath my feet. "You act like you're this nice, good girl. A shy little victim. You've even convinced yourself."

I lower the gun, my chest aching.

Lacey laughs, so loud and sharp that it startles me into aiming again.

"See?" She stares down the barrel. "Sweet little Kira is ready to put a bullet in my chest. Better watch out, Max. Your girlfriend's a firecracker."

She looks at him, and all at once, I understand. Even through her boldness, I see her: that fifteen-year-old girl who gave a boy the most delicate of things, her trust, and watched as he smashed it to bits in front of her. And the longing. That slim, whispering hope that maybe, just maybe, things would work out better if he'd only let her try again.

"I'm sorry," I breathe. "I'm so, so sorry I made you feel that way."

She drops her smug grin so quickly, it's like someone slapped her.

"You're sorry I feel that way," she repeats. "You're sorry I *feel* that way? Oh my god, do you hear yourself? You still can't take responsibility for what you did. You can't accept that *you're* the reason you're here!"

And just like that, I don't feel so sorry anymore. Yes, I've made mistakes, but I didn't do *this*. I didn't torture people, make them kill each other, and then laugh in their faces like a sick, twisted puppet master.

I speak slowly. "You're right. I should have been more careful with my words. I should have thought about the impact they could have. And I'm sorry I didn't. But you don't get to blame me for *this*." My fingers curl around the gun's handle. "You're the one who lured us all here. You're the one who took it too far. *You're* the reason people are dead. I didn't do any of that, Lacey." My heart thumps as I throw her own words back at her. "I just gave you the idea."

As soon as I've said it, I know I cut too deep. With a growl, she lunges forward like she's going to rip the gun from my hands, but I jolt out of her reach, aim unwavering. She stops, breathing hard, and wipes her forehead, leaving a smear of what must be Max's blood behind. Looking up at the sky, she smiles.

"Go ahead. Shoot me. You really want them to come and find you with six dead bodies and a smoking gun?" She laughs. "I'm empty-handed, babe. You can't call this one self-defense, can you?"

Blood pounds in my ears, my hands shaking, but I'm frozen. Paralyzed.

"You're not innocent, Lacey." Max speaks up, his voice cutting hard. "Do you actually think you're better than the rest of us?" He walks toward her, unafraid. "This is about me. Right? Don't bring them into this."

"God, you're so obsessed with yourself," Lacey tells him, but she's trying too hard to put on her bored Elody affect. Max is hitting a nerve.

"I'm sorry that I hurt you," he says. "Okay? I take full responsibility for that. But I didn't ruin your life. You want to talk about 'obsessed'?" Max gets right up in her face. "You ruined your own life because you couldn't let go of a middle-school crush."

Everything drains from Lacey's face until it's nothing but a stunned mask. And I see it happen, like a gear grinding behind her eyes, but she's too quick.

Lacey surges toward me, her weight knocking me back onto the sand. The gun falls from my grip. We both scramble for it, but I'm faster. Closing my hands around the gun, I stumble back, and my elbow cracks against her face. She cries out, holding her nose, and I stand up, aiming the gun with shaking hands.

Lacey grins, blood trickling from her nose. She wipes it away, smudging it like war paint.

"Go ahead." She laughs. "Kill me."

Her eyes are wild, broken, and I realize with a shudder that takes over my whole body: there's a part of her that wants me to. And I won't. Even with everything she's done, I won't fight this girl's hurt with more hurt. I won't let her turn me into what she thinks I am.

I lower the gun, and that's all it takes. Lacey's hands close around mine, pulling hard enough that it wrenches from my grip. She stumbles back and then rights herself, swinging it back and forth so I can't tell who she's even aiming for. I'm not sure if she knows, either. All I can do is watch, frozen, my heart and the waves roaring in my ears as Lacey swings the barrel to Max's chest.

"Sorry," she tells him. "But I need you to know how it feels."

She pulls the trigger.

Click.

Lacey stares at the gun, looking just as blank and confused as Max.

That's when Corinne unfurls her fist, revealing the unloaded magazine.

"No one else is dying tonight," she says firmly.

Lacey's jaw drops. "You—"

"Just caught you attempting murder," Logan finishes, nodding at the camera in Corinne's other hand, and then at the discarded knife. "For the second time tonight, by the way."

I breathe out, trying to release the adrenaline pulsing through me. Even though I knew the gun wasn't loaded, I wasn't prepared for how it would feel to aim it. To make someone believe the only thing standing between their life and death is a twitch of my finger. It didn't feel badass or heroic—only wrong. And looking at Lacey, her shocked expression, I have to believe some part of her felt it, too.

"It's over, Lacey," I tell her softly.

And then she grins.

"Wow," she says, clapping. "You really got me. And you know I *love* a performance. But the thing is, babe . . ." She bends slowly to set the gun on the ground. "I'm done with all the fake shit."

When she springs back up, the knife is in her hand. It happens so fast, a blur of motion broken up by moments in high definition. Lacey lunging at me. The glint of the blade raised above my head. Max rushing forward just in time to block its path. The swinging arc of the knife as it plunges into his skin.

Horror floods Lacey's face.

"Oh my god," she breathes. "Oh my god!"

Max buckles, clutching his side. We all rush toward him, crowding around as the blood starts to bloom through his shirt.

Everything is noise. The sea, our panicked voices, Lacey's cries, but then it's deafened by a new sound, one that kicks up the breeze and shakes the ground beneath my feet.

I look up as the first helicopter takes shape in the sky.

TRANSCRIPTION: A JOURNAL HIDDEN IN A WEST HOLLYWOOD HOME

Welcome, followers, to my last will and testament.

Oh my god, kidding! Don't worry, I'll be alive for years to come, if I have anything to say about it—me, and the best lawyers Mom's money could buy. My trial isn't for a few more months, but I'm hardly rotting in prison, since Mom's money was also great for posting bail. And thank god, because orange really doesn't agree with me.

Anyway, I'm not too worried about ending up behind bars, at least not for long. They have me on a few weak-ass charges, but they couldn't get me on literal first-degree murder. Even if they could, I wouldn't be worried. Girls who look like me have a way of getting away with ... well, murder. Literally.

My lawyers have a super smart strategy laid out for me: besides reminding people that I *didn't murder anyone*, our plan also involves a lot of pretty crying, remorse, and being all broken up about everything I endured as a preteen, or whatever. I'm sure I'll sell it. Like I said, I know how to work an audience.

Max is alive, by the way. Don't get all stressed. He was in the hospital for, like, a day after he got all stitched up, but he's totally fine now. He blocked me on all of his socials, but I made some fake accounts—funny how karma works, right?—and from what I can see, he's milking the drama for all it's worth.

After the story broke, Max was pretty much public enemy number one, the catfish-exposer-turned-catfish, but you know what they say. There's no such thing as bad publicity, and believe me, Max is drowning in it, even if it *is* an apology tour. He posted this long-ass YouTube video about taking a "hiatus" from his channel while he "reflects on everything he's learned"—which maybe I'd buy, if he didn't also take a fat check from a top podcast in exchange for an exclusive interview. Whatever. Max is a hot white boy, so like I told Logan, I'm pretty sure he'll be fine. That's how it always works, isn't it?

Ugh. I still get embarrassed even writing about him. Now that I've had time to process it all, or whatever, I know it was never really about Max. I was projecting stuff onto him, because I liked the *idea* of him more than I liked *him,* and blah, blah, blah, I'm basically boring myself to death. The point is, my Max phase? Done. Dead. Buried.

I guess I'm glad I didn't kill him, though. Or Kira. I still feel a little bad about my snap decision to run at her with the knife. If I'm really psychoanalyzing things, maybe I thought hurting her was the only way to make Max feel as hurt as I did—and yeah, I know it's problematic, but like I said, snap decision. Anyway, it didn't work, and neither did Max's heroic little jump in front of her. He and Kira aren't talking. They don't even follow each other. Maybe she just couldn't get past what Max did to me, even if he took a literal stab for her. Ouch, right? That's got to hurt. And maybe I'm a bitch, but it gives me a warm fuzzy feeling.

But like I said, this isn't about Max or Kira, or anyone else. It's about me.

When I walk into that trial, I'll do what I've always done: be exactly who everyone wants me to be. Here, though, in this confession meant for no one's eyes but mine, I get to tell the truth. Even if my lawyers find it and make me burn it, at least I'll know I got the words on paper, got to feel the bumps and ridges under my fingers. At least, for a moment, they were real.

And here's the truth: I don't regret any of it. Not for a second. Because the *IRL* project did exactly what I wanted it to do.

It blew the fuck up.

Seriously, it's all anyone's talking about. The camera footage and recordings are technically police property, but there *may* have been a leak or two. Don't look at me—as an officially charged criminal, my hands are tied. Tilly's, too.

Anyway, the point is: *IRL* is everywhere. We've started a multi-generational *discourse,* babe. News segments, tweets, TikToks, and articles everywhere from *BuzzFeed* to *The New York Times.* People of all ages are condemning "influencer culture" and everything it stands for. There's Instagram infographics and everything. Honestly, it's a little annoying, and also totally not the point, but whatever. I get to sit back and be proud of the fact that I *did* something. I *made* this.

Oh, and also, despite being #*canceled,* we're still totally famous. If anything, we're even bigger than before. All of us got huge jumps in our follower counts, even our fallen influencers—which, you know, ew, but apparently people are morbid as hell.

And I hate to say it, but those five have it so much easier now than they would have if they'd survived. In death, they're celebrated. Missed. The darkest parts of them blotted out by "RIP"s and tribute TikToks. In life, they would have had to deal with the hard stuff, like owning up to what they did.

But I guess that's kind of the joy of surviving, isn't it? Fighting through the rough parts and coming out swinging. Still standing. Getting more chances. Realizing that you don't dry up and die if you don't have it all figured out by the time you turn twenty-one.

God, I sound like one of McKayleigh's self-help books. *RIP*.

A few days ago, I was scrolling through TikTok, and I saw a compilation of Aaron's best moments from *The Magnificent Millers.* It made me so sad, to think of that happening to me—if I died, and the only thing people wanted to remember me for was something I did six years ago. But I wouldn't let myself cry for Aaron, because I did what I had to do. I think Aaron understood that. He knew how the world is: sometimes, it's you or me.

And maybe a little part of me is glad to see him gone. In the heat of the moment—you know, the whole gun thing—I never actually got a chance to tell him why I picked him for *IRL*. I don't know if he'd even remember, but I'll never forget it.

Confession time: there was a hot second where I wanted to be an actor. I only ever had one gig, though. I was thirteen, and I was an extra in (gasp!) *The Magnificent Millers*. I didn't have any lines or anything, but I got to be on set with Aaron in this school-cafeteria scene. I thought it was huge. The first step in my big movie-star career.

Well, it wasn't. I ended up on the cutting-room floor. Mostly, what I remember from that day is what Aaron said after we wrapped, when I chased him down and asked if he'd autograph my shooting schedule. While he signed, I asked if he had any advice for me as an actor. He took one look at me, laughed, and said, *Either get hot or get funny. No offense, but to be a girl actor, you have to be one or the other.* He handed back the paper, the marker bleeding through. *But maybe it'll happen for you.*

Well, guess who turned out to be the better actor after all?

Honestly, I'm kind of surprised it was Aaron who figured me out first. But now, I know why: I was sloppy. Again. Mom was right about my stupid birthmark. Some things you just can't fix. But it wasn't all my fault. When the gun went missing, it freaked me out, threw me off my game. Later, I watched the tapes back and realized it was Graham who'd stashed it. (Plot twist, right? He might not have been smart enough to figure me out, but he was smart enough to do the math: if the Bounce House was going down, he was probably next.)

The next bit took some piecing together, since Aaron covered up the cameras—another thing that threw me off, not knowing for sure who'd killed Graham. That was the first time I wasn't sure if I should keep going with the plan, if someone was really one step ahead of me. I figure after Aaron went all stabby, he found the gun in Graham's things, snagged it, and then went through Max's stuff. That must be how he found the DMs—right where I left them in the camera bag, birthmark in full view.

I'm still kicking myself for those little slipups. The birthmark. Missing the *Elody Ever After* DVD in the TV cabinet, the photo album that must have been somewhere on the bookshelf for Aaron to find. I should have known better. I mean, I was basically asking for it when I gave them the safe. Part of me really thought they'd never figure me out, that time would run out and I'd leak all their secrets without anyone ever knowing who I really am. Or maybe part of me wanted them to know. To finally open up their eyes and see what was right in front of them.

But either way, I guess I had it coming. I don't know what I believe about the afterlife, but if Mom is still with me, even a little, she never would have let me get away with this without a few screwups along the way.

Whatever. When it comes down to it, I can't be too stressed, because really, everyone turned out fine. Better than before, even.

Corinne and Kira got extra lucky. Neither of them were charged with anything, since *technically* Kira didn't commit any crimes, and *technically* Corinne didn't either, because she didn't know that anyone would die, and she was being threatened or coerced or whatever. So they're both totally free, mostly guiltless, *and* getting all the benefits—which they have me to thank for, even though they never will.

Oh, and if you thought Kira's little reckoning would make

her delete her socials, you're wrong. She's more committed than ever, except instead of fitness, she's shifting into mental health. Apparently, she's going to college for psychology and dance next year. It's all very *nice* of her. Using her trauma to help others. I guess it doesn't hurt that she broke two million subscribers on YouTube this week.

Corinne's Twitch channel is back up and running. She's in college now, but she's still doing her streams on the side. Oh, and she started a podcast with Kira. Something about looking at the influencer industry through a "critical lens," or some smart-person crap like that. People are obsessed with it. I only listened to one episode, but when I got to the first sponsored ad—online therapy or personalized vitamins, something like that—I got bored.

Logan's probably had the most to deal with, besides me. She has a trial coming up, too, for killing Zane. I feel a little bad about that, but it worked out for her, in a way, because Logan's fan base is bigger than ever. And I have a feeling she'll come out of this okay. Even if she ends up doing time, she'll have interviews and TV spots lined up for the rest of her life once she's out. There's already, like, ten fan accounts for Logan and petitions to get her acquitted, her little sister Harper leading the charge. Really, this is the best possible outcome for Logan, since she was already guilty of concealing a murder. I like to think my little project even taught her a lesson.

And me? I guess I'm enjoying the infamy, too. I have some die-hard fans now, which is pretty cool, because they like me as *me*. As Lacey Warren, the brilliant, cute-but-psycho mastermind behind the *IRL* project. That's what they're saying, and it's a little problematic, but I'll take it. They think I'm *iconic*.

Elody has more followers than ever, too, but I haven't been on that account lately. My lawyers are basically forbidding me from logging in until this is all over. Honestly, though, I'm not sure if I'll ever go on again. Elody Hart was everything I wanted to be, but as much as I loved her, even with all of the things I hated, I'm starting to realize that she wasn't enough. She couldn't ever be, because she wasn't real.

So, I guess it's time for me to have a taste of my own medicine, as gross and cliché as that sounds. I need to unplug. Wake up to real life.

Elody will always be a part of me, like the marks and scars that prove how hard I worked to become her. Like the island, where some part of us will always live, either in death or survival.

Sometimes, I wonder if I'll ever feel guilty for what I did to them, even the ones I didn't kill—maybe especially them. I wonder if it's wrong that I don't think I will. Maybe it's because deep down, I know I gave them exactly what they wanted: A story. A platform.

I let them be *known*.

If that makes you uncomfortable, then go ahead and turn on the TV, open your phone, follow the version of me and my story that you're hungry for.

But here?

Sorry, babe. I'm just being real.

ACKNOWLEDGMENTS

For the past year or so, whenever someone has asked me about my debut novel, I've often fallen into the same sort of frazzled, self-effacing response that so many authors rely on: "Oh, my silly little book? I don't know, it doesn't feel real yet!" While it's still a bit surreal, what has never felt silly or little is my immense gratitude for the people who have been a part of this journey.

To the absolute dream team—my agent, Claire Friedman, and my editor, Sarah Grill—I can never thank you enough for making my dreams come true! I couldn't have imagined two smarter, more badass people to bring this book to life (and talk reality TV with). I would like, subscribe, and follow y'all to the ends of the earth.

To Alexa Donne, my fabulous mentor: this book would not be what it is without your guidance, wisdom, and support. You were the first person in this industry to believe in me, and I will never stop being grateful that you convinced me to write this book first.

Another huge thank-you to the team at Wednesday Books, which, despite my dubious attempts to play it cool, has been my dream imprint from the moment I knew it existed: Kerri Resnick, Alexis Neuville, Brant Janeway, Alyssa Gammello, Eric Meyer, MaryAnn Johanson, Jen Edwards, Melanie Sanders, and Diane Dilluvio—thanks, y'all! And of course, I want to thank the team at Inkwell Management. You are all working magic, and I'm so grateful for everything you've done for this book.

I also wouldn't be here without the beta readers and critique partners who took the time to read early drafts and offer their wonderful thoughts: Britney Shae Brouwer, Jessica VanAllen, Miranda, and Haley Grage. Another huge thank-you to Margeaux Weston for her thoughtful feedback. Thank y'all for helping me shape this book into something I'm proud of.

And to the wonderful authors who blurbed this book—Goldy Moldavsky, Katie Zhao, Laurie Elizabeth Flynn, and Dana Mele—thank you so much for your kind words. It's truly an honor that y'all read my work.

Thanks also to Debbie Deuble Hill at APA for seeing film potential in *People to Follow*—I'm so excited to see what's down the line!

And to my friends: I don't know if I can express how grateful I am for y'all in a single paragraph. It's very easy to convince myself that I'm a TikTok manifestation–style lucky girl when I have people like you in my life. Alanna, Ali, Annie, Brianna, Cailyn, Carly, Casey, Cat, Elena, Emilie, Emma, Emmy, Hannah (both of y'all!), Jessica, Lauren, Libby, Madison, Megan, Melissa, Michelle, Sophia, Veronica, and all of the other amazing people who I've had the pleasure to call friends—thank you. You're all the coolest and the smartest, and also you're, like, really pretty. An extra special shout-out to Emilie, who read an earlier draft of this book, and Carly, who read an even earlier draft of another book that will certainly never see the light of day—thank y'all for making me feel like a real writer.

To my family: y'all are the best hype squad a girl could wish for. Mom and Dad, thank you for letting me major in theater and then not even batting an eye when I decided to be a writer, too. I wouldn't be who or where I am without y'all and the way you've encouraged me to always do what I love, no matter how impractical. Grayson and Eugenie, thank you for being my resident Youth Experts™—you are the coolest siblings to bool with. Another special shoutout to Papa: it's not Broadway orchestra seats, but I hope you like it, because I like to think I got a little bit of my love of storytelling from you. And to all the other Worleys, Fransens, Ottelins, Wirths, and the rest of my New Orleans family, blood and otherwise: I love y'all. Thank you for believing in me!

And finally, to everyone who has taken the time to read this book: thank you, thank you, thank you. I hope we get to share so many more stories together.

ABOUT THE AUTHOR

OLIVIA WORLEY is an author and actor born and raised in New Orleans. A graduate of Northwestern University, she now lives in New York City, where she spends her time writing thrillers, overanalyzing episodes of *The Bachelor,* and hoping someone will romanticize her for reading on the subway. *People to Follow* is her debut novel.